D0251133

THE BROKEN UNIVERSE

Tor Books by Paul Melko

Paul Melko

The BROKEN UNIVERSE

A Tom Doherty Associates Book
New York

THE BROKEN UNIVERSE

A Tor Book
Published by Tom Doherty Associates, LLC
175 Fifth Avenue
New York, NY 10010

www.tor-forge.com

Tor® is a registered trademark of Tom Doherty Associates, LLC.

Library of Congress Cataloging-in-Publication Data

Melko, Paul.
    The broken universe / Paul Melko.—1st ed.
       p. cm.
    "A Tom Doherty Associates book."
    ISBN 978-0-7653-2914-1 (hardcover)
    ISBN 978-1-4299-4660-5 (e-book)
    1. Space and time—Fiction.   2. Doppelgängers—Fiction.
 I. Title.
 PS3613.E4465B76 2012
 813'.6—dc23

                                                        2012009387

First Edition: June 2012

Printed in the United States of America

 0 9 8 7 6 5 4 3 2 1

THE BROKEN UNIVERSE

CHAPTER 1

John's ears popped as he and Grace transferred from Universe 7651 to Universe 7650.

Grace tossed the duffel bag of weapons and gold onto the scraped stone ground. She scanned the horizon and then slid the pistol in her hand into its holster. Grace's normally frizzy red hair was tied tightly in a ponytail. In her army fatigues, she looked nothing like the gawky woman John had first met in freshman physics lab nearly two years ago.

"I'll go back for Henry," John said.

She looked at him flatly.

"Sure, I'll be right here," she said, as she dragged the duffel outside the transfer zone. John couldn't help feeling guilty for all that Grace had gone through. If it wasn't for the transfer device, she never would have been kidnapped and tortured by Visgrath.

John reached into his shirt and toggled the switch on the transfer device. Instantly he was inside their small warehouse at the stone quarry in Universe 7651. He swallowed to clear the pressure in his ears.

"Is Grace, I mean, is everything all right?" Henry said. He sneezed and wiped his nose with a tissue. "Is it all clear over there?"

John nodded to his friend. He'd met Henry on the same day he'd met Grace. The three had ended up lab partners in freshman physics at the University of Toledo, and that partnership had led to their building a company that manufactured head-to-head pinball machines, an arcade game that had never existed in Universe 7650. Unfortunately that anomaly had been what Visgrath had detected.

"All clear."

Henry seemed to deflate with relief. He was as tall as John, but it was hard to tell with his slouch. While John was slender and sandy blond, Henry was even thinner and dark haired.

"Send us through again," John said.

"Let me set the timer." Henry was their backup. If a party of Alarians had been waiting for them in 7650, he'd have come running with guns blazing when John had failed to return to give the all clear.

"You sure that thing will work?" John asked, as Henry turned the dial on a mechanical timer. It began ticking.

"So far in every test," Henry said. He ran to join John in the center of the transfer zone.

"How many tests have we run?" John asked.

"One."

The timer dinged, and the inside of the shed was replaced by the bare rock of the quarry site.

A light drizzle had begun to fall, odd for a July day in northwest Ohio.

"Let's go let Janet and Bill know we're back," John said. Janet and Bill were his parents, or rather they would have been if John had ever been born in this universe. Bill and Janet were childless in 7650, and they'd taken John in when his broken transfer device had marooned him in this universe.

Henry reached to grab the duffel but Grace beat him to it.

"I got it," she said, and tossed it over her shoulder.

"I can carry it for you," Henry said.

"I got it, I said."

Henry cast a quick glance at John, whether for sympathy or in embarrassment, John didn't know. John shrugged. Grace hadn't been herself during the six weeks they'd spent in 7651 trying to build a transfer device to get them back to 7650, Grace's and Henry's home universe. She'd always been quick with a pun or a bad joke, which she was more than willing to laugh at herself. Her withdrawal from Henry, however, had been painful and obvious. Once they got back to her home universe, everything would be all right. Even as John thought it, he felt how hollow it seemed. Grace had been tortured. There was no easy way back from that.

The quarry was across McMaster Road from Janet and Bill's small farm. It was nearly identical to the farm where John had grown up in Universe 7533, his home universe. This farm had been a little more run-down than his own, but when he'd come to stay with the Rayburns, he'd done what he could to fix the place up. The Rayburns had become a surrogate family for him, and for that he was grateful. When he had been tricked out of his life by his own doppelganger, John Prime, when he found he couldn't return home again because the device Prime had given him was broken, Bill and Janet had taken him in.

They crossed the road and passed through the line of trees that marked the border of the Rayburn farm, situated at the corner of McMaster and Gurney roads. A hundred meters in front of them was the main barn and next to it was the house.

"Car's here," John said. "They must be home." He glanced across Gurney Road. He couldn't see the Rayburns' second barn, where he had built his own transfer gate. His car would be there, waiting for him, where he'd left it six weeks earlier. The trees were too full of green to catch a glimpse of the barn.

John tried the front door, but it was locked. He knocked and waited.

Grace peered into the front window.

"It's dark in there," she said. "You got a key?"

John shrugged. "No," he said. "But there's one around back, hanging from a nail."

"Maybe they took a walk," Henry said. He looked up and down Gurney Road.

"Uh-huh," Grace said.

Henry coughed again, loud in the quiet.

"You all right?" John asked. Henry had been unable to shake the cold for the last couple days. Now he looked pale and lethargic.

"Yeah, just tired."

"Yeah," John agreed. They'd pulled a few all-nighters to get the transfer gate in 7651 working.

John led them around back. He plucked the key off the nail and unlocked the back door.

It squeaked as he pushed it open ten centimeters.

"Bill? Janet?" he called. There was no answer.

He pushed the door the rest of the way. It thunked into something and would go no farther.

John squeezed himself through the small opening. The house was too hot, as if it had been closed up all day long.

"Bill?"

He looked down at what was blocking the door. Two tarps were bundled on the kitchen floor, each about two meters long. He reached down and nudged one. It was heavy. John moved the tarp aside and recoiled in horror.

Bill's bloodless face stared up at him.

"Oh, shit," he said. "Oh, god." He stumbled backward against the kitchen table. Grace squeezed into the kitchen. She reached down and moved the tarp on the second bundle.

"Don't," John said, but she ignored him.

Janet Rayburn had been shot in the side of the head. Black blood ran down her face. One eye stared in the wrong direction.

Henry pushed into the kitchen, took one look, and turned white.

"If you're gonna barf, do it in the sink," Grace said.

"I'm . . . okay," Henry said. He glanced at John. "John, are you okay?"

John looked away from the two corpses. They weren't his real parents, he repeated to himself. They were just one of a near infinite number of Bills and Janets. He'd met versions of them, he'd met versions of himself. This didn't matter. This didn't matter.

But it did.

They weren't just dups: what Visgrath and the Alarians called people who weren't unique in the multiverse. They were his parents. They were good people.

"You okay?" Henry asked again. He touched John's shoulder.

"No, no, I'm not," he said. "We need to call the police."

"Hell, no," Grace said. "No police."

"They need to be buried!" John said.

"No police," Grace said. "They'll think we had something to do with—"

She stopped and stared at the sound of a key in the front door.

"Go!" she whispered.

She pushed Henry through the back door, and then followed. John took one look at his dead parents and left them. He pulled the door shut after him, gently setting it tight against the frame. He didn't have time to lock it.

They ran from the house toward the orchard. It was the only direction they could go if they wanted to remain unseen from the front of the house.

"The tractor," John said.

It was old and rusted and surrounded by a clump of uncut grass. Grace slid around it on the wet grass, and Henry awkwardly settled next to her.

From behind the tractor, John peeked out at the house.

Shadows moved inside. There was no noise.

"Police?" Henry asked.

Grace shook her head. "There'd be warrants and examiners and ambulances. There'd be bullhorns. That is not the police."

"Murderers," John said. Whoever had killed Bill and Janet had come back.

Grace nodded.

Minutes passed, and John saw no more shadows against the window nor any other sign of movement in the house. He chanced moving out from behind the old tractor and ran diagonally toward the barn. Using it as cover, he peered around toward the front of the house.

Four men were carrying the corpses across the road into the woods.

"What are they doing?" Grace asked.

"Heading toward the other barn," John said.

"Why?" Henry asked, panting.

"It's where I built my first transfer gate," John said. Because his own transfer device was broken—it only went forward from one universe to another and never backward—John had had to reverse engineer the device and build his own in order to go back to Universe 7533 to recruit John Prime. The original transfer device fit on John's chest and moved from universe to universe with the transferee, but the ones the team built were several meters tall and remained in the universe where they were stationed.

"They're using your transfer gate," Grace said through gritted teeth. "Let's go."

John caught her arm. "Hold on. Let them get ahead." The second barn was about three hundred meters into the woods along a rutted dirt road. The summer growth would make it easy to follow the four and remain hidden, as long as they were far enough ahead. John counted to thirty.

"Let's go."

They ran across Gurney Road. Slowly they crept up the overgrown road until they heard voices. Then John led them through the brambles into the trees. Maple and ash trees rose up above blackberry shrubs that caught at their clothes and hands. John ignored the thorns, intent on the men who had murdered his surrogate parents and hauled them away.

John motioned Grace and Henry down. He could see the open barn door from where he crouched, just twenty meters away. Bill's and Janet's bodies had been tossed against the barn, and the sight of it filled him with anger.

A van was parked next to his car. Besides the four men he had counted already, there were four more people in the barn. He heard words. One of them was shouting.

"Alarians," Grace said. She slowly unzipped the duffel bag and withdrew an M4 carbine.

Visgrath and the Alarians were marooned universe travelers. Decades prior, they had been trapped in Universe 7650 by an organization of multiverse police called the Vig. They had had no transfer gates nor the ability to build one and had been forced to make the best of it. They'd created a huge conglomerate—Grauptham House—and "discovered" in 7650 inventions that they knew existed in other universes. They'd even pretended to author one of Beethoven's symphonies.

When John and the Pinball Wizards had created their head-to-head pinball machines, Visgrath had noticed. He'd found John and invested in their fledgling company, trying to determine if John was a marooned traveler as well. When Visgrath discovered John had a device, he had snatched Grace and Henry as bargaining chips against John.

John had built the transfer gate in the barn and used it to recruit his own doppelganger, Prime—who had given him the broken device in the first place and stolen his life—to help him save his friends. They'd done it, but marooned themselves in Universe 7651, at least until they had built a transfer device there.

"Hold on," John said. "They're armed." All the Alarians wore pistols, and some of them had rifles. Eight against three wasn't good odds, especially since the Alarians probably knew how to shoot. Grace could shoot too, having spent hours firing her weapons into the empty quarries for target practice in 7651. But Henry was no expert shot, and he was sick. No, the odds weren't good.

"Let's go back and call the police," John said.

"And then explain the transfer gate to them how?" Grace asked.

"We can—"

"They're using it," Henry said.

Two Alarians stood in the middle of the transfer zone holding one of the corpses.

"Ready?" someone said in English. A technician stood at the controls of the gate.

One of the Alarians nodded.

"Three. Two. One!"

The two Alarians and the corpse disappeared.

"Six against three," Grace whispered.

Two more Alarians took the second corpse and stood in the transfer zone. They disappeared.

"The perfect way to get rid of a body," Henry said.

John stared at him, momentarily outraged at the cruel statement.

"Sorry," Henry added.

"Four against three," Grace said. "Odds are getting better."

She stood. John grabbed her shoulder and pointed. Two more Alarians stood in the gate transfer zone.

"Where are they going?" Henry asked.

"Who cares?" Grace said. "Away is fine with me."

"Let's go," John said. He took a shotgun from the duffel, made sure it was loaded, and stuffed a handful of shells in his front pocket.

Grace and John ran, heads ducked low, toward the barn door.

They were only a few meters away when the first Alarian—the technician at the controls—noticed them. He looked up, his mouth an O.

"Freeze," John said. The man raised his hands.

The second Alarian was talking on a phone. Apparently they'd had enough time to rig a telephone line into the barn. The second one turned and looked at John and Grace.

He said into the phone, "They're back. The vermin are here."

"Drop the phone," Grace said.

"Yes, you heard me," the Alarian continued. He started to say something in Alarian.

Grace raised the M4 and fired a burst of shots into the wall near the phone. The Alarian dropped the receiver.

Henry trotted up behind John and Grace, heaving and dragging the duffel. He wheezed, and then stopped with his hands on his knees while he coughed.

"Hands behind your heads," John said. "Do it."

The second Alarian paused, glaring at him, and then slowly raised his arms.

"Where do you all think you're going with my transfer gate?" John asked. "Must be somewhere special."

The standing Alarian said something hateful in his own language.

Grace grinned, but in no way pleasantly.

"I'm gonna have to learn that language," she said. "It's so mellifluous."

"Over here," John said, motioning to a spot on the other side of the control panel.

The two Alarians started forward, and then both stopped, looking toward the barn door.

John heard it too, another car coming up the road.

Grace spun and took a spot by the door.

John kept his shotgun pointed at the two.

"Kneel," he said, but he kept looking out the door of the barn. "What is it?"

"Another van," Grace said. "Maybe four more bad guys."

"Henry, cover these two."

"Right," Henry said, digging in the duffel bag for a weapon.

John turned and took the opposite side of the barn door.

"Wait for them to come closer," Grace said.

But they didn't. The driver must have seen Grace or John by the door. He stopped short and pointed.

The Alarian in the passenger seat opened the door and rolled out.

He had a pistol.

Bullets slammed into the barn wall, making holes of sunlight.

John dove to the ground, realizing how thin the walls were.

He fired one burst of shot into the van's grille. The windshield chipped and starred.

More bullets slammed through the barn.

Behind him, Henry cried out and dove for the ground.

Grace couldn't seem to get a good shot from her position on the dirt floor. She fired a series of rounds into the air, posturing fire making certain the Alarians knew they were facing big guns.

John pumped the shotgun and fired again.

Behind him he heard the hum of capacitors.

He twisted on the ground. The Alarian technician was starting the transfer gate.

"Henry! Stop them!"

"I can't!" Henry was covering his head.

Bullets ricocheted through the barn.

John stood up, trying to see where the two Alarians were.

He spotted the leader, the one who had been on the phone, and he had a gun now. He pointed it at John. John rolled away, taking himself out of the barn and near his car. Henry scuttled after him.

Grace slid around to get a better aim on the new van and filled it with M4 rounds. She had no clear view of the two Alarians inside the barn, however.

John glanced up. The two Alarians were running for the transfer zone. The leader fired at him wildly.

The technician clutched a handful of rolled-up engineering prints.

They squatted in the transfer zone and the leader fired covering slugs at John and Henry. John had no clear shot from his vantage point behind his car.

They disappeared as the transfer gate triggered.

"Damn," Henry said.

All of the Alarians in the van except the driver were out now and firing at them.

Grace slid backward on her belly. She reached into the duffel and pulled out one of the hand grenades that they'd purchased from a shady arms dealer in 7651. She pulled the pin and threw it at the van. It skittered and rolled, disappearing under the van's front axle.

The driver watched the grenade disappear under his vehicle with a look of disbelief. He dropped the van into reverse and backed down the road. His associates, who had been taking cover behind the van, found themselves in the open. One flopped into the passenger seat. Another dove into the rear. The last ran into the woods for cover.

John hid behind his car waiting for the explosion.

"Down!" he yelled at Henry.

Nothing happened.

He peeked from over the hood of his car. Grace met his gaze from behind the barn door.

"I guess that gun dealer was pulling our legs about the hand grenades," she said.

"We paid five hundred dollars for that," Henry squawked.

"It did its job," John said. He listened as the tires of the van screeched as it accelerated onto Gurney Road.

"What do we do now?" Grace said. She nodded at the transfer gate.

"We take it apart and get it out of here before they come back," John said.

CHAPTER 2

"John!"

Casey slung her arms around his neck and squeezed.

"I guess you're okay," he said.

She didn't let go for a long minute.

John had dropped Henry and Grace off at their Toledo apartment with a promise to meet at the factory in the morning. He'd phoned Casey, and she'd demanded he come see her immediately.

Casey started undoing her blouse buttons.

"Hold on! Not in your parents' house," John said. It felt awkward to be this close to her after so long apart. He'd had no idea for six weeks if she was safe or not. She'd been shot by the Alarians during the kidnapping of Grace and Henry.

"Shut up," Casey said with a smirk, brushing aside a strand of blond hair. She undid the buttons far enough to slip the blouse over her shoulder. A puckered circle was etched into her skin just below the clavicle.

"Wow," John said. "That's a pretty nice scar."

"I'm still wearing a bikini," she said.

"No one would knock over your sand castle if they saw a scar like that," John said. "Are you really okay?"

"I am, John."

"I'm so sorry I left you," he said. "I had to rescue—"

"Grace and Henry, I know."

"I came back as soon as I could," he said.

"I know," she said, buttoning her blouse back up. "The police were very perplexed. But there were no suspects and no witnesses, and it was just a flesh wound. They stopped looking for you guys after a couple weeks."

"They couldn't have found us anyway," John said. "We were elsewhere."

"I know."

"So you believe my paranoid delusions now?"

"John, I know something's happened. I know I was shot. I know you had to go somewhere to save Grace and Henry."

"I can prove it to you now," John said. "We have a transfer gate in 7651. And one here too, only it's in pieces in the trunk of my car."

"I have no idea what that all means," Casey said. "But I *am* glad you're back."

"Me too."

John wrapped his arms around her and kissed her. He couldn't help thinking of Prime's Casey as he did so. Would kissing her feel identical to kissing the Casey in this universe? Would she taste the same? He remembered Visgrath's laughing mockery when he'd found out John wasn't a singleton, that he was a *dup*. Was someone with a single instance in all the multiverse, someone unique, living a more special life than someone with a million instances? How could that be? His emotions were just as real no matter how many other John Rayburns were out there.

What did it matter if there were he and a million other Johns scattered across the universe? Did that make him any less intrinsically valuable as a person? To Visgrath, it had. To be unique made a life more valuable. What twisted logic brought a society to that point? But even as he asked himself, he knew that scarcity implied value. A person who was scarce could be construed to be more valuable than one who wasn't.

"Bill and Janet are dead," he said.

"What?"

"The Alarians killed them."

"The who?"

"The people chasing us."

"Are you going to the police?" she asked.

"I expect they'll come find us," John said. "And they'll want answers, no matter what Grace thinks."

"Grace doesn't want to conform?" Casey said. "How odd."

"You don't know," John said, realizing that Casey hadn't lived with Grace at the transfer gate build site for six weeks, listened to her nightmares in the tent next to his, saw her normally sweet nature turn inward, even to Henry.

"Know what?"

"Grace, she was . . . tortured." John's mind turned to the image of her strapped to a table and covered in cuts. It could have been Casey that Visgrath had kidnapped. That it had been Grace, that it was ultimately his fault, made him queasy.

"What?"

"Visgrath thought she might know where my transfer gate was. He needed answers."

"My god."

"She killed him."

"What? Grace?"

"She shot him through the eye as he held Henry right in front of him. Coldest thing I've seen anyone do."

"Poor Grace, poor Henry."

"I don't think she can deal with what happened to her, or what she's done."

"And you guys didn't find her a psychiatrist?"

"Uh . . . we didn't exactly have a health-care ID in that universe," John said.

"You could have done *something*!" Casey pushed him away.

"We were doing everything we could to get her back here!"

Casey calmed herself. "I know. But six weeks of suffering over that. The guilt. The pain. She needs help."

"She doesn't talk to anyone now."

"Maybe she'll talk to me. . . ."

"If Henry couldn't get through to her, what makes—"

"What makes you so smart?" Casey asked.

"Uh . . ." John closed his mouth. "I'm sorry. You're right."

"Usually. Apology accepted," Casey said. "Take me to dinner, and we can discuss what happened in more detail. Now that I've taken a bullet for the team, I guess I better start believing you and this parallel universe crap." She paused on the steps. "I'm so sorry about Bill and Janet. I know how much they meant to you."

"Thanks."

John found himself waiting in the foyer for Casey to do whatever she did to ready herself to go out. Her father emerged from his office, looking startled for a moment.

"John! You're back!"

"Yes, sir, I am."

He began to smile, and then frowned. "Where'd you go, John?"

"Um, I had a trip out of town, Mr. Nicholson."

"I see," he said. "Somewhere where there weren't phones? Is that it?"

"Well . . ."

"You left my daughter lying in a hospital bed, shot. And you leave for six weeks."

John felt his face flushing. "I'm sorry, sir. I would have returned if I could—"

"It's not acceptable, John. No man can treat my daughter like that," he said. "She was shot!"

"I know, sir! I did everything I could to get back here."

"A letter if not a phone call? Something, John."

"I—"

"I don't know what your intentions with my daughter are, John," he said, "but I know she fancies you quite a bit. I, however, don't fancy you. What you did was unconscionable. I doubt any explanation will justify your continued presence in this house."

John steeled himself. He could lie. He wouldn't be believed if he told the truth. "I know it looks bad from your point of view. But the last thing I wanted to do was leave Casey. The only reason I did was because my friends were in danger and needed me more than she did. She was safe, as far as I could tell, and my friends were not."

"I see."

"I came back as quickly as I could."

"If your first priority isn't my daughter, I don't want you around her."

"It is, sir. It is."

"You're not mixed up with thugs, are you?"

John nodded. "I didn't know they were thugs, but yes, our investors turned out to be not very nice people." Not nice people from another universe, actually.

"Is it straightened out now?"

"I don't know—"

"Don't worry, Daddy," Casey said from the stairs. "He's not going anywhere without me again."

"That's what I'm afraid of," Mr. Nicholson sighed.

"You trust my judgment, don't you?" Casey asked.

"More than your brother's, that's for sure."

"Then you should know I trust John with all my heart," she said. "And that should be good enough for you."

"You're right, honey." Casey hopped down the last step, landing next to her father. She reached up on tiptoes and kissed him on the cheek.

"Yes, all the men in my life properly understand that I am usually right."

She led John out the door.

"Have fun, baby."

"Yes, Daddy."

As the door closed behind them, John said, "How long did you let me suffer before you cut in?"

"Long enough," she said with a smile.

He sighed. "Let me tell you the whole story."

CHAPTER 3

"As far as I can tell," Henry was saying as they walked across the parking lot of the pinball factory, "at least ninety percent of the top managers and executives of Grauptham House have disappeared. The stock is in free fall because no one knows where they are."

"We know," Grace said.

"Nowhere they can be found," John added. He unlocked the door and ushered them into the reception area that they never used. Grauptham House was the huge conglomerate that had funded Pinball Wizards, Inc., through a venture capital company called

EmVis. They owned Pinball Wizards. The company was effectively controlled by the Alarians, who had wanted very much to get out of Universe 7650 where they had been trapped for a long time. Now they'd done it, thanks to John's transfer gate.

John pushed open the swinging doors that led into the factory. He hit the light switch and huge overhead fluorescents flickered to life.

"Oh, crap," Grace said.

The floor of the factory was strewn with wreckage. Half-finished pinball machines lay tipped over, their glass covers shattered. Buckets of parts had been dumped on the floor. Kilometers of wire had been unrolled off their spools.

"They trashed it," Henry said. "The bastards."

"They were looking for the transfer gate," John said.

Grace peered at the mess, her face inscrutable. Then she found her way through it to the metal stairs that led to her office. She shut the door behind her without a word.

Henry stared after her for a moment. "What do we do now?"

John, unsure if he was referring to the mess or to Grace, said, "Start cleaning up, I guess."

They started in the back room, sweeping, ordering, sorting, until there was enough space for John to bring in the box of wires, circuits, and metal that was the remains of the transfer gate from the Rayburn barn.

Henry reached into the box. "I can't stand to look at another circuit board."

"I know," John said. They had spent weeks trying to reproduce what John had done in one feverish night. They had his plans for a transfer gate, but it had been far from easy to make a new one in Universe 7651.

As they sorted the pieces, John asked, "Is Grace all right?"

"Yesterday was the most animated I've seen her in a while," Henry said. "When she was shooting things and throwing grenades."

"Oh."

"I can't even touch her," Henry said softly.

"What do you mean?"

"Intimately," Henry said. John found himself blushing. "She can't stand to be touched."

"Henry. I'm sorry."

"Yeah, well . . ." Henry seemed to shake himself. "Sorry for bringing it up to you."

"It's okay. Maybe we can get her some help now that we're back in our own universe," John said.

"She won't do that," Henry said. "I mentioned it last night. She screamed at me."

"Maybe if I did."

"Don't."

"Okay, but Henry . . . She can't go through this alone."

"I'm here with her. That should be enough."

"Okay," John said. After a moment, he added, "Hand me that circuit board, will ya?"

"Yeah. Sure."

After an hour, Grace came down and leaned against the table they were working on.

"All our records are ripped up or gone," she said. "They took everything of any value from the office. Even my typewriter."

"I'm sorry, Grace," John said. "I—"

She cut him off. "For what? It's just some stupid company we built. Some stupid idea we had when we didn't know there were other more interesting universes out there."

"Yeah, I guess it isn't that important," John said.

She glanced at him. "I got ahold of Viv," she said. "She's on her way over." Viv was the floor foreman.

"No one else?" Henry asked.

"She was the first one I could get ahold of," Grace said. "The bank account is overdrawn. I have no idea what orders came in, what shipped, and what's in build." She shrugged.

"We can figure it out," John said.

"Or what?" Grace said. "Does it even matter?"

"Grace—" John started to say, but she walked off before he could add anything more. He had the same feelings—what did it matter? Why didn't he want Grace to think that way?

"I'm tired of this," Henry said. "Let's see if we can get a pinball machine working."

They managed to find two panes of glass that were unbroken, a wonder in the shambles. The pinball machines that Pinball Wizards built weren't the single-player models John remembered from his universe, though that's what they were based on. The Wizards had modified the design to be a head-to-head model played by two players at a time. John still preferred the traditional pinball, but the head-to-head version was what sold.

The door opened again, and there was Viv, the short, compact foreman who'd kept all the assemblers in line.

She shook her head at them. "Don't just show up here and expect that we'd all be slaving away for you as if nothing had happened."

"Um," John said.

"We're not waiting around when there's police involvement and shootings," she said. "We're not putting ourselves in jeopardy for a job. Right?"

"We didn't expect that, Viv," John said.

"Doesn't matter what you did or didn't expect," Viv said. "It happened, didn't it. And there was violence . . . right here. I don't like violence."

John realized how angry Viv was, and how scared she must have been. The guilt he felt for getting Grace and Henry wrapped up in all this was blown bigger by what had happened to Viv and the workers.

"You're right, Viv," John said. "I'm sorry I put you through all that. It wasn't fair to you and the other workers."

"Yeah, there's no place for violence," she said, but softer.

"You're right."

She blinked at John, and then said, "Where have you guys been?"

"We had to run for our own safety," John said.

"Is it safe now?"

"I don't know," John answered honestly. "Safer."

Viv nodded. "I see."

John waited for her to go on, but her anger had ebbed. "What happened while we were gone? We don't know, and we're only back as of yesterday."

"Well, after the shooting, the police came," Viv said, her eyes unfocusing as she remembered. "They asked a lot of stupid questions, but we didn't know anything. We didn't know who had taken Grace and Henry or who had shot Casey. We didn't know anything." She paused. "I don't like police much, and this was just like them. Nothing happened at all.

"So, not much work got done that day, and I didn't even bother pushing the guys. I just let them jaw. But the next day was payday. So everyone came back. Only, no one is here to cut the checks. Grace, Miss Shisler, she cuts the checks by hand. No payroll company or nothing, and when you all are gone, there's no one else to ask about pay. So the boys all left. No way they're staying for another week if last week wasn't paid for."

"We owe them all money," Grace said. "We'll get it to them."

"Good," Viv said. "So, we all went home. I told the guys I'd call them if I could get their pay."

"Any chance any of them will come back to work?" Henry asked. "You know, in case we need to build some more pinball machines."

Viv shook her head. "The ones that you want back have jobs again. The ones that don't have work, you don't want back. If we're back in business, we should just start from scratch. We lose some ramp-up time, but I can train any group of guys to do this."

"Don't you have a job?" John asked.

"Yeah, I got another one," Viv said. "But they don't let a mouthy broad be foreman like you guys do. So . . . I guess you can have me for a second chance. But if there's violence, I'm outta here, big job title or not."

"That seems fair," Grace said.

"You guys gonna start building again or not?" she asked, scanning the disarray.

"We don't know," John said. He looked at Grace. She was looking at the shop floor. Then she looked at John with a wan smile. He nodded at her slightly, and she returned it after a moment.

"Can you tell me which orders were built on that last day?" Grace asked Viv.

"Sure, I remember that," Viv said. Viv and she climbed the stairs to the office.

"Looks like we're six weeks behind," John said. "And no workers to help us. We need to get the pinball machines rolling out the door again."

"Do we?" Henry asked. "Do we need to do anything? What if we just stopped?"

"Is that what you want?"

"Everything seems so futile," Henry said. "Now that I know we're living in just one of a million universes, and I'm just one of a million Henrys. I wonder . . ."

"What?"

"I wonder if there are Graces out there who aren't . . . broken," he said. "Is that wrong? I know it is. I know it is."

"Henry . . ."

"She's not the same anymore, and I can't do anything about it."

"Henry, I'm so sorry. It's my fault."

"Of course it isn't," Henry said. "It's my fault. I could have fought harder when they grabbed us. I could have offered to talk first. I could have traded you for her life. But I didn't! I was scared."

"Henry, you gotta stop that," John said. "You can't blame yourself for what Visgrath did. We were all powerless. John Prime is the one who saved us all."

John had spent months hating Prime, trying to find some way back to his home universe and pay Prime back, but when the time came that he could travel back—after he had built his own transfer gate—John found he needed Prime.

"Yeah, but why did it have to be Prime? Why couldn't I have saved us? And does it really matter if I do anything? When there's all those duplicates of me flailing about doing the same things?"

"But you're not doing the same thing as them," John said. "You're here building a company and doing something good and helping Grace get by. All those things are important right here, right now."

"I guess."

Upstairs in the office, the phone rang.

"No, this company is like nothing else," John said. "It's a transdimensional company. With offices in Universes 7650 and 7651!"

Henry laughed despite himself.

"Think what we can do," John said. "We have three transfer devices, one here on my chest and one transfer gate in 7651 and another here in 7650. We can use that."

"To do what?"

"Whatever we want."

"Yeah, I guess we could do a lot," Henry said, his eyes looking off into space. "We could—"

Grace stuck her head out the door of the office and shouted down. "That was our Vegas sales guy. He's wondering where his order for fifty machines is. It was due there yesterday, cash on delivery."

"Fifty?"

"Yeah, apparently he didn't even notice that we weren't here for six weeks while he worked the deal."

John looked around. Fifty?

"Come on, you apes," Viv said as she trotted down the stairs. "We better get it together if we want to ship some units today."

"Is this what you want to do, Grace?" John asked.

Grace looked at him. "It's our company, isn't it?"

They managed to find, fix up, and scrounge seven machines by evening, with all of them working assembly on the floor. Everyone except for Henry, who started sneezing halfway through the afternoon and retired to the couch in the upstairs office.

"I hab the flu," he said as he climbed the stairs.

While they ate delivered pizza, Grace called shipping companies, trying to find one that would load the first part of the shipment to Las Vegas that night.

"No way tonight?" she said into the phone. "First thing in the morning then. Fine. Good." She hung up. "We can get these out tomorrow. Arrive in three days. What about the rest?"

"We don't have the parts for forty-three more," Viv said.

"Maybe ten more," John said. "Then we start running out of stuff."

"And we can't build more than one per day per person," Viv said. "Less because you guys aren't on top of the game and don't know my system."

"Hey, we built the first one," John said.

"You R and D guys think you know the best way to put your gadgets together," Viv said. "Well, you're wrong. Putting something together isn't the same as assembling it. You hired me to manage your assembly."

"Can we get more people?"

Viv shrugged. "Maybe. There's always workers if you got money. Whether you got money . . ." Another shrug.

"We'll make a payroll," Grace said, though John wasn't sure. "And we have the money from this order."

"I'll make some calls to some guys I know," Viv said. "Put an ad in the paper for tomorrow, if you can. It'll take time away from the build work to interview the guys, but we can do it." She turned around and laid her screwdriver into its spot in the tool chest. "Well, I'm outta here. Got a date." She sauntered out. "See ya all tomorrow."

Grace collapsed into a desk chair.

"That felt good," she said.

"You sound surprised," John said.

"Don't take that tone with me, John Wilson, John Rayburn, John number 7533, or whatever your name is."

"I'm just worried about you," John said. "Because—"

"Yeah, I know you are," Grace said. "And yeah, I appreciate it. But how about we just leave Grace alone for a while and let her sort things out."

"And who's going to help Henry sort things out?"

"Henry can—"

The door from the reception area swung open. A sheriff walked in followed by a man dressed in a dark business suit.

"I'm going to have to ask you all to vacate this building," the sheriff said.

CHAPTER 4

The sheriff held a piece of paper in one hand. His other hand was on his hip near his sidearm. The man behind him met John's look of disbelief and smirked.

John wanted to fly at him, but he forced himself to relax. This was no time for aggression.

"Why is that?" Grace said. She sounded far calmer than John felt. Henry pushed open the door to the office and looked down. His hair was standing up and he looked fever-drenched in sweat.

"Who's he?" he muttered.

"I have an injunction here that states you need to remove yourself from the premises," the sheriff said.

"We have a lease for this building," Grace said. "We're the legitimate occupants."

"This injunction says otherwise."

"Just get them out of here," the man in the suit said. John recognized the accent. He was an Alarian.

The sheriff turned only slightly to address him. "Mr. Gesalex, please let me do my job." He turned back toward Grace. "This injunction states Mr. Gesalex is the owner of the business residing at 9812 South Crevinger Way, and that includes all the materials herein. This is signed by a judge in this county."

"We've never heard of Mr. Gesalex, never met him," Grace said. "I'm the president of this company, and we own all of this."

"This document says otherwise," the sheriff said.

John realized that Gesalex didn't care a whit about the company; he wanted the transfer gate back, the same gate that sat half-assembled in the back room. John couldn't let them get their hands on it.

"I'm the chairman of the board of this company," Gesalex said. "I own all this."

"Mr. Gesalex, I will have you wait outside if you interrupt me again," the sheriff said.

Henry sat heavily at the top of the stairs. He muttered numbers in his feverish state, "Ninety-eight twelve, ninety-eight fourteen, ninety-eight twelve, ninety-eight fourteen."

John was worried they'd have to take him to the hospital soon, but there was no time for that now.

"He's not the chairman of the board," Grace said. "Ermanaric Visgrath is."

"He's dead and you know it!" Gesalex cried.

"This is your last warning," the sheriff said. "Stay quiet, Mr. Gesalex." To Grace he said, "All I know is that a judge signed this order and you need to vacate the premises."

"Not if he's staying," Grace said. "This is all ours."

"Ninety-eight twelve, ninety-eight fourteen, ninety-eight twelve, ninety-eight fourteen," chanted Henry from above.

"Listen, I just do what the injunction says," the sheriff said. "I will remove you all by force if necessary."

"You—"

"Hold on, Grace," John said. "Can I see the injunction, please?"

The sheriff nodded and handed the paper to John. There it was in print. Henry's fever-addled brain had found the clue.

"You're in the wrong building," John said. "This is 9814 South Crevinger, not 9812."

"That's ridiculous," Gesalex said. "This is clearly the place. This is clearly where you should not be."

The sheriff took the injunction back and read the address again. He pushed open the door to the reception area and looked at the address in bold letters above the front door.

"This letter has the wrong address," the sheriff said.

"It doesn't matter," Gesalex said. "It's just a typographical error. There isn't even a 9812 so it must be this place."

Gesalex tried to push the sheriff forward. The man did not move.

The sheriff turned toward Grace and tipped his hat. "Sorry to bother you, ma'am. This appears to be an invalid injunction."

"I'm the CEO of Grauptham House," Gesalex said. "You've probably heard of it. We are a billion-dollar company. We have a lot of power and money. And I want you to take care of these vermin."

The sheriff looked at him for a long moment. "You'd think a billion-dollar company would have someone who could write a decent injunction."

He walked out.

Gesalex watched him go, and then turned with a start, seeming to realize he was alone in the factory with Henry, John, and Grace.

"You're trespassing, Gesalex, you murdering son of a bitch," John said.

He sneered. "You can't stand against us. We will crush you and all your duplicates."

"Tell it to Visgrath," Grace said quietly.

Gesalex paled.

"Now go," Grace continued, "and count yourself lucky there's a witness to your being here, or you'd not make it out alive."

Gesalex opened his mouth to speak, and then turned and left.

As they watched him drive away, John said, "We better get that transfer gate out of here."

"And we better get Henry into a bed," Grace added.

"We're going to run out of glass tops, microprocessors, and LED score boxes," Grace said. She, Henry, John, and Casey sat around her desk in the office. Grace had managed to get the help-wanted ad in the paper just in time for the next morning's edition, and Viv had interviewed and hired ten assemblers, none of whom had worked there before. They heard her yelling below, correcting the slow, error-prone work of the new workers. "We can't make the order."

"When do the parts get here?" John asked.

"Glass tops we can get anywhere," she said. "But our cheapest supplier won't ship until next week. The score boxes are out of stock at the local place. The microprocessors we use, the MPU-12s, are nowhere to be found."

"Out of stock? Back-ordered?" Henry asked. He paused in mid-question to cough. A night's sleep had broken his fever.

Grace said, "No one has them."

"Maybe we can use a different model," John said.

"The MPU-24s are three times the price!" Grace said. "We're eating into profit."

"We have no profit if we don't ship," John replied.

Grace glared at him. "More expensive parts are the last resort. We already have to get the glass for more. And if the score boxes are more too, there goes the margin. We need the profit, not just the volume."

"We need the cash flow," John said. "You said we could make payroll, but can we?"

"At least one," Grace said with a grin. A real grin. John had noticed all day that she was more animated than she'd been since the incident with Visgrath. Was she pulling out of her depression due to hard work on something she loved?

"Do you guys have to work so hard again?" Casey asked. "You just got back to this . . . uh . . . universe."

Grace didn't say anything, so John said, "We need a certain volume to make a profit. If we don't push hard now, it'll all fold up from overhead costs. We could give up, but I don't think anyone wants to." He glanced at Grace.

"We've worked too hard for that," Henry said. He looked at Grace too.

Grace shrugged. "Maybe it doesn't really matter," she mused. "What we need are those little processors we bought in Universe 7651. What were they, five dollars each? They could handle the processing."

The microprocessors had been more advanced in 7651. The transfer device they'd built there had been smaller than the one in 7650. Not only were the processors more compact but it was the second time John had done it, and he knew shortcuts he could take now.

"We used up most of our cash in 7651," John said. "I don't think we have enough capital to do much there."

"But we've got cash here," Henry said.

"My bank account went into the gold we used to fund ourselves in 7651," John said.

"We own our town house," Henry said. "We can mortgage it again."

"Will the processors even work with the voltages in this universe?" John asked. He hated anything that seemed like exploitation between the universes. It reminded him of what Prime had dangled in front of him.

"They should. Same voltages. I don't see why not," Henry said.

"I wonder what else is cheaper in 7651?" Grace said.

"Hold on—" John said.

"Maybe shipping too," Henry said. "We could build here, ship there, and use a transfer device at our two destinations to move them back and forth."

"But—" John said.

"Or we build them in 7651," Grace said, "if labor is cheaper there."

"I wonder what the price of a microprocessor in 7649 is?" Henry asked.

"Stop!" John shouted. Henry and Grace looked at him quizzically. "We're not doing that. We're not setting up some network of devices between dozens of universes. We're just . . . not."

"Why?" Grace said. "Seems like the obvious thing to do."

"There are bad people out there," John said. "They'll notice—"

"Worse than the Alarians?" Grace asked. "Because we can deal with them."

"There could be. Corrundrum indicated there were," John said. The marooned traveler had hinted at a force called the Vig in the multiverse. Corrundrum had died before he could explain, shot by John Prime as he tried to steal the device from John.

"We can be careful," Henry said.

"We were careful last time, and we got found out," John said.

"We know what to look for," Grace said. "I wonder how many stranded travelers there are in the universes. I wonder if they have conventions."

"Do you think someone takes a census?" Henry asked.

"There are billions of people in billions of universes," John said. "Wouldn't we notice if travel between them was commonplace?"

"No one noticed that EmVis had scuba and Beethoven's Ninth Symphony, not even you," Grace said.

"I didn't know what to look for," John said.

"Could you spot it now?" Grace asked. "If we dropped you in 7652, could you tell if there were extradimensional travelers exploiting the universe?"

John considered it. "If I knew enough of what is common technology across a span of universes, I could spot the exceptions."

"If you knew," Grace said. "But you don't."

John thought. "Prime knows. He kept a notebook of information about each universe he visited."

"A notebook! We should have kept a notebook," Henry said.

"Prime even had me ship a huge footlocker of stuff to 7533," John said. "Probably included an encyclopedia, since it was so damn heavy."

"An encyclopedia from every universe!" Henry said. "That would be a good start." He scratched his head, and his red eyes held a faraway look. He wiped his nose absently. "It would be an exception-based analysis. We'd scan the encyclopedia looking for differences, and that would give us a list of things to examine and exploit."

"And for modern data," Grace said, "the day's *Wall Street Journals* would show us everything that we could buy low and sell high."

"Just hold on!" John said. "Prime couldn't do it easily. We all know how his Cube idea panned out. And we can barely do it with pinball here. It's not easy at all, and there's all four of us working at it. The Alarians took thirty or forty years to do it here and they had dozens, if not hundreds, of people."

"You're right," Henry said. "We'd need an army of people to do it."

There was a moment of silence, and then Grace said, "Let's get back to the problem at hand. We have machines to ship, and we need some parts. Unfortunately, they need to come from this universe . . . for now."

The next day, John and Casey drove into Detroit where Grace had found a cache of cheap MPU-12s that a distributor was trying to unload. For a change, Casey let him drive. She placed a hand on his thigh as they drove.

"I was thinking about what Henry said yesterday," Casey said.

"About what?"

"About an army to help manage a company across universes," she said.

"That was just talk," John said. "We can't really do it. We're too busy here."

"What about the other John, this Prime guy?" Casey said.

"Prime," John said. "It's complicated. He . . ."

Prime had arrived on the Rayburn farm in Universe 7533 offering something fantastic to John, the chance to see another universe. He'd flashed money, told him stories, proven that he was who he said he was. But in the end, he'd stolen John's life. John had been lost among the universes, while Prime slipped right into his life. He'd married the Casey there, the Casey that John had had a crush on.

John had spent a long time hating Prime for what he had done. But when he had needed help in saving his friends, Prime had come willingly. John couldn't have done it without him.

"And doesn't he have a Casey of his own?" Casey said.

"And a child too."

"The more the merrier," Casey said.

John felt a bit of discomfort discussing his old Casey from 7533. "Um."

"I'd like to meet her," Casey said.

"I don't want him involved in this," John said.

"Why? Isn't it clear after what he did that he's a good guy? He's you, and you're a good guy."

Was he? John wondered. Prime and he were identical and Prime was immoral. He lied, cheated, and had even killed. But John could never say with any certainty that he wouldn't have done the same thing in the same situation.

"I don't know if he is," John said.

"He risked everything for you," Casey said.

"Everything he stole from me in the first place."

"Including the other Casey?"

"Um. I hadn't even asked her out yet. Or even talked to her."

"She clearly had a thing for you," Casey said, "or she wouldn't have fallen for Prime."

"I guess so."

"So you regret that you never talked to her?"

"I— No."

"No?"

"No, she's a whole other person. I don't even know her. Never did. You're the Casey I love."

"Really?"

"Of course."

"That's rather sweet of you," Casey said. "But what if I had died when I was shot? Would you have gone to find another Casey?"

"No! Never!"

"Why never?" Casey asked. "I'm probably a really nice person everywhere."

"Yeah, but . . ."

"You're uncomfortable with this conversation, I see that."

"No, I'm not. Well, yes, I am," John said. "Visgrath mocked me and my friends for not being singletons. He proclaimed that these versions of myself, Henry, and Grace were intrinsically less valuable than he was because there were no parallel selves of his."

"How can he have no doppelgangers, if there are an infinite number of universes?"

"Because, first, maybe there aren't an infinite number of universes and, second, once you start traveling between universes—me—or interacting with someone who does—you—you can no longer be parallel with any other versions of yourself."

"What?"

"Travel between parallel universes pollutes the synchronicity of the universes. No other John Rayburn is experiencing anything of what I've experienced once Prime showed up with the device. My life took a radical divergence, because there can't be any other universe where other versions of me traveled the same sequence of universes that I did. Once you start moving beyond your current universe, you become a meta-person, a meta-event, beyond what normal versions of me experience."

"So you think travel is discouraged to maintain the synchronicity between the universes?" Casey asked.

"Hmmm. Maybe. I hadn't thought of that, but that would be a good explanation. Maybe it isn't about control. Maybe there is some value in maintaining lots of synchronized universes that we don't see."

"Too bad there isn't someone we can ask," Casey said. "Maybe the people in Universe One will tell us."

"You mean Universe Zero. The device starts counting at zero."

"Uh-huh. Whatever," Casey said with a smile. "In any case, wouldn't they know more? We're in the boondocks out here in the seven thousands."

"That's certainly true."

"No, I'm serious. We should go to Universe One or Zero, whatever the first one is, and ask."

John nodded his head. "We will, once we know more."

"You're the cautious sort, aren't you."

"I just like to know what questions to ask before I get there."

"Yes, cautious," Casey said with a laugh. "I'm more of let's-jump-right-in kinda gal."

"Yeah, I know. I like that about you."

"Really? I figured you'd rather have a calmer girlfriend around."

"Nope."

"Good," she said. After a few moments, she added, "If something does happen to me, you can go find another Casey somewhere. I won't mind."

By hook and by crook, the team shipped the machines to Las Vegas quickly enough to avoid peeving the customer. Grace managed to procure a line of credit with the bank to meet payroll. Henry, Casey, and John called all the sales reps and upped the commission by five percent. They used freelance salespeople in all the locales they were interested in selling; it was cheaper than keeping a dedicated sales force on their own payroll. They paid more in commission, but less in overhead. Some of them, like the one in Las Vegas, hadn't even noticed the home office was empty.

"Tells you what they think of our product," Henry said. "If they didn't even know we were gone."

"Another five percent commission will get their interest," Casey said.

Grace nodded. "If we can get the volume back to where it was before we left, we should be okay."

Henry peeked out the office window at the floor below. "Viv says the new team of assemblers is coming together," he said. "Though a few of them are out sick."

"A summer flu bug is going around," Casey said. "I heard it on the radio."

"That flu sucks," Henry said.

"Maybe Viv should get a raise," John said.

"Maybe," Grace said. "If we make our quota." She had set a quota that was the same for the new quarter as the old. It was aggressive with all that they had to make up.

"I'd like to give the sales thing a shot," Casey said suddenly.

"What?" John said. He hadn't ever thought of her as anything but back-office support, someone to handle odd jobs.

"Yeah, remember that arcade and restaurant we passed on our way to Detroit?"

"Yeah, at the Ohio border after Toledo," John said. "It was called Old Gus's." As they'd flown by on the highway, they'd seen that its parking lot had been full. The sign said that the arcade had offered miniature bowling, minigolf, and games of skill. "But—"

"But what?"

"I was thinking you'd just help out . . . here," John said.

"Running errands?" Casey asked sweetly.

"Yeah," John said.

"Getting coffee? Sweeping up maybe? Being ready to make out whenever you need a break?"

John realized he'd made an error and stared blankly at her.

"Um . . ."

"I think it's a great idea," Grace said. "Regardless of what John thinks."

"No, I just never thought—"

"Yes, John," Casey said, "for all the thinking you do, you don't think so much."

"Yeah, you're right. I think you'd do a good job at sales," John said.

"Thanks," Casey said. "Me too."

"Hey, boss!"

Grace stood and peered out the window. The voice belonged to Viv. They'd yet to find a receptionist to replace their last one, and so anyone who was brave enough to venture past the outer foyer usually ended up face-to-face with Viv.

"Yeah?" Grace replied after sliding one of the office windows open.

"Lawyer here to see you."

"Lawyer?" John wondered. "Was our lawyer coming over?"

"No," Grace said darkly.

The four climbed down the stairs, their eyes on the well-dressed man holding a sealed envelope.

The man handed the envelope to Grace. "Official notice from your stockholders. Sign here."

Grace snatched the pen from the lawyer and signed. The man gave the factory a once-over, then spun on his heel and left.

"Sorry, boss," Viv said. "I guess I should have kept him out."

"It doesn't matter, Viv," Grace said. "He would have gotten the papers to us some other way. It would only have delayed the inevitable."

"What is it?" Henry asked.

Grace tore open the manila envelope. Inside were several stapled sheaves of paper.

"Notice of stockholder meeting," she read. "Notice of stock transfer. Notice of option to recover investment." She glanced through the first. "We'll have to run this by our lawyer, but it looks like we have a new board of directors, they want a meeting in one week, and they intend to get their capital back."

CHAPTER 5

"How are we going to raise fifteen million dollars?" Henry asked, not for the first time.

Grace, somewhat exasperated, said, "We've been over this. We get additional capital, either through other investors, a bank, or revenue." John, Henry, and Grace sat at a table at their favorite Chinese place not far from John's apartment. Casey was on her way, and John kept glancing at the door.

"Revenue? If we continue to sell on the current projections for five years, then maybe we'll break fifteen million in revenue that year," Henry said. "Maybe."

"We're not going to do it with revenue alone," Grace said. "We'll get additional financing based on those sales projections. We did it once, we can do it again."

"By next week?"

"Calm down, Henry," Grace said coldly, sharply enough that John felt a pang of concern for Henry's feelings. He paused in his rant.

"I'm just worried they've outmaneuvered us," Henry said. He squeezed the edge of the table until his fingers turned white. "I'd hate for that to happen."

"What's the worst that could happen?" Grace said. "We bolt to 7651? We've done that once. We can do it again."

"The worst is that they get the device again," John said. "It's what they want."

"Is it safe in the new warehouse?" Grace asked.

"I think so," John said. "Our lawyer rented it for us. It can't be traced to me easily." John had rebuilt the transfer gate in a warehouse on the outskirts of Findlay.

"It's good we have two transfer gates," Grace said.

"Yeah, it gives us more possible solutions," Henry said.

"What's the optimal solution?" John asked suddenly. "What are we trying to do?"

Grace looked off into space for a second. "I want to know why," she said. "Then I want revenge. Then I want to help people."

Henry looked stricken. "You can't—"

"Stop it, Henry. I can want revenge. I can want to kill every last one of those bastards. And don't tell me it's not healthy. Because it certainly feels healthy to me."

"John and I—" Henry started. "We were thinking if you saw a psychiatrist . . ."

Rage clouded Grace's face. John wanted to backpedal and say he'd said no such thing. Maybe Henry had interpreted what he had said poorly. But if she was hurting, perhaps she did need a guiding hand.

"Really?" Grace said scathingly. "You think I should hire a psychiatrist, let her know I was tortured by a universe-hopping band of madmen, and that I have trouble now touching another person? That'll go really well for me, I bet."

"Grace, your voice," Henry said.

She stared at him and was on the verge of saying more when Casey appeared at the entryway into the dining area.

She waved at John, and then paused when she saw the tension in Grace and Henry.

"Hi, guys," she said softly. "Sorry I'm late."

"Hey, Casey," John said. "We waited to order."

"Good."

"I need the powder room," Casey said. "Grace?"

"What? Oh." Grace swatted the back of her hand at her cheek, wiping away tears that had slowly trickled there. "Yeah."

"Order me some chicken lo mein," Casey said. "And a spring roll!"

Henry watched their backs, and then let out a long sigh once the two women had disappeared into the restroom.

"Sorry," he said. "I thought she would consider it . . . if she thought you . . ."

"Sure, it's okay," John said. "Maybe you need to let things go for a while. Grace is a smart woman. She's trying to work things out."

Henry shrugged. "I don't know what else to do."

"She's not a problem to solve, Henry. She's a person."

"I know that! It's just that—"

The waiter appeared, and they ordered. By the time the waiter ran off to the kitchen, Grace and Casey had returned to the table. They were actually smiling.

"Tell them," Grace said.

"What?" John asked.

"I may have sold a hundred machines!" Casey said.

"What? How?"

"Old Gus's is a franchise," she said. "I had lunch with the manager there two days ago, and he'd seen one of our units. Had no idea who sold them or how much they cost. But he had dinner yesterday with the company president. They stopped off on Gross Ile on the way home."

"At the casino where one of our machines is?" Henry asked.

"Exactly," Casey said. "The president loved it. They have fifty Old Gus's across the country, and they want two per location."

"Wow."

"Yeah, I rock," Casey said.

"I agree."

Grace sat back down next to Henry while Casey sat next to John. There was no trace of the anger in Grace's demeanor, and John wondered what Casey had said to calm her.

"Not even close to fifteen million," Henry said, but he was smiling too. John calculated the profit in one hundred machines, about seventy thousand dollars.

"No, but it's a good thing to have in our accounts receivable ledger when we go for that loan," Grace said.

John put his arm around Casey. He couldn't believe he'd ever doubted her. He felt a bit foolish, but he was glad she was as good as she was.

"Of course," she added, "we're in the same boat we were before for raw materials. To build this many machines we need a bigger supply chain."

"Start now," John said.

"When we sign the deal," Grace said. "But I think we should look at getting items from 7651."

John sighed.

"Hear me out!" she said over his objections. "That transfer device represents a huge amount of our collective capital. All of your profits from a year of work, plus six weeks of our time, just when the company was taking off. To leave it unused is irresponsible."

"Using it is dangerous," John said.

"How so? More dangerous than leaving it active, sitting there in that makeshift barn we built at the quarry? We haven't been back in days to see if it's still there and safe. What's dangerous is if someone gets ahold of it instead of us. The Alarians were exploiting it for weeks before we got here. Who knows what havoc they've unleashed upon the multiverse."

"We should check on it," John agreed. "But that doesn't mean we should exploit—"

"There it is," Grace said. "That word 'exploit.' Exploiting something is a perfectly valid course of action. I'm not sure why you want to take the hard way on everything, John."

"It's not the hard way," John said. "It's the conservative, ethical way."

"Ethical? What possible ethical concern is at issue here?" Grace said.

"Theft of ideas is wrong. Using someone else's hard work as your own is wrong," John said. "If we don't do the work, we shouldn't take the benefit."

"I'm not suggesting we don't do the work," Grace said. "But maybe we should work smarter. Guidance counselors and teachers say that the whole universe of possibilities is open to you. But to us, two whole universes of possibilities are open."

"And more, if we make more devices," Henry added.

"We definitely don't have funds for that," John said.

"That's true," Casey said. "Yet. For now, we should just use the ones we have."

"You've clearly thought about this," John said. "How?"

"7650 and 7651 are pretty similar, right?" Grace said.

"Yeah."

"We've talked of using 7651 for supplies, but what about as a sales territory?"

"How?" John asked.

"Casey just made a deal with the CEO of Old Gus's, right? What if that same CEO is in 7651, looking for the next big thing?"

"And if he isn't?" John said. "Universes vary on the small details."

"If not him, then someone like him," Grace said. "It's like virgin territory. Undisturbed."

"Unless pinball already exists there," John said.

"You've already said, our head-to-head models are totally different than anything you've seen. We've made something unique based on the original idea."

"True."

"Virgin territory."

"But who lives over there to sell," John said. "That takes away from the people working here. If I move to 7651 and handle logistics and sales there, that's one less person here to help build."

Grace, Henry, and Casey shared a glance.

"What?" John asked, feeling like the three were plotting against him.

"There's a Grace over there," Grace said.

"But we agreed not to disturb ourselves!" John said. When they had first arrived in 7651 in the alternative Columbus, they had all four agreed not to contact their doppelgangers.

"We agreed not to contact them," Grace said quickly. "We didn't agree not to look them up."

"Grace!" John had wanted the Johns, Graces, and Henrys in 7651 to live on in oblivious happiness, without ever being looped into any multidimensional madness.

"Don't scold me, John Rayburn," Grace said sharply. "I didn't call her on the phone and listen to what a normal Grace sounds like, or visit her and watch her with binoculars to see how she laughed, talked, and smiled. I didn't do that. But I could have."

"Okay. I'm sorry."

Their food arrived, and John was left to ponder Grace's statement. A normal Grace. She thought of herself as broken, as abnormal.

"Who else?" he asked.

"What?"

"Is there a Henry? A John?"

"There was a Henry, but you didn't exist, as far as I could tell."

"What about me? Did I exist over there?"

"Sorry, Casey, I didn't look for you."

"Oh," Casey said with a smile. "That's okay."

"But we could look."

"But why?" John said. "Why do you want to get those versions of us mixed up in this?"

"I'd want to know," Henry said. "All of me would want to know."

"Me too," Grace said.

"Really?"

"Yes, we didn't experience what you did, John," Grace said. "We only see the good we can have from the device, not the bad."

"But if something goes wrong—"

"Then we'll deal with it."

John was silent. What if they hired Henry-7651 and Grace-7651 to man their transfer gate there? Who else can you trust if not yourself? That hadn't worked out so well in the case of John Prime.

"Where are they?" John asked.

"University of Toledo," Grace said, grinning. "Just like here."

"Do you think they know each other?" Henry asked.

"They must," Grace said. "We were in all the same classes."

"But do you think . . . ?" Henry stopped.

Grace gave him a sly look. "Oh, I think so. You are a handsome man in every universe, I'd say."

Henry blushed and Casey laughed.

For a second they were all silent. John realized he'd been wielding the device like a dictator. Because Prime had done that to him. But these were his friends, his best friends in the universe, or rather universes.

"Okay," he said. "We do it."

"Really?"

"It makes sense," John said. "And it'll—" He almost said that it would be good for Grace. "And it'll be smart for business. And safe for the device."

"Good. When?"

"The sooner the better," John said. "We need to move some machines."

"We had an encyclopedia in 7651," Henry said. "But it was impossible to spot the differences from memory alone. If we could go through an encyclopedia from there and here, side by side, we could spot everything that's different."

"Everything that's exploitable," Grace said.

"How?" John asked, looking from Henry to Grace. "How are you going to convince them?" He recalled how he had once confronted his one-armed self, ready to steal back his life from some other John. How would they react?

"I don't know," Grace said. "Or rather, I have no plan. What better evidence than myself?"

"When?"

"Now."

"How about tomorrow?"

"Fine," Grace said. "I'll convince Grace-7651 tomorrow."

It was raining in both universes. Drizzle collected in the scraped lines on the top of the quarry, forming gray puddles in 7650. John activated his portable device, and the huddled friends were in an identical place, only now the shack they had built around the transfer gate was there.

Same rain, same water molecules falling on them for all John knew.

He let go of Grace and Henry.

"We're here."

"Wow," Henry said. "I never get used to that." He turned toward the shack, unlocked the door, and went inside.

Grace stood for a moment, peering out over the bright blue water-filled quarry. No plants grew, driven away by whatever leached from the walls of stone into the collected water. Then she followed Henry.

John saw that the transfer gate was undisturbed, as was their small cache of 7651 money in a strongbox on the floor. They had selected the quarry because it was near John's house, near Toledo, and in a stable, isolated area. They had managed to lease the land for twelve months in 7651 for next to nothing.

John opened the strongbox.

"Two thousand one hundred and some change," he said. As far as they could tell, exchange rates between 7650 and 7651 were pretty even. A dollar there seemed worth a dollar here.

"All clear here," Henry said. "Let's go."

They had rented a generic white van in 7651, after procuring fake driver's licenses. It had been amazingly easy to find someone who could provide the documents for a price. How much scrutiny they could withstand, John didn't know, so he drove the speed limit and no more as they traveled to Grace's hometown of Akron. It was summer break, and Grace was certain Grace-7651 would be home working a low-paying job at the local Dairy-D-Lish.

"Dairy-D-Lish?" John asked. "That's a little different than being CEO of a small company."

"I didn't have a whole lot of options," Grace said. "And we do get free ice cream."

"Oh, fringe benefits."

"Yeah," Grace said. She was sitting next to John as he drove, looking off at the Ohio scenery. Her leg kicked faster than the rock music on the radio.

"You nervous?" John asked.

Grace shrugged, looking down at her leg, as if it had betrayed her. "I guess so. I hope she likes me."

"You think she won't?"

"You remember how I was as a freshman," Grace said. "Shrill."

"Shrill," John said at the same time.

"Yeah, shrill. Maybe she won't have matured and will see me differently than I see her."

John was silent for a mile or two. Then he said, "Why are we really doing this, Grace?"

"Oh," she said. She smiled gently. "For all the reasons I said, but also because it's therapy for me. I want to see what I was, you know. What I used to be."

"You think it'll help?"

"Who knows." She glanced back at Henry, asleep in the back.

"I'm treating him horribly, you know. I'm sharp with him, distant. I do things on purpose to push him away."

"He loves you so much he blames himself for everything that's happened."

"Love-struck boys," Grace said. "He needs to find a hobby other than me for six months. Not leave or anything, but stop obsessing."

"I don't think he knows how."

"It's always Casey and you in every universe, isn't it?"

"I don't know," John said quickly, unsure where Grace was heading.

"You were my first choice," Grace said. "But you were love-struck too. Only Casey exists for you. And I'm just some gawk."

"Grace!"

"Some shrill gawk, who is always quoting dumb movies, not knowing how to act socially."

"You're someone a little different than that now," John said.

"Yeah, I guess so," she said. "We'll see in a couple hours how different I am."

Grace's house was in an older suburb of Akron, full of split-levels on medium-sized lots with huge trees in the backyards filled with trampolines and aboveground pools.

"There it is," Grace said. "That one."

John pulled the van to a stop in front of a yellow house. A station wagon sat in the driveway.

"Looks the same," she added.

"You gonna go knock?" Henry asked.

"And what if my—her—parents answer?" Grace said. "How do I explain that?"

"I'll go then," Henry said.

"And if she recognizes you from school? How will you explain that?" Grace said.

"That just leaves John," Henry said.

"Me?"

"You don't even exist in this universe," Grace replied.

"And what do I tell her?" John asked.

"The truth," Grace said. "Just get her out to the van where we can talk in private."

"Okay," John said, breathing deeply. "Let's give this a try." He got out of the van and walked across the dandelion-covered lawn.

The doorbell was out of tune. He heard a dog yap somewhere in the house, then a woman appeared, wiping her hands on an apron.

"Yes, can I help you?"

"Hi, Mrs. Shisler?"

"Yes, that's me."

"My name is John," he said. "I'm a . . . friend of Grace's from college. Is she around?"

"Oh, a friend from college." Mrs. Shisler peered around John at the van out front. Grace had ducked low, but Henry was there looking out the window. "Is that Henry too? I didn't know he was coming to visit." She called out, "Hello, Henry!"

"Hello, Mrs. Shisler."

"Uh, yeah, road trip," said John.

"Well, you've missed her," Mrs. Shisler said. "Grace is at the Dairy D Lish."

"Oh, where is that?"

"Just take Long to Wilson and turn right at Main. You can't miss it. Oh, she'll be so happy to see you!"

"I bet," John said. "Thanks."

John climbed into the van. Grace was huddled in the well of the passenger's seat.

"That was my mom," she said "My doppelmom."

"Uh-huh," John said. "You're at the Dairy-D-Lish."

"Oh, the Dairy-D-Lish," Grace said. "That bastion of the swirly cone. I've worked there every summer since I was fourteen, mostly because I could bike there."

"Oh," John said. "Your doppelmom knew Henry."

"Then Grace and Henry here know each other," Henry said excitedly.

"Enough that she brought Henry home at least once," John said.

"Or, she met him at the university, because he's some creep who's always hanging around Grace," Grace said.

"Hey!" Henry cried. "I'm a nice creep!"

"Indeed."

The Dairy-D-Lish was packed. A line of six people stood in front of each of the two windows. John parked the van in the last spot in the lot, and they tried to peer through the windshield into the shop.

"I can't see anything through the mesh," Henry said.

"Keeps the flies out," Grace said. "But not the heat."

"We're not going to be able to talk to her with all those people around," John said.

"Not till after eight, which is when she gets off," Grace said. "If I know her schedule."

"I guess we wait," Henry said.

"Go get us each a swirly cone," Grace said to John. "She won't know you."

"Right."

He spied Grace-7651 through the front glass, working the line to the right, so he edged into that line though it was longer. She looked the same, same smile, same laugh.

Of course she was the same. As similar as he and John Prime. More identical than identical twins. Twins had the same genetic makeup but different environments, no matter how closely you dressed them. This Grace and their Grace had lived the same life through high school. Closer than twins.

"I'll have three swirly cones," he said to her.

"Three swirly cones coming up," she said. "You want chocolate and vanilla or vanilla and chocolate?"

"Uh."

"Just kidding," she said with a donkey laugh. "It's the same swirl either way!"

"I'll take three with double chocolate and double vanilla."

She paused then screeched another laugh. "That's funny. Coming right up."

"Thanks, Grace," he said, then paused. Was she wearing a name tag? He looked. No. Oops.

"No problemo . . ." She paused. "Do I know you?"

"Um, I was a couple years ahead of you in high school," John said. "You know. Small town."

"Sure, yeah."

John hurried away, but felt her eyes on him the whole way.

"Well, she didn't know me."

"She's in there for sure?" Grace asked.

"Yep. It's you . . . or rather her. It's Grace."

"She's the same?"

"Kinda shrill, yeah."

"Oh."

The three ate their swirlies in silence.

"I don't know if I can do this," Grace said. "Maybe you're right and we should let this all go. No need to get this Grace wrapped up in all this—"

The back door opened and Grace-7651 walked out. She looked right at John, without looking at Grace.

"Hey, you forgot your change," Grace-7651 said. "Three swirly cones, right?"

She walked right up to the window, holding out the two dollar bills and the handful of coins. Her eyes traveled across John's face to Grace's.

"Hi," Grace-7650 said to Grace-7651. "I'm Grace."

CHAPTER 6

John expected fireworks. He expected disbelief. Maybe anger. Something other than enthusiastic acceptance. Perhaps he just needed to face the fact that he was a pessimist.

The Graces became fast friends and fell in with one another in a truncated form of English that left Henry and John out.

"Pinball?"

"Yeah, arcade-style game with flippers and a ball."

"Never heard of it. Why?"

"Big market. Fun to play."

"Oh, I see."

"You want in?"

"Yeah."

Grace-7651 had finished her shift—only half an hour more—and run out to the van afterward. The two had sat in the back while Grace-7650 explained it all to Grace-7651. She had no problem believing.

"This went better than I expected," John said.

Henry gazed at Grace-7651. "Isn't she amazing?"

"Uh."

"Your Henry?" Grace-7651 asked.

"Yeah. Yours?"

"Yeah. Like Steve Ciaratha."

Grace-7650 giggled.

"What does that mean?" Henry asked.

Grace-7651 smiled. "Steve had braces. He slobbered a lot when he kissed."

"I slobber?" Henry exclaimed.

"Within tolerances," Grace-7650 said.

"Uh," Henry said. He looked at John. "I don't think I like this."

"It's too late now. Genie is out of the bottle."

"You in?" Grace-7650 asked.

"Sell here?"

"Yep, and procure materials."

"Interesting."

"Dairy-D-Lish is the backup."

"Henry too?"

Grace-7650 shrugged. "Sure."

Grace-7651 paused, looking at John and Henry, then back at Grace. "I'm in."

Grace-7651 quit her job that day, told her mom she was taking a road trip, and left with them for Henry's hometown of Xenia. They drove through the night and scared Henry as he walked the family dog around the block.

The three from 7650 sat in the van while Grace-7651 explained. Henry-7651 kept looking at them.

"Is my chin really that weak?" Henry-7650 asked.

"It's a fine chin," Grace-7650 said.

"Do I sound like that?" Henry asked.

"Obviously," John said.

"I thought I was taller," Henry said.

"Shush!"

Finally Henry nodded and walked over to the van.

"I'm gonna have to see it," he said.

"The device?" John asked, knowing that just looking at the device wouldn't prove anything.

"No, I need to see it work."

"Okay."

John decided on Universe 7535 to prove the device. First they drove to the quarry in 7651, and then they used the transfer gate to travel to 7535, the Pleistocene world.

"My god!" Henry-7651 cried. "It actually worked!"

Henry-7650 shared a glance with John. "Obviously."

Henry-7651 stared off in the distance, oblivious to the sarcasm. "Is that a mastodon?"

"I guess it is," John said. A huge hirsute elephantine beast lumbered in the distance between two trees, using its tusks to shred the leaves from the upper branches.

Henry-7651 took three involuntary steps toward the mastodon.

"Don't stray," John said.

"It's a kilometer away! No way it can get to us," Henry-7651 said.

"There are smaller things around here," John said. The cat-dog beasts that hunted in packs had nearly gotten him the first time he was in this universe. Sweeping his eye through the tall grass, he wondered how common they were. With all five of them present and together, though, he expected there would be no trouble. The cat-dogs were probably opportunistic hunters.

Henry-7651 dropped his knapsack, pulled out an old camera, and started snapping pictures.

"Hey," John said. "Those are going to be hard to explain when you develop them."

"No one will notice," he said. "And I'll explain that they were models for a school project."

John shrugged.

"Can we get closer?" Grace asked.

John searched in the grass until he found a stick. Then he used it to beat down a circle, centered on where they arrived. Here there was no quarry to mark the destination.

"Okay, stick together."

They walked slowly toward the beast, which took no notice of them at all.

"Look! Two more!" Grace cried. John realized with a start that it could have been either Grace-7651 or Grace-7650. He had no idea which. "A calf and a cow!"

"Any zoo—"

"Any zoo—"

The two Henrys looked at each other and laughed. They had started the same sentence. John was glad that Prime wasn't there too, but still he felt a little lonely being the only singleton on the trip.

"Any zoo would pay dearly to have this trio in their exhibits," one finished.

"Though it would be hard to explain where they came from," Grace said.

"A million dollars, maybe," Henry said. "That would solve some of our cash problems."

"And raise a lot of questions," John said. "One of our objectives is to stay under the radar from any other cross-universe travelers, right?"

"Yes," Grace said. "It's safer that way, until we know more."

"Or, forever," John replied.

"Forever is a mighty long time," Grace said.

"That's Prince," John said.

"Who?"

"In my universe, he's a . . . Oh, never mind."

The mastodons gave them a casual inspection, but otherwise didn't vary their course through the thicket of trees. They pulled saplings from the ground or broke limbs from bigger trees and denuded them of leaves.

When they were twenty meters away, the male planted himself in between them and the cow and calf.

"I guess that's as close as we get," John said.

"Probably not used to seeing us humans," Henry-7650 said.

"So there's no humans here? None?" the other Henry said.

"I don't think so," John said. "Megafauna extinctions in North America corresponded to human migrations into the continent from Asia. Lotsa megafauna here, ergo, no humans. If they're not here, then maybe none in Asia either. And in any case, there's no human technology great enough to get here from Europe, Africa, or Asia."

"True," Grace-7651 said. "If there's a niche available on the planet, humans will be there."

"A whole world to ourselves," Henry-7651 said. "We need to start a vacation club. 'Visit the Lost World!'"

"It's certainly better than the nuclear winter world," John said.

"The what?"

"I passed through a world—while I was arguing with Professor Wilson—that was frozen over due to nuclear winter," John explained. "7539, 7540, something like that. Due to a limited nuclear exchange which had kicked up a lot of dust into the atmosphere. It was only October, but there was already a meter of snow on the ground. Everyone was hoarding food and the army was rationing."

"Wow."

John nodded.

"Was that Professor Wilson from the physics department at U Toledo?" Grace-7651 asked.

"Uh, yeah. We had a little bit of a run-in," John said. "I tried to convince him that parallel universes were possible. He didn't believe me, so I transferred out right in front of his eyes."

"No!"

"Yeah, it was a pretty stupid thing to do," John said.

"Because now he knows travel between universes is possible," Grace-7651 said. "He won't stop until he figures it out."

"You think?" John said. "He'll use Occam's razor to convince himself it was all a fake."

"Maybe," Grace-7651 said. "He might, or he might spend the next decades trying to break open the secrets."

"Let him," John said.

After Henry-7651 had taken a few more pictures of the mastodons, John said, "It's getting late. We should get everyone back to their home universes. We've been gone from 7650 for twenty-four hours. Who knows what's gone wrong while we were away."

"Hopefully not much," Grace-7650 said.

They walked back to the transfer zone and used John's portable device to reach Universe 7651.

"So here's a couple thousand dollars," Grace-7650 said to Grace-7651.

"Whoa, that's a lotta cash!" Henry-7651 said.

"It used to be a lotta gold," John joked. "Now it's just a little bit of cash."

"Rent an apartment in Findlay, and a car," Grace-7651 said. "Tomorrow John will deliver the encyclopedia from 7650. You can buy the same set from the university bookstore."

"Right," Grace-7651 said. "And we need to incorporate the company here. Scour the two encyclopedias for discrepancies. And search the electronics catalogs for the parts you listed."

"Exactly."

"Two apartments or one?" Henry-7651 asked. When the other four turned to look at him, he began to blush.

"One, silly," Grace-7651 said. "With two bedrooms. To save money."

"Oh."

John saw Henry-7650 and Grace-7650 share a look. He wasn't sure what the status was between the Grace and Henry of 7651. They knew each other, and Grace had kissed Henry. But were they dating? It almost seemed as if his Grace and Henry were setting this Grace and Henry up on a blind date.

"Then we'll have you over a couple times in the evening to show how the machines are built," Grace-7650 said.

Grace-7651 smiled. "These pinball machines, or these transfer machines?"

John started to say something, but Grace-7650 said, "Both!" Again John felt he had unleashed forces beyond his control. Grace clearly wanted something more than one or two gates between worlds. Didn't he want that too?

Grace-7650 kissed her counterpart and Henry-7651. Henry-7650 awkwardly shook hands with Henry-7651 and Grace-7651. Then the three left the doppelgangers for their home universe, using the transfer gate.

"They seem like nice enough people," Grace-7650 said.

John merely raised an eyebrow.

Viv's new crew of builders increased their skills quickly, and the pinball factory had no problems meeting the quota for Casey's new order. John was no longer surprised when she appeared at the office at the end of the day with a handful of order sheets. She had a knack for sales, more so than he ever had. John and Henry were engineers.

The date of the board meeting arrived quickly, and though sales were rising, there was no chance they'd raise enough capital to buy themselves free of EmVis. The two meetings Grace had with banks were successful only in as much as the banks were willing to loan the company small amounts of money based on their income statement. The three meetings she managed to obtain with venture capitalists went nowhere. The last sixty days' lack of revenue made their pro forma statements look a little odd. Grace had no good enough explanation for the dip to persuade the venture capitalists to invest millions of dollars in them. Interested, yes. Willing to fund, no.

"How are they going to play it?" John asked on the evening before the meeting.

"They want our company, out of spite, I think," Grace said. "They can't expect to get access to any transfer device data now that we know what they're up to."

"True," John said. "Or they plan to use it as leverage. Anything in the papers?" he asked Henry.

"EmVis's stock is at an all-time low," Henry said. "But there's nothing to explain why. Most of it, pundits think, is due to the CEO and past board's disappearance two months ago. We all know why, but no one at the company is talking. Stockholder confidence is low."

"And our lawyer?" John asked.

"Says there's little we can do to stop the meeting," Grace said. "EmVis can appoint any board members they want, in any fashion they want, and we can't do anything about it. They have four seats. We have three."

"So there's nothing to argue there," Henry said.

"Not until the meeting is over, and we've heard what their play is," Grace said. "Then it will be time to fight them, once we know the game."

"I hate waiting," Henry said.

"Who's waiting?" Casey said. "I'm selling."

"Which reminds me, Casey," Grace said. "Here's your first commission check." Grace handed a check to Casey.

"No, really, I'm just helping out," Casey said. "You guys need this cash." She looked at the number on the check. "Holy smokes! That beats working at Dairy-D-Lish!"

"Tell me about it!" Grace said.

"Really, it's not necessary."

"Actually, it is," Grace said. "You're our best salesman at the moment, and I want you to work as hard as possible."

"I wonder if Casey in 7651 will work this hard?" Henry said.

"We're not going to find out!" John said.

"Isn't that my decision?" Casey asked.

"It doesn't matter," Grace said. "I asked that Grace to find out. Casey-7651 doesn't exist, at least not in the Findlay of that universe."

"Ah, too bad," Casey said. She met John's worried look with a grin. "One is enough?"

"Um."

"Don't answer that!"

Grace paused. "So tomorrow at noon at the Hyatt in Toledo. The Lawoughqua Room. Casey, please be there, though only John, Henry, and I are board members."

"All right."

"Let's get this over with, and see what they want."

"Oh, we know what they want," John said. "And we won't ever let them have it."

·   ·   ·

Grace paced nervously outside the conference room at the hotel. It was ten minutes before noon, and no sign yet of Gesalex.

"Calm down, Grace," John said.

"Sorry, I'm a little tense."

"Really?"

She smirked. There was no doubt she was more the Grace he remembered, ever since she'd come back to 7650, ever since she'd taken over the running of Pinball Wizards, and especially since she had met and befriended Grace-7651.

Henry and Casey sat in the conference room, nursing ice waters. John found himself wondering how they could exploit the Alarians. They knew a lot that he didn't. How could he gather the information that Gesalex knew?

At precisely noon, Gesalex appeared in the hallway, leading three other men. These would presumably be the other new board members.

Gesalex did not even look at them as he entered the conference room. Nor did two of the others. However, the fourth member stopped confusedly. He raised his hand as if to shake, and John wondered why he bothered.

Nonetheless, John took his hand and shook.

"Hello, I'm Jack Banks."

"Hello, Jack, I'm John Wilson, and this is Grace Shisler," John said, using the alias he'd been using since arriving in 7650.

"Good to meet you," Jack said. "I've been appointed a board member for this meeting."

"Are you . . . uh . . . from around here?" John asked. Jack had no accent, as he expected from the Alarians. But he was unsure how to ask if he was in on the secrets of the multiverse.

"Buckeye born and raised," he said jovially. "Grew up in Delaware, Ohio. Fine little town."

"I've traveled through it," John said. "Are you an EmVis employee? Do you work with Grauptham House?"

"Uh, no, I do not," Jack said.

"Then what are you doing here? You are on our board of directors, aren't you?" Grace asked.

"Oh, yes," Jack said. "I'm an investor. I usually invest in scientific and technology companies. But when Mr. Gesalex called and said he needed some help, I agreed to serve on the board."

"Interesting," John said. He was going to be the only outsider in the room.

"I think it—"

"Can we start the meeting now, Banks?" Gesalex appeared in the doorway of the conference room.

"Yes, sir, Mr. Gesalex," Jack said. "I was just introducing myself to my fellow board members."

"That isn't necessary," Gesalex said. "Let's proceed."

"Of course." Banks shrugged and smiled weakly. "After you, Ms. Shisler."

"Thank you."

They took places on opposite sides of the conference table, Casey, Grace, Henry, and John on one side, Gesalex, Banks, and the two others on the other. Four against four, though Casey had no basis and no vote at the meeting.

Gesalex noted that first.

"Why is she here?" he asked, pointing at Casey.

"She is our best salesperson and is here to present the pro forma income statement through last week," Grace said.

"That won't be necessary," Gesalex said. "We are here only to vote on the dissolution of the company and the recovery of our funding."

"That seems premature," Grace said. "We're a moneymaking venture, and we will recoup your initial investment."

"We wish to liquidate immediately," Gesalex said.

"Why?"

Gesalex said something in another language. "It is our prerogative!"

John glanced at Banks, who looked clearly uncomfortable. John wondered if the Alarians had no one else to man the board with, if all their people had transferred out of 7650 by the time John had recovered the device. Had Gesalex made a mistake in bringing in Banks as a neutral third party?

"Wanting your money back after less than twelve months," John said, "seems to be fraudulent." He was speaking for Banks's benefit.

"Nonsense," Gesalex said. "We need the capital back for other investments."

"Grauptham House must be under some terrible pressure if they need our capital," John said.

"That is irrelevant!"

"It seems you would be better off letting us generate income," Grace added. "If, that is, your motives were pure."

"What are you insinuating?"

"I think you know," Grace said.

"Motion to liquidate the company immediately," Gesalex said. The room was quiet for several seconds, until Gesalex nudged the lackey to his right with his elbow.

"Second," he rumbled in a thick accent.

"All in favor?"

Gesalex and his two cronies said, "Aye."

"Opposed?"

"Nay!"

"Motion carries," Gesalex said, standing up.

"Point of order," cried Grace and John at the same time. John grinned at her. They had both seen the same thing. Banks hadn't voted.

"I call a vote by voice," Grace said.

"Ridiculous!" Gesalex shouted.

"If you don't, our next stop will be a judge," Grace said. "To get an injunction against you."

Gesalex glared at them. "All in favor, raise your hands." He glared at Banks when the man didn't raise his arm. He sat there with his arms across his chest.

"Vote!" Gesalex shouted.

"You asked me to be on this board, and I will do so in as best a capacity as I can," Banks said.

"I will replace you!"

"Not today you won't."

"Why?"

"I want to hear what these people have to say before I rush to any vote," Banks said.

"The motion doesn't carry," Grace said.

"I table the motion," Gesalex said. "Until later." He glared at Banks.

"We'll present our pro forma financial statements," Grace said with a smile. "Casey?"

Casey stood and handed out a thick packet of financial statements, prepared the night before with as much of the data as they could include from recent sales figures.

As Casey walked through the charts and figures, John was attuned to her words. Not only was she the woman he loved, she had a way about her that drew in anyone listening. Or maybe it was just him. Gesalex wasn't listening, fidgeting with the pad of paper in front of him. But Banks was listening, and perhaps that was all that mattered. Gesalex had expected a yes-man. He'd gotten a free-thinking, honorable servant. This would have been an entirely different meeting if Banks hadn't been there.

"This is our projected revenue," Casey was saying. "Our conservative estimate shows us recovering the invested capital by the end of year two."

"How conservative is that estimate?" Banks asked.

Casey turned to Henry, who cleared his throat. He was clearly uncomfortable with the idea of speaking. "Um, exponential growth through year one, followed by linear growth in years two and three, doubling each year. We'll saturate the market in the fourth year, and see competition of the base models."

"You have a bit of a dip here these last few months," Banks said, pointing at the sales history and projections.

"We had some personal issues to deal with," Grace said calmly. She stared pointedly at Gesalex. "Those have been cleared up now."

"Certainly the recent sales look good," Banks said. "But what assurances do we have that these personal issues won't rise again? A CEO and her staff need to be stable, especially in a start-up."

"Please note that we've added a succession plan for all the major positions in the firm," Grace said. "This was something we hadn't done before, since we thought nothing like that would ever happen to us."

"Excellent," Banks said. "It's always good to have your backup around, isn't it?"

"It is, sir," Grace said with a smile.

Casey ran through the income statement, balance sheets, and cash-flow statement. As far as John could tell, she did it perfectly, with only a handful of business classes behind her. No wonder people were willing to buy anything from her.

When she concluded her presentation, Banks asked several more questions.

"Fine presentation," he said finally. "Seems like a good investment, Mr. Gesalex."

"I have little care for that," Gesalex said. "EmVis wishes to recover its investment, immediately."

"Well, Mr. Gesalex, you can certainly liquidate the company," Banks said. "But in this case, you'll recover, as far as I can tell, some intellectual property—patents and such—about thirty thousand dollars in cash, a few leased buildings, and assorted accounts receivable of maybe a hundred thousand dollars. More trouble than it's worth. In a year or two, you might get your millions back, with interest."

Gesalex slammed his fist on the table.

"No! We won't allow these vermin to continue on!" he cried. "They have something of ours. We demand it back!"

John leaned back and laughed.

"Vermin? Not singletons?"

Gesalex cursed in his own language.

"Really, Mr. Gesalex," Banks said. "That's enough. They seem earnest enough kids. What's your problem with them?"

"There's a motion on the table to dissolve the company!" Gesalex said. "How do you vote?"

Banks's face turned red with anger.

"Will you excuse us for a few minutes?" Banks said finally. "Seems we need a private conference."

"Of course," Grace said. The four left Gesalex and the other three in the conference room alone, shutting the door after them. They wandered down the thickly carpeted hallway to the window and looked out over the parking lot. Even with the door closed, they could hear the shouting, though they couldn't make out the words.

"Well, we know what their game is now," Henry said.

"Revenge," John said. "Gesalex must know he can't get the device by simply taking over our company. He's trying to pressure us into giving it up by taking away the company."

"Did Charboric leave the most intelligent lackeys behind?" Grace asked. "Probably not." Charboric had been Visgrath's second-in-command.

The door opened and Banks walked out. He glanced over at the four.

"Well, I bought you about a week," he said. "He's removed me from the board, but it'll take a while for him to find a replacement."

"Thanks, Jack," Grace said. "Sorry you had to waste your time."

"Not a waste at all," he said cheerfully. "I learned quite a bit about you all and your business."

"You don't happen to have fifteen million dollars, do you?" Grace asked. "You did say you were an investor."

"I wouldn't have taken this job if I had that kind of money," he said, laughing. "Not sure why he hates you all, but he won't stop until he's destroyed your company."

Grace shrugged. "EmVis and Grauptham House are under a lot of pressure."

"I guess so," Banks said. "Good luck!"

He disappeared down the hallway.

"A week won't do us much good," Casey said.

"More time to talk to investors," Grace said. "More time to—"

The door to the conference room opened and Gesalex and his two cronies exited. Gesalex stopped and stared at them.

"Gesalex," John said. "How about a deal?"

"John, what are you doing?" Casey asked.

"Getting them out of our hair."

"What deal?" Gesalex said.

"We'll transfer you to any universe you want," John said. "As many of you as you want, as long as you never come back."

"You dare make an unsuitable offer?" Gesalex shouted.

"Bite me, Gesalex," John said. "We have a transfer device, and you don't."

"We have—" Gesalex started, and then stopped. "If you give us the transfer device and show us how to build more, we will let you live."

John cocked his head. "Uh, no."

"Multiples," Gesalex spat. "We want the device."

"You mean the one you used after you killed my parents?"

"We take what we want."

"Why didn't you make copies of it?" John asked. "Why didn't you make another one? Too stupid?"

Gesalex took a step forward. John laughed.

"A lawsuit would solve this in our favor just as well," John said.

Gesalex growled, and then turned away.

"The offer stands," John called. "Transport anywhere. It must suck to be the last ones left."

Gesalex and his friends didn't answer.

"It was worth a shot," John said.

"They're idiots," Grace said.

"I expect Charboric doesn't want to see them unless they have a functioning device," Casey said. "Come back victorious or don't come back at all."

"They must have transfer devices in their universe or wherever they went," Henry said. "Right?"

"If they did, they wouldn't need ours," John said. "But they aren't talking. At least not to us."

Grace nodded. "Well, we have maybe a week. Let's make it count."

CHAPTER 7

Twice that week, John took Grace to 7651, dropping her off and letting her return via the 7651 transfer gate. Grace-7651 and Henry-7651 came once to the factory to watch how the pinball machines were built.

Henry-7651 said, after the car ride from the quarry site to the factory, "You should locate the factory at the quarry. It'll make the transportation issue easy."

"Yeah," said Henry-7650. "No need for transport if we're all located atop one another."

"Atop?" John asked.

"Sure. All the universes occupy the same space, just shifted," Henry-7651 explained. "7650 and 7651 are on top of each other, like all the universes."

"Oh, I see."

John and Henry had ripped apart a new pinball machine and were putting it back together in the factory. It was past eight, and all the workers were gone, to prevent them from seeing the duplicate Henry and Grace.

Grace asked, "Have you two found any discrepancies that we can exploit?"

Henry-7651 and Grace-7651 had been perusing the copies of the encyclopedia for just that purpose.

"Well, we know the differences in the two universes in detail," Henry-7651 said. "The major events are the same. The presidents. The wars. Modern scientists and philosophers are different, but the technology remains equivalent."

"The prices of commodities," Grace-7651 said, "appear on par with those here." She had been reviewing copies of *The Wall Street Journal*. "The biggest differences are those created by Grauptham House."

"Scuba gear," John said. "Beethoven's Ninth."

"Exactly! 7650 and 7651 may have been identical until the Alarians appeared and tipped them away," Grace-7651 said.

"So we can exploit everything they did here," John said.

"And pinball."

Grace nodded. "Unfortunately it'll take time. We can't just turn on a new company in 7651. Scuba was introduced in 1978 in 7650. But in 7651, alternative products that do the same thing have been created."

"The universes are just too similar," Henry-7650 said.

"If we had a bigger set of universes to compare, we could exploit more things," his counterpart said. "The differences would increase as a permutation."

"We need more gates!" Henry-7650 shouted, getting on the bandwagon with his doppelganger.

"Yes!"

"All that is moot," John said, "if we don't have base capital to start with."

Grace-7651 nodded. "A chicken or an egg problem."

"We're farthest advanced here," Grace-7650 said. "This is where I want to stay."

"Until Gesalex and his ilk are gone," John said, "we'll always be on guard."

"Too bad they didn't take your offer," she replied.

"Do we have any nibbles on the investors?" Grace-7651 asked.

"Things seem tight all over," Grace-7650 said. "We're in a recession, and investor capital is scarce. No one wants to take a chance on a company that Grauptham House is trying to unload."

"It looks bad for us," John said.

They had spent hours brainstorming ideas. There were possibilities, but it seemed that every one required seed money and time. The cancer treatment in 7651, the three-wheeled motorized bikes that were the new fad in 7650, all would make money if they already had money. Time would create money if they added hard work. They didn't have time, either.

"We could sell smilodon and dire wolves to zoos!" Henry-7651 said.

"Do you really want to catch those things?" John asked.

"Maybe just giant sloths, then."

"Too conspicuous," John said. "Megafauna can't just appear one day in a timeline where they're extinct."

"What are we hiding from?" Henry-7651 asked. "Are these Alarians the worst there is?"

"Someone put them here," John said. "That's who I'm worried about. Corrundrum was scared of the Vig. Whoever that was."

"Who's Corrundrum?" Grace-7651 asked.

John took a moment to explain how John Prime had found another stranded traveler who had given them some vague clues about the multiverse. Corrundrum had seen the Rubik's Cube that Prime had tried to create and knew Prime for a multidimensional traveler too. He tried to blackmail Prime, but had realized Prime knew very little about the multiverse.

"Where is he now?"

"Dead," John said. "Prime killed him." Right before he had almost killed John. Prime had saved his life, feigning sleep until Corrundrum had made his move.

"And Prime is another version of you?" Grace-7651 asked.

"Yes, he gave me the first device," John explained.

"Where did he get it?" Grace-7651 asked.

"From another me?"

"But where did he get it?" Grace-7651 asked again.

John shrugged. "Neither Prime or I know."

"You could find out," Grace-7651 said. "That might answer some questions."

John shook his head. "I'd just as much prefer to leave Prime be."

"John has some conflicting emotions regarding his doppelganger," Grace-7650 said.

"Hey!" John said, but he took the words with good humor. It was true. John was scared of how similar he and Prime were. Prime was devious, dangerous, and deadly. And that meant that John could be all those things too. Maybe he was all those things and he was fooling himself that he was good person.

"But—" Grace said.

"What?"

"Prime knows a lot," she said. "He's been to more universes than you. Maybe he has some clue on how to exploit them."

"I'd hoped we could go our separate ways after 7651," John said. "We're not the same person."

"Yeah? But he's still you," Grace said.

"We've diverged," John said. He tried to laugh, but his throat was dry. They'd spent six weeks with Prime in 7651, and he'd never gotten over his sense of revulsion over the person who had stolen his life, his universe, his Casey.

"Sure, you're not him," Grace-7650 said. "Just like I'm not her." She nodded at Grace-7651. "But he knows stuff that we can use. For no other reason than they suck and don't deserve to win, we don't want Gesalex to gain our company. And if he does, he won't stop there. He wants a gate, and we're the only shop in this universe. Nor do we want to give up Pinball Wizards and start over somewhere else. It'll be harder somewhere else."

John sighed.

"Don't we have any other possibilities?" he asked. "What about a loan?"

"There's always an off chance for a loan of fifteen million dollars," Grace-7650 said, "but I doubt it."

He and Prime *had* diverged, as soon as Prime had used the device the first time. He had had a whole year to change, to morph into the deviant he was. A whole year to justify stealing John's life. And when John had been faced with the same choice, he had *not* done it. He had come to live with his fate. But it was only by the slightest chance. They were the same, to a point. The same to the point of moral failure. John had chosen correctly. Prime had not. They were one person, save for that one decision.

John nodded. "I'll ask Prime," he said. "When I take these two back to 7651, I'll use the gate to get to 7533. We'll see what he says. But he may have no magic answers."

Casey-7533 opened the door and recognized him immediately. She had seen through him the first time he came looking for Prime too.

"John," she said. "Back so soon?"

"Yes," he said. It had only been two weeks since they had returned Prime to 7533 with his huge trunk of whatever he'd stolen from 7651.

Casey leaned forward and hugged him. Her smell—Casey's perfume—jolted him. He tentatively hugged her back.

"Thanks for bringing him back," she said. "I was worried, and then he was back and everything seems fine . . . here."

"I need him again," John said.

"So soon?"

"There have been . . . ramifications," John said.

"Of course. There always are with what you two do."

She stepped aside. Upstairs the toddler cried. "He's in the den," she said. "I have to get her." She paused as she climbed the stairs. "When are you and your Casey going to have children?"

"Uh, we're not even married."

"Ah, then you should marry her. I'm sure she wants you to ask."

"Sure," John said, uncomfortable to be talking to a version of Casey about his own Casey. But she would know for sure what Casey wanted. "Really?"

"Of course," she said. "Casey doesn't waste her time on something for the meantime. I know."

"Yeah."

John entered the den. Prime sat at the desk, reading a book. The shelves were lined with physics books and manuals. A volume of an encyclopedia lay on the desk in front of him. A cup of coffee sat next to it. The room smelled of books. Well-thumbed books. John would have liked a den like this and wondered why he didn't have one.

"John," Prime said.

"John."

Prime tapped the encyclopedia. "I read this all the time, and two newspapers, just to make sure I understand this universe. I still get caught up. Something stupid, something everyone here knows inherently."

"I know," John said. "It's like you moved to a foreign country at the age of ten. You can pass for native, except when you don't. Yeah, I know how it is."

"Of course, you do," Prime said. "I heard you talking with Casey. I wasn't eavesdropping, but I listened to your voices rising and falling. It's like a dream, like I'm watching myself in some surreal environment, especially when you talk to her."

"Yeah, I feel it."

"You're back soon," Prime said. "Frankly I wouldn't have been surprised if I never saw you again. What happened?"

"The Alarians found my gate in 7650," John said.

"Damn!"

"But we got it back," John said. "Most of them left 7650. The rest are trying to force us out of business, take us over, and steal back the gate." He paused. "They killed Bill and Janet."

"Bastards."

"Yeah." They were silent for a moment, considering.

"So?" Prime asked.

"We need money, a lot, fast."

"Ah, that's why you're here. Filthy money."

"Yeah, you're who we thought of first," John said. Prime laughed. "I know you kept notes, and thought you might have ideas if you had access to other universes."

Prime nodded. "You can't just walk away? Go to 7652 maybe?"

"No, we won't go."

"Yeah, that's never easy," Prime said. "How much?"

"Fifteen million."

Prime whistled.

"Any ideas?" John asked.

"Steal it."

"What?"

"Sure, find two universes where a bank exists in one and doesn't in another. Walk into the bank, grab a pile of money, and transfer to the blank universe. Repeat as necessary."

"I think theft is out of the question," John said. He didn't mention that he had had that same thought when he first had been lost in the multiverse. But he hadn't been able to bring himself to do it. How long would it have taken before he'd reached that point if he hadn't been taken in by Bill and Janet in 7650?

"That makes it harder," Prime said. "Then it has to be something available cheaply in one universe and expensive in another."

"Like?"

"Furry Buddies in 7501. I saw the same boxes of Buddies in 7502 for a dollar apiece. Went for twenty in 7501."

"We don't have the infrastructure to sell anything in 7501," John said. "Not quickly, anyway. And we'd still be left with the process of converting the money from 7501 to 7650."

"Gold," Prime said. "Easy medium of transfer."

"And we don't have gates in either of those universes, which means me running material back and forth. I'm limited by what I can carry."

"You're putting a lot of constraints on me," Prime said. He

ticked off on his fingers. "Need fifteen million. Need it next week. Can't sell something. Can't arbitrage. Can't steal."

"Do you have any ideas?" John asked, exasperated.

"That leaves finding," Prime said.

"What do you mean?"

"Treasure hunting," Prime said. "Surely you wouldn't object to just finding wealth?"

"Unless it's in Fort Knox," John said.

"Blackbeard's treasure," John said. "His ship is found only in some universes. *Queen Anne's Revenge* was sunk off the coast of North Carolina. Silver and gold in such quantities that we couldn't count it."

"Do you know how to scuba dive?" John asked.

"Uh, well."

"Sounds like a gamble anyway."

Prime said, "It's a matter of probabilities. We keep searching until we find it." He opened up a binder and flipped to a tab. "John Jacob Astor's cache of diamonds. Found in a toilet in the crews' section of the *Titanic* by chance."

"Do you have a remote-controlled submersible?"

"Okay, fine. How about Herihor's tomb in the Valley of the Kings in Egypt? Undiscovered in most universes, Herihor's tomb was filled with treasures from dozens of other pharaohs."

"And how do we operate in Egypt without being noticed?"

"You're adding a lot more constraints!" Prime flipped pages. "How about the Ark of the Covenant, hidden behind a wall in a building in Jerusalem."

"And we would sell that how?"

"Maybe the Vatican would buy it," Prime said. "Fine." He flipped through more pages. "Ah, here it is. Civil War gold."

"That sounds promising. Where?"

"Right here in Ohio," Prime said. "Johnson's Island in Lake Erie was used as a prisoner of war camp for Confederate officers. Fort Johnson was also used as a treasury for funds. When the USS *Michigan* was captured by Confederate spies, the Johnson's Island prisoners escaped on the ship and took a huge cache of gold with them. Only a squall crashed the ship onto the shores of nearby

Kelleys Island. With a handful of survivors, Confederate Colonel Nelson Franks buried the gold on a farm on Kelleys Island. Unfortunately for him, he died of pneumonia, as did most of his men, and the gold was lost. Except where it wasn't."

John nodded his head. "Civil War gold, lost in Ohio. I like it. We just need a universe where the prisoners escaped, then died, and the gold was never found."

"I have that universe," Prime said. "Universe 7458. I was going to try and find the gold, but I had to, uh, move on before I could dig it up. I never found another universe where the Confederate officers even escaped."

"So where is the gold?"

"Uh, well," Prime said. "I know the general vicinity."

"There's no exact location?"

"I know within a few hundred meters," Prime said.

"That's gonna make it hard to find."

"Metal detectors," Prime said. "We'll need metal detectors."

"We?" John asked. "I'm just asking for ideas, not volunteers."

"Ten percent finder's fee," Prime said with a smile. "Seems fair."

John shook his head, but still he laughed. "Fine."

"What's that? Another adventure without me?" Casey stood in the doorway, holding Abby to her shoulder.

"This one is just digging holes," Prime said.

"I've dug holes for you before," Casey said coldly.

John watched something pass between the two. Prime nodded. "Really, it's nothing dangerous. I'll just be gone a couple days."

Casey met his gaze for a moment, and then nodded. "I guess. All our problems are cleared up here, what with Ted Carson suddenly showing up a week ago."

"A week?" John asked. "He was missing here?"

Ted Carson was a bully, a sociopath, that had tormented John in high school.

"Mysteriously," Casey said.

"The police thought I might have something to do with it," Prime said. "Fools."

"Fine, a few days," Casey said. "It's not like you have a job at the moment."

To John's raised eyebrows, Prime said, "Disappearing for six weeks puts a damper on your career. That and the murder charge. But the severance is enough to survive for a couple years. But ten percent of a lot of gold will be better."

"If we find it," John said. "What are the real chances? I need this to work."

"I have no idea. The gold could be at the bottom of Lake Erie for all I know," Prime said. "The event is rare, but given that the escape happened at all and the ship disappeared . . . I have to assume the gold is on that island."

John turned to Casey. "Can you spare him for a few days?"

"Yes, of course, if you need him," Casey said. "I know what he owes you." She turned away then, and John thought he saw the streak of a tear on her face.

"Maybe I should do this myself," John said. "Just tell me where the gold is. You'll get your percentage."

Prime looked after Casey, a look of real concern on his face.

"No," Casey said, her voice muffled with her face snuggled close to Abby's neck. "I want him to go." She glanced up with glassy eyes. "I suppose he has to go now."

"Yeah, the sooner the better," John said.

"And you're doing it for your friends, and for your Casey?"

"Yes."

"Instead of just running away? You're doing whatever it takes?"

"I guess so."

"Would you do just about anything for your friends?" Casey asked.

John felt the gravity of the question, and paused. "Yeah, I would."

"Okay," she said. "He can go. But same as last time, bring him back in one piece. Or you have to take his place." John laughed, but Casey only smiled.

"Well, we need some supplies," Prime said. "Luckily I have some cash in this universe, so let's make a list."

John and Prime filled a shopping cart with supplies at the local Creble's Sporting Goods: a tent, two sleeping bags, a lantern, cooking supplies, and, the most important items, two top-of-the-line metal detectors and enough batteries to last a week.

"So your legal trouble is over?" John said as they packed the trunk of Prime's car.

"Surprisingly, when I returned the police had dropped all charges," Prime said.

"Why?"

"Ted Carson suddenly appeared, and not even an apology from the police," Prime said. "Do you believe it?"

"Yes, I believe that," John said. "They thought you had murdered him?"

"Yeah. The guy was just missing."

John studied him for a long moment. "So what was in that trunk that we brought back with us from 7651?"

Prime leveled him a hard stare. "Do you really want to know?" he said. "Because I'll tell you if you do."

John looked away. Why did he prod Prime? Why did he look into that mirror every time he could? "I think I know," he said. The police were suspicious enough of Prime to charge him in the disappearance of Ted Carson. Then suddenly all those charges were dropped when Prime returned six weeks later . . . carrying a huge crate that might have contained a living human body.

But he knew Prime was capable of atrocious things, whether justified or not. He had watched him shoot Corrundrum. Prime had stolen everything from John. And now this business with Carson. What John hated was that he would have done similar things in the same situation.

"Let's go."

Casey dropped them off at the quarry site, not waiting to see if they transferred out or not. Abby was crying in the backseat.

The late-afternoon sun did not change position as they transferred to 7651. One hundred meters to the northwest of them now sat the wooden building housing the transfer gate where nothing had existed in 7533.

"God, I hate this place," Prime said.

"We spent far too much time here," John said.

John looked around them to make sure their sudden appearance had gone unnoticed. No one saw them.

Grace appeared at the knock on the door.

"John!" she cried. "And John, I presume." She stared at Prime. "The illustrious John Prime."

John looked at her for a long moment, and said, "Grace. Good to meet you, I guess. Though I think I know you."

"A little bit," Grace said. "You know me just a little bit."

"So they hired you to watch the gate here?" Prime asked.

"That and sell pinball machines," Grace said. "We sold ten this week!"

Prime looked at this Grace and nodded. "You aren't like the other Grace, that's true."

John said, "You met her after she had gone through a lot."

"Yeah," Prime said. "I hope she's getting better."

Grace-7651 said, "She is." To John she asked, "Where to, boss?"

"Universe 7458," John said. "We're looking for some Union gold."

"You want to leave a message for Grace and Henry in 7650?"

"You run as courier?" Prime asked.

"Easier than that," Grace said. "Anything in the transfer zone swaps places with whatever is on the other side. We just put a box in the zone and place a satchel on top of it."

"Oh, I see. Each gate is a two-way transfer; where you are and where you're going change places," Prime said. "The Alarians never figured that out?"

John shrugged. "I don't think so. It's not obvious."

A bright red circle had been painted on the wooden floor of the warehouse. There was a divot cut into the floor and into the rock below from the first time they had tried the device and taken a bite from this universe to 7650. The device itself was a metal contraption that hung above the red circle. Wires connected it to its control circuits and the most important matrix circuits that determined the destination.

"Yeah, tell Grace that we're off to 7458 to look for gold," John said. "I'll be back to 7650 tomorrow after we get Prime set up on his scavenger hunt."

John dragged a transfer platform over to the middle of the transfer field, right on top of the red circle. The shape of the transfer field created by the gate was a sphere, and standing on the edge of it seemed dangerous. The edge of the gate didn't *seem* to move, but who knew if it would for some unknown reason. So they stood on a box, placing their centers of mass as close to the center of the sphere as possible.

"Come on, John," he said to Prime.

Prime hopped up, and squatted down in the middle of the platform, pushing John away from the center.

"We've done this dozens of times since last you were here," John said.

"Sure, sure," Prime said. "Once it's approved by OSHA, I'll be cool."

Grace handed up the bag of camping and detector gear.

"Universe 7458," she said, dialing the matrix circuit. "You guys have some fun, okay? Hey, do you have gold for incidentals?"

John patted his pockets. "Uh, no."

Grace laughed. She went to the small, open safe they had on the floor and pulled out a couple of gold coins. She handed two to John. "If you don't spend them, bring them back. We don't have a lot of petty gold," she said.

"Don't I know it."

"Positions!" she shouted. Then she ran to behind the console. "Universe check."

"7458," John replied.

"Power on!" she shouted. "Charging!" John didn't know why Grace-7651 made such a production of the transfer. She wore a white lab coat, and if she had goggles, she would have pulled them over her eyes. "Transfer imminent! Clear the transfer zone!"

"No one else is here but us," Prime said to John.

"She has her script," John replied.

"In three . . . two . . . one . . . Transfer!"

Grace-7651 disappeared and they were outside again. The two of them dropped about five centimeters. They staggered off the platform.

"There's got to be a better way to do that," Prime said. He patted his body, as if to make sure his limbs were all still there.

John surveyed the area. The same abandoned rock quarry

existed here as in most of the universes they knew. He squinted into the setting sun.

"We need transportation," he said.

"Let's hike into town and catch a bus to Toledo," Prime said.

John gazed across the road at the Rayburn house.

"Was he here in this universe?" he asked.

"I don't know," Prime said. "I didn't check every time, and I don't remember this one in particular."

"Let's cut through the back," John said.

It would take a little longer, but the back end of the quarry abutted against Steller Road. Sometimes there was a development of little box houses on the road, and sometimes it was just farmland. Steller ran into town too, but curved here and there on the way, running past the reservoir and sailboat marina.

The hike into town took an hour, and, except for a few farm trucks, they saw no one. The town looked little different than what John knew of Findlay. Clearly things were similar between the universes. They bought sodas and found the money in John's wallet to be identical to the local currency. Cash would not be a problem, and if they needed more than the couple hundred he had, there were the gold coins Grace had given them.

Prime stayed outside as John bought two one-way tickets to Toledo and then on to Sandusky. Twenty-two dollars each. He kept expecting the ticket agent to have some look of recognition, but she didn't even bat an eye at him.

The bus got them into Sandusky at just before midnight. There was no ferry to Kelleys Island until the next morning, so they found a cheap motel near the terminal.

The next morning they hiked to Marblehead and caught the first ferry across to the island. The weather was hot and muggy. The spray from the lake over the rail was welcome even that early in the morning. Mostly summer workers were on the ferry, coming over for the day of work at restaurants and bars.

The island was just over ten square kilometers in area, little of it inhabited. They passed touristy bars and restaurants, and then entered areas of the older established homes of the year-round residents. Huge quarries had been dug to get to the limestone, laid bare by the last glaciation. They passed through a dry quarry, filled with broken rock and patchy vegetation.

"Lucky the quarry diggers didn't find the cache," John said.

"The site is on the north side of the island," Prime said. "I think it's actually in the state park."

They stopped at the ranger station and paid for a primitive lot at the back of the site.

The ranger stared at them.

"Twins?"

Prime nodded. "Yeah, identical twins."

"Have a good time! Careful with your campfires!"

"Will do."

Prime said, "We want to see Bird Rock. Can you tell us where that is?"

The ranger paused. "Bird Rock? Oh, yeah, the old boulder covered in petroglyphs. There's a trail that runs behind all the lots. Follow it toward the lake. But don't stop at the water. Follow the lakeshore and you can't miss it."

"Thanks!"

After they left the ranger station behind, Prime said, "I'm surprised more people haven't commented on our twinness."

The site was empty, and none of the lots near them were taken. Raising the tent had seemed easier in the store when the salesmen had been showing them than in the wild. Eventually they got the tent up, but only after they had done it once with a bad slant to the left.

"Ready?" Prime asked.

They took the metal detectors and strode off toward the northern shore. Birds and small rodents scurried away in front of them. Twice they saw deer staring unconcernedly while they chewed grass, their mouths churning in circular motion.

"The article said it was within a hundred meters of Bird Rock," Prime said. The path opened onto the lake, a rocky shore that forced them to jump from rock to rock to cross.

Snakes, sunning themselves in the morning light, slithered away from them. Mollusk shells crunched under their feet and the smell of dead fish was overwhelming.

"That must be it," John said. A boulder sat on a bar of rock that jutted out into the water. John jumped from his current rock to the bar, nearly slipping on the algae. The boulder was etched deeply with simple line drawings and geometric shapes. They were so old that thick moss had grown over the shapes. John ran his finger over the lines.

Prime scrambled up the boulder and peered back at the land.

"One hundred meters puts us about where that big tree is over there," he said. "And near those shrubs over there."

"I doubt it was exactly one hundred," John said. He followed Prime's gaze, marking the extent of the area they had to explore. Then he noticed the house. "Uh-oh," he said.

"What?" Prime asked.

"It could be on their property." The state park ended at the edge of someone's home. Occupied, John guessed, based on the hanging laundry.

"Yeah, but it won't matter."

"Why?"

"If we find anything, we'll dig it up in the middle of the night, and leave for 7650," Prime said. "But it's probably not. More likely over there in that higher area. Let's grid this off and start looking."

"Should have brought some flags," John said.

"We'll use rocks."

Starting from Bird Rock, they marked five-meter increments along the shore with rocks. One hundred meters away was a small patch of sandy beach. They turned on their detectors and swept them over the sand. Immediately the detectors flared at them.

Digging with their shovel, John turned over the sand. The shovel struck a beer can. It sloshed onto the beach, draining of dirty water.

"Gold!" Prime said. "Malt gold!"

"Funny," John said.

Walking parallel and separated by three meters, the two walked into the woods. The brambles and tightly growing bushes made going in a straight line difficult, and when they turned back toward Bird Rock, they realized they had walked off at a diagonal.

"This is going to be hard," Prime said.

"Yeah," John said. They'd taken thirty minutes to walk one dissection of the plot. It was going to take four or five days at that rate to cover the whole area one hundred meters from Bird Rock.

"We should have brought string and stakes to mark it out," Prime said.

"That would make what we're doing noticeable," John said. "The last thing we want is a slew of treasure hunters walking around here, following us."

"True," Prime said. He took his knife out and notched the nearest tree. "Is this far enough?"

"I guess so," John said. "Let's work backwards."

They stepped over a couple meters and began working their way back toward the lakeshore.

They broke for lunch in the early afternoon, with a handful of soda cans to show for the work. They had also found a quarter from 1965. Lunch was a couple of sandwiches they'd picked up at the store just off the ferry.

"Well, twenty-five cents doesn't quite cut it, does it?" John said.

"We'll find it," Prime said. "There's some good spots over that way that we haven't gotten to yet."

"Right," John said. "I'll work with you for the rest of the day, and then I'll catch the last ferry to the mainland. I've got to check in with Grace and Henry."

"Sure. I can handle this," Prime said. "I am after all just a treasure hunter."

John looked at him. There had been some bitterness in his voice.

Prime met his gaze. "Casey was my treasure. Your life. Everything I have, I plucked from someone else."

"What are you saying?"

Prime's face was dark, and John realized he was about to cry. John felt uncomfortable, but he didn't look away.

"I suck," Prime said. "I don't just do the wrong thing, I do the evil thing. You know what was in that trunk, don't you?"

"I . . . think I know."

"It was an accident," Prime said. "I didn't mean to do it, but he was menacing us, menacing Casey and the baby. I don't know if he meant to attack or he was just moving his arm up. But I killed him. I swear I saw a knife." Prime let out a single sob.

"So you kidnapped another Ted Carson to replace the one you killed."

"The police were looking at me! I had to. For Abby's and Casey's sake!"

"Or for your sake."

"He deserved it! You know what he is! In half the universes, he's an animal killer, a serial killer wannabe! I did a service to that universe!"

John was silent for a moment. "You've built up a lot of justifications for what you did. I don't know what happened, I wasn't there. But I can see situations where I could have killed him for what he might have done to me."

"Might have? Could have?" Prime said.

"I wasn't there," John repeated.

"No, just me, and then Casey."

"You're carrying a lot of guilt around, trying to justify what you did," John said.

"I know," Prime whispered.

"I can't absolve you."

"But you're me," Prime said. "If I can't forgive myself who can?"

"Often the last to forgive us is ourselves," John said.

Prime dipped his head, shaking it from side to side. John looked at his doppelganger. He feared sometimes that he was becoming more like Prime, that his moral sense was eroded away by the huge power the transfer technology gave him. Any universe was his to visit, to plunder, to exploit. But, he was *not* John Prime. He was his own person, and his decisions would be the right ones.

John stood, offering his hand to Prime to help him up. "Let's get back to it."

"Thanks."

"I don't know how you gain absolution, John," John said. "At least not with the dead."

"Me neither."

CHAPTER 8

The next day in 7650, John arrived at the factory to find Grace ranting about the summons to the new board meeting. John had left Prime to his fortune hunting, taking the last ferry across to Marblehead, and then boarding the bus back to Findlay. He decided he'd have to see about a car if he was going to make that trip often.

"Friday!" Grace cried when he entered the office. "Three days from now!"

"Friday what?"

"Gesalex and his board meeting," she said. "He must have found a board member who'll do whatever he says." They had hoped that the delay of a few days without a certified letter from Gesalex indicated that he had given up on his plan to destroy the company.

"We knew it would happen sooner or later," John said. "Any news on a loan or angel investors?"

"Some nibbles," Grace said. "No one wants to move quickly. And no one wants to piss off EmVis or Grauptham House. You know, I grew up knowing that Grauptham House existed, like Westinghouse and GE, but I never really thought about it. It was just some huge conglomerate. Now we know what they truly are, and they're trying to squash us."

"Not that they don't have problems of their own," John said. "The stock is still in the basement." He had gotten a financial update from Henry. The stock had reached an all-time low. Stockholder confidence was low. Profits were down. "But only a small portion of the company is actually owned by the public. Through a limited IPO back in the 1980s. I guess they needed some cash."

Grace-7651 walked in, and John did a double take. She walked over to Grace-7650 and gave her doppelganger a kiss on the lips.

"Hey," he said. "I'm still not used to you being around. Why'd you come over?"

Grace-7651 flopped on a couch.

"I came over last night with a shipment of comic books."

"Comic books?"

"Yeah, any discrepancy we find in the encyclopedias seems to lead back to Grauptham House," Grace-7651 said. "Everything else is identical! So we started looking for smaller differences. We're reading *The Wall Street Journal* and *The Findlay Bee*. Anyway, we see this story about a lady in Findlay who finds a cache of old comic books in her attic, worth a hundred grand altogether."

"More treasure hunting," John said, seeing where this was going.

"We sent the packet over, with that article circled," Grace-7651 said.

Grace-7650 picked up the story. "Henry goes over to the lady. She hadn't even looked in her attic yet, here. Offered her one hundred dollars for the box in her attic."

"*The Opal Owl* number one," Grace-7651 cried. "*All-American Comics* number sixteen. A complete run of *Candy Apple Blue*. *Bling Comics* number three, where they introduce Father Eel for the first time. A hundred titles. We sold them for thirty thousand dollars at the shop up in Toledo."

"You took that woman's comic books that were worth thirty thou?" John asked.

"We gave her a hundred dollars!" Henry protested.

"And in 7651, she sold the box at a garage sale for ten dollars," Grace-7651 added.

"She's ten times better off in this universe!" Henry said.

"She'd be three thousand times better off if she'd sold them herself," John pointed out.

"She didn't care!" Henry cried. "She was more than happy to have someone to talk to for ten minutes."

John stared at them. "Why am I always the conscience of this group? Why do I have to point out the moral flaws in what we do? What we should have done was told her about the comic books and offered her a good fraction of the money. Now we're no better than Gesalex and Visgrath!"

He turned away, angry that his friends were taking glee in cheating a poor woman out of her money.

"John," Grace-7650 said. "We don't have the luxury to be so kind-hearted. We're in a fight for this company."

"When was doing the right thing a luxury?"

"We need the money," she said. "We're running out of cash, even with the inflow of money from Casey's sales. The lawyer fees are killing us."

"I won't let us do the wrong thing," John said. "I'll take the transfer gates apart and throw mine away if that's how it's going to be."

"John, we're not raping and pillaging the multiverse," Grace-7650 said. "We can't do good if we don't have the funds to operate. Now, I agree that we should always strive to do the right thing, but when our fundamental capability is hampered by others and a lack of money, then we should do what we can to achieve our ends. That woman is no worse off than when we took the comic books off her hands. She'll never know! Ever."

"Grauptham House conspired in secrecy too," John said. "So do these Vig people, policing the multiverse. I don't want us to be like that. I want . . ." He stopped. What did he want? "I want us to do something better than that. I want to help people. I want to use this technology to do good."

He met Grace's eyes, and she looked away.

"Okay, we'll give the lady the money back," she said.

"Wait," John said. "How bad do we need the cash?"

"It doesn't matter, John. Friday they take it all away from us," she said.

"Then we'll build a new company," John said. "And we start again."

Grace-7650 shook her head. "I'm too tired to start over. We don't have your bushy-eyed attitude and hellish optimism."

Grace-7651 chimed in. "I think John is right. We need to take the higher road, but we need the money right now. What can we do?"

Henry asked, "Will Prime find the treasure trove?"

"If it's there," John said.

"Then maybe we treat this like a loan," Henry said. "Until we find our fortune."

"And if he doesn't?" John asked.

"We'll pay her off with our scholarship money," Grace-7651 said.

"That's 7651 money," John said with a laugh. "Won't work here."
"Close enough."

John thought for a moment. She'd get her money for the comic books, he thought. Sooner or later.

"Okay," he said. "It's a loan for now."

"Thank you, John," Grace-7650 said.

"But we better make it up to her, with interest!"

"We'll be more careful from now on," Grace-7651 said.

"It looks like we need to find that gold, more than ever," John said. "I better go help Prime finish the searching."

"Not before you spend some time with Casey," Grace-7650 said. "She'd be mad if you passed through without seeing her."

"Right."

Casey had been staying at his apartment most nights now, unless she was on the road to Chicago or Cincinnati or Pittsburgh. She was the star salesperson now, and claimed as much territory as she could, calling on riverboat casinos, game rooms, restaurants, and truck stops. Two weeks on the job and she was earning enough commission for Grace to rethink the sales plan.

But the apartment was dark when he unlocked the door.

"Casey?" he called.

No answer. He flicked the light switch. Nothing.

He froze.

A normal person would think a bulb had blown. John's mind went to worse things.

He turned and pulled the door shut in front of him. A hand in a black glove reached to halt its swing. Someone had been waiting in the apartment. John pulled with all his might. The door slammed on fingers. There was a howl of pain.

John turned and ran for the stairs. He reached into his shirt for the device trigger. It was always set for 7651 in case he needed to make an escape.

But he couldn't throw the switch! He had no idea what was on the other side in 7651.

He cursed himself for not planning his escape. He had told himself since he returned to see if the apartment building in 7651 was the same as in 7650. He didn't know. If he jumped from the second story here into nothing in 7651, he would fall ten meters and break his legs. If it was a giant hole or an intersection, he'd be worse off. He just didn't know what was on the other side.

Ground level was his best bet. He ran for the stairwell. A man in a dark leather jacket appeared in front of him and he stopped fast. He turned for the back flight of stairs. He'd have to toggle the device now, ten-meter fall or not.

Something slammed against his head, and he tumbled to the orange hall carpet. His stomach churned at the pain in his temple. His breath came in gasps.

Hands turned him over.

Words in a foreign language. Alarian.

Two thugs looked down at him, laughing.

One pointed at this chest and said something.

The other ripped open his shirt.

The two ogled at him, then pawed at him frantically to get the device off his chest.

The pulsing of his heart sent sheets of red across his vision.

He tried to grab the device as they tore it away from his chest, but he couldn't move fast enough. His back screamed as the buckles tore loose and ripped across his skin. A thug pushed him back to the carpet with a booted foot.

They were arguing over the device.

In English, the one thug said, "Ask him!"

"Gesalex said you had this," the other said to John. "No one believed him. Where did you get this?"

"Bite . . . me," John spat. He tried to squirm out from under the boot, but the thug was too big, too strong. He reached down, grabbed him by the shoulders. He lifted John up and slammed him down, this time with a forearm across John's windpipe.

"Your last minutes can be easy and pain-free," the man said. "Or . . . not."

"Police are on the way," John bluffed.

The thug grinned. "Just in time to find a corpse."

"This is a damn Prime artifact," the other one said. "No one has seen one of these in millennia."

"You a Prime?" the first asked.

"Doesn't look like a Prime."

"Primes don't die under my boot." The first pulled a pistol from somewhere and aimed it at John's head. "You got a Prime cache you dug up, dup?"

For a moment, John was confused by the word Prime, because it was the same nickname he'd assigned John Prime.

"Who are the . . . the Primes?" he asked, struggling for air. "The Vig?" He was grasping for some logic to what he thought he knew.

The thug on top of him leaned back. John gasped for breath.

"The Vig? Hell, no! The Vig just found the biggest cache of artifacts. They think they're in charge, but they're nothing."

"How come he doesn't know that?" the second thug asked.

The first stared down at him. "Who the hell are you, kid?" The gun came back and aimed right at John's face. "Who doesn't know all that already?"

"Someone who just found a device," John said. "I never knew about anything but my own universe until two years ago."

"You *are* just a dup," the first one said.

"But we sure took care of Visgrath," John said. He felt no fear looking down the barrel of the gun. What did it matter at this point?

The two thugs shared a glance, and then laughed. "It was time that bastard went! You did us a big favor."

"Too bad you didn't deal with Charboric too."

"Is that why he left you behind?" John asked.

"They didn't take us," the first said, "because we're half-bloods. Doesn't matter to Gesalex that we're singletons."

"My mum's from Pittsburgh," the second said. "The bitch."

"Mine's from New York," the first said. "Just breeding stock for the singletons."

The gun was pressed against John's cheek. "But that's about all you get to know for this lifetime."

BAM!

John expected nothingness, but instead the first thug was flung around wildly. His gun skittered away, and he fell to the floor.

John pushed himself against the wall, away from the two. He

turned. Casey stood in a marksman's pose, her purse at her feet, dressed in a business suit, holding a gun that seemed longer than her forearm.

She pointed it at the second thug. The man turned and ran, carrying the device.

John lunged for it, catching a strap.

The second thug yanked, trying to get the device away. Then another shot slammed into the ceiling next to him. He winced, dropped his grip on the device, and ran, grabbing his slouched-over partner and half carried, half dragged his companion down the stairs and out the door.

John stood, his ears ringing. The hallway smelled of gunpowder.

"When did you get the gun, Tex?" he asked.

"I figured they'd try strong-arm techniques again," she said. "It was just a matter of time. I wasn't getting shot again. Neither were you."

"The gun?"

"Oh, right after I got out of the hospital," she said. "I had to take a class, and they were very nice at the shooting range. I guess a lot of people who get shot at come by afterwards for a gun."

"How come you didn't tell me?" John sputtered.

"I do a lot of things that I don't tell you about, John," Casey said. "Come on inside. I'll get you an ice pack, and we better call the police."

Two officers arrived first and, while one looked around the parking lot as if the two Alarians might still be there, the other took possession of Casey's gun and began asking questions about time and location. Then a man arrived and introduced himself as Detective Duderstadt.

The officer said, "Attempted burglary, two suspects, both white males, about two meters tall. They were in the process of robbing this male here, when the female arrived home to the apartment and shot the first suspect. A second shot was fired and the two fled."

"Did she miss twice with this thing?" Duderstadt asked, hefting Casey's gun in his palm. "Very big gun for a little thing like you."

"I missed once, on purpose," Casey said with a tight smile.

"Oh, you missed once?"

"Yes, the first shot winged the first guy," she said. "The second shot was so they kept running."

"You could have hurt someone with that second shot, honey," he said.

"Really? You think there's some moonbathers on the roof, Detective?"

"So you think you winged one of them?"

"She did," John said.

"I'm asking her," Duderstadt said sharply.

John bit his tongue to hold back the quick remark, and then smiled. "Whatever you want," he said, then leaned back and repositioned the ice pack on his head.

"Yes, one I got in the upper arm," Casey said.

"Because you were aiming there?"

"No, but I must have pulled away subconsciously, since he was close to John."

"So you winged one, and he got up and walked off."

"Apparently."

The first officer, the one who had looked outside, said, "There were blood drops all the way to the parking lot. They just stopped like he got . . . into . . . a . . . car. . . ." The officer trailed off when he saw the look on the detective's face.

"Thank you, Officer," Duderstadt said. He turned back toward Casey. "I remember your face. You were involved with a shooting a few weeks ago."

"Yes, I was shot."

"Ah, yes. You couldn't identify the assailant then?"

"Correct."

"Maybe you've since identified them, and they were here tonight for some reason?"

John expected Casey to erupt, but she remained calm. "No, these weren't the two who shot me."

"And maybe you're one of the three who disappeared at the same time?" Duderstadt asked John. "All very perplexing that was. Three local young businesspeople all disappearing at the time of a shooting."

"We were away on business," John said.

"And you couldn't come back when your best girl was in the hospital?"

"I saw her before I went," John said.

"Indeed. So the nurse said. And where did you go, actually?"

"None of your business."

Duderstadt looked at him. "Maybe you don't like my manner," he said. "Maybe I ask probing questions, you think. Maybe I should mind my own business, yes?"

John said nothing.

"Well, the peace, prosperity, and safety of this town are my business," he continued. "And you seem to be mussing up that peace, prosperity, and safety. That's what I think."

John shrugged.

"A shrug, a shrug. That's what I get for my trouble." He stood. The officer looked at him.

"Sir?"

"Check the hospitals for a wounded male," Duderstadt said. "Winged in the shoulder by this girl here."

"What should I do with . . . ?" The officer held out the gun.

"Is it properly licensed?"

The officer nodded.

"Well, give it back to the young lady. She might need it again."

With that Duderstadt left the apartment.

"I don't think he liked us much," John said to Casey.

The officer glanced down at them. "He doesn't like anybody much."

"Maybe you need a gun too," Casey said. The police had left, and the two were sitting at the kitchenette table.

"They're not going to stop, are they?"

"I don't think so," Casey said. "We should have anticipated this, when the legal ploys didn't work."

"Starting over doesn't seem so bad now," John said.

"It does, and we won't, except as a last resort," Casey said. "You lost your original parents, didn't you? Do you want the rest of us to go through the same thing? Lose our families and friends?"

"Of course not," John said. "But these people will cause us to lose our lives. If you hadn't arrived in time, I'd be dead. If you hadn't decided to get a gun."

"I guess you owe me your life," Casey said.

"I do," John said. "What can I do to repay you?"

"Hmmm."

John paused. "I saw Casey and Prime in 7533. They have a baby there. Abby."

"Yes, I know."

"Maybe, you and I . . ."

"Is that a proposal, John?"

"Um."

"Because unless you have a ring hidden somewhere on your body, I don't want to hear another word about that," Casey said.

"But if I bought one, would you . . . ?"

"Sorry, a lady won't answer those kinds of hypotheticals. You just have to ask and see."

But she reached around his head and kissed him firmly on the lips. "You just never know what the answer will be until you ask."

"Got it."

"How's the treasure hunting going?" she asked.

"We've got nothing."

"We're going to lose the company, aren't we?" she said.

"If we do, we'll make a new one. Either here or in 7651."

"I guess so," Casey said. She wiped a tear from her eye. "I kinda like this universe." She paused. "What's the other Casey like?"

"You know the answer to that. She's just like you."

"Really? She's had a baby. She's had to deal with Prime. She can't be the same."

John thought about it for a moment. Yes, on the surface, the two Caseys were identical, but there was an edge to Casey-7533, a darkness that Casey-7650 didn't have. Her experience with Prime—the death of Ted Carson, whether accidental or murder—had hardened her.

"She's . . . different. Prime changed her."

John reached up and felt the puckered hole of the gunshot wound in Casey's shoulder. She touched his hand.

"You think . . . ?" she started. She looked at him.

"Yeah, I think I'm a bad person sometimes," John said. "I think I'm going to get you hurt."

"Oh, I see," she said. "No, John, you haven't corrupted me. And, no, you aren't John Prime."

"But we're the same!"

"Up to a point," Casey said. "The John I love is a million times different than John Prime. He gave up. You kept going. You kept going until you found me."

"I gave up too. It was just dumb luck."

She smiled. "You can think that if you want." She kissed him on the lips. "Come on. Let's go to bed."

John transferred into 7458 using the fixed gate, after running documents and Grace-7651 from 7650 to 7651.

"I'm beginning to feel like a taxi service," he said.

"I'd slap a taxi driver that held me that close," Grace said.

The half day lost to bus travel made him wish he had a car in 7458. One more trip, and he'd see about getting one.

He did rent a bike on Kelleys Island, and that made the hike to the campsite easier.

Prime wasn't there, but the sleeping bag was laid out within the tent. The fire was smoldering, warm from breakfast or the night before. John assumed he was at the search site. He grabbed his metal detector and hiked through the woods toward the beach and Bird Rock.

"John!" he called.

No response.

He called several times, crisscrossing the search site. Had John left for lunch? Or found an area beyond the original site to search? No, he wouldn't have had time to finish the first area at his rate of search.

John rounded a small hill, covered in saplings, and found a recently dug hole. Prime had started digging here for some reason. Digging deep too. John ran his metal detector over the bottom of the hole. It beeped and whirled. Something was down there.

He narrowed in on the spot, marked it with a stone. Then he

jumped out of the hole, setting the detector aside. He needed the shovel, and found it, tossed aside in the bushes. Prime had been digging, and then he'd stopped, taking the detector with him, leaving the shovel. But whatever he had found was still buried. Where had he gone?

He stood and looked around the area. He couldn't see anything beyond the green of the forest.

John started digging with the spade. Something crunched under his blade.

He reached into the pit, rooting in the dirt, and pulled out a small coin. The obverse said C. BECHTLER, ASSAYER in a circle around the rim. The opposite side said NORTH CAROLINA GOLD. There was no date, but the coin said 150 G. That meant 150 grains. A third of an ounce of twenty-carat gold. The gold alone was worth a few hundred dollars, but John had a feeling that the age of the coin gave it much more value.

John stood up again and looked around. They'd found their gold, but in the process they'd lost John Prime.

CHAPTER 9

John Prime wiped sweat from his eyes again. A rain shower had blown through, and, instead of refreshing the forest, it had left it so muggy and humid that the perspiration refused to evaporate from his forehead. The detectors were guaranteed waterproof, and so was he, but that didn't stop the sweat from streaming into his eyes and stinging.

He was maybe halfway done canvassing the area. For his trouble, he'd found fifteen coins, some as old as 1943, amounting to $2.15. Not one of them was gold. Slowly he'd been working his way closer to the house on the adjacent property. He'd seen no one near the house, but when he glanced over once, one of the curtains looked like it had been moved.

How pissed would they be if they found out all that gold had been sitting right next to them all these years? But they'd never find out.

What if the gold was right on their property line? Or even over the line?

Perversely, Prime took a turn from his line directly toward the house. The detector beeped.

He bent down, as he had done a dozen times already, and cleared away leaves, humus, and dirt. A pop-top, from the seventies, lay half buried in the dirt.

"Find riches beyond belief," he whispered. "Pirate treasure, old coins, the wedding band you lost last year."

He continued on, right up to the edge of the property, where the shrubs gave way to lawn. He was over a hundred meters from Bird Rock at this point, beyond their target area.

Prime turned, took two steps over a small mound, and the detector began to vibrate.

"Another pop-top," he said. "This'll be the most pristine tract of forest in Ohio when we're done."

He cleared away the upper layer, running his detector over each shovelful. Nothing. He pulled out a larger chunk of dirt. Still nothing, but the detector chirped over the same spot. He threw his shoulder into it and excavated another chunk of dirt.

Something was wedged into the dirt. He dug it out with his finger. Something heavy and metallic rolled onto the ground. A button.

Prime held it in his palm, poured a little water over it, rinsing it. It was a button, and etched into it were the letters CSA.

"Confederate States of America," John said.

Prime didn't let himself get too excited. Buttons didn't mean anything. Johnson's Island, just on the other side of Marblehead, was a Union prison. There were any number of ways a button might have arrived on this spot. And only one way that gold might have.

Prime ran the detector over the bottom of the hole. Still it beeped. Something else was down there.

He started shoveling dirt from the hole, deepening and enlarging.

Every ten shovels full, he ran the detector over the debris. He found three more buttons, and then there was no more sound from the detector.

"Four buttons," he said. "That's it. Four buttons."

But then he paused. This was a sure sign that there were *some* Civil War artifacts on the island. Instead of continuing his linear path into the woods, Prime decided to circle around from the hole. Maybe there was something nearby.

On his second circumference, just as he stepped over an old mound of mossy dirt, the detector exploded with sound. Mapping it out, Prime found the area of interest to be a meter in diameter. Something big was down there.

He marked the area with the shovel, dragging it through the leaves and debris. Then Prime started digging in huge strokes. He forgot the heat for the moment. He ignored the pain in his feet and the blisters on his palms.

Something dinged on his shovel.

He jumped into the hole, now about half a meter deep. Brushing dirt aside, he found a glint of metal. A round coin the size of a nickel.

Prime grinned.

"Found it!"

He heard the sound of a shotgun pumped once. He looked up into the face of a grimy man dressed in dirty jeans, a white T-shirt, and a cowboy hat.

"You sure did," said a second man on the other side of the hole. "Now why don't you tell us how you came to hear about our Civil War gold?"

One dragged him out of the hole, while the other kept his gun pointed on him.

"I'm just looking for metal," Prime protested. "I didn't know about any Civil War gold until I found this coin."

The first man grabbed it out of his hand. "Our gold."

"This is federal land!" Prime cried. "That's mine to keep." Prime had no idea if that was true or not.

"Not if you're dead," the one with the gun said.

"Uh."

"Grab his stuff, Russell," the one with the gun said.

Russell grabbed Prime's detector and the small trowel. He missed the bigger shovel, and Prime wasn't about to mention it to them.

"Come on, digger," Russell said. "You can tell us all about it when we get you to the barn."

"Don't think about squawking. No one will mind a stray gunshot out here. Turkey season."

"And he's the turkey, right, Amos?" Russell said.

"Yeah, he's the turkey."

They dragged him through the woods toward the west, emerging onto the lawn of the house that marked the edge of the park. They led him to a barn behind the house.

"Cuff him to that pole," Amos said.

The barn was dim, etched in sunlight knifing through the cracks in the old weathered walls. Russell dragged Prime to a post and cuffed his hands behind his back and around the post. Amos then set the gun next to his feet on the ground.

"So, you're looking for gold, and we want to know how you found out," Amos said.

"I told you, I was just looking around for souvenirs and stuff," Prime said. "I don't know about any gold. Not until I found that coin. Which you can have. Looks like it was on your property anyway."

Amos laughed. "Our property!"

Russell guffawed.

"We saw you crisscrossing that land for three days," Amos said. "We was watching you. You don't spend that time crisscrossing without having some plan, right?"

"Some plan to find Civil War gold," Russell said.

"So there's some Civil War gold," Prime said. "So what? You want it? You can have it. I'm outta here. Just uncuff me and I'm gone."

"Yeah, well, that could have been the plan, until you found that coin," Amos said. "Now, we need to know who else knows. We can't have people nosing around all day and night for our gold."

"I won't tell anyone," Prime said. "I promise."

"You don't have to promise," Amos said. "We can take care of that."

The threat cut through Prime. He didn't see any easy way out of this. He had to buy time until Farmboy found him.

"Everyone knows about the gold where I'm from," Prime said. "And people know where I am, so don't think you can get away with anything!"

"People go missing all the time in the woods," Amos said. "We'll clean up your search site, hide all your camping gear. It's like you've never been here."

"People know I'm here. They'll find me."

Amos glared. "We'll just leave you here for a few hours. You think about telling us what we want, and we'll make it painless for you. Otherwise . . ."

"Yeah, I get it. 'Otherwise' is bad."

"Oh, and look how close you got to the gold!" Amos said. He walked over to a pile of boxes covered in a white cloth. He whisked it away. On the top of the pile was a steamer trunk open and filled with gold coins.

"You morons," Prime said. "What good does keeping all that gold in a box do you?"

Amos glared again. "You'll be sorry. You'll see!" They left the barn.

"What the hell," Prime said, and tried to reposition himself on the dirt floor. He figured he'd be there for a long time.

John stood up and looked around again. Prime would not have wandered off in the middle of the day with the dig in progress. No way. Something happened. Maybe he'd hurt himself and had gone in search of medical assistance. Though there was no hospital on the island. John had no idea where to look. He could check in with the police, he guessed. The island did have one police car.

"John," he whispered. "Where'd you go?"

For just a moment, he wondered if Prime had absconded with the gold. No, there was no way to get back to his Casey if he did. Nor did John believe Prime would steal the money even if he could go back. But John wondered for a second if Prime could build his own device. He had been armpits deep in building the machine in

7651. Maybe he'd copied the plans or memorized them. It was no harder than building a kit airplane or submarine.

John bent over and ran his detector over the bottom of the hole again. It continued to beep. Still more down there.

He dug the shovel into the earth and turned over another pile of dirt. With the side of the spade, he broke the pieces into smaller chunks. This time he didn't need the detector to see the coins. A small handful of dull metal circles clung to the clod.

"Geez!" John hefted the pile of coins in his palm. They were heavy like gold. He poured a little water over them. They glittered as the dirt came off them. Each was bigger than a dime, smooth edged, and printed with the same words in an arc around the edge of the coin: C. BECHTLER, ASSAYER. And on the opposite side: NORTH CAROLINA GOLD. He was holding a fortune in gold in the palm of his hand. The gold alone was worth thousands of dollars, but he had a feeling the coins as antiquities would be worth even more. Civil War gold.

"John!" he shouted. He climbed out of the hole. "John!"

He scrambled onto the small hill next to it. John stopped. The small hill was an old pile of dirt. Someone a long time before had dug there. He paused and looked closely at the pile. It was moss-covered, with leaves atop and small ferns. But it was clearly not a part of the original terrain. Someone had piled that dirt there, years before. Looking for gold.

He turned at the sound of someone moving through the brush.

"John?"

The sound stopped, but there was no response.

John froze. Prime would have responded.

He carefully walked to his left, trying not to disturb plants or make noise with his feet. He slipped the coins into his pocket.

Backing carefully down the gentle slope, he found a small bush and knelt behind it.

Two shapes emerged into the clearing with the hole.

"I swear I heard something, Russell."

"Ain't no one here now, Amos."

One stared into the hole. The other stood with his arms on his hips and looked around.

"This shovel wasn't here before," Amos said. "I'm telling you, he has a friend."

"Then where'd he go? Ain't here now."

John presumed something had happened to Prime, and these two knew what. Maybe he could bluff them. He looked just like Prime.

He stood up. "What do you two want now?"

The two jumped, staring at him. They stared into the green cover as John emerged.

"Who . . ."

"What . . ."

"I asked what you wanted now? Why are you bothering me again?"

"How'd he get away?" Amos asked.

Russell didn't answer but pulled a gun from his belt.

John turned and ran. Bluffing hadn't worked so well.

A shot went off. Something thudded into a tree nearby.

John reached into his shirt to activate the device. Then he misplaced his foot and slid on a patch of moss.

"I think we got him!" someone yelled.

"How the hell did he get away in the first place?"

"I dunno. You cuffed him!"

"Don't blame me!"

Pain stabbed John's ankle where it had slid out from under him, and it was so intense he had no thoughts except to sit there in the dirt and breathe.

"There he is!"

John turned to see the two running down the slope toward him. He reached in and toggled the device, transferring to Universe 7651.

John Prime looked up as Amos and Russell slammed open the barn door. They'd been gone no longer than thirty minutes.

"He's still here!" Amos cried. Amos's arms flailed and waved as he walked toward Prime then back again.

Russell just stood by the door and glared at Prime.

"Where else would I be?" Prime asked. "You cuffed me to a goddamn pole in your goddamn barn."

"Check the cuffs," Russell said.

Amos edged around Prime, as if he was scared that he might lunge at him. The man tugged at Prime's cuffed hands.

"He's still cuffed!"

"Sounds like you saw a ghost," Prime said.

"It wasn't no ghost," Russell said. "You just got a brother or something."

Prime knew what had happened. These two buffoons had stumbled onto Johnny Farmboy.

"How do you explain him disappearing into thin air?" Prime said.

"How'd you know?" Amos cried. Prime smiled. He hadn't, but had guessed that John transferred out to evade the two, and he hadn't waited to do it in hiding when confronted with a gun.

"Ghost, I said."

"It was a ghost!" Amos cried.

"No such thing!" Russell said.

"Think how bad it'll be if you kill me," Prime said. Amos looked at him with mostly white eyes.

"Shut up, I said!" Russell yelled.

Prime stared right at Amos. "Don't tell me you don't hear those Confederate soldiers at night, moaning after their gold."

Russell smashed his fist across Prime's jaw. He hadn't seen it coming. Russell swung the other way, and though Prime saw this one coming, he couldn't move much. He rocked his face back with the blow, but it still hurt.

"Shut . . . up. . . ." Russell said through gritted teeth.

The two left him in pain and darkness, but as Prime leaned his aching head against the rough wood pole, he decided it was worth it.

John found himself on the same sloped hill in the same humid heat. He stood, grabbing a tree trunk for support, and stumbled toward the ranger's office. Maybe Grace or Henry in this universe could meet him halfway to the transfer gate. He'd hate to go by bus all the way to Findlay.

He jogged, favoring the bum ankle, through the wilderness

preserve to the campground. The ranger station was deserted, so he stuck his head into the open door and pulled the phone off the wall mount. He pulled out his cheat sheet of numbers, organized by universe, and dialed the shack by the quarry. Grace and Henry in 7651 had had the building wired for phone service.

The phone, however, beeped at him, and John realized the ranger's phone disallowed long-distance calls. He jogged from the camp, down the main street toward the cluster of restaurants and bars near the main ferry drop.

There was a phone booth on the main drag. He pulled the door shut and rooted through his pockets. Then he pushed the door open again. It was too damn hot to be shut in a confined space. His hand had a fist of coins, but he had no idea whether they were 7651, 7650, or 7458 coins. Half of them were gold coins that he knew would never work.

"Damn!"

He tried a quarter and a dime at random and the phone clicked. He dialed the number at the shack.

"Hello?" It was Grace.

"Grace, this is John," he said. "John-7650," he added after a pause.

"Yes, I know which John," she said. "What's up?"

"I need a lift. I'm on Kelleys Island. I had to transfer out of 7458," John explained. "Some crazy rednecks have Prime and they ended up pointing a gun at me."

"I hate that."

"No kidding. I need to transfer back to 7458 right away."

"Okay," she said. "I'll send Henry with the car. He'll be there in ninety minutes."

"That should allow me to get the next ferry. I'll meet him at the dock in Marblehead."

"You got it," Grace said. "I'll have the gateway warmed up."

John had to wait only forty minutes for Henry to show.

"I broke some laws getting here," he said. "Let's get you back to Findlay."

"Let's go," John said. "But let's not get pulled over on the way."

"What happened?"

John started to explain.

"Wait, you found gold? Let me see!"

John handed Henry one of the coins. "This isn't Union gold. It's Confederate gold."

"Gold is gold," John said.

"Sure, it's still gold, but this is worth more as a coin than melted down to gold."

"You think?"

"Can I keep this?" Henry said. "I'll try to find out what it's worth on the open market here."

"Sure, I have a handful."

John continued the story.

"You think they have Prime?" Henry asked.

"They must."

"And you must have scared the crap out of them transferring out like that," Henry said.

"I hope they don't do something rash," John said. "That's why I have to get back there quickly."

"Right."

They pulled into the quarry drive just before six.

Grace-7651 had a backpack ready for him.

"Smoke bombs, mace, knife, food," she said. "Did your money work?"

"It seemed to," John said.

"Do you need more?"

"No, I'm okay."

"Do you want a gun? We have one."

John paused. "No, I guess not. No guns."

"How are you going to get to the island?" Henry asked.

"Bus, I guess."

"But you'll miss the last ferry," Grace said.

"It's at ten o'clock," Henry said. "Or it is in this universe."

"Can we afford to lose twelve hours?" Grace asked.

John shook his head. "I don't want to."

"Can you get a car in 7458?" Henry asked.

"I don't have a license or an address in 7458," John said.

"How about we transfer through the car?" Grace said.

"No way it'll fit in the transfer zone," Henry said. John remembered the Jeep from the EmVis compound. When they'd escaped 7650 to 7651, they had been squatting behind a disabled Jeep. Only part of the Jeep had come through to 7651.

"If not a car, how about a motorcycle?"

"I can't ride a motorcycle," John said.

"Maybe you should learn," Grace said. "You could take it everywhere. You'd be the cross-dimensional hog rider."

"Uh."

"We need some sort of transportation," Henry said.

"Well . . ." Grace said.

John looked at her, knowing instantly what she meant.

"He's there, but . . ."

"Prime needs us. He needs you, or rather all of you."

"Let's hope he's home," John said.

"Let's hope."

Grace powered up the machine and John transferred through to 7458.

CHAPTER 10

Twice John had passed by the house that sat across the road from the quarry. Twice he had averted his eyes, as if knowledge alone of his doppelganger in 7458 would contaminate him.

Now he walked toward the house with purpose. He paused after crossing the road, in the same copse of trees he'd knelt in months before when he was going to do to the one-armed John what Prime had done to him. But waiting there in the evening sun for some sign or portent seemed wrong. He had no time for skulking.

Instead, he just walked toward the house.

The Trans-Am was in the gravel driveway. No way would Dad or Mom have that for a vehicle. John-7458 existed here, and he was at home.

John patted his keys in his front pocket. Maybe his keys to the Trans-Am would work. Maybe he could just take the car. No, an ally would mean as much as a car.

He stood at the shut front door, at the screen door that he remembered from a past life.

John knocked.

He heard someone stomping down the front hall. He heard his mother in this universe call Bill's name and say something indistinct. A shadow moved across the rectangle of the door.

"John! What are you doing knocking? The door's unlocked."

"Mrs. Rayburn," he began.

"Always fooling around! I thought you were in your room."

"Your son *is* in his room, Mrs. Rayburn." He remained on the front stoop, though she had left the door open.

She turned then and stared at him. Her eyes ran up and down his length, noting the clothes she had never bought or washed. She raised her hand to her mouth.

"John!" she cried, but not to him. She directed her shout to the back room where John-7458 probably was messing with electronics or reading a physics book.

"What, Mom?"

"Come here, please." Her voice was shaky.

"Coming."

John-7458 appeared from the back of the house. He glanced at the screen door, stopped, and did a double take.

John nodded, then stepped back so that he was off the stoop and out of sight.

John-7458 appeared at the door.

"Who . . . who the hell are you?" he asked.

"I need your help," John said.

"You look like . . ."

"I am you, just not from this universe," John said. He smiled as he said it. The last time he had tried to confront a version of himself, he'd wanted to use violence and lies. This time, he was telling only the truth. "Step over here and I'll explain."

John-7458 looked back down the hall, and then shrugged. He had no shoes on, but he followed John to the middle of the lawn.

"Go on."

"There are a lot of universes out there," John said. "I'm from one like this one, but a little different. I have a device that allows me to travel between universes. Right now, another version of us is in trouble and we need to drive to Kelleys Island to help him."

"That's . . . ridiculous."

"I know. I felt the same way when I figured all this out," John said. "I know that you're skeptical. I know you don't want to believe me, but you can come with me and have the adventure of your life, or you can let me borrow your car, or you can turn me away."

"My car?"

"Like I said, I need to get to Kelleys Island, as soon as possible."

"This makes no sense!"

"Yeah, it's tough to comprehend," John said. "Did you go to college last year?"

"Yeah, University of Toledo."

"Did you study physics?"

"Yeah, I did."

"Was Dr. Wilson your advisor?"

"Yeah, he was. How do you know all that?"

"Did you meet Grace and Henry?"

"They were a year behind me, but I know them. She's kinda weird."

"Are you dating Casey Nicholson?"

"Uh, well . . ." John-7458 blushed.

"It all happened to me too," John said. "Only it was another universe, and slightly different because I have this device." He lifted up his shirt.

John-7458 bent low to look at it. He peered at the device, its buttons and switches.

"Show me," he said.

John nodded.

"Okay, put your arm around my shoulder," John said. "Tell your parents not to worry."

John-7458 turned back toward the house, where his parents stood in the doorway.

"I don't know what's about to happen," John-7458 said. "Maybe nothing, but if something does, don't worry."

John added, "We'll be back in a few minutes."

He put his arm around John-7458's shoulder and pressed the button, taking them back to 7651.

The house disappeared, replaced by the empty field where John's house should have been in 7651.

"Oh my god!" John-7458 cried.

"Calm down, it's okay," John said. "Let's start walking over this way."

"Why? Take us back!"

"We need to walk over here to get back. Come on."

John-7458 stood there as John walked off across the road toward the quarry. Then John heard him run to catch up.

"What's that building?" he asked. "The quarry by my house is abandoned."

"It usually is," John said. "We have a fixed transfer gate in that building to get us back to your universe."

Grace and Henry popped out of the shack.

"Hey, John and John," Grace said. "Is he convinced?"

"Henry, Grace?" John-7458 said. He seemed a little wobbly on his feet.

"Not quite yet," John said.

"So there's a third one of us," John-7458 said, "who needs our help?"

"Yeah, I'll explain things on the way to Kelleys Island. You ready?"

"I don't know. It seems so far-fetched," he said. "But . . ." He spun around, looking at the building, staring back at where his house wasn't. He finally nodded, coming to some conclusion. "Okay. I guess you can borrow the car," he said. "But I'm driving."

Grace smiled. "Let's get you back to 7458 so you can catch the last ferry."

John found himself warming to John-7458 as his doppelganger drove him across the back highways of Ohio in the hope of catching the last ferry to Kelleys Island. He'd always had an adversarial relationship with the other John, John Prime. He'd been unable ever to like that version of himself. But John-7458 was far more amiable, far more likeable. John had always thought it was the long months on his own that had hardened Prime, but now he wondered if he was just a slightly different John Rayburn from birth. John-7458 shared John's own fascination with the universe and his general optimism. Prime and he had never meshed in that way.

"So why don't you just use the one gate as a two-way communication device?" John-7458 asked.

"What?"

"It swaps the space between the two universes, doesn't it? I mean what's in one universe on the platform transfers with whatever's in the same spot in the other universe, right?"

"Yeah, I guess so," John said. "But you have no way to know for sure if you're going to cut something or someone in half when the gate is powered up."

"Sure, it'll take some coordination," John-7458 said. "You would just have to schedule a time that the gate will be activated. Every three hours on the hour. Use some atomic clock to coordinate the universes. Then Grace and Henry in 7651 cycle through all the universes over an hour period. They send things through, and whoever is in the remote universe—me, for instance—would get what they had on the platform and they'd get what I had on the platform."

"It would save me having to ferry people back to 7651 every day," John said.

"But I like the idea of having gates in a lot of universes," John-7458 said. "It ups the chance that you could find something useful. The combination grows as the handshake number."

"The handshake number?"

"Sure, two people, A and B, in a room," John-7458 explained, "there's only one way they can shake hands—with each other. Add one more person, C, to the room, and now A and B can shake, B and C can shake, and C and B can shake. Add one more person, D, and you add three more shakes. One, three, six, ten, fifteen, and so forth."

"Oh, I see," John said. "You end up with forty-five combinations by the time you get to ten gates."

"And if each universe has a small chance of a variation with every other one, you have a bigger chance of finding some exploitable difference," John-7458 said.

"Yeah, but I hate the word 'exploitable,'" John said.

"Like finding Confederate gold isn't exploiting the universes?"

"We need seed money," John said.

"Sure, and once you have seed money, what do you plan to do?"

"I don't know."

"You do know," John-7458 said. "I can see it in your face."

"I want to . . . I want to help people," John said. "I don't know why this technology isn't known by everyone. Who is suppressing it? Why don't we see travelers every day? Why aren't the Pleistocene universes used to grow food for all the people that need it?"

"I knew you had some ideas," John-7458 said. "If you need a recruit to man the station here in 7458, count me in."

John looked over at him. "Yeah, you seem like a solid fellow."

They found themselves behind a slow dump truck on a double-lane county road leading toward Marblehead and the ferry dock. John was certain they wouldn't make it, but John-7458 urged the Trans-Am into the parade of oncoming headlights, passing the truck with a chorus of car horns. They turned into the ferry driveway just in time, a minute before ten.

The ferry was deserted, just a few locals catching the last trip to the island. John sat tensely in the car while they made their slow way across Lake Erie. John-7458 stepped out, however, and stood in the night air.

"You see this?" he called through the window.

"Yeah, this morning and this afternoon," John said.

"Not the lights then. Come on, John. We'll not get there any faster sitting in the car."

"Yeah."

John opened the door. The smell of water, a strong fishy smell, invaded his nostrils then was swept away by the wind. The ferry bounced over the waves, rising in the chop, and then settling slowly down again. John inhaled and felt his body relax.

They were going to make it. John Prime was safe for the moment. He had to be. No yokels were going to stop that sly dog. No way.

As if knowing what John was thinking, John-7458 said, "You got here as fast as you could."

"Yeah."

"If you'd taken the bus, you'd be in Toledo still."

"Thanks for helping, John," John said.

"You know my price," John-7458 said. "I get to man this outpost of Pinball Wizards, Transdimensional."

"You got it."

"So, what's the plan when we get there? Do we even know where he is?"

"No, but I think I know how to find out."

They climbed back into the car as the ferry approached the dock. In the shelter of the island, the waves faded and the bouncing ebbed. They slid into the dock with a grace one wouldn't expect from a hundred-meter barge.

John-7458 eased the car off the boat and onto the local road. They neared the first four-way stop.

"That one," John said. "That bar."

John-7458 pulled the car into the first parking space he could find, right across from the bar that was blasting country and western.

"The Shaft?" John-7458 asked.

"We're looking for locals. That one looks like a local bar. Sounds like one too."

"You want me to come in? People might remember us if we look alike."

"Doesn't matter at this point," John said.

He pushed the door open and the music blared out. Yeah, it looked like a local crowd. Not the suntanned touristy people he'd expect on the weekends. No, these were the local residents of Kelleys Island letting loose on a weekday.

John took a spot at the bar next to a whiskered older fellow. John-7458 stood beside him. John was worried that the bartender would card him; he was only twenty. But the man just nodded when he asked for two beers.

The guy on the stool next to him looked John and John-7458 up and down.

"You two fellers twins?"

John was glad he'd had John-7458 come in with him. It made starting a conversation easier.

"Yeah, we are."

"You two should wear the same outfits!" John realized the man was drunk.

"Yeah, not since we were kids," John said.

"Sure, sure."

"Listen, we're looking for people," John said. "You a local?"

"Yeah, sixty years a local!" he proclaimed. "I'm a handyman, fix the bed-and-breakfast places all over the island. Also have a water truck that I use to fill up people's cisterns."

"So you know just about everyone on the island?"

"Just about, unless they have piped water. The only people with piped water is everyone in these couple blocks downtown!"

"Then you gotta know who I'm looking for," John said. "Two guys, a little bit yokel—no offense— one is named Russell and the other is named Amos."

"Oh, you mean Russ and Amos Smerndon," the guy said. "They have a house out by the forest preserve. Near the beach and the glacial grooves."

"Yeah, over there. They inherited some money, didn't they?"

"Money? I don't think so. They don't work much of late. Used to do handy work like me, but they don't bid the jobs against me anymore. I thought they was just lazy."

"Where do they live now?"

"Old white house off Titus Road."

"Right up against the forest preserve?"

"Yeah, that's the place."

"Thanks, man. Let me buy you a beer," John said.

"Yeah, Russ and Amos are usually here this time of evening," the guy said. He turned around on his stool and John panicked, wondering what he would do if the two were there in the Shaft. But the guy just shrugged his shoulder. "Naw, they ain't here."

John paid for their beers and he and John-7458 left the bar.

"Glad they weren't there," John-7458 said.

"Would have been interesting."

Before getting into the car, John found the same telephone booth he had used that day in 7651.

"It's 3290 Titus Road," he said, consulting the phone book.

They drove slowly toward the forest preserve and past it onto Titus Road.

"I feel as if I'm about to get in a fight," John-7458 said.

John nodded. His stomach was tense too, filled with butterflies, and he felt hyperalert.

"This might get rough," John said.

"For them!"

John felt a bit of the tension ebb away as he laughed.

"There it is."

John-7458 slowed the car, noting the dark drive that disappeared into the woods.

"There's a pull-off up ahead," John said.

John-7458 eased the Trans-Am onto the dirt berm. He flipped off the lights and the two looked at each other.

"Flashlight's in the trunk," he said.

"I have one in my ready bag," John said.

They stood by the car for a moment, both of them listening to the crickets and waiting.

"Ready?" John asked. "You can wait here, you know."

"No, I'm going," he replied. "As if you could stop me."

"Yeah. I know how it feels to be in your shoes."

"You said it."

They trotted up the gravel driveway, eyes open for some sign of human presence. There was nothing, no lights at all. The white of the house loomed ahead of them. No lights shined in the windows. No porch light, not even a mosquito light.

John paused and John-7458 knelt beside him. Then he motioned him to follow him around the edge of the yard. He remembered another building beyond the house, a barn or shed.

The ground was lumpy and he almost fell in the darkness. On the other side of the house was a small barn, and a light was on within. The windows were papered over, but the door didn't fit squarely against the earth, where feet had worn away a path and the light slipped out from under it. As they watched, shadows danced within.

Someone was in the small barn.

They continued around the edge of the yard so that if someone emerged from the barn, the two wouldn't be seen. Now they were close enough to hear voices, someone shouting.

They crouched and crawled on hands and knees closer.

"He's not gonna say anything," someone said.

"He'll talk," someone else said. "Won't you, punk?"

There was an incoherent reply.

John and John-7458 shared a worried glance.

"Tell me, punk. Why you digging for our gold?"

"Piss . . . off. . . ." The words weren't clearly articulated.

"And where's your twin brother at?"

"Was a ghost . . . dimwit."

There was a dull thud, as if someone had been kicked in the stomach.

John-7458 stood at the same time John did. They shared a glance, then ran.

John hit the barn door first and it gave. He stumbled and fell, felt John-7458 run past, screaming like a banshee. He tackled one of the two men—Russell.

John scrambled to his feet and tripped, ran, staggered at Amos.

If the man hadn't been staring at the two Johns in horror, John would never have reached him.

"Ghosts!" Amos screamed.

John slammed into him and screamed into his face as he pummeled him with his fists. Why hadn't they brought a gun? John wondered as Amos curled into a ball and screamed. Because they were ghosts.

John stood and looked down on Amos as he murmured and

squealed. Then he spun as he heard Russell curse. He had John-7458 in a headlock, but his doppelganger was striking the back of his head weakly with a fist.

John saw the two-by-four on the floor. He grabbed it and swung it down at the top of Russell's head. The man looked up just in time for the wood to slam into his eye socket. He fell to the ground like a crash dummy.

John-7458 stood up rubbing his neck. They both looked over at John Prime, tied to a post in the middle of the barn. He was bloody, his eyes bruised, his nose broken, and his lips cracked.

He smiled.

"I'm seeing double," he slurred just before he passed out.

John-7458 trussed the two men with the same rope they had used on John Prime and was none too gentle about it. Amos merely whimpered and remained in his fetal position. Russell was unconscious long enough that John began to worry.

Prime, however, recovered enough to stand unsteadily.

"Who's this?" he asked, pointing at John-7458. "Or rather which universe is he from?"

"This one," John said. "I needed to get back fast, and he gave me a ride."

"I assumed they'd run across you earlier when that lunkhead kept going on about ghosts," Prime said, nodding at Amos.

"Yeah, I had to ditch and come back the long way."

"Well, I'm glad you did." Prime walked over to a pile of old boxes covered in canvas. "And now you're glad you did."

He pulled the canvas away, revealing a steamer trunk filled with gold coins.

"I found the treasure and didn't have to dig for it," Prime said.

John tried to guess how much there was, but he couldn't figure the volumes in his head. There had to be thousands of gold coins in each box.

"My god," he said. "That's millions of dollars in gold!"

"It's our gold!" Russell spat out.

"Not anymore," Prime said and swung a kick into Russell's exposed stomach. It would have done worse damage if Prime hadn't wobbled as he'd stepped up to kick. Still Russell woofed and curled up as well as he could in his tied position.

John put a hand on Prime's shoulder and pulled him back from a second kick on the helpless Russell.

"I know you're pissed right now, but let him be," John said.

"Sure, sure," Prime said, but it didn't sound like he meant it.

"Why don't you bring your car around?" John asked John-7458.

"Okay."

John helped Prime sit down on a hay bale. "You need to relax a bit."

"I will, I am." He sighed. "I hate almost getting killed."

John put a hand on his shoulder.

"We thought this one was going to be a simple dig and run," John said. "And we promised Casey you'd be back safe and sound."

"We always make that promise." He looked at the boxes of gold. "Well, that's going to make your life easier, isn't it?"

"Yep. Yours too." He heard the Trans-Am coming up the drive. "Let's pile this in the car."

The car was noticeably lower in the back when they had finished putting the chests into the trunk.

"Don't drive over any bumps on the way off the island," Prime said. "Let's go."

"What about them?" John-7458 said, nodding at Amos and Russell. Russell had rolled over and was glaring at them.

"Leave them to rot," Prime said.

"No."

John looked around the barn and found a serrated knife on a hook. He picked it up, and then tossed it into the yard.

"You can crawl out and find that in the morning," he said to Russell. "By then we'll be long gone."

"Screw you all," he said.

"You tried, you failed," Prime said.

"Let's go."

CHAPTER 11

"Where'd you get this?" the man asked.

"Why does that matter?" Grace asked. The man frowned and looked at the coin again through his magnifying glass. John and Grace had found Toledo Gold and Coins in the yellow pages, arriving as the owner was opening his storefront. The stockholders' meeting with their investors was the next day.

"I don't deal in stolen goods," he said.

"If the police come looking for it, feel free to turn us in," Grace said. "They won't."

The man took a book off the shelf and flipped through it.

"I'll give you a thousand dollars for it," he said.

John laughed despite himself. He had expected to be ripped off. When Grace had consulted the yellow pages at the library, John had paged through a numismatics book. The North Carolina gold coins minted by the Bechtler Mint were exceedingly rare.

"We know how rare it is," he said.

"It's not even in a coin case," the man said. "And I have no idea what the provenance is. I have risk that you have to pay for."

"By a factor of forty? These have gone for forty thousand dollars."

"At auction to dedicated coin collectors," the man said. "You want that kind of money, you need to take it to auction."

"We don't have the time," Grace said. "We need a better price."

The man shrugged.

"At least we can buy coin cases from him," John said.

The man shrugged and laid a single case in front of them.

"Fifty cents," he said.

"No, we're going to need ten thousand of them," Grace said.

The man's jaw dropped open. "What did you find?"

Grace shrugged at him.

"Hold on, hold on," the man said. "You have ten thousand Bechtler coins from the 1830s?"

"About that many. We didn't count."

The man typed some numbers into his calculator. "That's hundreds of millions of dollars you have. Do you realize it?"

"Yes, we had an inkling. Now we need to sell them for cash," Grace said. "Can you help us or not?"

"This might be the greatest coin discovery of the decade!" the man exclaimed. "You can't just lug the coins into a coin store and sell them!"

"We need the money now," John said.

"You need four hundred million dollars right now?" the man asked. "I don't think so."

"Well, we only need about fifteen million," Grace said.

"We don't have to auction them now to get that money," he said.

"We?"

"Yes, you let me handle the auction at three percent, and I can help you assess the coins at a reasonable value. A bank will loan you cash on that collateral."

"That makes a lot of sense."

"We just need to establish the provenance," the man said.

"How do we do that?"

"We need to show where you found the gold."

"We dug the coins up," John said.

"Where? On public land, private land? Do you own the land? Does your grandmother?"

"It was public land," John said.

"Federal, state, or county?" the man asked.

"State land," John replied. They had decided to go with the story that they had found the gold coins as if they were lost during the Civil War in the same place on Kelleys Island in this universe as 7458.

"Did you have a permit?"

"Nope."

The man rubbed his chin.

"We can get around that. There's no law that requires you to have a permit on state land, unless it's posted as you enter the area."

"We didn't see anything."

The man had begun to sweat, and his gestures were wild and exaggerated.

"Uh, I think we're good," John said. "Thanks for your time."

"I can help," the man said. "I really can."

"No, we're good."

John and Grace left the store, running back to the car.

"He seemed a little desperate," John said.

"But he had a good idea," Grace said. "We don't need to sell them. We just need to appraise them. Then any bank can give us a loan with the coins as collateral."

"Who's going to appraise the coins?"

"I don't know. Let's call my guy at Ladora Savings."

"Who?" John asked. Ladora was the bank that Grace had set up all their business accounts through.

"Clay Burgess," she said. "He's kept us going with lines of credit during the bad times. Maybe he'll know what to do."

"Um, maybe we should cover our tracks, too," John added. "Get Henry to buy a plot of land on Kelleys Island near the forest preserve."

"I see what you mean," Grace said.

They stopped at a pay phone and Grace called Henry.

"He'll call a Realtor," Grace said. "But if anyone looks closely at the timeline . . ."

"Why should it matter? We have the coins and no one can ever claim they had them first," John said. "They never existed on that island in this universe."

"True, but when we're talking about a half billion dollars, people do stupid stuff," Grace said.

"Wait, turn here," John said. "There. Coin shop. It was second on the list. Let's buy the coin holders."

"You mean, let's look like we know what we're doing?"

"Yes."

Ten thousand coin holders wiped the shop owner out. He also sold them small cartons that held a hundred coin holders each. It made carrying the coins easier than lugging them around in a cardboard box. They spent two hours sliding the coins into coin holders and then the coin holders into the boxes. John's fingers began to hurt, and he accidently dropped one of the coins into the space between his seat and the center console of his car.

"Careful," Grace said. "That's forty grand down there with the bubble gum wrappers and old French fries."

John extended his sore fingers and managed to grab the coin.

"Got it," he said.

Clay Burgess was a young man, too young it seemed to be a business banker, but he greeted Grace with a hug.

"I still haven't heard anything from Mr. Gilbert in Investments about the funding," he began, but Grace shook her head.

"We're here on something else," she said. "We've stumbled upon some coins, and want to see if we can use them as collateral for a loan."

"Coins?"

"Civil War–era coins," Grace said.

"But you were looking for an investment of twenty to twenty-five million, weren't you?"

"It's a lot of coins."

"That's not my area of expertise, Grace," Clay said. "I'll need to talk with someone else."

"Of course, but as you know, we're in a bit of a hurry. Our corporate meeting is tomorrow."

"Hold on," he said. He disappeared from his desk in the open area of the bank, going upstairs.

"We may not make it by tomorrow," John said.

"That's fine," Grace said.

"It is?"

"Yes, we have capital now. With capital we can do anything," Grace said.

"I expected you to be more agitated with the meeting tomorrow," John said.

"No, I'm calm," she said. "Don't get me wrong. I don't want them to have my company, but we have bigger fish to fry, and now we have the money to do it." She paused to look at John. "In how many other universes are those coins just sitting there, do you think?"

"How many more have Amos and Russell?"

"We know how to deal with them," Grace said.

"Grace, are you . . . well?" John asked.

"You mean, have I snapped finally due to my torture at the hands of Visgrath?"

"I—"

"No, I'm fine, John. More fine than ever before."

Clay appeared with an older woman, dressed in a skirt-suit.

"I'm the bank manager, Margaret Carlisle. Mr. Burgess says that you wish to secure a loan with coins as collateral?"

"Yes, that's correct."

"May I see the coins?"

Grace took a box from her satchel and thunked it onto Clay's desk. The other boxes were in the trunk of John's car.

She took a coin from the middle. She held it up to her face, lifting her glasses off her nose.

"From 1834?"

"They are all pre–Civil War coins, of the same mint," Grace said.

"How many?"

"Ten thousand."

The woman looked shocked. "The gold alone . . ."

"Two and a half million dollars, best guess."

"We can arrange a loan of the amount of two million dollars," she said. "Based on the weight in gold."

"We need fifteen million," Grace said.

"I have no idea how much these coins are worth," she said. "We'd need to assess their value."

"Let's do that," Grace said. "Do you have a valuator who can assess these coins immediately?"

"I'll have to ask our district manager," Carlisle said.

"It is very important to us that we have the fifteen million dollars tomorrow," Grace said slowly. "We have a stockholders' meeting during which we want to buy back the shares of our company held by our investors. Fifteen million is the set price for the recovery of their investment this year."

"I don't know if we can do it that fast," Carlisle said.

"Assess the coins, Miss Carlisle, and then determine the value of our continued use of Ladora Savings Bank as our prime financial institution."

"I . . . um . . ."

"Do you need a calculator, Miss Carlisle?" Grace asked.

The woman's face became stone, and for a moment, John was certain Grace had pushed her too far. Instead, the woman nodded

"We'll get someone in here right away," she said. "May we store the coins in our vault until then?"

"You may store a sample of coins in your vault," Grace said. "The rest can reside in our safe-deposit box."

"That seems reasonable, Miss Shisler."

"Excellent," Grace said. "I will call you at noon to assess your progress."

"Certainly."

With the help of two bank guards, John lugged the remaining cartons of coins into the bank vault. He kept a couple dozen, however, in his bag. Carrying gold wire was a good way to transfer wealth between universes. But a coin worth $40,000 had a far greater density of wealth, even if the value was only of the gold itself. Wouldn't most universes have had a Civil War and a mint in North Carolina? Of course if Corrundrum was to be believed, worlds like his, where the United States was dominant, weren't the most common. Just apparently around the universes he'd traveled in, clustered in the 7000s maybe.

"Well, we've done as much as we can here," Grace said as they walked down the bank steps. "Let's get back to the warehouse. I think I need to have our lawyer there tomorrow. That's going to cost." She stopped herself.

"What?"

"The cost of a lawyer's day doesn't really matter to us anymore."

"True."

This time, Gesalex's board members made no attempt to converse with the Pinball Wizards. At 11 A.M., they marched into the meeting room at the Hyatt and sat down.

"Meeting called to order," Gesalex stated.

Immediately, the Alarian on his left said in a heavy accent, "Motion to dissolve the company via liquidation."

"Second," cried the Alarian on the right.

Grace said before Gesalex could call a vote, "Point of order! The board members have not identified themselves."

"Is this necessary?" Gesalex said.

"Of course," Grace said. Her call that morning to the bank had said that they were processing the loan check, but had no idea when it would be ready.

John glanced at Fred Ultrech, the junior lawyer that their firm had sent over on short notice. Ultrech had scratched his head at Grace's request, but had come up with at least a dozen stalling techniques that they could use according to corporate procedure to delay the end of the meeting.

"We can't do any *more* than delay it, I'm afraid," he said. "But we can delay it for a bit."

"All in favor of the motion on the floor," Gesalex said.

Ultrech stood up. "Sir, no vote can proceed until the point of order is addressed."

"It's ridiculous!"

"But required by law. Otherwise, the vote will not be binding."

"Fine. I am Reccared Gesalex, chairman of this board."

He looked to his left.

"I am Suintila Theusenand."

Gesalex pointed to his right.

"I am Sesedoric Agila."

"I am Wamba Liugica."

Gesalex pointed at Henry.

Henry stood slowly.

"I am Henry Philip," he said, pausing. Gesalex looked to John, but Henry cleared his throat and raised a piece of paper to read from. "I am chief engineer of the company, and have constructed or assisted in construction of over three hundred pinball machines. I was born—"

"This is just a stalling tactic," said Gesalex.

"He may speak for five minutes for his identification," Ultrech said.

Henry smiled and continued, tracing his roots to his hometown in Xenia, his years in high school, time as the captain of the chess team, and his interest in physics.

"It's been five minutes," Gesalex cried.

"Four minutes and thirty seconds," Ultrech said.

Gesalex threw up his hands.

There was a knock at the door of the conference room.

A man in bicycle pants and a hat that read HERMES DELIVERY entered and spied Grace. He handed her a thick envelope, for which Grace signed.

"Get on with it," Gesalex cried.

John glanced over Grace's shoulder and saw a check with a lot of zeros. Grace and John shared a smile.

She stood and said, "I have a privileged motion."

CHAPTER 12

Two weeks later, on a Saturday in the empty warehouse, the first meeting of Pinball Wizards, Transdimensional, was called to order. Present were John Prime, John Rayburn, and John Rayburn of the Civil War gold, or in John's suggested nomenclature John-7423, John-7533, and John-7458. Also in attendance were Grace-7651, Grace-7650, Henry 7651, Henry-7650, and Casey.

"I feel all alone here," Casey said with a laugh.

"Don't worry," Prime said. "There are other Caseys out there."

"Oh, really? How many have you known?" Casey said, sharply.

Prime actually blushed.

"I should be used to Casey's barbed tongue," he said. "I married a Casey."

"I still think this naming convention is ridiculous," Grace-7650 said. "I'm never going to remember all these numbers."

"Do you have a better idea?" Prime asked.

"I'm working on it," she said.

John stood up. He unstrapped the device from his chest and laid it on the table. All the banter stopped and the eight of them looked at the thing.

"For months we've been running helter-skelter," he said. "First from Visgrath, then from Gesalex. We've needed money and allies, and now we have both of those things." He paused. "It's time to figure out what we're going to do."

Henry-7650 spoke up. "Well, this auction thing isn't bringing in the money we need." He was right. The dream of four hundred million dollars had faded away when the auctioneer they had hired explained that a deluge of the nearly identical coins on the numismatic market would drop the price of each coin to its value in gold.

"The first one may be worth forty thousand dollars," Elmer Prescott had explained, "but the next ten won't be worth that, maybe ten thousand. And the next ten only five thousand. By then you've saturated the market for Civil War coins. Maybe there's a few museums and institutions that will buy a coin. But the equilibrium price of the coins is going to be two thousand dollars at most. Probably closer to fifteen hundred. And I bet we'll sell no more than five hundred."

"I know how we can sell the coins, at near full value," Grace-7651 said.

"How?" Henry asked.

"Sell a hundred in a hundred different universes," she said. "That way we don't saturate any one market for the coins."

"Of course," Henry said. "We'd buy the plot near the forest preserve in each universe and pretend to discover the coins! Then we can convert the coins to commodities in that universe and ship them anywhere!"

"Then we could pay off the bank loan, and get down to business," Grace-7650 said.

John raised his hands. "I know our immediate problems are solvable. That's not what I'm talking about. We can accumulate money in any universe we want. There's no doubt of that. My question is, do we want to?"

"Well, of course, we do—" Henry-7651 said.

"I see what John is saying," Grace-7651 said. "We've got this amazing device. What should our *purpose* be?"

"Making money seems reasonable," Prime said.

"You want to help people," Grace-7650 said to John.

"Yeah, yeah, I do."

Casey leaned close to him and squeezed him. "I like that idea," Casey said.

"You can help more people with more money," Prime said.

"I will grant that money is a means to many ends," John said. "But it shouldn't be our end all."

Henry-7651 said, "We should map out all the nearby universes. Find out why they're different. Document it all!"

"I do like science for science's sake," John said.

"I know what I want," Grace-7650 said. "I want to find the Alarians." Her voice was grim. "We have some unfinished business."

"I don't know if revenge is a good plan," John said gently.

"When you disassembled the transfer gate in the barn," Grace asked John, "did you write down the universe it was set to transfer to?"

John looked at her for a long moment. He had noted it. It had been set to Universe 2219. "I know what it was," he said.

Grace didn't ask, but she held his gaze.

"I've got one," Civil War John said, after a moment. Everyone turned toward their newest member. "You ever hear of the I-75 Ripper?"

"Yeah," John said. "That serial killer who was targeting girls between Toledo and Cincinnati."

"I wonder if there's a universe where he was caught," Civil War John said.

There was silence for a moment. Then John nodded. "That's worth finding out, my friends," he said.

"As long as we're sure the guy is the same in all universes," Prime said.

Civil War John added, "We'd have to do our due diligence, sure."

"I've got one," Prime said.

"More money-making ideas?" Henry-7650 asked.

"No, not this time," Prime said. "I want to find the first John."

"The what?"

"The first John. The John who gave him the device," John said. "No revenge."

"That's not what I meant," Prime said. "I want to find the John who first found the device. Maybe it was the John I met—John Superprime—but maybe Superprime got it from a prior John and that John got it from a prior John, et cetera and so forth."

"Where did this all start?" John said.

"Yeah, exactly."

John nodded. "I think we've touched on everything I want to do, at least in some small way. First, I'm giving up the device. It's not mine to use, except if we all agree to it. It needs to be taken care of and babied and learned from. We can't let the Alarians get anywhere near it.

"Second, I want to do *good*. I want to do things with this technology that will better people's lives. I can't even get my mind around the human suffering in any one universe, let alone an infinite number of them. Yet, we have to do something to ease the pain we know of.

"Third, we have to figure things out. I want to understand not just the technology, but the science behind our multiverse. The two gates we've built, they're just bad imitations of that." He pointed to the device on the table in front of them. "I have no idea of how it actually works. I want to understand how.

"And lastly, I want to understand why. Why aren't we overrun with cross-dimensional travelers? Why isn't there some huge multi-dimensional empire that controls our lives? Where did the device come from? Who put the Alarians here?"

John sat down. "Those are the things I want to do. And I hope you all will help me."

There was a moment of silence, as the rest of the group all looked at John.

Grace-7650 was the first to speak. "I'm in."

Grace-7651 nodded. "We're in." She tilted her head at Henry-7651.

Civil War John and John Prime shared a look. "There's no doubt I'm in," Civil War John said. "My life was a little bland before two weeks ago. I doubt I'll get an opportunity like this again."

John looked at Prime.

"As if you could get rid of me," Prime said.

Casey squeezed John tightly. "Wherever you're going, I'm going too, honey."

"I've got it figured out," Grace-7650 said.

"What?" John asked. "How to stop the Alarians?"

"Nope. This stupid numeric naming convention you came up with."

"Uh . . ."

"He's John Prime," she said. "He's never going to be John-7423, because he's living in Universe 7533 now. But you're John-7533, though you're living in 7650, which is the company's home office."

"So how do we keep track of ourselves?"

"Nicknames. He's John Prime. His Casey is Casey Prime. We're John, Casey, Henry, and Grace Home. He's John Gold. Everyone from 7651 is Top since that universe is the goalpost until we add more transfer gates beyond it."

"But the numbers are so simple," John Home said.

"I don't like the numbers," Casey Home said.

"I don't either," Henry Top and Henry Home said at the same time.

John Home shared a look with John Prime and John Gold. They each shrugged.

"Fine. I guess that's our first order of business," he said. "All in favor of shucking the numbers, say aye."

"Aye!"

They spent the evening hashing out the details. John wanted to run things as a company, with a charter that outlined the points he had made. Grace agreed, but refused to allow him to specify a pure democracy.

"We'd never get things done," Grace Top argued. "We need a CEO, a president to run things on a day-to-day basis."

"I call head of engineering," Henry Home and Henry Top cried in unison.

"Maybe they should fight for it," Prime said.

"Oooo, Henry fight," Grace Top said. "I like it."

"What we need," Casey said, "is a mission statement and bylaws that we all can agree to. Something loose yet binding. Flexible to deal with all sorts of strange things."

"What's the difference between a mission statement and the by-laws?" Grace Top asked.

"The mission statement is what we plan on doing. The bylaws is how we go about doing it," Casey explained. "I guess I did pay attention in Corporate Organization class," she added with a smile.

"What John said earlier," Grace Top said. "To help other people, to understand the technology, and to understand the multiverse. That's our mission statement."

"That's pretty good," John Gold said.

"Let me write that down," Grace Home said. She scribbled quickly on a pad of paper.

They started to throw around ideas for bylaws.

"I say we make it a law we can't tell anyone about the device or the technology," Henry Home said. "Keep it all a secret."

"Why?" Grace Top asked.

Henry shrugged.

"I think we should differentiate between settled and unsettled universes," Grace Home said. "Settled are those that we have operatives in: 7458, 7533, 7650, and 7651. In Gold, Prime, Home, and Top. Unsettled are those we don't."

"And have different rules in each type of universe?" Prime asked. "Why?"

"We want to be more careful in unsettled universes, don't we?"

"We need rules on how we recruit new universes and new . . . uh . . . associates," Grace Top said. "Who gets to be an associate? What universes do we settle? How many do we settle?"

"I think that's important," John Gold said.

They threw out ideas for an hour, with Grace scribbling notes on her pad.

"This is a lot of ideas," she said when the suggestions finally petered out. "I don't know how to make sense of it all. Some of these ideas are contradictory."

"Maybe you and I should type them all out," Grace Top said. "Categorize them, and see which ones make sense and which ones don't."

"And the rest of us—" Henry Home asked.

"—can play some pinball," Henry Top finished.

"Why don't we ever do that?" John Gold asked John and Prime.

"I hate when they do that," Prime said.

"I kinda like when they do that," Grace Top and Grace Home said at the same time.

Grace caught John in the hall.

"I think you should be the CEO, the president," she said.

"Why?" John asked. "You're doing pretty well with Pinball Wizards in 7650."

"Yeah, but this is so much bigger," she said

"I think you can do it, Grace," John said.

She frowned. "I know I can do it!" she said. "But I don't . . . trust myself to be fair about it."

"What do you mean by that?" John asked.

Grace looked at John closely. "Do I seem normal to you? Do I seem like my old self?"

"More so than when we were in 7651," John said.

"The depression is gone at least," Grace said. "I'm glad to have something to do with the company. I'm happy to be busy. I . . . feel safer when I confide in my twin."

"Sure," John said, remembering the conversations he and Civil War John had had on the way to Kelleys Island.

"But all that dark emotion has been replaced with something darker still," she said. "If I had all these resources at my disposal, I'd hunt the Alarians to the ends of the multiverse and eradicate them."

"We don't know for sure where they are," John started.

"I'm sure Gesalex would confirm the destination universe once I place red-hot pincers on his testicles," Grace said matter-of-factly.

"Oh."

"Which is my way of saying, you should be in charge of this thing," she said. "It's safer."

"You seem so . . ."

"Calm?" she said with a laugh. "My rage is quite rational." She leaned in close and put her arms around John's neck. "I don't blame you, John. Don't ever think that. I know how Henry feels. He blames himself too. But don't think for a second that my anger is because of you."

"Grace—"

"It's mine, it's all mine, and nurturing it gives me solace."

"Grace—"

She stroked his face, and kissed him on the cheek.

"I appreciate what you're going to say, but shut the hell up and just accept this for what it is," she said.

"Okay, fine."

"Good."

In the end, John became president of Pinball Wizards, Transdimensional. All the rest of the team became board members. Each universe was managed by a single one of the board members, Prime in 7533, John Gold in 7458, Casey in 7650, and Grace Top in 7651. Those were the settled universes. They adopted Grace's nomenclature for the universes. Instead of Universe 7533, they called it Prime. 7458 became Civil War Gold, truncated to Gold. 7650 was Home Office, or just Home. And 7651 was Top, their upper goalpost universe. Going beyond 7651 would always be risky since there was no guaranteed way back. If they went too low, the portable device could always take them higher.

Their mission statement was a more elegant version of John's speech. The company existed to help people, whatever people each universe manager decided for his or her universe. For people in unsettled universes, it required a board vote. To open a new settled universe, the board voted as well. John and the Henrys would handle the research and development of the technology. All other projects would be at John's discretion, with majority veto power of the board.

Their final bylaw provided membership into the company of any version of John, Henry, Grace, or Casey in any universe they deemed settled.

"It is our company," Grace Home explained when she proposed the bylaw. "And by 'our,' I mean every version of us. Who else shares our beliefs, our mores, our vision? Who else will help us in what needs to be done?"

And so they voted, adopting the bylaws unanimously, and each signed their names. Under each signature, they printed the number of their universe. In this way, Pinball Wizards, Transdimensional, was born.

John decided that for 7458 and 7533—Gold and Prime—they would start construction of a static transfer gate immediately. He was reluctant to keep the old transfer gate operating in 7650, to prevent the Alarians from stealing it.

"I think we can get around that through obscuration," Henry Home said. "Make it nearly impossible to run the gate without know-how."

"Security by obscuration—" Henry Top said.

"—is no obscurity at all," Henry Home said. "I know."

"They probably have plans of it already, don't they?" Civil War John said.

"And seeing another completed one would show them the error of their ways," John said.

"We can't risk them having an operational transfer gate," Grace Home said.

"It makes travel in and out of 7650 hard," John said.

"Maybe," Henry Top said. "We have a solution for that, I think. Civil War John and I have been working on this."

"What?"

"A precise timetable."

"Huh?"

"The fixed gate—and I assume the portable one—doesn't just go from one universe to the next," Henry Top explained. "It swaps the matter in the transfer zone between the universes."

"So?"

"It's why we don't have a sudden pop of air rushing into vacuum. The air in one universe changes places with the air in the other." John remembered when he powered up the transfer gate in 7650 to a universe where there was still topsoil over the quarry area instead of bare rock. A huge sphere of dirt had appeared and slouched over immediately.

"Oh, I get it," Henry Home said. "We just have to place whatever we want to move between universes in the right spot at the right time and it'll get transferred over."

"Yeah, exactly. If 7650 is the Home Office universe, it doesn't need a working gate, just the timetable of when the transfer needs to take place."

"This universe is Grand Central Station," Casey said. "Grand Central Universe."

"Sorta, yeah," Henry Top said.

"I like it," John said. "So, it sounds like in each settled universe we need to do the following. One, buy the land near the quarry and build a large factory or work structure. Two, buy the land near Bird Rock on Kelleys Island and 'accidentally' discover a few gold coins."

Grace Home nodded. "That'll get us seed money in each universe."

"Then we can start building gates in 7458 and 7533," John said. "The Johns there can start managing those universes."

"And recruiting the Caseys, Henrys, and Graces in those universes," Casey said. She looked at Civil War John. "Is there a Casey in your universe?"

Civil War John blushed. "Yes, but we haven't . . . haven't . . . uh . . . dated."

"Well, you don't have to date her," she said with a smile, "but you'll have a chance to talk to her."

"Yeah, sure, but I don't think she'll believe me," said Civil War John.

"She'd believe me!" Casey said.

"Which is a good point," John said. "Recruiting our doppelgangers won't always be easy."

"That's true," Civil War John said.

"We need to figure out the best way to get them on board," John said. He paused. "So, for the near term, we have our assignments. Any questions?"

Prime cleared his throat. "What about the expedition to find John Superprime?"

"Not for revenge—"

"No, no," Prime said. "I just want to know where the device came from."

"Corrundrum was shocked when he saw the personal device," John said. "He only knew of devices that were also vehicles, ones that transferred multiple people inside them."

"Thomas and Oscar," Prime said. He paused. "Two . . . renegades I met in my travels felt the same way. The personal device isn't normal."

"Nor is the standing gate," Henry Home said.

"No," Prime said. "It's a lead we should follow up on."

"I agree," John said after a pause. "All in favor of launching an expedition in search of John Superprime say aye."

It was unanimous.

CHAPTER 13

John and Prime sat in the thicket near the Rayburn house in 7423, trying to spot John Superprime.

Prime watched intently, while John's memory drifted, remembering bits and pieces of his childhood. He'd played in these brambles, picking blackberries in summer, tracking hares in winter. He reached out and plucked a succulent berry from the thorned bush. He crushed it between his tongue and the roof of his mouth, feeling the hard seeds. He let the juice fill his mouth and then crunched the seeds.

Prime sighed and looked away from the house. They'd been there for three hours, hunched in the thicket about a hundred meters from the house, and had yet to see anybody around. Bill Rayburn's old truck sat in the driveway, but there was no sign of any other car.

"You're sure it was 7423?" John asked.

"As sure as you are that yours is 7533," Prime replied.

"Was."

Prime didn't answer.

They'd left a few days after their first meeting, long enough to order the parts for two more transfer gates, one for 7458 and one for 7533.

"The grass is long," Prime said. "It hasn't been mowed. That isn't like Dad."

"Yeah."

"The barn needs paint. He should have come out to feed the animals at least. Something."

"If he's home," John said. "He could be away for the day, running errands. We've been here only a couple hours."

"I know."

Prime leaned back, picked one blackberry after another, then he jammed the entire handful into his mouth.

They waited another hour, and still there was no sign of movement in the house. Finally, Prime stood up. "Let's find a pay phone."

"Okay."

They dashed across the road and crossed the old quarry lot to the far side where the new subdivision was. There was a gas station at the end of Bell Avenue, an old Clark station. Next to the air-pressure valve stood a pay phone, bolted to an overhead lamp. Hanging from a chain in a plastic sleeve was a phone book.

"Look, John Rayburn, Franklin Street," Prime said.

"He's living in town," John said.

"Come on."

Prime wore a baseball cap, while John went hatless. Still he was certain they appeared identical from any distance. The same gait, the same height, the same face. But even if they were seen by someone who knew John Superprime, did it really matter? They were practically pros at transdimensional travel now. They knew what to do, what to say if they were spotted, questioned. How many worlds had they been to combined? Hundreds.

Franklin Street was part of the oldest area of Findlay. The bigger houses had been broken up into apartments.

"Casey and I used to live around here," Prime said. "Not here, but you know what I mean. One street over." He paused, seemed to shudder.

"Not good times?"

"No," Prime said. "Carson." The one word explained it all. Ted Carson was John's nemesis in every universe, it seemed, a troll, a petulant bully.

They found the house, and John spotted a yellow Trans-Am in the alleyway behind the house.

"Look," he said. "Some things don't change."

"He's here," Prime said.

"Let's knock."

They entered the vestibule of the house. A table under four mailboxes built into the wall was covered in magazines, newspapers, and circulars. J. Rayburn and E. Finch were in 2B. They climbed the stairs.

"He has a roommate," John said.

"Yep. You know any Finch?"

"No, do you?"

"No."

They stopped at the door to 2B, listening through the door to a TV blaring a baseball game. They shared a glance, and Prime knocked.

They heard a voice. "You wanna get that, Elliott?" Even muffled through the door, they recognized the voice.

"Yeah," someone replied.

The TV volume slackened and someone clomped to the door. Prime took off his hat as the bolt slid away.

"Yeah?"

Elliott Finch was a tall, stringy fellow with a scraggly beard and bloodshot eyes.

"Oh, shit, man," he said. He turned and called, "It's for you, John."

"I'll be right there," John Superprime called. Then he appeared from the bathroom at the end of the hall wiping his hands on his pants.

His smile faded to a look of shock as he saw Prime and John standing in his doorway. He took a step, stumbling as his knee failed to hold him.

"Oh, two of you. Yeah, sure." He caught himself on the edge of the couch.

Elliott shook his head as if he had water in his ear. "Whoa," he muttered.

John watched Prime for some sign of intent or aggression, but he seemed relaxed.

Prime said, "John, we need to talk."

John Superprime was shaking as he took the steps one at a time, both hands gripping the rail. Prime watched him intently, staying at the top of the stairs until he had made it halfway. John followed Prime, casting a quick glance at Elliott Finch; he returned the look with wasted eyes and slack features. John had not failed to notice the drug paraphernalia on the table—a water bong, matches, leafy substances—and the smell of incense.

"Yeah, we do," John Superprime mumbled. "We do need to talk. Got a lot to talk about. Helluva lot." His foot missed the last step and he stumbled, almost landing face-first on the wood floor.

"He's wasted," Prime whispered.

"Or scared to death," John replied.

"Both."

"Better take his arm," John said.

Prime took the rest of the steps three at a time, reaching John Superprime as he flung about for a hold on something.

"This way."

He walked him out the front door and around the side of the house toward the alleyway. A small wooden shed painted the same tan as the house abutted the alley. The Trans-Am sat next to it.

John Prime pushed John Superprime against the wall of the shed in disgust. Superprime kept touching his face, looking up at them, and touching his face again.

"This is real, right?" he said finally.

Prime snorted.

"Yeah, it's real," John said.

"Yeah? But why are there two of you? Huh? Why two?" John Superprime put his face in his hands and started sobbing. "I'm so sorry. I didn't mean to do it."

"Yeah, well, you did," Prime said.

"I didn't mean to kill her," Superprime continued.

Prime stared at him. "What? Did you hurt Casey? What the hell?"

"It was dark, you know? Rainy. I was fine, but she—"

Prime grabbed Superprime by the collar. "What did you do to her? What did you do?"

"I was fine, totally fine. But she got thrown and she was dead right there."

"How could you have done that to Casey, you bastard?"

John pried Prime's hands off Superprime's throat. Superprime slumped against the shed, landing hard on the ground.

"Not Casey," he said, sobbing. "It was Mom. But the worst thing is, I know she's still alive somewhere else. I know she's still alive."

Prime and John shared a look. Prime's face clouded up and his forehead wrinkled.

"Mom," he said. "It was my mom."

Prime kicked Superprime in the stomach before John could stop him. John threw himself between the two.

"Don't, John," he said. "Can't you see he's suffering enough?"

"Not enough for me," Prime said through gritted teeth. "He killed my mom!"

"It was an accident!"

"He was drunk, I bet, or high as a kite!" Prime cried.

"Just calm down for a minute," John said. "You still have a mother in 7533! My mother."

Prime looked away. He took two steps toward the house and stood there, staring up at the roof.

John bent down next to John Superprime.

"How long ago was this?" John asked.

"Eight months ago, I guess."

"And you've been self-medicating since?"

"I, uh, dropped out of school. Moved in with Elliott. Dad won't even talk to me!" He paused, looking up at John and then at Prime. "Wait, if he's the John from this universe, who are you?"

"I'm the John he kicked out of my universe."

"He did it to you too? Just like I did it to him?"

"Apparently."

"I didn't know what else to do!" Superprime cried. "I didn't!"

"And someone did it to you first."

"No," Superprime said. "No one did it to me."

"No? How'd you get the device?" John asked.

"We found it."

"You found it?" Prime cried. "Where?"

"Me and Billy Walder found it," Superprime said. "At the old quarry."

"You better—"

"Stop it," John said. "Let's go get some food and you can tell us the story."

John Rayburn and Billy Walder ran across McMaster Road and slipped through the hole in the chain-link fence around the abandoned quarry.

They noticed the cave when they heard the deep, echoing plop of a stone falling into the water.

"Did you throw a rock?" John asked.

"No, did you?" Billy edged closer.

Then they saw the burgeoning waves.

John said, "A rock slide. Cool." Rock slides were one of those things that always happened when no one was looking, and all that was ever seen was the cone of debris. Rock slides were like tornados or Santa Claus.

As they watched, another rock shifted and a shower of pebbles bounced down the wall and trickled into the water.

"Do you see that hole there?" Billy said. John saw a dark crevice near the top of the wall. "That looks like a cave."

"It's just a shadow."

John had seen caves before, the limestone caverns up by Toledo called the Ottawa Indian Caverns. His father and mother had taken him a year before on his thirteenth birthday. At first he'd been excited, but the tour had been through the well-lit parts. The dark and inviting passageways all had been roped off. They hadn't seen a bat or a skeleton from a lost spelunker or a sparkling outcropping of crystals. It had been only milky, oozing stalagmites and stalactites, which were okay, but nowhere near as interesting as bats.

"Yeah. Is that a ledge there? I think we can climb down to it."

"Climb? I don't know about that," John said.

"Come on." Billy led him around the quarry to the far side and got down on his belly, wiggling backward to the edge. Machines had long ago scraped the topsoil away, leaving the scratched rock surface bare. John watched him disappear over the edge of the cliff, Billy's short cropped head tilting once to flash John a grin.

"You coming or not, Johnny?" Billy called, but John stood rooted at the edge of the quarry. Six feet in front of him was the abyss of Quarry #3. The sign that named it also read NO TRESPASSING.

The limestone quarries had been mined for eighty years by Desmond Rock and Stone, but abandoned since before John was born. Billy's dad and uncles had worked there, been laid off, and now spent a considerable amount of time cursing Desmond's name. For the boys, the quarry was a wonderland. Stunted shrubs and pines adorned the slag piles that sat between the water-filled quarries.

John's own father had told him how he and his friends had played near the quarries at night, after the quarry men headed home. They'd gone swimming in #3, jumping off the quarry edge to the water fifteen meters below. His father also told him how Roger Martin had drowned there, his body tangled in the water vines.

He knew his father had told him the story to scare him away from the abandoned quarry, but the place lured them.

It was Billy who always wanted to ditch his sister and come over here. John followed, despite his father's stories of Roger Martin, his slime-covered corpse, pulled from the clinging plants, his body blue and bloated. The quarry was like an alien landscape, not farmland, not street, not grass, but bare rock, like a desert, like Mars maybe. How could they stay away? How could they not climb down the cliff wall to the cave below?

John got down on his belly and inched forward to the edge. Billy stood on a thin ledge, two and a half meters below the top. Dust covered his fingers.

"Gonna need the rope?" John asked. He wanted to run back to the barn and bring back a loop of rope. Then maybe his mom would see him and give him a chore, and then he'd not have to come back at all.

"Naw. It's right below me." Beyond Billy's head gleamed the green-blue of the quarry water, striking contrast to the white sheer cliffs of stone. John could make out the snaking forms of water vines, like those that had clung to Roger Martin's body.

"Careful, Billy," John said. The only thing worse than John falling into the quarry water was Billy doing it and John having to run home to tell their fathers.

"Jesus, Johnny, you're a scaredy-cat," Billy said, looking up, squinting at him. "You've been a scaredy-cat all day."

John blushed. They'd come to the quarry from the Walder barn where they'd been looking at the *Playboy* in the loft, ogling Miss June, trying to figure out the dirty jokes on the other side of her. Billy had stolen the magazine from his dad's nightstand, daring to take just one from the stack of dozens, picking Miss June because she looked so much like Mrs. Fonza, their teacher from fourth grade, with the jet-black hair and slim figure.

Billy had wanted to get another issue, but John had said no, worried that they would get caught.

Billy said, "I can see it."

Looking down, John was seized with vertigo. He tasted his lunch at the back of his throat—Mom's tomato soup. He closed his eyes and gripped a crack in the rock. Billy was always doing fool stuff like this. John still felt the pain on his backside from the time they snitched a jug of Billy's father's wine and drank it in the hayloft. Swimming in Mrs. Jones's pond had been Billy's idea too, but John was the one who'd tripped over the barbed-wire fence. His calf ached where he'd gotten the three dozen stitches.

John opened his eyes and forced himself to watch Billy's progress down the cliff face. Someone would have to help him if he fell.

"Almost there," Billy said, his foot stretching. He lowered himself another meter. "I can see into it."

Billy disappeared.

"Billy?" John called. There was no splash.

"Billy?"

"I'm in," Billy called up. "There's enough room for two. Come on down."

John edged closer to the abyss, his fingers biting into the scraped stone.

"This cave goes way back. Like twenty meters," Billy said. His head popped out of the cliff wall. "You coming or not?"

"I don't know."

"Did I mention there are cave-dweller paintings on the wall?"

"There are?"

"Yeah. Get down here."

John sat up, his legs dangling over the edge, not looking down.

"There ain't no cave-dweller paintings," he said to himself. "But you're going down there anyway, aren't you?"

He rolled onto his belly and felt with his feet for the first ledge, a five-centimeter jut in the wall.

If he didn't look down, if he ignored the fact that he was fifteen meters up, it was like being on the balance beam in gym class. He reached down with his foot and found the next small ledge.

John stepped lower, his face flat against the rock wall, his fingers aching from the force of his grip. As he pressed his foot down, a rock shifted and skittered down the side of the cliff. He slipped, dangling for a moment by his arms.

Blood pounded in his ears, and his shoulders screamed. How easy it would be to let go and plummet into the blue-green water below, just like Roger Martin. John hung there, his breath stopped for that second. Then he flexed, exhaled sharply, and dragged himself upward until his feet found a crevasse in the rock face.

A gentle wind tugged at his shoulders and cooled the sweat across his back.

The top of the cliff was just ten centimeters above him. He could climb back up. Up and back to the farm, and screw Billy Walder.

"Keep going," he whispered.

He forced himself to step down once, then again. He saw the opening below him and Billy's face grinning up.

"Don't worry, even if you fall, you'll just land in the water."

The dust tickled his nose. He took another step down, and Billy grabbed his leg.

"There you go." He pulled John into the cave mouth. "I was kidding about the cave-dweller paintings."

"I figured so," John said. He stood for a moment, letting his heart slow. He summoned up enough saliva to spit once, even though his mouth and nostrils were caked with dust.

"Look over here though," Billy said, pulling him deep into the cave. The air leached the heat from John's cheeks. The light faded away before the cavern did.

Billy pulled out his key-chain flashlight.

"This is so cool. So much better than a tree fort. We have a new command post, and there's no way Sheila will find us here."

"I'm not climbing down here every day," John said.

"We'll get a ladder."

At the far end of the cave, dark holes gaped, leading deeper into the stone. There might have been a large complex of caves beyond this one cavern, and John felt the urge to explore each tunnel, mapping them out with graph paper, compass, and string. The limestone walls reminded John of the cave he'd visited with his parents. Its walls had the same rippled, milky texture, but this cave was nothing like that one, because there was no roped-off trail here. In this cave there might really be bats and outcroppings of jewels.

"What's that?" he said. Something reflected the light of Billy's flashlight.

"Jewels?"

They edged closer, finding footholds on the slippery rocks. John peered closely at the thing, a disk of metal embedded in a column of limestone.

"Not jewels," he said. Then he saw the skeleton. Or rather, the half skeleton, its right side sealed into the rock, as if the limestone had absorbed it. Across its chest was the disk of metal, strapped in place.

Billy began to back away, the light jiggling.

"It's Roger Martin," he whispered.

"No, it isn't. They found his body," John said. He almost called Billy a scaredy-cat, but remembered his own fear on the cliff wall. "Don't worry, Billy. He's long dead. Hold the light steady." Falling was something to be scared of, not a skeleton, stuck in the limestone, dead years ago.

John pulled out his pocketknife and began chipping away at the wet limestone. In a few minutes the disk was loose. He removed the straps on the back and brought it closer to the light.

"What is it?" Billy asked.

It was a thin disk, with buttons and a digital readout that said 7312 on the face. Around the edge were a one-inch-long lever and a couple of dials.

"I don't know," John said with a smile. "But I'm going to find out." His finger lightly touched the finished metal of the lever. "Whatever it is, it's ours now."

"My dad told me those same stories about Roger Martin," John said. They sat in the Friendly's on Pike Street, three look-alikes drawing stares and attention. John didn't care.

"Yeah, me too," Prime said.

Superprime had wolfed down his dinner, as if he hadn't eaten in days. By his skinny appearance, John guessed that was true.

"So what happened then?" John asked.

"You can guess. We figured out how to dial a new universe," John Superprime said. "That was cool. I know we pulled the lever, but the universe counter must have been lower than 7312 so the device didn't work. And then we dialed it up higher and—poof I was gone."

"What did you do?"

"When?"

"When you transferred out?" John said. "What did you do?"

"I was scared shitless!" Superprime said. "The first place I ended up was this crazy world where everyone spoke French. I almost got caught, because I had no idea what had happened. One minute I was in the barn at Billy Walder's and the next I was in this huge stone-paved area that looked like ancient Greece."

"French?" John asked Prime.

"Saw one like that once. I think the French and Indians never lost the war with the British," Prime said. "No General Washington. The United States is all balkanized. I didn't stay long. It was useless to me if it was too far different."

"Yeah," Superprime said. "It was different. Bastards started chasing me when I tried to ask some questions. They were chasing me, shooting at me! I ran, ran for a corner. I was sure I was out of my mind.

"But then I came around the corner, right? And there were these guys in brown shirts and they waved me into this little lawn-mower-engine car. 'American? American?' they kept saying. They drove me out of the center of the city.

"By then my mind had settled a little. They threw a cloak over me as we went through this checkpoint. We didn't even have to stop. I started thinking. We had been playing with the device. It was in my pocket, so I took it out.

"They started shouting, like it was a bomb or something. They jammed on the brakes and I flew into the seats in front of me. They scrambled out and I reached for the device. Toggled it back to 7312 and of course nothing happened. Then I tried some other number and pulled the lever.

"Splat! I fall a meter or two on my ass. No car in that universe. But this one was closer to ours, right? America at least. Not some crazy French place."

"So what did you do then?" John asked.

"I tried to tell people," he said. "I tried to walk home first, but my house wasn't there. It looked the same, same roads and all, but no house. I was sure I was insane. Then I walked to the police station, and told them I couldn't find my house. They took everything down, tried to find my parents. No Rayburns of any kind in the area.

"They began to think I was crazy too. But I wasn't some bum. I had clothes and I was well fed. They put me up for the night at the precinct. But then they had some psychiatrist look at me. The house address I was repeating just wasn't there.

"I gave him the device."

"You what?" Prime cried.

"I didn't know then!" he cried. "I had no idea what it was!"

"What did he do?" John asked.

"He looked at it, touched it, but didn't press any buttons. Then he handed it back to me and asked me to tell him how it worked. I said I didn't want to, that everything would disappear. He told me in a calm voice that, no, it wouldn't. I argued until I was in tears. He insisted. Finally he put it in my lap, turned the dial, and put my finger on the trigger."

"No," John said in horror at what he knew would come next.

"I had no idea, you gotta believe me," Superprime said. "I didn't know."

"He made you press the button."

"He seemed so sure, and I wanted to believe him. He said it was all in my mind, that the device was just a toy. That if I pressed it, nothing would happen. I so wanted to believe that. So I let him push the lever."

"Jesus," Prime said.

"No," John said.

He hung his head, nodding it. "So much goddamn blood."

"How much of him—" Prime stopped his question halfway through.

"His arms, some of his chest." Superprime turned away, and his stomach heaved. He wiped his mouth with his sleeve. "I was in a field. With cows, and two goddamn arms.

"I panicked. I tried everything on the device to get back to my universe. But it wouldn't work."

They paid and left the restaurant, driving back to the apartment building.

"Did you guys break it when you took it out of the cave?" Prime asked.

"You've seen it. There's nothing to break."

"How old was that skeleton?" John asked.

"It was a fossil. It could have been decades, centuries old."

Prime glanced at John. "We need to see it," Prime said.

"Yeah," John replied. "What did you do then?"

"I started jumping universes, looking for some answer," he said. "I hoped there was some advanced civilization in the next universe over that could get me back. But none of the universes had technology any more advanced than mine. Some of them were backwards. Steam engines, horses and wagons. I tried—tried talking to myself once. But what good was that? I scared the hell out of my—our parents there. The John there thought it was cool.

"I stayed there for a few months. I was hungry and tired. I should have stayed, but . . ." He paused.

"What?" Prime said.

"We were only kids. I was jealous, okay? I was jealous of the other me!

"So I left one day. Didn't even tell them. Just left," he said. "I guess I had the idea then of . . . you know."

"Yeah," Prime said.

"So I started looking for a place that looked like home," Superprime said. "Some place where I could fit in. I found you." He nodded at Prime.

"Yeah," Prime said. "I know."

"How'd you do it?" John said. "I never knew."

"It doesn't matter," Prime said.

"I knocked him out with a shovel," Superprime said. "I tried to get him to try it, but he wouldn't. He was too suspicious. So I pretended like it didn't matter and then whacked him on the head. I dialed the device ahead one universe and triggered it with the handle of a shovel."

"Wow," John said. It was almost his exact plan when he was going to do the same to one-armed John.

"So, you can take me back, can't you?" Superprime said. "If you're here, then you figured the thing out, right? You gotta take me back."

He stood up, then, and put his arms on John's shoulders. He smelled of vomit and beer, plus a sweet pungent odor.

"No!" John shook him off.

"Why?" he said, shrugging at Prime. "Doesn't he want his life back? Here it is for him to have. I don't want it."

"You can rot in it for all I care," Prime said.

"Screw you both!" He turned away. "I did what I had to do. You both did it too."

John didn't reply. He hadn't done it, but he almost had. He wasn't any better than either of the two.

"We're not going to do anything for you in your current state," John said. "You're drunk, stoned out. What good is giving you back your old life if you'd just screw it up again?"

"Screw you," Superprime said.

"Fine," John said. "Let's go."

He and Prime turned away and started walking toward the street.

"Cathartic enough for you?" John asked Prime quietly.

"No. Not at all."

"It doesn't make it any better looking the person in the eye. Not at all."

"He killed my mother," Prime said.

"It was an accident. And you can take cold comfort in her being still alive in your home universe," John said.

"Cold comfort," Prime repeated.

"Hey! What are you going to do?" Superprime cried. "Why did you find me? Just to torment me?"

John turned on him. "We wanted to know where it came from. Now we do. Now we're going to go look for ourselves."

"You could take me back. Please! Take me back."

"Not today, John," he said. "Get your life back together and maybe we will."

CHAPTER 14

John ruminated on his last comment as they walked back to the quarry. What right did he have to deny Superprime his desire to return home? Why did he judge him unworthy?

"I guess we can't settle this universe," Prime said. "Otherwise he gets to be on the board."

John looked at him. He shouldn't have been surprised that they were thinking about the same things at the same time.

"Yeah, I was just thinking that," John said.

"I know."

They found the spot on the rock where they had come through, a blank piece of floor in the warehouse in 7651—Universe Top. Henry Top had taken to painting out circles as drop zones for travel between any universe and Top. That way there was no problem with someone materializing into an object. John and Prime transferred through to 7651.

Grace Top looked up.

"Gentlemen," she said. "How was your trip?"

"Angsty," Prime said. "Frustrating."

"But we know where we're going next," John said. "7312 is where Superprime found the device."

"He found it? He didn't get tricked by some Superduperprime?"

"No, he found it."

"Interesting." She checked her watch. "Hey, can you wait a few minutes? We're testing out the mail system."

"Cool," John said.

"Mail system?" Prime said.

"Watch and see."

Grace rolled a platform into the transfer zone for the fixed gate. She placed a small satchel on the top of the transfer platform.

"Mail!" she said.

"What do you need to send?" John asked.

"That James Bond film that was made here but never in 7650, a letter for Grace, a letter for Henry, a silly limerick I wrote."

"Is that VHS tape going to work?"

"Yep. We checked!"

"A transdimensional movie rental system," Prime said. "Now, that's entrepreneurship."

Grace counted down on her watch. She set the gate controls.

"Oh, almost forgot!" She took a second watch, made sure it showed the same time, and slipped it into the satchel. "We need to stay synced!" She paused, waiting. "Three . . . two . . . one!"

The lights dimmed. The machine hummed. Suddenly Henry was standing on the platform.

"Henry!" Grace cried. "I thought we weren't going to practice with people yet!"

"I know!" Henry said. He hopped down from the platform. "Hi, John. Hi, John. But we had successful transfers five times in a row. I figured we could do a real person on six." He grinned. "It worked." He gave Grace Top a kiss on the lips.

"They found Superprime," Grace said. "Now they're heading to 7312."

Henry said, "Oh, yeah? How'd he get the device?"

"Found it," John said. "In a cave, not too far from here."

"Mark it down," Grace Top said.

"Right," Henry replied, and marked a note in his notebook.

"What is he marking down?" Prime asked.

John shrugged.

"Universe 7312 is Universe Cave," Henry said.

"Universe 7423 is Universe Superprime," Grace Top said.

"Oh, right."

"We're building our corporate culture," she said with a smile.

"Okay," Prime said. "I still like plain numbers," he added to John quietly.

John said, "Grace, set the gate to 7312. We have some exploration to do."

"You got it."

John and Prime climbed atop the platform. Prime crouched a little, as if he was unsure that the radius would include his head.

"Three . . . two . . . one! Transfer!" Grace cried.

John's ears popped. He looked around at the bare landscape.

"I hope we never find a universe where they decided to dig the quarry here," he said.

"They're usually water-filled," John said.

"Usually."

It was late afternoon, and the sun was reflecting off the white scraped stone. Prime walked to the edge of the quarry pit, some fifty meters away. He peered down into the gaping hole.

"I don't see anything," he said.

John followed the edge of the quarry with his eyes, about three meters down, all the way around. Much of the quarry was covered in shadow, and he had no clear view of it.

"Kids," Prime said.

"What?"

"Kids are coming." A car pulled into the driveway of the quarry, skirting the old rusted rail that blocked the way. John watched them for a few moments, and then shrugged. They were just kids, looking for fun and probably a place to make out.

"I'm going to walk around the edge and see if I can spot the opening," John said.

"If it's still there," Prime said. "There are a lot of gravel spill-ins that could have covered it again."

"We'll find it, even if we have to drag Superprime out here to show us where it is."

"He can rot in my old universe for all I care."

John shielded his eyes from the sun as he walked the east side. Prime was walking the other way. Halfway around, he thought he saw something, a half-covered hole in the wall of the quarry, darker than the surrounding stone. He noted where it was, taking a bearing by a boulder farther back in the quarry and a distinctive streak of dark gray in the granite.

The kids had eyed the two of them for a few minutes, and then gone about their business. John heard a whoop as one of the boys— there were two boys and two girls, maybe in their early twenties— jumped from the cliffside into the water below.

The splash sent ripples across the blue water.

"Ahhh!" he cried.

"Is it cold?" one of the girls called.

He replied with chattering teeth, "No!"

They watched John as he passed, giving him a measured look. The girls were dressed in bikini tops and cut-off shorts. The boy just had shorts.

"Whatcha doing, man?" the boy said.

"Just looking for fossils."

"Sure, lots around here."

They turned back to watch their fourth make his way up from the water, via a zigzagging path of stone near their jumping point.

"What did you see?" Prime asked, meeting him as he came around.

"I think a hole in the wall. Hard to tell," John said.

"Did you ask those kids?"

"Naw."

John found the colored streak of granite that he'd spied from across the quarry.

"Here," he said. "About three meters down."

Prime grinned at him. "You going?"

"Sure." John lay on the edge of the quarry and slipped over the side until his feet found the ledge. "Here I go." Fingers gripping the edge, he lowered one foot until he found the next ledge. Then the other foot, and then once more.

"Well?" Prime asked.

"Yep, there's a cave opening here. A little to the left of where I am. I can reach it." He scooted along the ledge until his foot could reach the floor of the cave. He swung in and landed awkwardly on the cave floor.

The cave was chilly, and, by the weak light through the opening, covered in milky white stone ceiling to floor. Stalactites and stalagmites reached up and down. He had a flashlight and pulled it from his pocket. The cave disappeared into the dark, its walls opening wider than the beam played.

John stepped carefully over the rocky floor. Light from the cave opening flickered and he turned to see Prime dropping in from above. He was glad for the company suddenly.

"Anything?"

"Not yet."

Prime and he walked farther in. The cave floor dipped and suddenly there it was, the petrified universe traveler.

He was half embedded in the rock of the wall. It was no skeleton, but rather a desiccated corpse. The face was in rictus, the skin shrunken across the well-preserved muscles. He looked as if he had died in agony.

His clothes clung to him in shreds, bits of gray fabric, that John expected should have decayed away years before.

"He transferred right into the wall," Prime said. "The poor bastard died unable to reach the device."

It was true. The man's hands were both trapped in the rock. It appeared he had transferred in from another universe partially embedded in the rock and unable to move his hands to reach the device. One arm, his right, was reaching across the chest, but was encased in rock at the elbow.

"But why would he have transferred into rock?" John asked. "Transferring underground would have been a death sentence."

"Unless he had no choice," Prime said.

"Or he didn't think he would have a problem," John said. "Remember, the device is broken. Maybe going just one direction isn't the only way it's broken."

"Sabotage?" Prime asked. "Murder?"

"You've probably thought about it as much as I have," John said. "Why would a civilization as advanced as one that could create multidimensional travel create a device that fails as easily as this thing did?" He pointed to where the device sat strapped across his chest. "It only goes one direction, and we know that's easy to get around. We built a device that goes both ways. This thing beams you into solid matter, if such exists on the other side. What advanced civilization would allow that sort of failure to happen?"

"None I can postulate," Prime said.

"Exactly." John pointed at the cadaver. "This guy died a horrible death because his technology was either broken or sabotaged."

"What do we do with—"

"Hey!"

They turned to see someone entering the tunnel. John's hand went to the device, and then he pulled it away. There was no way he'd ever transfer under solid rock. Not after viewing the body of the first traveler.

Prime shined his flashlight at the approaching figure, and John realized it was one of the swimmers. The guy was still dressed in dripping trunks.

"What are you doing back here?" he cried.

"What concern is it of yours?" Prime asked.

"It's a big concern," the guy said. He pointed at the cadaver. "I'm the appointed guardian of this guy, and I don't like you poking around him 'looking for fossils.'"

"Appointed guardian, huh?" Prime said. "Then you should have called the police to let them know about this."

"Get that flashlight out of my face!" He swung his hand and

knocked the light aside. Prime let it drop, and its reflection illuminated both their faces.

The guy stopped in shock. His eyes went from John to Prime
and back again.

"Johnny?" he said softly, looking at Prime. "Johnny?" he said
again, looking at John.

John peered closely at him. The face had aged with the change
from adolescence to adulthood, leaner, more rugged. He was six
centimeters taller and more muscular. The tattoo was new, but
John recognized his boyhood friend. Only it wasn't really his boyhood friend.

"Hello, Billy Walder," he said. "But we're not the John Rayburn
you knew."

"So, he's still alive?" Billy Walder asked. They had climbed out of
the cave, when Billy started shivering in the cold underground air.
They stood on the bare rock above. His three friends were watching from a distance. He'd waved them off when they started toward them.

"Yes, he's alive."

"Damn," he said. "That could have been me. It could have been
me who disappeared like that."

"Yeah, one of you had to press the trigger," Prime said. "Good
thing you weren't too close to him when he did."

"Why?"

"It would have taken half your body with it," Prime said. "Leaving the rest here."

Billy Walder shuddered.

"And so you two are here why?"

"Looking for answers," John said. "We want to know where the
device came from."

"Space aliens," Billy said.

"Uh, aliens?"

"Yeah, I been thinking about it longer than you two have," he
said. "It's the only explanation. Cause if humans made that sorta
teleporting thing, then everyone would know about it, right?"

"It's not a teleporter," John said.

"Whatever. It moves you from place to place, right? Teleporter," Billy said. "If the U.S. government did it, it woulda leaked out. No one keeps a secret like this, right. So, aliens."

"Uh, sure," Prime said.

"So, you guys see 'em?" Billy asked. He leaned in close to them. "The aliens, I mean."

"We've seen some weird things, but no aliens," John said.

"Yeah, I guess they'd want their stuff back if you found them," Billy said. "You still have it, so you must not have found them."

"Good logic," Prime said.

Billy Walder paused for a moment, looking away. "His mom took it real hard," he said. "I mean he was fourteen, and just gone. No trace. They were pissed at me for a long time. Even though I had no idea."

"What did you tell them?"

"Nothing. What could I tell them?" Billy said. "I still have some of his stuff." He nodded down at the ground, toward the cave where the petrified man waited.

"His stuff?" John asked.

"Yeah, he had other things on him than the thing," Billy said. "You want to see them?"

"Yes, we do."

"Sure," he said. He scratched his head. "I can't remember where I put them. Oh, yeah." He pointed across the street where his parents' house stood. "Hid the stuff in a trunk at my parents' house. Come on."

He led them over to his three friends.

"What's going on, Bill?" one of the girls asked.

"These guys are old childhood friends of mine," he said. "We're going to walk over and talk to my parents for a minute. I'll be back in a few."

"Bill, you said we were going to swim," the girl said petulantly.

"And we will," he replied sharply. "Come on," he said to Prime and John.

The Walder house was across the street from the Rayburn house technically, though you couldn't see one from the other due to the line of intervening trees. The Walders had always had a yard full of old cars, tractors, and appliances. And this universe was no different.

"Stay here," Billy said. "I'll be right back."

John and Prime leaned against an old tractor and waited.

"I wonder what other artifacts the traveler had on him," Prime said.

"I wonder if there's more under the limestone," John said.

"You want to chip him out of there?" Prime asked.

"I think we should," John said. "If for no other reason than to give him a proper burial."

"Yeah."

Billy appeared a few minutes later carrying a box.

"Sorry, Mom wanted to talk." He handed the box to John. "Those are things that he had on him. On his wrist, around his neck, on his finger."

John opened the box. There was a ring, a wristwatch, and a simple chain necklace with a pendant hanging from it. John picked it up and saw that it was a curled snake in a figure eight, eating its own tail. The wristwatch had a display, but nothing showed on it.

"Couldn't ever get that thing to work," Billy said. "You're welcome to that stuff. I was afraid to touch much, afraid I'd disappear too."

Prime reached for the items, but Billy pulled them back.

"Can you bring John back?"

Prime stared at him, but John said, "Maybe. He's made a life for himself somewhere else."

Billy shrugged. "Well, you ask him for me," he said. "I'll give you this stuff, but you ask him if he wants to come back. And if he does, you bring him back."

"I'll ask," John said.

Billy handed the traveler's items to Prime.

"Thanks, Billy."

"Naw, thank you," he said. "I've always wondered. Now I know. But you ask him."

CHAPTER 15

John Rayburn let the door slam behind him. It rattled in its frame, and then dropped an inch on the handle side. He should have fixed that, but he had little enough time as it was. He'd promised to help his parents out during the summer, while he took a couple summer courses at the University of Findlay. But with his father's stroke, it looked likely that he'd be dropping those courses. Going back to Case Western in the fall seemed unlikely as well.

The day had been sweltering, and his body ached from the hours he'd spent spraying the cornfields. At least the crop looked good this year. A bad yield, combined with his father's health issues, and his parents would have had to sell everything. John touched the back of his neck. It stung where he was sunburned.

Any way he looked at it, he was stuck here, helping his parents. At least for a year, while Dad recovered. He knew Mom was assuming the worst. But John was sure that Dad would work through it. He was home now, against the doctors' wishes, but there was no way they could afford any more nights at the hospital. They had a nurse coming in to help with the rehab. She said he was doing better. And he seemed to be. John could understand most of his words. He was all there upstairs; controlling his body just wasn't so easy.

John kicked at the dirt. He headed past the barn. A swarm of gnats swam around his head at the corner near the lamp there. He loved his parents. He did. But he had his own life to live. Getting into Case Western hadn't been easy, and swinging the work-study meant he had no time for anything but bussing tables at the Faculty Club and studying physics. But it had been worth it. His parents did want him to do something other than farming, and though they'd never come out and said he should stay in the fall . . .

What choice did he have?

Something moved in the woods.

"Who's there?"

A stick snapped.

John whirled. He should have brought a flashlight.

Then a light swung left and right. Someone was in the line of trees along the road.

"Who's there?"

"Hi," someone said. "John Rayburn?"

"Yeah, that's me," John said. He forced himself to relax. It was just one of his friends maybe, someone from high school. Yeah. Sure, and whose phone didn't work.

Someone stepped out of the woods, shining a flash at the ground. He strode confidently toward John.

"Who are you?" John asked. "What are you doing out here?"

"John Rayburn, John Ten?" the person said. "I'm John Home." He flashed the light on his own face, and John gasped. It was his own face.

John wasn't sure when he went from believing the man was a loon, to believing with all his heart that what he said was true. The handful of Civil War gold coins hadn't been it. Nor had the detailed story he had told. The identical facial features, and the same jagged scar on his calf had gotten him part of the way. But it was the calm passion, the intensity of purpose that this foreign John Rayburn—this John Home—exuded that finally brought John to believe.

"I'm really glad you're going to Case Western," he was saying. They had wandered back to the barn and were sitting among the hay bales. John Home had brought two bags of cheeseburgers; ketchup, pickle, tomato, just like he always ordered them. John took another bite. "If you could take some cosmology courses, that would be awesome. Quantum physics too. No way there'll be a class on what we need to know, but that's the foundation we need."

"Do you have the plans for the . . . uh . . . transfer gate?" John asked.

"Oh, yeah, sure," he said. He pulled out a plastic binder from his backpack. "This is the original diagram of the device as we mapped it out. We've annotated what we think we know. This mass of connections is the state machine that controls the destination. I've marked the controls that we've figured out." He turned to another sheet of paper. "This is the step-by-step instructions for building a transfer gate. You'll notice there are huge parts of the original design that aren't in here."

"Why?"

"I was in a hurry," John Home said. "I cut anything that I couldn't understand or get to work. Our design is pared down to the basics. Understanding what else is in the original design is something we need to do."

"Right."

"Here's the parts list," John Home said. "Here's the part list by universe. Sometimes the integrated circuits we need go by different names in different places. It may go by a totally different name here. If it does, note it."

"Note it."

"It's just like freshman physics lab, but more intense and more important than that. We're trying to figure out the nature of the universe, and I need you—and all the Johns we recruit—to help." He smiled wryly. "I'd like to do it by myself, as you know, but that just won't happen."

John smiled. "Yeah, I guess you would want to do it yourself."

"Yeah, you understand," John Home said. "Here's your checklist."

John took the sheet of paper. It was an enumerated list:

1. Convert gold coins. Need plausible story for discovery.
2. Purchase quarry lot. Often owned by holding company named Sultan Rock and Gravel in Toledo. Negotiate a price of 17,500 in 7650E$ (7650 Equivalent Dollars).
3. Build a structure over the exact location of the 7651 transfer point.
4. Purchase the parts for a transfer gate in this universe.
5. Purchase an Encyclopaedia Britannica. Review summary sheets from 7651.
6. Recruit Grace and Henry.

"What's a 7650 equivalent dollar worth?" John asked, the most inane of all the questions in his mind.

"Probably very close to what a 7601 dollar is worth," John Home said. "Things aren't that different between our universes."

John looked back to the list, his mind boggling.

"Who are Grace and Henry?" he asked.

"Uh, well, their addresses are in there in the front," John said. "You'll like them. I promise."

"Okay," John Ten said. "But what is the 7651 transfer point?"

"Oh, yeah," John Home said. "There's a diagram." He flipped pages in the binder to a diagram marked with precise latitude and longitude. "This is every universe we've settled, and how it maps to 7651, which is our station universe."

John counted the numbers. "Ten, you've recruited ten of . . . me?"

"You're number ten," John Home said with a laugh. "We couldn't find a better name for this universe, so you're John Ten."

"You've done this nine times, already?" John asked.

"Yeah. I'm pretty convincing, aren't I?"

"You've got it down."

"I know what sounds good for John Rayburn," John said.

"Does this plan work?"

"Seems to," John said. "You're not that far behind the first."

John nodded. Suddenly his suspicions rose. "Why me? Why did you pick me?"

John Home shrugged. "It was random in many respects. You exist in a universe close to mine. You've had similar experiences to me, up to a point. You'll understand what I want to do, after you work through your suspicion."

John was suddenly angry, and then he laughed. "You've done this before."

"Couple times."

"My dad . . ." John stopped.

"He's had a stroke," John Home said. "Yeah, I know. A couple other Johns have experienced the same thing."

"Will he be all right?"

John Home shrugged. "None of these other universes is the future. But money isn't going to be a problem. Use anything from the sale of the coins to pay for whatever procedures he needs."

John looked away. He wasn't used to anonymous help.

"Listen," John Home said. "I'll be back in a week or so. You try selling the coins. Tell people you found them in the fields in an old box or something. Or in the attic. It'll take a while for experts to verify the coins."

"A week?"

"A week or so," John Home said. "It's okay to doubt me. You'll see proof in the results. You can back out any time, you know. It's not a binding contract we have here."

"What if I run to the police?"

John Home shrugged. "And what will you tell them? What law am I breaking?"

"I'm sure the U.S. government would want to know."

"Which U.S. government? Which president? Nationalism suddenly seems a little hard to maintain when you know there are tens of thousands of United States of America out there."

John shook his head. "It's a lot to comprehend."

"That's why I'm gonna let you think about it for a week." He stood up. "Okay. Time for me to go. Wanna watch this?"

"Yes, go ahead."

"I'm going to do it over here by the quarry." John Home opened his backpack. "I think I gave you everything. Let's go."

They walked over to the quarry. John Home searched the quarry surface for something, finally finding a spray-painted marker on the ground.

"Here," John Home said, handing John the flashlight. "You'll need this."

"Where . . . where are you going?" John asked. Being on his own with that daunting list of things to do suddenly seemed impossible.

"Back to Universe 7650, the home office," John Home said. He opened his shirt, exposing the strange device again. He dialed it until the front showed the number 7650. "You'll be all right, John. Even if you decide you don't want to do anything else, you can keep the coins. We have more than we know what to do with."

"Thanks."

"And it looks like you could use the money . . . for your dad."

"Okay."

"I'll be back in a week or so. So long, John." He disappeared.

John Rayburn had had doubts up until that very moment. Until John Home disappeared before his very eyes. He walked slowly around the spot, waving the flashlight back and forth. He was gone.

John sighed. If this wasn't the strangest thing that ever had happened to him, he had no idea what was.

But to let it go, to ignore it, as John Home suggested? Keeping the gold coins and doing none of the things John Home had listed for him? No, there was no doubt what he would be doing for the next week. John found himself grinning with pleasure as he walked back to the farmhouse.

CHAPTER 16

John appeared inside the quarry warehouse in 7650, in a zone marked as the 7601 transfer site. With ten settled universes in action, making sure each had its own zone was crucial. But 7650 was pretty simple compared to 7651. Grace Top ran the universe depot with precision, since she maintained connections—or would when their gates were complete—with every settled universe. Only one settled universe—Universe Gold: 7458—had a gate online so far, though nine John Rayburns had been recruited. Ten, if John counted John Ten. But that John seemed ready to sign on. They'd finally decided to build a gate in 7650 too, even with the chance that the Alarians might get hold of it. That meant they had three transfer gates—in 7458, 7650, and 7651—as well as John's transfer device.

Ten universes visited in three weeks; ten John Rayburns convinced to join the company. It had been a busy end to their summer. Though, when had he not been busy since he had received the device?

"Hey, John. How'd it go?"

Henry Home was manning the desk. He reached up and dialed

a number next to the label JOHN HOME, changing it from 7601 to 7650. John was back in 7650, so the big board showed it. The next satchel to 7651 would have that information, and when Grace Top sent her satchels out to the settled universes, they would know too where John was, all within two hours.

Also in the satchels were any deviations between the universes that anyone had found. Anything that differed in price or availability between any two universes was something they'd arbitrage.

"Pretty well. One conversation," John said.

"Case Western? Stroke? Summer at the farm?" Henry asked.

"Yep." Those simple characteristics were enough to know it had been an easy recruitment. Those John Rayburns were the ones most likely to jump at the offer to join the company. Those were the Johns who were ready to build.

"I'll add a reminder to visit in seven days," Henry said.

"What's new here?"

"Crazy Rubber Bands."

"What?"

"It's a fad in 7510, not so much here. We're shipping through twenty crates with a markup of three hundred percent. We buy a pack of twenty-four for two dollars and sell for six." Universe 7510 was home to John, Henry, and Grace Quayle, a universe where Dan Quayle had become president after the assassination of Bush I. The United States had avoided the Second Depression and experienced a renaissance of science, education, and arts.

"But what are they?"

Henry handed him a colorful circle of rubber. It was shaped like a mouse.

"This is it?"

"Yeah, kids trade them."

"Aren't we going to saturate the market?" John asked, thinking of the gold.

"Naw. The thing is, all our designs are unknown in 7510. They're unlisted, making them super rare," Henry said. "We're gonna make close to one million dollars in 7510."

"For rubber bands?"

"Fad items, John. Fad items."

John opened the outgoing satchel and leafed through the contents. Administrivia. Who was where, reminders for tasks, lists of arbitrage numbers on the items they were tracking. All of them like the rubber bands. Knickknacks, novelties, untraceable, cheap. Casey was especially good at spotting a fad they could exploit.

"What's this?"

John read the newspaper clipping. It was the court report for the *Toledo Sword*. One listing in particular was marked and starred.

Findlay resident Palmer Helmon was arrested Tuesday on charges of aggravated sexual assault. He is being held at the Findlay county jail on bail of $450,000. He was arrested for the July 15th rape of a Findlay teenager, a minor and attendee of Findlay High School. Her name is being withheld. Speculation of Helmon's involvement in three other rapes last year prompted the high bail amount. Additional charges are expected.

"What universe is this from?" John asked, and then he saw the 7458—Universe Gold. "Grace has this going to 7510?"

"All the settled universes, actually," Henry said.

"What if this guy is innocent? What if the police in 7458 are wrong?" John said. It was the same argument he'd had with Casey a year before, based on the fact that he and Prime were such different people. Though he had come to believe it was wishful thinking alone that differentiated him from Prime. Casey was convinced they were anything but similar.

"What if they're not?" Henry replied quickly. "If the rapes happened in any other universe on the same days, then this guy did it in those other universes."

"Fine!" John said. "Damn! What's she going to do with this? Tip off the police?"

"Yes."

"But if we cause trouble for some innocent guy . . ."

"Yeah, yeah, sure, sure." An alarm chimed from the desk. Henry checked the clock. It was nearly eleven. "Time for the last shipment of the day." They wheeled a new platform into place and put the satchels in the center of it. With a minute to spare, the last shipment was ready. The two stepped back and waited. At precisely eleven, there was a snap.

The satchels disappeared and in their place was a woman. Grace hopped down from the platform.

"Hey, John," she said, and by the tone alone, John knew she was Grace Top.

"Grace, how are you? You have business over here tonight?"

"More like fun," she said, hugging him. She turned toward Henry and planted a solid kiss on his lips. Henry returned the kiss with vigor, one of his hands squeezing her butt. John had been certain that this had been Henry Home, but perhaps it was Henry Top. It would explain their familiarity. The Henry and Grace of 7651 had formed some sort of relationship, John was certain. Henry tossed the new satchel to John, who rifled through the contents.

"Oh, Grace says to tell you the restraining order has been filed," Henry said.

"Not that it'll matter," John said. Twice they'd seen cars lurking in their parking lot, filled with blond-haired hulks who they could only assume were Alarians or Alarian agents. Grace had called the police the second time, and the police had arrested them before they could flee. The two brutes turned out to be full-time employees of Grauptham House. They'd decided to file a restraining order against the two as well as anyone else associated with Grauptham House.

"Grace was sure no judge would go for it," Henry said. "But those two assholes wouldn't even speak. The judge found them in contempt and passed the order."

"They've got nothing left to do but skulk and lay in wait," John said. "But a court ruling won't stop them."

"Okay," Henry said, looking around at the room. He'd powered down the transfer gate, and everything of value was locked in the safe, a common item in all settled universes. Often shipments were gold or other precious valuables. "Looks like we're good to go."

"I'll drive you over to your house," John said. His was the only car parked outside the building.

Grace got in the back of the Trans-Am, and Henry took the passenger seat. Pulling onto McMaster Road, John saw a car sitting by the road.

"Kids making out," John said. "My dad used to chase them off every night." He sighed, remembering the Rayburns' deaths in this universe.

Grace reached up and touched his shoulder.

In his rearview mirror, he caught the brake lights of the dark car flaring red. The lights pulled into the driveway to the quarry. John assumed they were turning around. But the headlights didn't appear after a few moments.

"They turned into the quarry driveway and didn't come back out."

"Damn it," Henry said.

John spun the car around in a three-point turn. He doused his own headlights as he pulled into the driveway. There next to the warehouse was the car.

"Grace, go across the street to my parents' house and call the police," John said.

"No way," she said. "I'm coming." She pushed Henry out of the way. "Pop the trunk."

John climbed out, hitting the trunk release. Through the window of the building, a flashlight bounced around inside.

Grace took the tire iron out.

Henry picked up a rock.

John wished he had listened to Casey and bought a gun too.

"Fine, let's go," he said.

They ran to the door.

With a shout, they pushed it open and slammed on the lights.

Two black-clad thieves stood next to the transfer gate. One held a camera, the other a flashlight.

Grace ran for them, wielding the tire iron. Henry and John had to run after her.

The two men froze for a second, and then ran.

Grace launched herself at the camera-toting thug, and he fell, tilting at the neck from the weight of a woman dragging him down by the camera strap.

Henry landed on him with his knees first, smashing his nose.

That left the first for John. He ran for the back room, John after him.

He pushed the back fire door open and disappeared into the night. John followed, but stopped short. There were gaping open pits out there, and though he had a good idea where they were, he wasn't going to run blindly based on that good idea.

He heard feet pounding in the dark, heading directly toward the pit just sixty meters away.

"Look out!" He followed slowly. "There's quarry pits out there!"

The sound of footsteps ended abruptly, followed by a scream. John followed slowly, and then turned back to the building to fetch a flashlight. He found Henry tying the camera toter with a rope. The camera lay at his side, smashed, the film exposed.

"Grace is on the phone with the police," Henry said.

"Sure, after she tackles someone she's willing to call the police, but not before," John said. He found a flashlight on the hip of the lassoed thug. "I think the other one may be in worse shape."

John's light crisscrossed the bare rock. Suddenly, the ground gaped open. The quarry hole was so deep and dark that the flashlight barely illuminated the floor of it. John finally found the mangled body of the thug. His arm moved weakly as he tried to get upright. He'd missed the water, whether for good or bad, and lay in the gravel just a meter away from it, and ten meters down. He'd clearly broken some bones; no normal leg had an angle like that.

"Help is on the way," John called. "As well as the police, asshole."

The man screamed incoherent, garbled words in what John had come to recognize as the Alarian language. John considered climbing down and helping him, but he had no desire to scale the rocks in the dark. Let the rescue squad figure out how to get him out of there. He returned back to the transfer building.

"Did you call an ambulance?" John asked Grace.

"No, just the police," she said. "What did you do to him?"

"Nothing," John said with a smile. "He fell in the quarry."

"What an idiot."

"This one is named Baduela Muthgalic," Henry said, reading his driver's license.

"Really?" Grace said. "How do they get driver's licenses? Do they even have birth certificates?"

"This one may have been born here," Henry said. "He's young enough. Or maybe he was banished as a baby."

"Do they teach you Alarian instead of English?" John asked.

A string of Alarian words erupted from his mouth.

"I should get an Alarian-to-English dictionary," Henry said.

"How many of you assholes are left on this planet?" John said.

"Fuck you, multiple swine," he spat.

"Listen, before the police get here and haul your defective asses off," John said. "Tell Gesalex that I'll transfer every single last one of you assholes wherever you want to go. Any universe out there. A free one-way ticket. Just to get you guys outta here. The offer still stands."

"Die a slow death, dup pig," he said.

John stepped on his arm and pressed down, until the man gasped.

"Tell Gesalex that he and anyone who wants to can leave this universe for free," John said slowly. "Do you understand me?"

The man didn't answer, so John leaned harder until he screamed. "Ah! Fine! I'll tell him!"

"Here come the police," Grace said. Lights were flashing through the windows. John let his foot off the thug. It wouldn't do to be seen torturing their trussed thief.

After two hours, the rescue squad managed to raise the second thug from the quarry floor. He had multiple broken bones. The first was hauled away in the sheriff's car, to be charged with breaking and entering. Grace had mentioned the restraining order, and if they could prove that either man was an employee of Grauptham House, they'd add the charge of violating a judge's order.

"They know about our warehouse," Henry said.

"We shouldn't have built a device here," John said.

"It doesn't matter," Grace said. "They didn't get it open."

"I think we need a security guard on-site, all the time," Henry said.

"I think we need to deal with the Alarians once and for all," John said.

"You said it."

. . .

He dropped Henry Top and Grace Top at Henry and Grace's house in the suburbs of Toledo. Then he drove to the new apartment he and Casey were sharing. They'd moved after the assault by the other Alarian thugs. How long before the Alarians knew their new address?

They knew where the pinball factory was, they'd known where the Rayburns lived, and they now apparently knew the Wizards had something going on in the quarry warehouse. John felt no safety at all in Universe 7650. Maybe it was time to leave for some other location. He could move Casey and him to 7651. There was no Casey Top or John Top.

With ten actively settled universes, 7650 held little real value. Except that it was the clearinghouse for most of their money transactions. Any arbitrage was converted into gold, silver, or platinum and transferred to 7650 for conversion into cash.

"So what happened?" Casey asked. John had called her after the police arrived, but couldn't explain because the sheriff had wanted his statement.

"More Alarian thugs," he said.

"Again? We need to put a stop to this."

"My thoughts exactly," John said. "They won't leave us alone. They know where we work. It's just a matter of time before they hurt us in their attempts to get the gate technology."

"We don't even know who they are," Casey said.

"We can guess if we see a corporate roster," John said with a laugh.

"Yeah, they're all Crudadud, or Yuffamix, or Slartibartfast," Casey said, joining in his laughter. "All we need is a phone book."

"Did you want to comb through the Pittsburgh white pages?"

"No, not really."

Casey, dressed in one of his T-shirts and devoid of any makeup, looked absolutely heavenly to him as she stood in the doorway to the kitchen. He finished pouring his glass of milk, almost spilling it as he looked at her.

"Oops," she said. "You almost spilled it all."

"I know, I was just thinking, and I was distracted."

"Oh, yeah, what were you thinking?" Casey reached up and wrapped her arms around his neck.

He didn't tell her what he had been really thinking, that he should marry Casey, just like Prime had married his own Casey. Instead he said, "That there are a million universes without any Alarians at all."

"Yeah. It would be nice to take a permanent vacation from them," she said.

"But I don't think Grace wants to cede this universe just yet," he said.

"She's hired private investigators to find out the Grauptham House and EmVis employees and owners," Casey said. "She's pulled off this restraining order, and we managed to buy ourselves back from them. It's a good fight. But deadly."

"Yeah, but we're constrained by the law, and they aren't. They don't give a crap for law," John said. "Prime would know what to do."

"Prime? Why do you always invoke his name when something hard needs to be done?"

John shrugged. "I don't, but he knows what to do. He knows how to take action."

"Aren't you both the same person?"

"No," John said. "I wouldn't do the things he does. We're different."

"But you'd condone the dirty work you ask him to do?" Casey asked.

John shook his head. "I don't know."

"Prime is amoral," Casey said. "You are not. He's a dangerous man."

"But you just said we're the same person," John said. "That makes me dangerous."

"Well, you can't have it both ways," Casey said. "You can't be him and not be him. You can't be amorally dangerous and morally responsible at the same time. Or can you?"

Prime was John. John was Prime. He had always told himself that in the same situation, he would have done the same things that Prime had, desperate to get back to his home universe. John, however, had been subject to a different set of stressors, a different environment. But when John had needed him to save Grace and Henry, Prime had come willingly. He had redeemed himself in John's eyes. Perhaps he was a rogue, but he had saved his friends' lives.

Casey wrapped her arms around John's neck. "Something should be done, yes? Just not tonight, I think."

"I agree," John said. He bent to kiss her, but she evaded his kiss, slipped from his embrace, and turned toward the door. She paused at the doorway, gave him a single look, and disappeared down the hallway.

He left his milk on the counter and hurried to follow her.

CHAPTER 17

"What is that?" John asked.

Grace was crouched over a small television screen in the office above the pinball warehouse. She was typing on a keyboard as she peered at the screen.

"It's a computer," she said, not even looking up.

"What? No way that's a computer," he said. The computers he had used in the programming class he'd taken at the university were mainframes that took up whole rooms. In FORTRAN class, they'd toured the computer facilities; the rooms were all white and super cold. To control the computers, John had used punch cards, not a little typewriter.

"It is," Grace said.

"It's . . . too small!"

"You remember 6013?"

John paused. "No." They'd scoped out a lot of universes to settle. John would transfer in via a fixed gate in 7651 carrying the portable device and explore the quarry area. Once they had a stable, safe location, they could use the fixed gate to move in a reconnaissance team.

"There was no John, no Grace, no Henry, no Casey," Grace said.

"There were a lot of those," John said. A lot of the universes outside the 7000 range seemed radically different from their own, so much so that often the universe was one where none of them existed. The universes near 7000 all seemed similar in their histories, though there were always anomalies sprinkled throughout, such as the Pleistocene world.

"The recon team pulled a Sears catalog," Grace said.

"A Sears what?"

"Like a Macy's here."

"Oh."

"In there," she said, pointing to a long cardboard box labeled 6013. He opened it and pulled out a thick catalog. One of the pages was marked, and on the page was an ad for a personal computer, identical to the one Grace had in front of her. He read the wondrous ad, his mind jumping in amazement.

"It does . . . this?" he asked. "Word processing? What's a spreadsheet? Accounting?"

"Yes," Grace said. "I may be able to fire our accountant. This program handles a company's books."

"No!"

"Yes."

"I want one."

"I knew you would," she said. "Yours is in the corner."

"Mine," he said.

He pulled open the box, removed the manuals, and began to read.

Two hours later, he looked up, realizing he was alone in the room and had to pee badly. He ran down the steps to the shop floor and found Grace in conversation with the shop boss, Viv. Grace gave him a smile as he hopped from foot to foot, as if she had known what would happen when she gave him a personal computer. Finally, when the conversation ended, John said, "Do you know what we can do with those?"

"I think so," Grace said. "Henry says we can eliminate the paper transfer, do everything by floppy disk."

"Sure, we can use it to track stuff," John said. "But we can write a program to look for universe differences for us. It can be our arbitrage system, instead of us looking for things ourselves!"

"Oh," Grace said. "We could load a universe's data into the system—"

"The database."

"—and it would figure out what we could exploit."

"Exactly."

John's mind wouldn't settle down. He had gone his whole life without ever knowing of a personal computer, and now in two hours he couldn't envision a universe without it. They could do . . . anything.

"Grace Top thinks we could sell these," Grace said. "Buy them in 6013 and double the price here. There's no competition at all. We'd dominate the market."

John nodded, but turned suddenly as the door to the factory opened and a tall woman walked in.

Her features were striking: her hair was platinum blond and she was as tall as John was. She was not particularly beautiful, but the set of her face was so unique that a person passing her on the street couldn't help but look twice.

She looked at him with blue eyes when she saw that John was staring at her. She walked directly toward him.

"Mr. Wilson, sir?" she said.

"Yes, that's me," John said, always shocked when someone used his taken name in 7650 of Wilson instead of his given name of Rayburn.

"My name is . . . Clotilde," she said. John pulled back at the name, realized that she was Alarian. He would have known instantly if she were male and walked through the warehouse door. It would have been obvious. But he couldn't recall ever seeing a female Alarian. "Clotilde Visgrath."

Beside him, Grace gave an animal snarl and launched herself at the woman. Grace's elbow caught her in the solar plexus, and the woman woofed, falling on her rump.

Grace brought her knee up and slammed it into the woman's nose. There was a sickening crack. She rolled over on all fours and did not move or make a sound.

John caught Grace's shoulder and pulled her back. The woman was rocking back and forth as blood dribbled onto the concrete floor.

By then, Viv was there, looking on, as were a dozen of the line workers. John gave her a look, and she nodded.

"All right, you monkeys!" Viv cried. "Stop lollygagging and get back to work." The workers turned away sullenly, but not a one disobeyed.

John pulled Grace backward until she stopped fighting him and sat her forcibly in an office chair.

"Don't get up, Grace," he said into her face. "Don't move."

She met his eyes for a moment and nodded.

"I mean it," he said.

"All right," she whispered. "Get her out of my factory."

"We'll see what she has to say first," John said.

Grace said nothing, but she sat heavily back into the chair.

John grabbed a handful of napkins from a nearby desk and knelt beside the woman named Clotilde Visgrath. He handed the napkins to her, but she did nothing but remain on all fours, rocking.

"Ms. Visgrath," John said. "Clotilde, please take these napkins."

For a long moment she did not move. Finally she turned and looked at the napkins. She took them and dabbed them against her face.

"I am sorry to offend, master," she whispered. "I am sorry to offend."

John was unsure of the reaction. It was not how a bossy American female would respond to an attack. Not what he would have expected from an Alarian male. Then he remembered Stella, Visgrath's docile and seemingly brainless secretary. Had Stella been an Alarian too? Was there some difference in class based on gender in that society?

"It's all right," John said. He put some of the napkins on the puddle of blood beneath Clotilde. "Grace . . . had a problem with someone named Visgrath."

Clotilde looked quickly at Grace then down again. "My . . . my father."

"Oh," John said, and he felt less horrified by what Grace had done to her. She was an Alarian. Progeny of the most evil person he had ever known. John took her arm to help her up, but she remained on her hands and knees, rocking back and forth.

"I'm sorry, sir. Please forgive me, sir," she repeated.

John felt sickened by her submissive behavior. She had been beaten down, taught to submit to anyone showing force. And she was the leader's daughter.

"Stand up," John said.

Clotilde glanced at his feet, and then shook her head.

"It's all right," John said. "I want you to stand . . . now."

She nodded nearly imperceptibly, and stood slowly. John dabbed the napkins to her nose and lip. She frowned, uncomfortable with this attention. Her face was already swelling. By tomorrow, she'd have two black eyes.

"Why are you here?" John asked. "You know we're not particularly fond of you Alarians."

"I know, sir. I know," she said. "I came—" She paused then seemed to gather her strength. "I came because you said you'd send anyone of the People—us—who came to you anywhere he or she wanted."

"I did," John said. "I did say that." He looked at her closely. "You want to leave this universe? And go back to the Alarian home universe?"

"No!" she cried. "No, sir. I don't want to go there. I just want to leave this one."

John looked at Grace. She sat on the chair, arms folded, staring straight at Clotilde. "She wants to defect," he said.

"Don't trust her," Grace said coldly.

"I'm sorry for what my father did," she cried. "I had nothing to do with it. Please, mistress!"

"It's a trap," Grace said. "Some scheme."

"No, I'm sincere, mistress! I am."

Grace stood and advanced on Clotilde. The woman cowered as Grace approached. She would have fallen to her knees if John hadn't had a hold of her shoulder.

Grace peered closely at her. "I killed your father," she whispered.

Clotilde looked at her in shock with large blue eyes. "Yes, I know," she said. "Thank you."

. . .

Grace did not exactly warm to Clotilde, but nor did she attack the woman again. John fetched ice from the freezer and then made an ice pack for her face. Grace led them to the upstairs office and stood while Clotilde sat on the low leather couch. She answered their questions tentatively.

"I don't know where the Alarians have gone," she said. "No female knows where the home world is. And certainly no half-breed. I just know that Lord Charboric and most of the other Twelve—I mean Eleven—are gone."

"Gesalex is one of the Twelve?"

"The youngest. He was a boy when they were banished here."

"And he's all that's left here from the originals?" John continued.

"Yes, Lord Charboric left him to move the transfer gate to the laboratory, only something went wrong."

"Stop calling him 'Lord,'" Grace said.

"Yes, mistress," Clotilde said meekly.

"How many went through before they moved the gate?" Grace asked.

"Hundreds," Clotilde said. "Charboric and his favorite women. The other Eleven, except for Gesalex, and their favorites. Some of the oldest half-breed males."

"Did any come back?" Grace asked.

"None."

Grace and John shared a glance. *Why hadn't they come back? They had fled this universe to . . . somewhere. Surely they had a gate there.*

"And how many are left, of the People, I mean," John said. "How many are in the know?"

"Less than a hundred," Clotilde said.

"From the outside, Grauptham House looks like it's in chaos," Grace said. She stood apart from Clotilde, her arms crossed.

"It is, mistress," she said.

"Stop calling me 'mistress,'" Grace said. "Only Henry is allowed to do that."

"Yes . . . ma'am."

"'Grace' will do."

"Yes, Miss Grace," Clotilde said. "I am here because there are no chaperones at the seraglio. I could leave easily."

"How did you get here?" John asked. "Do you have a car?"

"No, I have no car!" she said. "I took a bus, of course. I have money! I know how to spend it." Her anger startled him, and her as well, because she immediately lowered her eyes and added, "I'm sorry, sir."

"I was just asking," John said with a laugh. "But I take it someone will miss you at some point."

"Maybe," she said. "Things have not been the same since the Second Exodus. Gesalex told us that we would soon be heading to the Home Universe. But that was months ago. Then I heard from . . . one of the half-bloods that you had made an offer of peace."

"Twice," John said.

"But that Gesalex would not take it."

"No, he seemed a little put out at the time," Grace said with a smirk.

"He has failed," Clotilde said, the same dark smile on her face.

"So you want to go to the . . . home universe?"

Clotilde paled. "Anywhere but," she said. "I hate what my father did! I hate everything about the Alarians!"

"Why?" Grace said.

"He . . . he . . ." Clotilde said, grasping for the words. She swallowed. "I know about the culture here," she said. "My privilege as Visgrath's daughter allowed me access to books and some movies. I know that we are different. But it's nothing I want."

"Do the other Alarian women feel that way?" Grace asked.

"Yes, we mostly agree," she said. "Some can't see beyond the seraglio, but most of us, especially the younger ones, understand."

"How are you treated at the . . . seraglio?" Grace asked.

"As breeding sows," Clotilde cried. Tears formed at her eyes.

"Oh," Grace said. She grabbed the box of tissues from her desk and handed it to Clotilde.

"Anywhere but here?" John asked. "You just want to leave."

"I can pay you," Clotilde said. She reached into her purse and pulled out an envelope. John expected to see cash, but instead inside was a folded sheet of thick paper. She handed it to John.

John read the words on the stock certificate, *Grauptham House, 10 shares, Clotilde Visgrath.*

"How many shares of the private stock does Grauptham House have outstanding?" John asked Grace.

She shrugged, and turned to her filing cabinet. She pulled a file, and inside was the report from the State of Pennsylvania on the company. "This says a thousand," she said.

"Do all the Alarian females have stock certificates?" John asked Clotilde.

"Yes, when the Second Exodus started, many papers were signed over," Clotilde said. "The stock was given to the women in case it was needed later. Charboric didn't expect to be back."

Grace took the stock certificate worth several million dollars and said, "I think we can come to an agreement, Clotilde."

John and Grace took Clotilde to an urgent-care facility where they set her nose and prescribed painkillers. The doctor eyed John suspiciously and asked to speak with Clotilde alone, as if John were an abusive boyfriend. No, John thought, it was the thin, gangly woman standing next to him who had broken Clotilde's nose. Never cross Grace. That was a good axiom for life.

"Do all the women at the seraglio have stock certificates?" Grace asked again. She leaned against the wall, her hands on her hips. Clotilde sat on the edge of the examination table, her slight nervous movements rustling the stiff paper covering.

"Yes, most of them," Clotilde said.

"And most of them will take us up on the offer if they could?" Grace said. "Transport to another universe. Any other universe?"

"Yes."

"And you'll explain the offer to all the others?"

"Grace," John said. "It's dangerous if she goes back. They'll know she's been gone."

"They have no idea," Clotilde said quickly. "I could be gone for a week and no one will know."

"But the black eyes?" John said. "They'll know."

"They won't," she said. She looked into John's eyes. "I'll be fine. Just drive me back tonight."

The seraglio was in Pittsburgh, a night's drive.

"We'll need a bus," John said. "Two buses. And drivers." His head was boggling at the magnitude of the operation.

"That we can cover," Grace said. "We'll send a message to the settled universes. Tell them we need drivers for a caravan to Pittsburgh." She laughed, and Clotilde smiled in return. "I'm sorry for attacking you, Clotilde. But when I learned who you were . . ."

"I understand."

The nurse returned with her discharge papers and prescription.

"Let's go," John said. It was after seven already, and the drive would be close to four hours. He hated Pennsylvania! In all universes!

"Do you go by the name Clo?" Grace asked.

"Tilly," Clotilde said. "You can call me Tilly."

"I like that," Grace said.

John Ten, Civil War John, and John Champ joined them in Grace's minivan for the trip to Pittsburgh. Clotilde looked at the four Johns, her mouth agape.

"I understood, of course, but I've never seen a dup before," she said. She lowered her eyes. "I'm sorry. I didn't mean to use that offensive term."

John laughed. "It's not actually offensive to us," he said.

"I knew it was true," Clotilde said, "but none of us born here have ever witnessed what that meant." She reached out to touch John Ten's face. He blushed.

"Um," he said. Grace made John drive, taking the passenger seat, and somehow positioning John Ten in the bench seat next to Clotilde.

"What are you doing?" John asked Grace softly.

"There's no Casey in 7601," she whispered back. "She seems like a nice girl."

"You're matchmaking him with an Alarian?" John asked.

"Shush!" Grace replied. "7601 is a fine universe for all of them to emigrate to."

"But—"

"Really, you're going to argue with me?"

"Okay, fine."

John sped them across Ohio toward the Crimson Livery Rental in Wheeling, West Virginia. Grace had reserved four minibuses.

"You guys can drive these, can't you?" Grace asked.

The Johns shared a look, scoffing at her. "We grew up on a farm!" John Ten said. "We can drive anything." He glanced at Clotilde, making sure she was listening to him. She was. John tried not to roll his eyes.

But as he watched John Ten maneuver near Clotilde, speak so that she knew he was speaking, and always be ready to assist her, John reminded himself that there was no Casey in his universe. In 7322 and 7351 (called Universe Low and Universe Champ, since one was the lowest settled universe and in the other, John's basketball team had won the state championship), John and Casey were an item for certain. And maybe they were in every universe where the two lived in Findlay. Prime had his Casey, and John had the Casey in 7650. It was almost as if it was always meant to be. Except for John Ten, who'd never had a chance to find his own Casey. But he certainly liked Clotilde.

John Ten agreed to lead the caravan since that meant Clotilde would ride with him. The four buses formed a convoy into Pennsylvania, and around midnight they pulled onto a dark road that led into a wooded lot on the east side of Pittsburgh. The road meandered until they reached a stone wall nearly three meters high. The road formed a circle in front of the gate, and all four buses lined up there as if it was last bell at some nocturnal grade school.

Clotilde emerged from her bus and walked to the gate. The metal gates were chained together, but she easily slipped between the two gates; the chain was too loose to hold them completely closed. There was no guard as far as John could tell. Clotilde disappeared into the darkness beyond the wall.

Minutes ticked by. Grace was silent beside him. John stood up and said, "This is driving me nuts."

Grace caught his arm. "Hold on." She peered intently into the darkness past the gate. "Here they come."

A flash of white in the darkness caught his eye. He thought it was a plastic bag blowing in the wind, then two more shapes appeared, then a dozen. But no, it was a line of women walking toward them, dressed in white skirts that covered their bodies from neck to toes. Leading them was Clotilde. She produced a key and unlocked the gate.

John counted fifty-three women.

"Let's go."

John realized that it would be a tight fit. Each of the women had baskets, bags, or handfuls of clothes and objects—utensils, radios, books. As the group neared the buses, they stopped and stared at the Johns. They were all tall and nearly all blond, with the Nordic look that was common to the Alarians.

It was Grace who rushed forward and took the nearest by the hand.

"Let's go, ladies," she said. "We have a long way to go tonight. Let's get going."

She led the first woman to the nearest bus and placed her things in the back. After that, each of the Johns helped stow their belongings.

The women, silent at first, were suddenly loud and boisterous, jostling to get their things packed in the back. As John loaded baskets and bags, the women reached out and touched his face one by one.

"John Wilson," one of them whispered. Then another said it. "John Wilson."

"It's John Rayburn, actually," he said self-consciously.

"John Rayburn," a woman said. "Thank you."

John looked over to see each woman handing Grace a sheaf of paper, payment for their passage. Some women had no paper, but Grace waved them onto the minibuses anyway.

"Quiet, please," John whispered.

"Don't worry, sir," someone said. He turned to see Clotilde walking toward him. "The single guard will not bother us."

"Did you . . . ?" John Ten asked.

"No," Clotilde said, blushing. "He's not dead. But his head will ache in the morning."

They managed to load all of the women, fifty-four counting Clotilde, though some had to sit on the floor, leaning against the plush seats. It took far longer than John expected, but no alarm sounded, no guards emerged from the dark, no Gesalex appeared to demand the return of the women.

The caravan departed with the rumbling of diesel engines.

Beside him, Grace grinned.

"We saved them all," John said.

Grace raised an eyebrow. She waved the sheaf of paper at John. "And we were well paid for it."

"How much?"

"Six hundred and change shares of Grauptham House," she said. "As soon as we have these notarized in the morning."

"Of the thousand?"

"Yes, we own a majority share of Grauptham House."

CHAPTER 18

The morning was a madhouse. The call had gone out to all the universes, and the pinball factory was the center of the craziness. Representatives from every settled universe were present, calming the Alarian women, calling to find notaries available on a Saturday morning, and making breakfast.

Luckily it was a weekend, and the factory was closed. The guard had been sent home, rather than allow him to see ten identical John Rayburns, six Graces, five Henrys, and three Caseys.

"Found one," John Gore said. "Said she'll be out here in two hours with her notary stamps." Universe Gore—Universe 7512—was an environmental nightmare universe, where big business had sacrificed the planet for profits, leading to global temperatures that were noticeably higher and weather more chaotic than any other universe.

"That's three notaries on the way," Grace Home said. "We need to make sure all these women have identification."

Clotilde nodded. "I made sure. We all have certificates of identification and social security numbers."

"Just no driver's licenses?" John asked.

"That was forbidden," Clotilde said. "But I'd like to learn," she added with a smile.

"I'll teach you," John Ten said.

John Prime and his Casey—Casey Prime—appeared, trailing a half-dozen Alarian women. They had raided the local Roebucks for clothing, suitcases, and toiletries, enough for all fifty-four of their guests.

"Let's line them up alphabetically," he said to Casey as he passed by.

"We'll label their spot with their name," Casey Prime replied. "Give them all a suitcase or duffel and the best match we can for size."

"We're going to need another trip," Prime said, brushing past John with a nod.

In the little kitchenette in the back of the factory, a gaggle of Henrys and Graces were making pancakes on a dozen griddles they'd purchased at Callahan's in Columbus on the way back.

John shook his head at the bustle around him. And yet they were all of a like mind. How could it be different? Most of them were the same person and had the same synapses, the same mores. Of course they would work well together.

It *was* a madhouse, but they were getting things done.

He glanced at Grace, who looked pensive.

"What's wrong?" he asked. "It's all coming together."

"Gesalex is going to respond," she said. "The question is how soon."

"We can move somewhere else . . ."

"No," Grace said. "Everyone is here. The notaries are coming here. The quarry site is too small and not safe for a large group. People would be tripping over the cords."

"I guess we'll just have to be quick," John said.

"He could be here any time."

"Maybe we need weapons," John said. He knew that Casey had her pistol. She always carried it now. Did anyone else have weapons?

He waved over Henry Low and said, "See who's carrying weapons and come up with an idea to get some more."

"We should also post a guard," Grace said. "Park the minibuses across the entrance to the parking lot. That should keep them from driving right into our front office."

John assigned the task to John Champ.

"First notary is here," someone shouted.

"I got this," Grace said. She rubbed her face, seemed to grab ahold of herself, and walked forward, suddenly the CEO of a company. "Hi, I'm Grace Shisler, thanks for coming on short notice."

She led the notary—who seemed a little dazed by all the frenetic activity—to a table. Grace started calling the Alarian women over one by one alphabetically.

"Aduswintha!" Grace called. "Please come forward."

It was a madhouse. But John felt like they were actually doing something. Grace's plan was gutsy, off the charts, out of the box. But if they pulled it off, everyone won, except for Gesalex.

John glanced at Grace, who was discussing something with the notary. The notary finally seemed to accept Grace's explanation, took Aduswintha's identification card, and then stamped the certificate. She handed the certificate to Grace.

Grace saw John watching and mouthed the words, "One percent."

John remained at the center of the chaos, coordinating action, making sure there was enough breakfast, finding tables for the notaries to do their work. The Alarians did not complain at the slightest inconvenience, and cheerfully pitched in with whatever task he assigned them.

"Here's a shopping list for the grocery store," he said to one. "Go with the Henry there and take two others. Here's cash." He pulled two hundred dollars from his wallet.

"Make sure the guards on the roof all have what they need," he said. "Coffee, soda, bathroom breaks."

When a dozen of the Alarian women had had their papers notarized, John had one of the other Johns drive them to the quarry. Until they knew the ramifications of what they'd done, the women would stay in 7601, guests of John Ten. He and Clotilde had already transferred over and were searching for a cheap hotel, a mansion, anything that they could rent for all fifty-four women.

Luckily funds were not a problem. Pinball Wizards had been placing cash and gold reserves in each settled universe, in case of emergencies. They'd have to transfer more gold to 7601 soon to cover some costs, but for the moment, they had enough to rent a location and keep the women fed. He made a mark on the transfer ledger to transfer ten thousand grams of gold to 7601. John handed the ledger to John Quayle, who was headed to the quarry office. The ledger was their method of tracking material goods transfers. A computer system—a networked computer system!—would have made the process easier. Though how they would network across universes, he didn't know. In any case, John Ten would need a constant stream of cash to care for his fifty-four guests.

"What are we going to do with fifty-four women?" John muttered to himself.

"Nothing," one of them said—Englavira. She was the oldest of those who had left the night before. Clotilde said a dozen more had stayed, refusing to go or not even being asked to leave. "You just give us a start, and we take it from there."

"But all by yourselves? In a new universe?" John said. "We can help you."

"We'll take some help," Englavira said with a faint smile. "But we've spent our lives in bondage, kept as chattel for breeding purposes, or, in the case of those not 'pure' enough, as slave labor."

"Some of you, Clotilde and yourself," he said, "seem very liberated for living in the society that you did."

Englavira smiled. She was only a few centimeters shorter than John, almost a platinum blonde, broadly shouldered, but voluptuous.

"They liked to think they had us cloistered," she said. "But you can't live fifty years in a place and not be influenced by it. We had a cache of books, magazines, and papers. We taught the younger ones. Clotilde is our best student, and I understand exactly why she ran to you when she heard the offer. We have been slowly liberating ourselves from Alarian culture for years."

"How much do you know about how they got here?" John asked.

"We hear rumors and stories," she said. "In them, Visgrath is a hero, who is maligned and unjustly sent away."

John snorted.

"Exactly," she said. "A hundred years ago, the Alarians—then only in a single universe—managed to obtain transfer technology. More than likely, they stole it from some poor traveler who didn't know what they were getting into."

"What universe?"

Englavira shrugged. "I have no idea." She shrugged again, looking away. "You believe because it's all you know, but it's all myth and ancient history. And I make it seem like we were slaves. But we were pampered too. Mothers of monsters. Sucklers of evil." Her laughter was cold. "I am not innocent. Neither is Clotilde. Look who her father was." She made a fist and seemed to throw empty air at the ground. "Good riddance to him." She looked embarrassed at her outburst.

"What was the myth?" John asked after a moment.

"Visgrath was Teiwaz's son, he claimed. He was the liberator," she explained. "He wanted to use the technology to enslave the multiverse. And he did it, he used nuclear weapons on a universe to subjugate them. Purifying fire. And it worked. He conquered entire universes. How can you fight an enemy that can appear anywhere with nuclear warheads?"

"Yes, how?" John Prime said. He had neared the two as they talked. In fact, all the Alarian women nearby were listening to Englavira's story.

"You can't, if you don't have the technology," Englavira said. "Two, three universes. Then five were vanquished. Not Alarian worlds. Worlds like this or with other histories. Not like ours. But it couldn't be ignored. People notice when universes are broken, destroyed, nuked."

"Who noticed?" John asked.

"The Vig noticed," Englavira said.

John and Prime shared a glance. It was the same word that Corrundrum used for some omnipotent patrolling force.

"What or who is the Vig?" John asked.

"They police the multiverse," she said. "They allow certain universes to use the technology in exchange for commerce rights, and stop others. And by stop, I mean they destroy cultures that violate their rules."

"Destroy?" John said.

"Yes, what they did to the Alarian world. Nuked it to oblivion, or so the story goes. But not before Visgrath was marooned here. His allies turned on him—can you blame them?—and exiled him to this universe—what he called the Prison."

"How did he know the home world was destroyed if he was exiled?"

"The Vig had already destroyed our conquered universes," Englavira said. "Cauterized the wound. It was only a matter of time. And when no rescue came, no punishment, no travelers at all, Visgrath knew that the home world was destroyed."

"Where did Charboric go then?"

Englavira shrugged.

Prime said, "He had a safe haven universe. Somewhere he had scouted out and hadn't told anyone else about. Wouldn't you do the same?"

"Yes," John said. But his mind wasn't on Charboric. He was thinking about what the Vig had done to the Alarians when they found out they had transfer technology. But there was a difference between conquering universes and using the technology to arbitrage goods. What would the Vig do if they found the Pinball Wizards? Would they cauterize the ten settled universes?

"Englavira?"

They turned as Grace called her name.

"Yes?"

"We're ready for you," she said, nodding toward the notary.

Englavira nodded. "I hope I've helped you understand our broken universe," she said to John.

"Yes, you did, thank you."

John Ten and Clotilde returned by the time the third group of Alarian women had been bussed over to the quarry site.

"We found housing for all of us," Clotilde said. "It's perfect."

"Camp Bobby Kavanagh," John Ten said. "Old Boy Scout campground. Hasn't been used in years. But safe, isolated, and cheap."

"We can live in a barracks," Clotilde said. "As long as no one is there to watch us all the time."

"We can probably buy it," John Ten said.

One of the Henrys suddenly called down from the roof through the small access hatch.

"Company!" he said. "Two black SUVs on the side of the road. Watching."

"Okay," John cried. "We load up the rest right now! Let's get these women out of here!"

"Hold on," Grace said. "We need two more."

"Grab the two," John said. "The rest of the women can get in the minibus."

"Here they come!" the Henry on the roof cried. "Eight of 'em. Looks like one of them is Gesalex."

"Oh, no," Clotilde said. Grace grabbed her shoulder.

"It'll be okay."

Casey appeared from the kitchen with her purse. In it was her gun, John knew. Their eyes met and he shook his head imperceptibly. She nodded, knowing to keep the gun from sight unless needed.

"Are they armed?" John cried.

"Not in the open!"

"Let's meet them in the lobby," Grace said. "Load the minibuses from the loading dock."

John started for the lobby, Grace falling in at his side.

"Shouldn't you be getting the last two certificates?" John asked.

She startled, then smiled. "Oh, yeah. I guess that's the play, isn't it?"

"Yep," John said. He felt calm at the coming confrontation.

"I'm coming," Clotilde said, following him.

"You don't have to," John said.

"I do."

He, Casey, Clotilde, and John Ten entered the lobby, stood in front of the double doors, and waited.

Clotilde's face was pale, her chin trembling. John watched John Ten take her hand and she smiled at him.

The eight appeared around the corner. They were dressed in dark suits; they didn't appear armed. But any of them could have weapons strapped under their jackets. Gesalex was in the middle.

The first goon opened the door savagely.

"Stop!" John shouted. "Stop right there, you bastards. You are not allowed to enter these premises."

Gesalex motioned the two men in front aside.

"You have something of mine, Wilson!" he cried.

"And what would that be?" John replied.

"The precious matrons of our society," Gesalex replied. "Return them."

John smiled. "Oh, it's okay to shoot, kidnap, and torture us, but you draw the line at our liberating your women?"

"Return them now."

"We're not going back," Clotilde said softly.

"Silence!" Gesalex cried.

Clotilde cringed, then straightened her back. "We're not going back," she said, louder.

"You have no say in the matter."

"Oh, really?" John said. "Is slavery suddenly legal here?"

"The laws of this place mean nothing. You should know that."

"Then you can explain that to the police when they get here," John said.

"We will explain," Gesalex said, "that you kidnapped fifty helpless women against their will."

The last minibus of women rumbled by behind the Alarians. Gesalex didn't turn, but if he had he would have seen the pale faces of fifteen women staring at him.

"What women?" John said. "They're in another universe now."

"What?" Gesalex cried. "What have you done?"

He motioned to two of his men to go forward. They advanced, but after they'd taken a step, Casey smoothly drew her gun and fired a single round into the wall above the door.

"No," she said. "You may not enter the premises."

"This will not . . . stand!" Gesalex cried.

The doors opened and Grace appeared. In her hand was a stack of paper, signed and notarized stock certificates of Grauptham House, Incorporated. She smiled at John.

"Mr. Gesalex," she said. "I now own fifty-three percent of Grauptham House, and you're fired."

CHAPTER 19

Maybe it was that statement from Grace or perhaps the wail of sirens in the distance, but Gesalex stared at them for a moment, his face a pale, stricken slab of flesh, and then he turned and ran. His entourage followed.

The sound of the gunshot still echoed in John's brain, but his heart had begun to beat again.

"Fifty-three percent?" he asked.

"Yeah, fifty-three," Grace said. "The price of that brick is coming out of your commission check, Casey."

"Sure, no problem."

"What do we do now?" John asked. "I mean, we own one of the largest companies in this universe. What do we do now?"

"In the multiverse," John Ten said.

"They're going somewhere," Casey said. "In a hurry."

Grace shrugged. "Meh, we'll deal with that after the Alarians are settled in. Though I should call our lawyers. They probably need to know about this."

"You think?" John asked. "And once the Alarian women are settled into 7601?"

Grace grinned. "We scrub that company clean of any sign of those bastards."

Monday found them in Harrisburg, Pennsylvania, explaining their case to a judge. No Alarians were present. The judge ordered a freeze of all Grauptham House assets and the start of meetings between the major shareholders and the current management of the company.

With the writ in hand and three federal marshals, they invaded the corporate office buildings in downtown Pittsburgh. They took the high-rise elevator to the top floor and barged into Gesalex's office. The Alarian stared at them for a moment, drew a gun, and shot himself in the temple.

Four days later, the party was boisterous and wild. Gesalex was dead. Grauptham House was theirs. As far as they could see, their enemies were vanquished.

The pinball factory thumped with music that Henry Case was playing from a huge stereo system that they had transferred in from his universe, Universe 7625 or Universe Case, which was one of the few universes where John had gotten into the Case Institute of Technology. The center of the factory floor had been cleared and Johns and Caseys, Graces and Henrys moved in rhythm to the sound. John found himself dancing closely with a Casey he couldn't be sure was his. After a moment of concern, he decided it didn't matter. Perhaps it was Casey Prime. He found himself momentarily aroused by the thought.

Even Clotilde was there, the only singleton among them. She was easy to spot on the dance floor, taller than any other woman out there, and platinum blond. She was dancing close to John Ten, John assumed. The rest of the Alarian women were in 7601.

Though they could have returned to 7650, the Alarian women chose not to. They were already looking for jobs in Toledo, as store clerks, cashiers, cooks, and maids. John made it clear that they could do whatever they wished; Pinball Wizards, Transdimensional, would support them indefinitely. This was firmly and politely refused. Englavira had spent the first three days in 7650 identifying all the remaining Alarian half-breeds by looking through the personnel files. Each Alarian was fired and offered a cash buyout, if they happened to own stock. The ticket to another universe remained open, and most took the offer. A dozen Alarians remained unaccounted for, and a hundred stock certificates, which was ten percent of the company.

The song changed, a faster tempo, more chaotic than before, and John extracted himself from the Casey he had been dancing with. He took a seat on the steps going up to the office. Things were wild. The media had had a field day with the takeover. Gesalex's death had been the main event. But the purging of the Alarian half breeds, their disappearance in many cases—hardly a crime but the Wizards couldn't explain the transfer of all the half-breeds to 7466—and the amazing takeover itself fed the Pittsburgh newspapers every day that week.

"Tired?"

John turned to see Grace—which Grace, he didn't know—peering at him through the iron railing.

"It's been a busy week."

"You know we own the Palladius Hotel in Columbus?" she said. "We could have had our party there."

"The Palladius?" John said. "That's the nicest hotel in the city."

"We own a dozen hotels now," Grace said. "That I know of. I'm still working my way through the books."

John knew it was Grace Home then, the CEO of Grauptham House, the media sensation of the week.

"We have enough frenzy around us," John said. "A picture of twenty Johns, Henrys, Caseys, and Graces at a party in downtown Columbus would be all we need."

"It would make things interesting," Grace said.

"More interesting," John countered. "Any luck finding those last hundred stock certificates?"

"None, and there's still Alarian male half-breeds we haven't found," Grace said. "Not that I care too much about that. They're cut out of the company now. A ten-percent owner is nothing."

"You own ninety percent after all."

"Ninety percent of a mess," Grace said. "It's gonna take us months—years, maybe—to figure out what we've got. They've been running this for fifty years with no oversight, with no real corporate goal except to exploit this world, and make themselves money."

"You mentioned the hotels," John said. "What else do we own?"

"Copper mines in Utah and Arizona. Banks in the Caymans and Britain. Aluminum smelting companies in Brazil. Construction companies in Boston and Chicago. Millions of acres of land in Canada."

"Canada?"

"Great fly-fishing, but otherwise useless for anything," Grace said. "The company has sixty thousand workers."

"And none of them knew they were working for sadistic bastards from another universe."

"How could they know?" Grace asked. "Profit from the technology exploitation went to finance these marginal companies. Many of them show no profit at all, certainly less than the cost of money. But the Alarians seemed willing to buy into anything that they knew might go big. Medical inventions, speculative technology, things they might have known about from other universes but didn't know exactly how they worked."

"How do we sort this all out?" John asked.

Grace shrugged. "With a little help from our friends," she said. "The upper layer of management may have to go. I met with a general manager of a cartage company today. Asked him for his P and L sheet. He had no idea what I was asking for or decided to play dumb."

"What did you do?"

"He has until Monday," Grace said. "Or he's gone."

"You can't replace everyone at that level."

"A few as object lessons," she replied.

"Is this what you want? To run a company like this?"

Grace shrugged again. "To run any company? No. To control Grauptham House? Yes. We've beaten the Alarians. Charboric is gone, never to return. Gesalex and Visgrath are dead. We've won."

"But?"

"But nothing. We have it all, John," Grace said. She reached over and squeezed his hand. "But if you're asking if my problems are gone, then, no, this doesn't solve that."

"I guess . . ."

"Don't worry about it, John," she said. "I'll be okay."

John nodded and looked away at the dance floor.

"What kind of music is this?" John asked.

"Henry says it's called grunge disco," Grace replied. "Very hip, very cool. In some universes."

John focused on the dancers, realizing that the Henrys and Graces were a single writhing mass. The Johns and Caseys had actually moved off the floor and were coupled together. John smiled at the dynamic, but frowned when he saw two Graces kissing. He turned away quickly, looking at Grace again.

Was she smiling at him?

"Um," John said.

Now he was certain Grace *was* smiling at him.

"I'm gonna go dance," she said. "I won't ask you to join me." She stood and disappeared into the swirl of Henrys and Graces, and John soon lost which of the Graces was her.

At the end of the night, slightly tipsy, he and his Casey were standing on the roof of the building, looking up at the starry sky. The September night was crystal clear. John rubbed Casey's goose-pimpled arms as she shivered in her short-sleeved shirt.

"Want to go back in?" he asked.

"No, I'll be all right." She pressed against him.

The door to the roof swung open and another John and Casey appeared. It was the second time they'd been interrupted by a John and Casey; the first couple had disappeared to the far side of the roof for privacy. This one waved and walked some distance away. If one John thought the roof would be romantic, so would the others. *My romantic overtures are not so unique anymore,* he thought.

"Have you ever partied with yourself so much?" John asked.

"Not that I recall," Casey said with a laugh.

Below was a sudden loud chorus of laughter. John looked down and saw the Henrys and Graces leaving, climbing aboard one of the minibuses.

"I hope one of them is sober enough to drive," John said.

"I don't think the Henrys drank too much."

Two of the Graces were locked in an embrace. A third joined them, and then a Henry too.

"What are . . . ?" John said. "Are they . . . ? What's going on?"

"You're a little oblivious sometimes," Casey said. "They've been doing this group thing for weeks. Maybe from the time Grace Top and Henry Top met Grace Home and Henry Home."

"Group thing?"

"As far as I can tell, the Henrys and Graces are interchangeable in their relationship."

"But—" John's mind churned as he watched the minibus drive away. "But—"

Casey shrugged. "Whatever floats their boat."

"You . . . we . . . won't ever."

"John, it seems we Caseys and Johns are pair-bonding monogamists," she said. "You won't have to sleep with Prime or his Casey."

"Oh, good," he said, though the thought of bedding Casey Prime, his first Casey . . . It aroused him. "I just didn't think that—"

"No, you didn't," Casey said. "I think it's what our Grace needed. And certainly our Henry got through some heavy stuff with the help of the other Graces."

"Yeah, I can see how that would help." The minibus disappeared with a rumble from the parking lot.

The door to the roof opened and two more pairs of John and Casey appeared and found an open spot on the roof to look at the stars.

John fumbled in his pocket for the engagement ring there. He knelt and flipped it open.

"Um, speaking of relationships," he said, "would you do me the honor of marrying me?"

"Of course, John," Casey said with a smile. "Of course." She squeezed him, and they kissed passionately. As he buried his face in her hair he saw five other Johns on their knees in front of their Caseys.

CHAPTER 20

John Prime watched the apartment for six hours. No one entered, no one left, and, when the sun set, no lights came on. It was his second reconnaissance. He'd seen no one enter and exit the apartment the first time either.

An inquiry at the building office indicated that apartment 23B at Odin Village was not available and that his information, sir, must not be correct. Yes, the tenant had been there for years and there was no indication that he would move soon. Perhaps apartment 2C would interest him?

The grass was mowed by the landlords. However, the mailbox was stuffed full. Prime wondered if the postal carrier had just stopped delivering and was holding the mail at the main office.

John Prime exited his car, walked across the dark grass, and let himself into Corrundrum's apartment, empty now since mid-May, four months, almost five. He had tucked Corrundrum's keys into his pocket then, lifted from the dead man's pockets.

Prime had watched the newspapers with interest for weeks, researched the severed foot found in the woods behind an office park in Columbus. But there had been no linkage to Corrundrum, no corpse found. How could it have been? It was in another universe.

The room smelled of dust and closed-in rooms. The air-conditioner was on, and the temperature was a tepid seventy-five. There was the faint smell of spoiled food.

He turned on the light in the living room. Nothing had changed from his visit at the start of the summer. Corrundrum couldn't have changed anything, since he had been with John and Prime from the moment he left the apartment until his death. He apparently had no housekeeper, no pet-sitter, and, hopefully, no pets.

John paged through the magazines on the coffee table. Nothing of interest. The bookshelf's contents were mundane. No advanced physics books. There was a book on Ohio's Serpent Mound, an

Adena Culture snake-shaped mound of earth, and that rang a bell for John Prime, but he couldn't recall from what.

The kitchen area was tidy and devoid of anything of interest. He checked the top of the refrigerator, the cabinets, searching each shelf. He found a pile of bills, but no personal correspondence. He took the electric bill from its envelope. Prime wondered why the power was still on if the bill hadn't been paid in four months. Perhaps Corrundrum had paid ahead.

The bread on the counter was moldy. The smell of spoiled food came from the cabinets and fridge. Prime moved to the bedroom.

The bed was unmade. The nightstand held a clock with tile numbers that flipped over. It was still moving, its motor turning rotors, but the time was wrong, as if it had slowly gone out of sync over the months.

Prime opened the first drawer of the nightstand. A magazine, scissors, paper, and pens. Under the paper was another gun. Apparently he had had at least two. The second drawer was empty.

Prime froze.

The doorbell had chimed.

He turned slowly, and then walked quietly to the doorway of the bedroom. A shadow moved across the front door. The doorbell chimed again. A second later, the person started pounding on the door.

"Corriander! Corriander! You in there?"

Prime couldn't pretend he wasn't. The light was on, and clearly that was something a neighbor had noticed after months of darkness. He shrugged.

"Corriander! It's Jerry from next door."

Prime unbolted the door and pulled it open. A wizened man stood there, over-tan and over-bald.

"Oh, hey," he said. "Thought you were Corriander." The man peered around Prime's head. "He in there?"

"Naw, Kent asked me to check in on his apartment," Prime said. He stressed Corrundrum's false first name, making it seem as if he and Kent Corriander were on a first-name basis.

"Oh, he did? He ain't been around in a while."

"No, Kent is in Europe for a year," Prime said. "On a job."

"Yeah? Europe? Wow."

"Yeah, Kent asked me to check in on things," Prime said.

The man continued to peer around Prime's head, trying to see inside. "I didn't know he had any European, uh, interests."

"I guess Kent forgot to mention them to you," Prime said.

"Yeah, I guess so," the man said. "You an old friend of his?"

Prime decided to push back a bit on the nosey man. "Sure, who are you, old man?"

The man jerked as if slapped. "Oh, me? I'm Jerry Herbert, from twenty-two. I'm the neighbor!"

"You don't say," Prime said. "Anything happen over here in the last few months?"

"No! Nothing's been happening. Nothing happens around here," Herbert said. "Though Miss Clark in fifteen had her laundry stolen from her deck last month." Herbert spat. "Perverts. It was her underthings they took."

"I'll let Kent know about the perverts," Prime said. "And your concern." He reached to shut the door.

"I'm not surprised that Kent went off to Europe," Herbert said. "He seemed always ready to go. Had a ready bag and everything. Like we had in the service back then. Always ready to go at a moment's notice. I remember—"

"Thanks, Mr. Herbert," Prime said. "I'll let Kent know we talked." This time he shut the door completely before Herbert could get another word in.

If a busybody like Herbert didn't suspect a thing, then Prime was safe to assume no one had. He returned to the bedroom, rummaging through the closet. He thought he'd found something when he found a box on the upper shelf of the closet, but it turned out to be only a bundle of old bills and a hundred dollars in cash. The bottom drawer of the dresser yielded another gun and a box of bullets. Prime let them be. He didn't want to be in possession of the gun of a missing person, even though the gun could have been unregistered. No, he was tired of police scrutiny.

The bedroom revealed nothing of Corrundrum's true nature. But there had to be something. Corrundrum would have kept notes, information, details of his life among the natives of universe 7533.

Prime spied an air vent. He found a chair and unscrewed the fasteners of the vent with his pocketknife. Nothing but dust awaited him. The other vents and ducts contained nothing. He tapped all the walls, looking for hollow areas. He lifted all the pictures on the walls. There appeared to be no extra space unaccounted for in the unit. Nothing.

Prime simmered. He couldn't come back. He had one chance at this. After he'd visited the apartment once, he didn't dare be seen there again. Especially with Jerry Herbert's watchful eyes on the neighborhood.

He scanned the apartment again. He didn't want to start tearing open cushions or ripping out walls. He'd prefer his visit remain undetectable. Though Herbert knew he was here.

Herbert . . . What had he said of Corrundrum? Always ready to go. With a ready bag. Where?

Prime looked at the hooks on the wall in the kitchen. House keys were in Prime's pocket, but there was a key ring for a car. Corrundrum had a car. Prime had known that.

Prime exited the front door and stared at the long row of garages. Which was his? Prime turned, saw Herbert looking at him from behind his shades. He motioned at the old man.

A moment later, Herbert appeared on his doorstep.

"Yeah?"

"Kent wanted me to check his car, turn the battery," Prime said. "But he didn't tell me which garage was his."

"Oh, yeah," Mr. Herbert said, nodding, glad to be needed. "Right next to mine. Number forty-five, right there." He pointed at one of the garages.

"Thanks."

A streetlight cast blue light on the lock, but there were only three keys on the ring he'd lifted from Corrundrum. The lock turned with the first key and he pulled up the garage door. Inside was the car Corrundrum had driven when he'd found him in Toledo. Prime unlocked the car door and popped the trunk.

Inside was a duffel bag.

Prime unzipped it, but the contents remained in shadow in the faint light of the streetlamp. It looked like clothes, another gun, money in a wad.

"Is it starting?" Mr. Herbert called from his doorway across the parking lot.

"Uh," Prime said. Shit. He couldn't walk out of the garage with the duffel if he hadn't walked in with it. "Yeah, maybe dead battery."

"It's been four months. He should have asked me to start it."

Prime pulled the duffel from the trunk and threw it into the backseat. The dome light came on weakly. Where was his flashlight? He'd left it in the apartment, damn it.

He pocketed the cash. Tossing the clothing to the floor of the car, he dug into the bag. The gun landed with a thud.

"I got cables," Mr. Herbert yelled. "I can give you a jump."

Prime's hand found a book—a dog-eared notebook.

He pulled it out, opened it, and flipped through the pages. Line after line of symbols and characters that weren't the Latin alphabet. The numbers were, however, Arabic. Sequences of four and five digits. Universe labels?

He tucked the notebook in the small of his back.

There was nothing else in the duffel.

He zipped it up, shut the car door, and reached up to close the garage.

"Yeah, you let a battery sit for that long, you're asking for trouble." Herbert stood right there, his robe flapping over his knobby knees. He had a ring of keys in his hands.

"Uh, yeah."

"Did it turn over?"

"Uh, no."

"Let me get my car and we'll try to jump it," Herbert said. "We'll have to push it out of the garage to get it close enough. Just have the two-meter cables."

"No, I'll just call AS," Prime said.

"AS?"

"Auto Service," Prime said.

"What's that? Like Three As?"

"Yeah, yeah, it's like that," Prime said quickly. Too many subtle differences were there to trip him up. He turned the lock on the door. "I'll have 'em come by in the morning. No need for you to bother, Mr. Herbert."

"No bother, but okay," he said. "Have the professionals come on out, I guess."

"Thanks, bye now."

Prime walked back to Corrundrum's apartment. He didn't want Herbert to see which car was his.

He took one more look around the apartment for any sign of his invasion. There was his flashlight. Some burglar he was. Prime peered out the window. Herbert's door was still open. Prime took the notebook out and opened it to the first page.

The strange characters filled the page. Numbers were at the top of the page. 7533. The universe code. Corrundrum knew where he was. The date was also clear. The first entry of this journal was dated fifteen years earlier. Fifteen years Corrundrum had been trapped here.

Prime suddenly remembered more of Corrundrum's story. He had tried to escape this universe. By traveling to the Serpent Mound. The book on his shelf made sense. He said there was a beacon there, whatever that meant, but there'd been an ambush of some sort. "A band of paths had the beacon area under surveillance," he'd said. Paths?

But what Corrundrum had said that interested him the most was the idea of Prime artifacts. Corrundrum had had a hunch that Prime had a couple in his possession, that the device itself, broken though it was, was one as well. Corrundrum's reaction to seeing the device, his description of the transfer devices he had used and Oscar's and Thomas's reaction. The device was something different, something special. So were the artifacts they'd collected from Billy Walder.

Prime opened the curtain a centimeter and checked for Herbert one more time. The man's apartment door was shut. Prime turned off all the lights in Corrundrum's apartment then locked the door behind him. He saw no one as he sauntered across the parking lot.

He wasn't sure what he had in the notebook, but he had something. There was treasure—of all sorts—in the multiverse and now he had a clue of where to look.

CHAPTER 21

John stood on the campus of the University of Toledo in Universe 7539, recognizing a place he had never visited and faces that did not know him. 7539 had no John Rayburn or Casey Nicholson. Nor was there a Grace or Henry. But there was a woman here, at least one, and a little girl, who weren't born here. The question at hand was, how would he find them?

"What do you remember now?" Casey asked. "Does being here help the memories?"

They stood on the footpath near the river. This is where he had transferred them. The woman had been shot by food looters, and the girl had broken her leg when she'd fallen down the slope to the frozen river. All for two cans of noodle soup.

"I think it was here," he said. "I'm just not sure."

He shut his eyes. He'd transferred the mother and daughter from 7538 to get here, huddled in the snow with the two. From winter to fall. From death to happy-go-lucky campus. Covered in blood, he'd asked someone to call the police, but the person had pointed him toward the emergency box.

He opened his eyes. There was the box. He'd called, waited for the ambulance, then run off to the field house to shower and rinse the blood from his clothes.

So he'd been about ten meters to the east of where Casey and he now stood. He walked toward the spot, weaving through the throng of students.

"Here," he said to Casey. "We were right here."

Casey looked down as if there would be a clue after two years. "Here?"

"Yeah." He'd left Kylie and her mother there. Kylie! That was the little girl's name. He couldn't recall the last name, however. Smith? No, not that common. "I remember the little girl's name."

"That's good. Do we search the papers with that? You know the date, right?"

"The date was October twenty-ninth," John said. Five days after Prime had tricked him out of his life.

"That should narrow it down," Casey said. "If we know the name and the date, we can find more. There had to have been stories written."

"Yeah, there had to have been," John agreed. A wounded body, a child with a broken leg. On an otherwise bucolic college campus. Yeah, there had to be news stories written.

"Come on," Casey said, grabbing John's arm. The journalism college had a building on the main quad. It published the University of Toledo newspaper—*The Dagger*. The main room had three microfiche readers and an archive of past issues.

"It's called *The Knife* in this universe," Casey said. "Huh."

Casey sat down at one of the readers, while John thumbed through the cabinet of fiche. He found the year and then the day when he had passed through this universe two years prior. He hadn't been here long. Just long enough to call the police and wash his clothes out.

The fiche was heavy in his fingers and felt as if it might rip. The top story was on the student council race.

"Nothing," he said.

"Should we try the next day?" Casey asked.

"Oh, right," John said with a laugh. "What was I thinking?"

He pulled the fiche for the next publication date, two days later.

"Here it is," he said. The top story was about the shooting and attack on campus. It *had* been a shooting on campus, just not this exact one. John scanned the article, with Casey over his shoulder.

"Her name is Melissa Saraft," Casey said.

"Yeah, Saraft, that's the name. Melissa and Kylie Saraft." John wrote the name down so he wouldn't forget it.

"They're looking for an unidentified witness who was seen fleeing the incident," Casey said.

"That would be me," John said. "They didn't find me."

"Let's assume after two years they've given up the search."

"Taken to General Methodist," Casey said.

The next edition of the paper was the Monday following. John had already reached 7650 by then and was staying with the Rayburns, working as a farmhand. There was no new information in the follow-up story, nor the scathing editorials on campus safety.

"Nothing," John said. "I doubt *The University of Toledo Knife* is the place to look for more information."

Casey looked at the student sitting behind the desk in the reference room. "Maybe he knows what happened to the woman and her daughter."

"He looks like a freshman," John said.

"Let's ask anyway."

Casey walked over to the desk and asked the student, "Do you remember that shooting from two years ago? The one where the woman was shot and the little girl had a broken leg?"

The student rubbed his chin. "In October, wasn't it?"

"Yes, that's right."

"I remember the story," he said. "She was shot, but it wasn't a serious wound. But there was something else." He tapped his chin. "I'm trying to remember. Hmmm. Ah, yes. She had psychological conditions. No family, no support system. There was a follow-up story, by Joe Cursky at *The Barker*, but that's all I can remember."

"Thanks," Casey said. They left and sat on the steps overlooking the quad.

"It freaks me out when I see someone I know and they have no inkling who I am," Casey said, as they watched the college students lounge or walk on the grass of the quad. Casey pointed. "She was in my dorm freshman year. He's in my psychology class. Tried to ask me out."

"You'd think he would remember that," John said.

"You'd think."

"Psychological conditions," John said. "What do you think that means?"

"If you were shot and ripped from your universe, you might have some problems too."

"Thanks for that."

"Oh, hush. You had to do it. For her sake."

"I know," John said. "What now?"

"I think we need to talk to Joe Cursky. And we should check the white pages at the main library while we're here," Casey said.

"Right."

The university library only had white pages for Lucas County, and there was no Saraft listed at all. But there was a number for Joseph Cursky and one for the news office at *The Toledo Barker* newspaper.

From the pay phone at the student union they called the news office. It was only a little after noon on a weekday.

"Barker News, how may I redirect your call?" a voice said.

"Joe Cursky, please," John said.

"Mr. Cursky is on assignment. Would you like to leave a message?"

"No, thanks."

"Do you think he's at home?" Casey asked.

"What does 'on assignment' mean?" John asked. He dialed the number they had for Cursky.

"Yeah?"

"Joe Cursky?"

"Yeah, who's this?"

"Joe Cursky the reporter for *The Barker*?"

"Yeah, who the hell is this?"

"I'm looking for Melissa Saraft."

"Who the hell is that?"

"She was shot on the University of Toledo campus two years ago. Her little girl broke her leg," John said.

There was a pause. "Yeah, she had some problems. I remember. Thought she was abducted by aliens or from some other universe. Something crazy."

"Do you know where she is?"

"How the hell would I know?"

"Anything would help us."

Cursky sighed. "Yeah, right. Who are you?"

"We're friends of hers, we've been trying to reach her."

"She didn't have any friends. She didn't have any family. Total blank slate. Figured she was on the run from the mob or something. Made her crazy. I remember now. She made up a weird story about nuclear war. She was in a hospital for a while. I talked to her a couple times."

"Any idea where she is now?"

"So you can take her back to whatever she ran away from? No way, bud."

"I helped her get away the first time," John said.

"You did? Then what's the real story?"

"I can't say," John said.

"Then neither can I."

Cursky hung up the phone.

They tried the main Toledo library, but the white pages included only major Ohio cities. There was no Melissa Saraft in Columbus, Cincinnati, or Cleveland.

"Maybe this is hopeless," John said.

"Don't say that. We've only just started to look," Casey said.

"Ah, well. I've screwed up royally this time."

"Because you saved her life? Because you did everything you could?" Casey said. "Stop kicking yourself because you did the right thing. I've never known someone to linger and mope on the past so much. You should be worried about what you can do, not what you can't change."

"Thanks for the pep talk," John said. "But I can't think of another thing that we can do. No one is going to tell us where she is."

"We could call the local hospitals. We could search for her records in the psychiatric facilities."

"If Joe Cursky didn't tell us anything, no medical facility will."

"Maybe we ask the police," Casey said. "Just tell them we're looking for an old friend."

John nodded. "We can try that."

They left the library and found a serviced apartment complex not far from downtown. They booked a room for a month and from there Casey called the precinct nearest the University of Toledo, fabricating a story of an old friend searching for Melissa.

"I guess that's the best we can do for now," John said.

"For now. You can check in for messages as needed."

They left the hotel, drove down to Findlay, returning their rental car. Then they rode their bicycles to the quarry site and transferred back to the Home Office.

. . .

John entered the fenced-off area of EmVis with mixed feelings. It was Pinball Wizards's property now. But it was the same secret complex where Grace and Henry had been held captive. The place where Grace had been tortured. The place where Grace had killed Visgrath.

The guard plaza was empty and the gate was open, but a team of workers were pulling up the tire deflation devices. This is where their Jeep had shuddered to a halt, where they had made their last stand before transferring to 7651.

"Does anyone know where Grace Shisler is?" John asked the workers.

"Yeah, she's in the far building over there." The worker pointed to the building where Grace and Henry had been kept in cells.

John walked through the parking lot. He pushed through the doors. The bullet holes were gone. The double doors opened onto the lab/torture chamber where they had found Grace. It was empty.

"Grace," he called.

He hoped she would not be lingering here. Perhaps he should suggest that the building be razed to the ground. Or sold.

"Grace!"

"In here!"

Down a hallway, John found a series of doors, all of them with dark rooms behind, until the last. Inside Grace stood over a transfer device.

"Look what I found," she said.

John glanced at the device, and then looked closer at Grace. "You shouldn't be here alone," he said.

"Because of all the bad memories that might jump out and yell, 'Boo!'?" Grace said. "I'm a big girl. I'm sure I'm not the only person in the world to be tortured by an evil warlord from another dimension."

"Grace, don't push me off with sarcasm," John said.

"Or what? You'll get all tough with me?" she said. "Slap me around and show me some tough love."

"Grace."

She reached up and wrapped an arm around his neck. "Or maybe you can take me to some distant universe, some place with dinosaurs, and nurse my soul back to health."

"Grace!" He lifted her arm off his shoulder.

"You're welcome any time at the Grace and Henry commune, by the way."

"You know Casey and I are engaged."

"She's welcome too."

"You think you're smart, don't you, Grace, changing the subject like that? You think you can deflect my attention by invoking some farmboy prudery you think I have? Won't work."

"Meh, I have many defense mechanisms," she said. She nodded at the transfer gate. "Does it work?"

"Let me look," John said. He let himself be distracted by the device. It was so crude compared to what they were building now. A diagram and pictures of his original device lay on a table nearby.

Already the team had come up with enough design simplifications and advances to make this model seem an antique. Perhaps the most bizarre change was a self-destruct mechanism attached to each transfer gate. "In case someone tries to steal it," Henry had explained.

He followed the circuitry. It was close, but he noticed several subtle problems, capacitors backward, circuit boards only partially soldered in place.

"Nope, no way," John said. "And this building is actually a little below the natural grade. They could have ended up stuck under ground if they used it here."

"Fitting," Grace said. "So there was no way any of them got out of 7650 to warn Charboric after we moved it from the barn."

"No."

"So," Grace said. "Where'd they go? Which universe?"

"Why do you need to know?"

"Curiosity."

"Grace, we don't need to know where they went."

"Yes, we do. There's a lot of universes out there, and we don't want to be running into the Alarians again."

John tried to see some deviousness in Grace's request. He'd

heard the bile in her voice when she spoke of the Alarians. But what she said was true; they didn't need to go running into them again somewhere in the multiverse.

"We need to know," she said again.

"I'm not disagreeing with you," John replied.

"We need to make sure we never find them again!"

"I know."

"I'm not going to march on them with an army of Graces!"

"Of course not."

"Stop agreeing with me!"

"Okay."

Grace laughed, and John joined her. This time he reached around her neck and pulled her close. She didn't shy away as she once would have. She pressed in close to him.

"I'm a nut, aren't I?"

"Since I first met you in freshman physics lab."

She laughed again. "Yeah. True."

She squeezed him for a moment, and then pushed him away.

"It was Universe 2219," John said.

"That seems far away," Grace said. "2219. Good."

John nodded at the gate. "We should dismantle it."

"I'll have Henry come down and take it apart," Grace said. "We can probably use the parts." She laughed. "I still think we're a little podunk company. We have millions of dollars at our disposal. Did you know that?"

"Yeah, I realized as I walked in that we own all of this building," John said. "Or rather, you do."

"Yeah, me. I hadn't told my parents, but they saw it on the news. They think there's another Grace Shisler out there."

"Do we know how much money we have? The accountants are done with the audit?"

"Not quite yet. But the coffers are anything but empty," Grace said. "Even though the company was riddled with misogynist ass-holes, Gesalex couldn't fail to make money."

"They were running out of ideas," John said, remembering how Charboric had tried to coerce new ideas from him when the Alarians realized he was a universe traveler. It wasn't until later that they found out he was from a universe as backward as the one he'd ended up in.

"Yeah, but the patents for a dozen things are still in play," Grace said. "They just divvied the ideas out in increments for years. And their diversifications would have kept them fat and happy for decades, if not forever."

"It's a wonder they wanted to leave," John said.

Grace nodded. "Makes you wonder what's in Universe 2219."

"No, not too much," John replied.

"Yeah, not too much."

CHAPTER 22

Prime turned on the four cameras, one at a time. They were digital video cameras that one of the Henrys had found in a universe around 6000, able to record hours of digital footage on small cartridge tapes. The film camera he remembered from his family holidays was nothing like these beauties. His dad had a clunky reeled monstrosity that created scratchy, off-color home films. These were pristine and better than the television in this universe. Of course there was nowhere to play the tapes in this universe except in the same camera that recorded them.

The gate was powered up and the cameras—lashed together to a wooden frame to keep them pointed in the four cardinal directions—sat on a platform. He checked his universe destination—1214—and powered the machine. The platform disappeared.

He started his stopwatch.

After sixty seconds, he reactivated the gate.

The platform reappeared. He reached to grab it and accidently tipped it. Prime lunged at it before the cameras smashed into the concrete floor. He didn't want to ask for new ones. One of the Graces might notice and wonder why. It wasn't his job to experiment with gate technology. He was the manager of this universe, not assigned to lab duty. No, it was better that no one else knew of his experiments.

Or the fact that this was an unauthorized gate.

He placed the camera structure on the nearby lab table and turned each one off.

"Damn!"

He'd forgotten which one was facing north. Some scientist he was. He tried to remember which way it was pointed when it toppled and which way he placed it on the table. But he didn't know.

He'd mark the directions next time.

"Let's see what 1214 has to offer," Prime said.

He picked one of the four video cameras at random and rewound the tape. He hit play and watched as the camera jiggled. He caught sight of himself turning toward the control switch. Then concrete walls were replaced with blue skies.

He'd had his sanctuary built on a parcel of land outside of Findlay, away from the quarry, away from any land he knew that Pinball Wizards owned. It was in the middle of farmland that he had bought at a cheap price. He'd had contractors build the Quonset hut on a flat bit of land, exactingly defining how the building would be built. No grading, concrete floor, industrial power. He was sure the builders had been perplexed. But he didn't care. Prime had enough cash to pay for it to be built exactly as he wanted it.

Brown grass and blue skies, exactly the view to his west from this building. A cloud slowly wafted closer. Otherwise, the scene in the video was motionless, a picture. Prime paused the camera and carried it outside. He walked around the building until his view of the west horizon was identical. There was a difference. A big difference. The huge power transmission tower wasn't there in the video. The horizon in the video was clear. He walked back into his lab, closing the door against the cold.

It had been simple to build his own gate. He had millions of dollars in cash now. And as much petty cash as he needed from the coffers of Pinball Wizards, Transdimensional. He just had to ask and Grace would send him gold. In Universe 7651, he'd watched closely as John and Henry had gathered the materials and built their new gate. Sure, he didn't have the college classes they did, but he was as smart as John was—exactly as smart and the plans weren't a secret. He'd made a copy of the originals in 7651 in the middle of the night when the other three had been asleep. And he'd looked at the plans for the new designs that John and Henry were coming up with: the larger effective sphere, the cleaner controls for the field radius, the remote circuitry, allowing better timing on start and stop. He hadn't bothered with a self-destruct device, something that John was insisting on now. Farmboy wanted to keep the technology out of the hands of anyone who might be snooping on them.

Corrundrum's journal was his most-prized extra-dimensional artifact, though he had the things that Billy Walder had given them, the things he and Superprime had found on the mummified corpse: a ring, a wristwatch, and an Ouroboros pendant. He and Farmboy had examined the three items, but had deemed them useless. The wristwatch was dead, the pendant just a simple chain and figure. The ring—when Prime had put it on—had pricked him with a bit of rough metal, though when he'd gone to file it down, he'd been unable to find the burr. Still it tickled him to wear the ring; it fit his right ring finger cleanly, and he wore it all the time.

Prime focused on the natural landscape shown on the video. Was Universe 1214 a Pleistocene one? Empty of human inhabitation? If so, why had Corrundrum marked it down? A world without humans was hard to exploit. But he found he didn't care so much about exploiting universes for money.

That was the funny thing. Now that he had all the cash he needed, he didn't care for it. Now that he could market any idea from any other universe here, he didn't really care to. Corrundrum's notebook perplexed him, mesmerized him. 1214 was one of the numbers he had seen over and over in the book.

He played the second camera, the one that had to have been pointed north. Most of the frame was stuck on a hill, the same hill behind his Quonset. Nothing moved, except the brown leaves on the ash trees.

The camera to the east showed the decline to the road in his universe, only there was no road in 1214. It was just more grassland.

He expected nothing else from the southern exposure. He

sighed. The problem with the transfer gate was that it didn't allow transfer to some other location in the remote universe it opened to. He was stuck sending objects between the corresponding spots in both universes. If he wanted to explore some other location with his apparatus, he'd have to build the transfer gate somewhere else.

Or he'd have to build some sort of roving camera that traveled about and came back after a certain time.

Or he'd need an accomplice. A dangerous situation, if ever there was one.

The last video was just about over, and he had given in to the fact that he'd have to try something else to explore 1214 or give up, when he caught sight of something in the sky.

It caught the sun as it banked. But had only short stubby wings. And it moved very slowly.

An aircraft of some sort, coming toward the camera?

The aircraft grew closer for a moment. It was just a kilometer away and seemed to be coming in for a landing.

Then the tape ended abruptly.

"What the hell was that?" he said aloud.

John Prime ran the video back and forth repeatedly, trying to determine the size, distance, and speed of the aircraft. Was it actually coming toward the camera? Had it seen the camera? Or was it just out flying on a beautiful day?

It was clearly not flying by aerodynamic lift. It was too big and too slow and the wings too stubby to fly like an airplane. Ultimately the length of time the craft was on the video—less than five seconds—made it impossible to know for certain.

He debated for a long time about sending the device back and taking another set of videos. But by the time he decided that he would, it was too dark. And the cameras wouldn't film well at night.

But was it coming toward the camera? He had to know if the thing had somehow spotted his camera device. He was struck with the thought that Universe 1214 was listed in Corrundrum's notebook as a universe to avoid.

He'd try again in the morning.

He locked up the lab and drove the fifteen kilometers to the quarry site. He owned the entire area now. Or rather Pinball Wizards, Transdimensional, did. But in this world that was him. There was no Grace or Henry to meddle with his work.

He waved to the security guard as he passed through the gate. No more kids would be swimming in his quarries. Prime wondered what Gabe, Dave, and Trudy thought of guarding an abandoned quarry and its one new building twenty-four hours a day. Probably nothing as long as the paychecks came every two weeks and they could read their paperbacks in the guard shack. The perfect job.

Prime saw the satchel on the transfer zone from 7650 as he unlocked the door. Probably more corporate notes and votes for him to sign and return. Awesome.

Checking the time, he pulled the satchel off the transfer zone. As expected, a dozen requests for information, thirty requests for synchronization, two votes, and a note from Grace Home on the current state of the Grauptham House takeover.

The information requests were for new data from his universe: prices, dates, people, places. The sync requests were things that the Henrys tracked in their computer looking for arbitrage possibilities. He had brought the sources he used most commonly to answer both of those: the Almanac, the Findlay newspaper, the Toledo newspaper, *The Wall Street Journal*, and the Montgomery Wards catalog.

Some he couldn't do right there, such as the court records from Columbus on one Simon Otralsky, serial killer and rapist. Grace Home was after another murderer. She'd done it a dozen times already, finding uncaught felons in one universe using information from another. If Otralsky had been caught and imprisoned in 7533, then Grace could use his court case to find corroborating evidence in any other universe. Grace Shisler, pan-universal detective.

He finished what he could with the information on hand, then waited for his scheduled time and transferred the satchel to 7650. There Henry would collate all the other data he received from the settled universes for whatever devious plan he had in mind.

It was nearly six when he arrived home. Casey had prepared

lasagna, which he dove into, though with not quite as much abandon as baby Abby did.

"Daddy? Noodles!" she said.

"Yes, noodles!"

"Anything in the packet?" Casey asked.

"About a hundred requests and two votes," Prime said. "Your ballots are in the briefcase." She unsnapped the briefcase and grabbed her ballots. Absently eating her meal, she read the packets.

"Oh, John wants to settle 7535 with people from 7538," she said.

"Who from where?" Prime said. He hadn't even read the ballot before marking it "Yes."

"He wants to move people from the nuclear winter universe, 7538, to the Pleistocene universe, 7535."

"There's no money in that," Prime said quickly, angry that he'd voted yes without actually reading the measure. "Sounds expensive."

"He's trying to do something good."

"How can he move billions of people from one universe to another?"

"Not all of them, honey," Casey said. "Just the ones that are desperate."

"They are all desperate in that universe," Prime said. He banged the table and Abby looked up at him from her lasagna with big eyes. "Why does he have to fix everything?"

"John? Because he does."

"What will helping those few people do in the long run?" Prime said. "What will finding one more murderer in an infinite list of murderers do? There will always be suffering. There will always be another killer to slice another throat."

"What can one person do?" Casey said. "Is that what you're asking? Well, we're all not just one person, are we? You're a John, one of a million. I'm a Casey, one of a million. If you and I help just one person, we've helped two million people. That's a lotta suffering we've eradicated."

"It's all about the karma, is it?" Prime said.

"Yes, it is."

"I'd prefer to worry just about our own," Prime said. "You, me, and Abby."

"We're all fine, aren't we?" Casey argued back. "We have everything we need. It's time to worry about others."

Prime shook his head, but he said, "Yeah, I guess you're right." To himself he added, *But I'll still worry about my family and myself first.*

John Prime went to his secret lab—he laughed as he named his destination—early the next morning, eager to try again with a reconnaissance of Universe 1214.

He found himself sweating as he powered up the transfer gate again. His hands were weak as he turned each camera on. They were marked this time—N, S, E, and W.

Stepping back, well away from the effective sphere of the gate, he checked the transfer coordinates and turned the gate on. This time, he'd decided, he'd let it go for two minutes, instead of one. The camera mechanism disappeared. He caught a whiff of something metallic. He wondered for a second if he had burnt out a circuit. The seconds ticked away on the stopwatch. At sixty seconds he found himself wanting to transfer it back early.

The next minute ticked as slowly as a week.

At two minutes he triggered the gate again, and the mechanism reappeared. That same smell hit him, stronger now, something burnt, something metallic.

His hand stung. The cameras were freezing cold. Prime dropped the camera unit on the lab bench quickly, where it clattered. A sheen of frost was on the exposed metal.

"What the hell?"

The temperature was a cool fall day, but there had been no chance of frost this morning. Not in his universe.

He took the northern camera and pressed play, tapping the keys quickly with his fingers to avoid the cold.

The camera flickered, and then the image firmed up. The hill was there, but the frame was empty. No snow on the ground. Where had the cold come from?

He turned on the camera pointed east. Grassland, off-color due to the shine of the sun into the lens. Near the end, he thought he saw some shadow cross the frame, but it was impossible to tell with the sunlight bleaching out the image.

Prime played the camera facing east. It showed nothing but the same brown grass and blue skies. No flying machine. He'd been foolish to think he'd see it again.

He played the last camera, the one pointed south.

"What the—!"

The silver airship was right there, ten meters away, and next to it stood a silver humanoid shape. It was too small to be an actual human in a suit, at least by comparing the thing to the same tree in his universe. Unless it was a midget in a suit.

As he watched, the head slowly rotated, and long, oval eyes stared toward him.

Not him, he thought. The camera.

It took a step toward him, lifting its arm. Something flashed, and then it took two more steps.

John Prime found himself wishing the scene would change, the film would end, that the two minutes would end suddenly. Even though he had the cameras in his hand right now. Even though everything he saw was in the past.

The robot—it had to be some mechanical device—stopped just a meter or two from the camera. Right at the edge of the transfer zone. It raised its hand, as if to speak, as if to communicate, and then it disappeared. The image was replaced by the south wall of his Quonset, his own face rushing forward to grab the device.

"What in the world was that?"

Prime rewound the video and cranked the volume.

The sound of wind on the microphone. The light tap of metal on dirt as the robot walked forward. No sound as its arm rose. Then something, some word that he couldn't recognize because it cut out too quickly.

It was trying to communicate.

Prime's mind marveled at the technology. To have that, to control that sort of technology! Maybe he could trade with the robot. Or control the robot. Or get ahold of the flying machine.

His own universes, the ones that Pinball Wizards played in,

seemed so mundane. Of course there were universes with more advanced technologies—mainline universes, is what Corrundrum called them. He'd called these United States of America universes— Yankee Doodle universes—backwaters. Other universes clearly had better technology. And that was how he'd gain an edge. Not Pinball Wizards, him, John Prime.

He moved the cameras around. He aligned one of them to point to the south, while the second would point its screen in the same direction. One would record, the second would play his message. He removed the other two cameras.

He started recording, waited twenty seconds, then said, "Hello, I am John Rayburn. I'm interested in a trade of technology. How can we communicate?" He repeated it once. The second recorder would record as before.

He set the recorders on top of it, and sent it through quickly. He didn't want the robot to leave!

Thirty seconds, forty-five seconds, sixty seconds. That was enough!

He powered the system back up, jumped forward to grab the cameras, and jumped back just as quickly. A black box, a half meter on each side, stood next to his video cameras.

"Was it that easy?" he said. "A trade for nothing? Just giving me stuff?"

Then he saw the red ticking symbols.

"Oh shit!"

He turned and ran, diving out the door of the Quonset. He ran for his life, dodging behind his car, where he knelt, one arm covering his head.

Sitting there, cowering behind his car, he felt like a fool.

It wasn't a bomb. The robot was probably just reconnoitering him as he was reconnoitering it.

"Damn," John Prime said.

He stood and started for the Quonset, just as it exploded into a fireball that bounced him down the gravel drive and into the soggy, wet ditch.

CHAPTER 23

John checked for messages at the hotel in Universe 7539—Melissa Saraft's universe—every couple days. There was no word from the police. Searching the phone books for all the major municipalities in Ohio, Michigan, and Indiana turned up nothing. A second call to the local precinct was met with a curt, "We looked, but there's no file. Sorry."

Finally John called Joe Cursky again.

"Yeah?"

"I really do need your help finding Melissa Saraft," John said.

"Who?"

"Melissa Saraft, shot on the University of Toledo campus two years ago."

"You again? I don't have time to help you find her so you can bug her."

"It's important!"

"So is my cold beer."

"Listen," John said, searching for some way to get his attention. "Her story was true."

"What story? Nuclear winter? I think I'd notice that."

"No, she's from another universe. I brought her here to save her life and now I need to find her."

The phone clicked dead.

They tried other precincts and police headquarters. No one seemed to have a record of the event or the case.

"This is useless," John said.

"She can't have just disappeared," Casey said.

John smiled at the joke. They stood in the sitting room of their suite of rooms, reading the latest letter from the police. No record of the case, try the Hill Bottom precinct. Only they already had.

"I can't think of what else to do," John said.

"Hire a private detective," Casey said. "It's the only thing we haven't done."

"We haven't searched 7538."

"Too dangerous," Casey said. "You know it is. And what chance have we to find a woman who disappeared two years ago in a world where the army stands by while people kill each other. At least life is valued here."

"You're right," John said. "I wanted her to be the first. To have the chance to go back or be a part of New Toledo. But I guess we go forward without her."

"How many of the Alarian women are going to do it?" Casey asked.

"Nearly half of them," John said. John had made the offer in person, traveling to the camp in 7601. He'd told them his plan to populate 7535—the Pleistocene universe—with refugees from 7538—the nuclear winter universe.

"But you all are refugees too," he'd said. "The offer is open to you all. You can go wherever you want to go. Any universe you want. Here or 7650 or anywhere. But if you want to start the colony in 7535—New Toledo—then that is open to you too. All of you."

"There's no one there?" Clotilde asked. "No humans at all?"

"I don't know for certain, but there are no Amerinds or other inhabitants in North America," John said. "I don't know if there is anyone in Europe or not, but the fact that there is so much megafauna makes me believe the world is unpopulated with humans."

"So no men either," Englavira said.

"Well, not yet."

"Hmmm."

"I have a job here," one of them said—Liuvia. "I like it here."

"You don't all have to go!" John said.

"Well . . ." Clotilde said. "We're used to each other."

"We'll talk about it," Englavira said.

In the end, the group had split in half, with half choosing to stay in 7601 and the other half choosing to emigrate.

"They're taking classes," John said to Casey. "Camping, hunting, woodcraft, frontier skills."

Casey laughed. "Really?"

"Yeah, we think we can start before winter," John said.

"Won't it be dangerous to start a colony in the middle of winter?"

"Henry is tracking the temperature," John said. "We think the temperatures are milder than in the other universes we've seen. It may not even snow."

"Maybe I'll emigrate too," she said.

"Sure! I'll come with you," John said. He cast one more look around the suite. "Let's go. We tried."

Though John should have been hip-deep in Henry's plan to bootstrap the entire computer industry in 7650, he found his mind wandering back to Melissa Saraft and her daughter.

"Silicon monocrystals, John! Did you hear me?"

"Apparently not," John said. They stood over an open computer from 6013. They were in the old Pinball Wizards factory, empty now of all pinball-making facilities. Grace had transferred that to a new facility in Cleveland where an assembly line built ten machines an hour. They had had access to a huge lab, with any electronics or gadgets they wanted from any universe they'd explored, but in the end they'd returned to the pinball factory to work and tinker.

"Logistics are putting a crimp in our profit," Henry said. "We need to figure this out."

For a month, they'd been reselling computers from Universe 6013 in Home Office. Unfortunately, one universe could hardly supply the necessary volume to feed the demand in two universes. Nor was transporting thousands of boxes a day particularly feasible for the workers of Pinball Wizards, Transdimensional. There were only a couple dozen Wizards, and they couldn't just hire stevedores in 6013 and 7650 to load boxes out of the transfer gates. Someone would notice.

"There's millions of circuits on this board," Henry said. "We need to be able to manufacture semiconductors. We need to develop photolithography here."

John listened as Henry made lists, but his mind was elsewhere.

Would a private investigator be able to find things they couldn't? he wondered. And going back to 7538, maybe there were clues. Maybe Melissa went back to her hometown in 7539, or maybe they could find who her relatives were in 7538 and track them in 7539. But Casey was right. Traveling to 7538 was dangerous. Too dangerous. Not without safeguards.

"You're still not listening."

"Sorry, Henry. My mind is wandering."

"Sure. I get it. Wanna pick up again tomorrow?"

"Yeah, sure."

They locked up the pinball factory and parted ways. John stopped at his and Casey's apartment. She was out, a note saying she was working on their business plan for marketing PCs to the automotive industry. John left his own note, then drove to the quarry and transferred to 7539. It was just after five in the afternoon.

Taking the car they'd left at the quarry, he drove up to Toledo and reached his destination just after six. The bar was just around the corner from the *Toledo Barker* offices. He was certain he'd find Joe Cursky there.

He was easy enough to spot. He looked just like his smiling byline photo, only he wasn't smiling. He was grimacing as he walked into The Loose Mongoose where John had sat and waited for fifteen minutes, drinking three Zingos, avoiding the bartender having to card him. He had no valid driver's license after all, not in this universe. But the bartender didn't seem to care if he sat there and drank sodas.

Joe Cursky was alone, but nodded greetings around the bar as he worked his way to the counter. The bartender placed a shot glass in front of him without his having to order. Apparently he was a regular.

John, on the far side of the bar, let him take a sip from his drink. Then he walked over and took the stool next to him. The bartender gave him a stern look, as if everyone knew that Cursky got his first drink alone and undisturbed.

"Mr. Cursky," John said, "I need your help."

Cursky looked at him for a long moment. "Jesus, not you again.

Shandy, Shaft, Saraft. That's it. Melissa Saraft," Cursky said. "I recognize your voice."

"I thought if you saw me, you'd know I was sincere," John said.

"Shit, what do you think I am, a bullshit detector?"

"I need to find her."

"Forget it."

"Her story wasn't made up," John said. "It's all true."

"Right, parallel universes," Cursky said. "So much shit. Get lost, kid."

The bartender leaned over the counter. "Time for you to leave, buddy."

John nodded. "Fine. But read these." He tossed three newspapers on the counter and left.

John was a block down Huron Street when he heard Cursky behind him.

"What the hell is this?"

John slowed but didn't turn. Cursky grabbed him by the shoulder. He spun John around and shoved the three newspapers into his face.

"What is this?"

"Newspapers."

"*The Toledo Dispatch? The Toledo Telegram? The Toledo Scabard?* That's all bullshit."

"Not in another universe."

"And Irv Trilpio is dead! Do you hear me? Irv is dead." Cursky ripped open one of the newspapers to the opinion page. A picture of an older reporter stared at him.

"I'm sorry, Mr. Cursky," John said. "He's not dead in every universe."

Cursky looked shaken. "He shot himself. After the Palmer Helmon trial, when that bastard went free. Said he was soul weary, tired of life."

"I'm sorry, I didn't know."

Joe looked at the editorial, began reading. "Jesus. This is him. This is exactly what he'd write. How'd you do it, kid? How'd you make this? What's your goddamn angle?"

"I stopped in some neighboring universes, Mr. Cursky, on the way here."

"Bullshit! He's dead! I . . . I spoke at his funeral!"

"Not in every universe," John said. "Listen, I'm sorry I brought it up. I'm sorry I disturbed you. Just forget it. I didn't know he was dead here and that he was your friend."

"No," Cursky said. "Show me."

John waited outside the small bungalow while Cursky went inside. He didn't want to see the emotions that played through Cursky's body when he saw his old friend. He shouldn't have brought Cursky to 7574. He shouldn't have opened so much emotion.

In 7574, Cursky existed and Irv Trilpio was still alive. Maybe no Palmer Helmon lived here, and so there was no way that Trilpio could lose faith and end his own life. Maybe . . . It could have been any combination of events that saved Irving Trilpio's life here.

The door opened and Cursky walked out. His face was puffy from where he'd been crying. Trilpio appeared at the door.

"You sure you're all right, Joe?" he asked.

"Yeah, sure, Irv. Just a little emotional right now."

"Sure, I understand."

"Do me a favor and don't mention this to . . . me, anyone tomorrow, okay?"

"Yeah, sure."

Cursky glared at John as he approached, as if it was his fault Trilpio had died in his own universe.

"Get in the car," Cursky said. They got into the car they'd rented in 7574 for a huge sum so there'd be no need for a credit-card hold. "Drive."

John headed the car back toward the car lot.

"Tell me again from start to finish."

John stood outside the diner in Sebewa, Michigan, peering into the window, wondering if it was her. Then he saw Kylie, two years older, sitting at the counter and drawing, while her mother worked. It was Melissa Saraft; he'd found her. He watched as she sat another

milk in front of her daughter and then took the order of a customer.

John entered the diner and helped himself to a counter seat.

"Let me know when you're ready," she said, handing him a menu
and hurrying off.

Cursky had known right away. "She went up to Michigan, said
she was from some little town near Lansing. I have it in my notes.
Said she was from there," he said.

"She was all right?"

"No! She was screwed in the head!" Cursky said. "She had been
institutionalized because of you. She thought she was from another universe, so she got put in the mental ward. Don't think you
aren't liable for that crap sack of luck."

"I know. That's why I'm here."

A crowd of breakfast customers came in, greeting Melissa as
they sat, and John found he couldn't say what he had been planning
to say, so he ordered instead, a breakfast of eggs, bacon, and corned
beef hash.

He ate it slowly, watching Kylie doodle at the end of the counter.
After three cups of coffee, the crowd left, off to work, and it was
just John in the diner. Melissa didn't dawdle over him even then,
keeping his coffee filled, but not engaging in any conversation.

Finally, he raised his hand for the check, and when she came
over, he said, "I know you."

Her smile was guarded. "Yeah? How's that? You're not local."

"From Toledo," John said.

Now her expression turned darker.

"You with the newspaper? Huh?"

"No, I brought you to Toledo," John said.

She responded faster than he expected.

"Get the hell out! Maurice! We got an asshole out front!"

She grabbed Kylie, who looked at him with big doe eyes.

Maurice, the cook, came out carrying a butcher's knife.

"Him?" he cried.

"Stop!" John cried. "Let me explain, Melissa!"

Maurice started coming toward him.

"I remember him," Kylie said.

"What?"

Maurice seemed hell-bent on hacking John to pieces and would have too if the counter wasn't between them. Maurice made for the opening, and John skirted the other way.

"Mommy, I remember him. He helped us."

"Wait. What did you say, Kylie?"

"When you were hurt and my leg was broken," she explained, "he helped us."

Melissa looked at John hard.

"Stop, Maurice," she said. Maurice didn't look like he wanted to, but he lowered the butcher's knife.

"You sure?"

"No, but maybe Kylie remembers," she said. "I need ten minutes, okay?"

"Sure, sure, Melissa. Whatever you want." Maurice stared at John for a long moment, and then said, "Be careful."

CHAPTER 24

John Prime built his second secret gate in a weekend. He'd expected a visit from the police, from the fire department, someone. But apparently demolition of tree stumps was a common enough occurrence that none of his neighbors—kilometers away to be sure—cared. After a couple days, he'd hired a crew to rebuild the destroyed Quonset.

Prime crossed 1214 off his list of universes to explore.

For whatever reason, it was patrolled and defended by robots.

Robots!

Perhaps he'd have to stay away from every universe listed in Corrundrum's notebook. Luckily, the notebook had been in the front seat of his car when the lab blew.

"9000," he said. "I'm going to Universe 9000." Pinball Wizards hadn't gone far from the 7000s. Why not try to go somewhere distant? Someplace really upstream?

He'd asked for one more camera, unwilling to ask for four more for fear of arousing suspicion. But instead of the four-direction mount, he built a small motorized lazy Susan that rotated the camera 360 degrees in just sixty seconds. This provided a full view of the surroundings.

Prime sent his single camera through to Universe 9000, counted sixty on his stopwatch, and brought the camera back, ready to run if there was an explosive charge attached to it.

The camera reappeared, still turning at one rpm. There was no surprise explosive with it.

He rewound the tape and played it.

A dilapidated farmhouse stood in the distance, and slowly panned away. A rolling hill, a fence and then a gate twenty meters away, the gate askew, a field of late fall grass, unmowed, the hills to the north, and then the farmhouse again. Then—flash—the image of him grabbing the camera.

Prime played the video again, searching the sky for aircraft, searching the frames for nearby human presence. Nothing.

He tried another video survey, this one five minutes long. Still no sign of anything human or robotic. Ten minutes. Twenty.

Satisfied that no robotic guardian awaited him in 9000, John Prime powered down the transfer gate and drove to the electronics store to figure out how to build a timer device.

It was far easier than he expected. A simple electronic timer did the trick, but as he talked with the salesman, he convinced himself he needed a backup in case of power failure. Though if the power failed, the transfer gate wouldn't power up anyway. But a mechanical fail-safe would work if the electronics reset for some reason. The salesman managed to configure an effective solution.

Prime spent a week testing it, letting it run on an hourly cycle, making sure the site in the remote location was secure. In all that time, he found no sign of humans on the remote site. No airplanes in the sky, not even a jet contrail. If it wasn't for the dilapidated farmhouse, he would have guessed it was a Pleistocene world, with no humans at all.

He planned his first excursion for the next day, a one-hour survey of the nearby locale, then back to Universe Prime, no worries, no fuss. His supplies included two watches—so he knew exactly when one hour was up—a handgun, a compass, a flashlight, a kilogram of gold in small ingots, and the video camera. In case things went badly, he had left a message on his desk at home for Casey to find.

Come find me in Universe 9000 near the new lab building on Glidden Road if you don't hear from me in 24 hours.

She was his final fail-safe.

He hoped it wouldn't come to that. He didn't want to explain. Hated the idea of explaining to anyone.

He set the timer for sixty seconds and took his place atop a platform in the transfer zone. His watch clicked down to zero seconds. The walls of the laboratory disappeared.

Prime stepped down from the platform, dragging it out of the zone.

He paused, waiting. Nothing. It was as desolate as he had seen on the video camera. No sound but the breeze in the branchless trees. The wind was chill against his skin. He rolled up the collar of his jacket.

Nothing here.

Prime glanced at the abandoned farmhouse. No need to explore that. He decided to walk the driveway to the main road and hitchhike into town, the same thing he'd done dozens of times before when he'd found a new universe. He just had to be careful that he didn't end up doing something stupid and miss the pickup time. He didn't have the device. He couldn't leave instantly. He had to go back to the transfer zone. Before he forgot, he marked the transfer zone—a scooped-out chunk of a sphere—with spray paint.

He found Glidden Road where he expected it. The farmhouse may have been a difference between universes, but the roads appeared laid out the same. Glidden Road was barren, but that was to be expected. The only things this way in the county were farms, spaced kilometers apart. He started hiking.

By the time he reached the first intersection, a kilometer down the road, he had yet to see or hear a car. Glidden crossed Van Wert Road. A farmhouse stood on the northeast corner. It too seemed abandoned. Screens hung from windows. The door stood open.

He turned northeast on Van Wert Road, taking up a jog. He hadn't meant to expend so much energy, but he had a sudden sinking feeling and he wanted to know what had happened here.

He stopped suddenly and searched the sky. No contrails. On any given day there should be at least three jet contrails in the sky over any place in North America. Nothing.

He spotted another farmhouse in the distance. He ran now. As he neared it, he saw that it was slanted off its foundation, tilted due to old age and lack of maintenance.

A recession of some sort perhaps had driven these people from their homes? A war?

There was a car in the driveway of the farmhouse. He tried the door and found it unlocked. The key was in the ignition. The car smelled of mold, and the windshield was caked in dirt and leaves. This car had been here at least a season.

He tried to start it. It cranked but refused to start up.

Prime didn't want to enter the house, worried that it would collapse. He continued instead toward Findlay.

He reached the outskirts, a subdivision to his left. He marveled to see the houses empty, quiet. No one was living here. No one at all.

Cutting across a fallow field, he reached the subdivision. Cars sat in driveways. Bikes lay in overgrown front lawns. Doors and windows were broken or ajar. People had left their houses at least a year or more before, left them vacant with all their possessions strewn about and gone.

Why?

He decided to enter one of these homes. They seemed less likely to collapse on him than the farmhouses he'd seen.

He picked one, tried the door, and found it unlocked.

"Hello?" he called.

This house had no open windows, no open doors. It smelled of dust. Clearly it was unoccupied. He called again.

"Anyone home?"

The first level was empty. He left the basement for last and climbed the stairs. Dust was caked on the banister. Something fetid reached his nose. He paused at the first door, pushed it open. Beyond was a child's bedroom, a girl's based on the pink, but it was empty. The next door was a sewing room. The last door was to the master bedroom. Something lay on the bed within.

"Hello?"

He squinted in the weak light.

Stepping closer, he saw a corpse on the bed. Long dead and nearly mummified.

Left dead or left for dead? he wondered.

He paused. Death? Everything left as it was. No humans.

Plague?

His stomach flipped, and he backed away.

At the door he turned and ran. Prime flung the front door open in front of him, and he was outside in the cool fall air.

Disease!

What had he done? Stumbled on some plague world?

And was he now infected?

What had he done?

He headed into town. As he walked, he paid attention to his heart rate, his temperature, his state of mind. Had he infected himself? Had he killed himself? Should he run as fast as he could to the gate and get his doctor to administer penicillin, streptomycin, and erythromycin, and any other antibiotic he could think of? Or would that risk Universe Prime by unleashing a plague there?

Stay or go? Carrier or not?

In the end he decided to wait and see if he developed any symptoms and, if he did, he'd deal with it then. Until then, he'd look around and stay in the open.

He passed the Burger Chef, its plate-glass windows shattered. He passed St. Paul's, and realized its roof was burnt through. The grocery store had been looted. He came across no more corpses.

He stopped before the News Shop, a tobacco and magazine store he had frequented as a teenager for its comic books. Prime entered, propping the door open to allow light in. Magazines lined one long wall, and he remembered how as a child he'd thought there couldn't have been one more magazine title in the world. At the start of the shelf, there were the racks of newspapers. He grabbed *The New York Times.*

MARTIAL LAW IN EFFECT! he read.

Martial Law is in effect across the entire United States. No travel except by military order is permitted. President Palin signed an executive order passing control of the nation into the hands of the local military leaders. Without a clear command and control structure in place, any top-down leadership is impossible. . . .

The story was dated two years prior. Two years. He skimmed headlines. ONE BILLION DEAD IN CHINA! VACCINE TRIALS IN BRITAIN FAIL! PLAGUE HITS NEW ZEALAND.

It had been worldwide, and here was the effect two years later. Utter destruction of the human population.

He left the store, leaving the door propped ajar. Across the street was the Ben Franklin. He found a tiny transistor radio and placed a nine-volt in its battery slot. The dial was stiff to his touch as he rotated it. There was nothing but static up and down the spectrum. He tried FM, and then AM. Nothing.

Prime stumbled out of the general store. There could still be pockets of humanity on this planet. In the large cities. Couldn't there be?

He spotted the Dynaco store a block down and ran there. The door was locked, the sign saying the store was closed until further notice. Prime looked around and found a brick near the road. He threw it with all his might, shattering the glass of the front pane. There in the display case was what he wanted, a shortwave radio. He grabbed it.

He plugged the radio into a wall outlet right there in the display case, but there was no telltale flicker of lights. The outlet was dead.

He walked back to the News Shop. The lights would not turn on. No power.

Prime scanned the downtown area. There was the police station, the library, the clothing store. He turned back to the police station. Maybe they had a portable generator.

He ran across the street. The front door of the police station swung open. He tried the power outlet right there in the lobby. Nothing.

The front desk wasn't walled off; he could walk right through a waist-high swinging door, and did so. A board hung on the wall with a list of patrol cars and their keys hanging from it. He looked back out the door and saw that car K-12 was in the lot. He grabbed the keys.

The car started, to his surprise, but maybe police cars were made to last years. He bent down and looked under the dash. There was a cigarette lighter adapter, and next to it a normal plug. He plugged in the shortwave radio.

The radio warbled and squeaked. He waited a moment. Nothing. There was a button that said SEEK. He pressed and the digital dial spun through the frequencies. And kept spinning. Nothing.

Prime's heart fell. If there was anyone, anywhere within a thousand kilometers, they would be broadcasting on shortwave. Something. The military would. Perhaps they were just taking a break from broadcasting.

He let the radio continue to seek and put the prowler into gear.

Driving slowly up Tippecanoe Street, he looked left and right at the desolate town. Not my town, he said to himself. Some other town entirely.

All these dead people, and possibly him too. Possibly him too. What had he done? Exploring worlds and not thinking it through? It was damned fool luck Pinball Wizards hadn't dragged a plague already between universes.

Prime saw the Bank of Findlay on his left. He stopped. The doors were open and off their hinges.

He climbed the steps and entered. The vault gaped open. He peered inside. Stacks of bills stood against the walls. He ignored them. Beyond the first vault door were the safe-deposit boxes. Several boxes had been pried loose from their slots. He played the flashlight around the vault. A drill and a crowbar lay on the central table. Someone had spent some time here looting. But to what point. The futility of it all must have become apparent as the plague ravaged the body of the thief.

Prime opened the bag, found jewelry, gold bars, watches encrusted with gems. A small box lay at the bottom of the bag. Within was a handful of diamonds.

He took the bag with him, stowed it on the passenger seat of the squad car. The shortwave radio still twirled.

He left the car there and walked across the street to the SupeRx. He grabbed a thermometer off the shelf. Prime drove slowly back to the transfer site. He'd have to make a decision soon before Casey realized he was gone and alerted the Wizards.

He parked the car next to the farmhouse, overlooking the transfer zone, and sat. He unwrapped the thermometer and slipped the tip under his tongue.

If he was infected already—if this world was swimming in plague virus—he and his rescuers were doomed. They would come looking and be infected immediately. Or he would return and doom his home world and ultimately any world that he visited. The plague would spread to all the settled worlds of Pinball Wizards, Transdimensional.

But perhaps the plague had passed away with the death of the last humans. Or perhaps it was a plague that humans in other universes were immune to. Perhaps he was utterly safe. He could pass back to Universe Prime and no one would know.

He pulled the thermometer from his mouth. Thirty-seven degrees Celsius. Perfectly normal. He checked his watch. He could wait another six hours. He would check again then. If he was normal, he'd risk it and go back through to 7533.

Prime dozed in the squad car. Every once in a while, he would start awake, look to the dial of the shortwave radio, check his temperature, and close his eyes once more. The temperature did not change in that time, but he found he had no knowledge of how long a virus would incubate in a human host before manifesting symptoms. Depended on the virus, he supposed.

He awoke with a start, shivering. He was certain he had contracted the disease, but then realized he was merely cold. The sun had slid behind the trees. He was late, he needed to get back to Universe Prime.

Checking his temperature one last time, he found it still to be thirty-seven. He had to assume he was uninfected. He had to.

Ten minutes to the next transfer, he saw after checking his watch. He shoved his platform into the transfer zone. Five minutes before the transfer time, he squatted on the platform and waited. He didn't want to be too late into the zone, getting cut into pieces by being halfway in and out. Nor did he want to squat in the cold for too long.

He knelt there, his bag of loot next to him, praying that he was not infected. That Abby would not die because of him. That Casey would survive. For a second, he was half convinced to just send a note through. *Good as dead. Don't come after me. Love, John.*

No, nothing would stop Casey from coming after him. Not even a plea for her safety.

His watch beeped. He crouched on the platform. One minute.

He hated this part. He hated this part. He hated—

The universe shifted.

He was back in the new lab. Stepping quickly away from the gate, he turned it off and deactivated the timer.

Prime had done it. He'd built a system to allow him to explore worlds on his own. But in the process, he'd possibly infected himself and all of Universe Prime.

He picked up the phone and dialed Casey.

"Hey, baby, I'm gonna be a little late," he said.

"Sure, Abby and I are having pizza," Casey said.

"Cool, save some for me."

"See you when you get here," she said.

Prime hung up the phone, feeling sick to his stomach. Not a symptom, just stress and anxiety.

He retched into the wastebasket, emptying his stomach of bile and fluid.

"Uh," he groaned. And then he was sick again.

CHAPTER 25

They walked silently a few hundred meters to a memorial park. Kylie ran off to play on the swings. Melissa sat on a bench to watch. John stood.

"You can sit," she said. "Tell me."

He sat next to her on the bench. "You got the last of the food, remember?"

"I remember. Tell me what I don't know."

"I was just passing through. I'd never seen a universe like that one. Never where the world was winter like that."

"Just passing through?"

"I was lost myself, trying to get back home."

"So there isn't just the two worlds? I always thought it was two."

"Thousands, if not millions, if not infinite," John said. "But that's the only one I've found that was like that. I don't think it's common."

"Thank god."

"I was trying to understand. I had been in a normal universe and suddenly I was in yours. I talked to the soldier there, asking what happened when the food ran out. They pounced on you . . . Rudy, Stan . . . shot you as you walked away."

"I knew them. From our old neighborhood."

"Kylie rolled down the embankment, broke her leg. I carried her back up to where you lay. The blood had turned the snow red. I didn't . . . know what to do. I was just a stupid high school kid. I took you to the next universe."

"The same but different."

"Yes, no war. It was a beautiful fall day. Snow was clumped around us, but it started to melt right away. I called an ambulance, and then I walked off." John paused. "I'm sorry I did that to you. I'm really sorry."

"Sorry for saving my life?" Melissa said. "Sorry for saving Kylie? She would have died right there with me."

"I know, but I ripped you right out of your world. Took everything away from you. Your life, your family."

"It's okay. It was a sucky world." She paused. "What's your name anyway?"

"I'm John Rayburn."

"My life wasn't so great back there. Kylie's father was dead. We were barely getting enough to eat. It was only a matter of time before it all fell apart. I just wish . . ."

"What?"

"I woke up in the hospital, looked out the window, saw the sun shining, and started screaming," she said. "I thought I had died. We hadn't seen the sun in months and didn't expect to until summer again. And there it was, and it was warm and comfortable. And Kylie wasn't there. I freaked."

"Yeah, I bet you did."

"They tried to calm me down. When I realized I wasn't dead, I thought I might be in Mexico or something. But then my ideas weren't in sync with the history here. They sent me to a psychiatrist. I explained everything clearly. Gave them the entire history of the war in my world. The psychiatrist listened and diagnosed me as suffering from post-traumatic delusional disorder. They took Kylie away and placed me in an institution."

"I'm so sorry."

"Stop, it's not your fault," she said. "I had no family, of course. No one I knew lived here. No one to claim me. No one to vouch for me. I knew I was right. Kylie remembered some things, but she was no reliable witness. Years of living with a delusional mother had shaped what she thought she knew, right? I realized I was either insane or the victim of some event I could never prove. So I gave in. Memorized the history of this universe, better than most natives." She laughed. "Convinced them I was sane. Told them I was from Sebewa, but without family, without a husband. They let me go, let me collect Kylie, and I came here, eighteen months ago." She waved her hand around. "It's the same but different."

"I know. People you recognize that don't know you. Familiar places you've never been," John said.

"You said you were lost. Did you ever get back?"

"I found a new home. But I could go back if I wanted to."

"I found a new home, or rather an old home that seems new," Melissa said. "So, why did you track me down after two years? It couldn't have been easy."

John thought for a moment of his own travels, of how far he'd come in two years.

"It's taken me this long to get back. Taken me this long to get back here," John said. "I knew I was leaving you in a lurch. But the alternative was to leave you to die. I'm trying to fix it."

"How?"

"I can take you and Kylie back if you want," John said.

"Back? To the long winter? No. That's no choice."

"I know, but if you had people there. I could take you back to them," he said. "I left people behind when I was whisked from my universe."

Melissa looked at him from the corner of her eye. "What else? You've come with options, haven't you?"

"Yes, we're colonizing a universe. One that has no humans in it at all," John said. "We're populating it with refugees. You're a refugee too, I guess."

"Refugee," she said, considering the word. "I guess so."

"We have less than a hundred refugees. All of them women," John said. "We plan to build some common shelter before winter, keep the colony supplied with materials during the winter."

"No men? That seems a little odd," Melissa said. "It's not some transdimensional lesbian experiment, is it?"

"Uh, no," John said. "One of the reasons I wanted you involved was to help bring people from your old universe there. People from 7538."

"7538," she said, rolling it around on her tongue. "That's this place?"

"This is 7539. Your home universe is 7538."

She paused, glanced back at Kylie in the park. "Before I had Kylie, I was a white-water rafter. I hiked daily in Colorado and then in Ohio when I moved," she said.

"Then this is perfect for you!"

Melissa looked at him, her face a frown. "I'll think about it," she said. She stood. "Kylie! Let's go."

John watched her walk off, certain she'd have nothing more to do with him. He'd tried at least.

Melissa turned and said, "Check with me in a week. I'll think about it until then."

By the end of November, before the first snow, they had erected six twenty-meter-long huts and a central house for cooking and meals for the Alarian women. The name was debated and came down to something in Alarian or New Toledo. In the end, they wanted nothing to do with the old Alarian ways, including the language, and chose New Toledo.

Game was plentiful and with the milder climate, a late crop in the greenhouse bloomed and produced vegetables. The colony was never meant to be self-sufficient, and daily transfers augmented the settlement with the benefits of an advanced society: soap, paper, oranges, and books. The transfers were handled by the largest, most advanced gate the Wizards had built yet.

The settlement was near where downtown Toledo would have been, not far from the Maumee River. Instead of transferring through at the Findlay quarry site—and lugging material overland in the Pleistocene world—they built a gate in a warehouse not far from the settlement. A kilometer walk was all it took to carry material there and back.

The elephant-snouted herbivores proved rather tasty, but the Alarians preferred not to hunt them, choosing instead to graze a herd of domesticated cattle on the open prairie. Guarding it became a concern, when a cow and her calf were brought down by a saber-toothed tiger. However, the tiger was no match for the long-bore rifle that the Alarian women carried, and, once dispatched, there was no sign of another tiger. Apparently they were solitary beasts and no other tiger was nearby, and probably wouldn't be until spring.

John was present, however, when Clotilde and John Ten came across a den of cat-dogs. The two came running back to town, saying one of the cows had been attacked and gutted. The spore had led back to a mound of dirt that looked like some kind of dug-up den.

"I think we'll need some gasoline to drive them out," John Ten said.

John and two or three Alarians followed John Ten and Clotilde. They stopped first at the cow's carcass. Bones, scraps of skin, and the last of the viscera were all that remained of the beast.

"How long was the cow gone?" John asked.

"Less than six hours," Tilly said.

"These beasts are quick and thorough," John said. He knelt and looked at the gray rib bones. Small teeth marks covered them. He worried for a moment there was some horrendous predator they had missed on this world—the real reason that humans didn't live here—some deadly Grendel-like predator. But then he realized what he was looking at, a victim of the cat-dogs, the pack creatures that had almost gotten him when he passed through this universe. He should have realized the colonists would run into them eventually.

He led the way to the den, a low mound of dirt, maybe a half meter tall, with entrance holes leading inward and down in all directions. In the tall grass, the den would have been invisible from across the plain.

The six of them circled the den. They were all armed; carrying at least a pistol was standard procedure in the Pleistocene world. John Ten dashed forward and leaped atop the mound. His boots sunk a few centimeters into the soft dirt. He splashed half the gasoline around the top of the den before emptying the rest of it into a hole.

Using a lighter, he caught flame to a makeshift torch of dry grass.

"Stand back!"

He tossed the torch and it floated awkwardly down, losing flares of sparks as it did so. John was certain the gas wouldn't light. Nothing happened, and then with a whoosh, the mound erupted in flame.

The smoke of the gasoline fire was black and heavy, rising in slow spirals. John had expected the cat-dogs to flee their home en masse, but there was nothing coming from the den, not even a keening sound, at least nothing over the crackle of the flame.

Then something shot out of the opening to John's right, a blur of tan. The cat-dog leaped between him and the Alarian next to him. She turned quickly, tracked the beast with her pistol, and fired a single shot. The cat-dog jerked, twisted, and collapsed in the grass.

"Careful! They're fast!"

Across from them, another leaped out of the flaming mass, right at John Ten. He batted the cat-dog down with the butt of his rifle, then took aim, and shot it once.

Then everything was too fast to take in. One appeared before John, a fat one, slithering out to peer around with dark, evil eyes. John wasted no time and shot the thing twice.

To his left, Clotilde screamed. A cat-dog had launched itself at her and was clinging to her shirt, its teeth latched deeply in the fabric.

John drew his knife, steadied the writhing thing's head with his left hand and slit it across its throat with his right. It spasmed and fell loose, still stuck to Clothilde's shirt. She was awash in blood, her shirt ruined. John ripped the carcass away.

No more cat-dogs were coming out, and the fire was dying down, except to the east where the wind was blowing it into the dry grass. John Ten stamped at the spreading fire with his shoes. John jumped to help, worried for a second that the fire would spread across the entire prairie, but the wind died down and they managed to stamp the entire fire out.

When John turned back, he saw that Clotilde's face was white. Her shirt was soaked in blood, and John realized it wasn't blood from the cat-dog. He ran toward her, just as John Ten saw. They steadied her, one on each arm.

"I think I'm . . ." she said. "I think I'm bleeding." They laid her on the ground, and John Ten opened her shirt. The cat-dog had managed to bite her shoulder, gashing the flesh at least ten centimeters from the clavicle to her forearm. The wound gurgled with the beating of her heart.

John applied pressure, pushing the shirt against the wound.

"Call for the first-aid kit," John said.

One of the Alarians drew out her military-grade walkie-talkie and raised the town.

"Hang in there, Tilly," John said. "We'll get you back to the settlement. We'll get you some bandages and some painkillers."

"Okay," she said. "I'm fine. I feel . . ." And then she lost consciousness. John felt for a pulse. It was steady and even, but she was in shock.

In a few moments, he heard the sound of the quad ATV, one of three they had transferred through. Any vehicle larger wouldn't fit in the transfer zone. Not until they built an even bigger gate.

Englavira was driving the ATV, the first-aid kit in the trailer she was hauling behind. She tsked at the sight of Clotilde's shoulder and said something in Alarian.

"Look out," she said. She lifted the shirt away to peer at the wound. Reaching into the first-aid kit, she grabbed the antiseptic powder and sprinkled it into the wound. Then she ripped open the gauze pads. They soaked red immediately, but she laid another package of them on and used a bandage to hold it in place, wrapping Clotilde's shoulder, armpit, and torso.

"Help me sit her up," she said. They leaned her forward, and Englavira continued wrapping Clotilde until she looked not unlike a mummy, from the waist up.

Once she had tied the bandage off, they gently lifted her into the trailer, and Englavira got in with her.

"You drive," she said to John.

Slowly, avoiding the bumps and ditches, he drove the ATV back to the settlement, while the rest of the hunting expedition trailed behind.

A bevy of Alarians rushed out at the sound of the ATV and carried her into the dormitory. John's eyes rested on the bloodied shirt that lay in the trailer. His heart sank. How could he justify bringing Melissa and Kylie here? It was a deadly world. He had been a fool to think this was a suitable location to raise a child.

CHAPTER 26

John Prime went to his doctor's office, claiming an upcoming trip to South America and Africa and asking for whatever injections that would require and anything that might be preventative for those locales. What else could he do?

His temperature had remained the same and he felt no symptoms after his stomach had calmed, after he had emptied his guts into the trash can. Every itch, every twitch, every pain was a sign to him of his imminent demise. After two weeks, however, and no sign that he was actually sick, John Prime realized that he had not brought destruction on the multiverse.

That relief and the million dollars' worth of gems and jewelry that he had found in Universe 9000 buoyed his spirits. He had managed to explore a whole new world on his own. He had a system to repeat the process. Better yet, the world was utterly devoid of human life, yet all the infrastructure was in place for him to exploit. How many banks did the United States have? And he had all the time in the world to break into each one and extract the valuables. He would be rich beyond belief. And free to pursue whatever further exploitation of the universe he wished.

Death had passed him over one more time.

But better than that, he wouldn't have to be a member of Pinball Wizards, Transdimensional, after all.

John Prime built a second gate in Universe 9000. Then he didn't have to worry about his timer. He could always come back to 7533 using the new gate in Universe 9000. He used the nearby farmhouse, reinforcing the decrepit structure, installing a gas generator, and making it livable again. Making a Mark 1 gate—what the team called the first generation of gates, very similar to the first one Farmboy built—was becoming easier and easier. He was fairly certain he could build one from scratch in any advanced universe. If he was trapped in a Pleistocene universe, however, he was doomed, but if not . . . He could create one in a matter of days with the right materials.

The area around the farmhouse became a collection point for various equipment: front loaders, fast cars, motorcycles, tractor trailers. He felt like Croesus, sitting atop a mound of material goods. Anything in the entire universe of 9000, he could have. Yachts, cars, houses, famous art. When his mind fell on that, he took a trip in Universe 9000 to the Cleveland Museum of Art. He drove the police prowler, the shortwave on the passenger's seat always scanning. He'd raided the police station's armory and wore a police belt, with firearm, mace, and knife. In the squad car, he had an assault rifle, a machine gun, and grenades. He'd practiced with each, destroying the statue of William Henry Harrison in the Findlay town square in the process. With the rifle, he'd removed all the windows that faced the square. The machine gun had ripped apart the diner across from the police station.

He didn't expect to see any humans, but he might. And he wanted to be able to return to 7533 if he did.

The roads were clear to Cleveland. He jammed to his tunes, singing at the top of his lungs as he drove 110 kilometers an hour down the highway. Near Sandusky, he came across a tractor trailer tipped over and blocking the entire freeway. Sudden fear destroyed his mood. He slammed on the brakes, dropped the prowler in reverse, and backed up a half kilometer on the highway.

His heart pounding, he waited. Nothing. He unholstered the pistol and held it against the steering wheel. Nothing followed him. Nothing moved. He opened the window and frigid air entered the car. No sound but the rumble of the prowler's engine.

Prime drove the car slowly across the brown grass median. Slowly he took the car down the opposite side of the road. As he came abreast of the tractor trailer, he noted the rust on the cab where the crash had scraped the paint off. This truck had been here for two years. There was no one lying in wait. This world was empty.

Prime drove on.

But he kept the music off and the car at a lesser speed.

As he neared Cleveland, he found more and more abandoned

cars. Some were burnt out. Some were just sitting there, as if waiting for their owners to return. When he reached the city proper, he found the freeway completely blocked by a multicar pileup, forcing him to exit into the looming heights of the city proper. He felt claustrophobic.

But still there was no sign of any human being whatsoever. This world was truly desolate.

He didn't bother to get back on the highway, but drove on, passing out of the high-rises, through poorer areas, until he came to the campus of Case Institute of Technology, where he had once planned to study physics.

The museum lot was empty, the building itself untouched. No one flocked to the museums when plague took the living. Perhaps the churches would be jam-packed with corpses, but not the museums. He climbed the steps and found the doors locked. The first blow of his sledgehammer starred the glass. The second knocked the glass from its frame. Prime reached in and unlocked the door.

It was dark within, but his hard hat held a light, which he flicked on. He knew what he wanted, Gallery 128, on the first floor. The painting was easy to find, right there in the middle of the gallery. Picasso's *Bull Skull, Fruit, Pitcher*. He had seen it on a school visit to the museum in the eighth grade. The eyes of the skull had looked cartoonlike, yet haunting. The teeth held an angry grin.

He stared at it for a moment, then stepped around the velvet rope, and lifted it off the wall. He half expected an alarm to sound. But nothing happened. He held the painting before him, looked at the brush strokes, so clear from arm's length. Yes, this is what he desired.

He carried the painting to the atrium and left it in between the inner and outer doors. Then Prime returned to the gallery and looked at the other paintings that had surrounded the Picasso. None of them spoke to him, so he walked to the next galleries: Egyptian and Oriental art. He passed these by too and passed into a room of sculpture.

His eyes fell upon a small sculpture—a Rodin, the tag said—called *Fallen Caryatid Carrying Her Stone*. The poor creature was crushed under the weight of its burden, and Prime looked at it with sadness. He smashed the enclosing glass with his sledge and lifted the statue from its place.

"For Casey," he said to himself.

He prowled the galleries then, searching for paintings and sculpture that evoked some emotion and dragging them to the atrium, where they leaned against walls and slouched in doorways. He took dozens of pieces, knowing he could only travel with a few in the prowler.

When Prime was done, fifty pieces of art lay at the entrance. He surveyed them slowly. In the end he took twenty of them, among them a Winslow Homer, an Edgar Arthur Tharp Junior, an Henri Rousseau, and a sculpture by Lino Tagliapietra that looked like a gondola. The last item was a brilliant bejeweled ring that he took for Casey. He wrapped the art pieces in blankets from the gift shop, feeling as he did so that he should be more careful with them. Then he placed them in the backseat of the prowler and in the trunk.

Millions of dollars in art shoved in the back of a police cruiser.

Prime checked his watch. Just past three in the afternoon. He could easily make it back. He started the cruiser and slowly slithered his way back toward the city, taking a different route than he arrived by, one that took him right toward the city again.

He passed an old fenced building, and realized it was a National Guard Armory. He braked.

Prime turned the car into the parking lot of the armory, a grin upon his face.

He ended up taking little from the armory; he had no room in the car. But Prime knew there were armories nearer to Findlay. There was Camp Perry near Clinton on the lake. Even Wright-Patterson Air Force Base wasn't far from his base of operation. He wondered if he could drive a tank . . .

As he unloaded the paintings and sculptures, his mind wandered to what else he could plunder from this world. Anything in this world could be his. Anything.

CHAPTER 27

John returned to Sebewa to let Melissa know he couldn't take her and Kylie to New Toledo.

She nodded when he came in.

"I was worried that you were a figment of my imagination," she said, pouring him water. "Or that you might not come back."

"I'm real. I'm back."

She stood and looked at him for a moment.

"We've decided," she said.

John hoped she had decided to stay, so that he wouldn't have to deny her and Kylie.

"We decided the hour after you left," she said. "Knowing we don't belong here made it easy . . . makes this all so empty, so not . . ."

John nodded. "I know what you mean."

"Yeah, I guess you do," she said. "So, we'll go. As soon as you can take us. It's better to make a positive choice than to live on at the whim of a random universe."

John could have said, no, we'll take you somewhere else, somewhere similar to this but different. But he saw what New Toledo represented. It was the optimistic choice, not the pessimistic one. It was the acceptance of responsibility.

He grinned. "Okay, but you can change your mind any time you want. Go somewhere else."

"Are you trying to talk us out of it, now?" Melissa said.

"No, no," John said. "But it's not permanent if you don't want it to be."

"That makes it too easy, John," she said, "if we make our decision so weakly. We'll go. Tonight."

John nodded. "Tonight, then."

John need not have worried about Melissa and Kylie. His concern should have instead been for Clotilde. The arrival of the little girl brought the maternal instincts out in the Alarians, and they bustled to find a place for Melissa and Kylie in the dormitory.

"We'll need to start a school," Englavira said.

A question popped into John's mind as Englavira said that, but he didn't have a chance to ask it. Melissa was whisked away to be shown the settlement.

John didn't follow. He was well aware that New Toledo wasn't his place, though he had helped found it. He remained in 7650 with Casey. New Toledo was the Alarian place. The refugee place. And that was fine with him. He turned instead to the inventory. New Toledo would not be self-sufficient for years and needed a constant flow of supplies from the settled universes. Modern supplies.

He stepped outside and walked to the supply hut. The temperature was above freezing, unlike 7539—Universe Cursky is what he called 7539—where a fine snow had covered the ground. Englavira was certain they could get two crops a year with the warm seasons in the Pleistocene universe. Food would not be a problem. But gasoline for the ATVs, paper, books, clothing, medicine, all were unavailable in the Pleistocene.

John hoped that he was not setting them up for failure. What if something happened to all the transfer gates? Would they survive or suffer a slow decline into subsistence farming, or, worse, starvation? But for all their gates to fail? No, that was impossible.

He was counting out the toilet paper when Englavira found him.

"We took Clotilde to 7351," she said. "She had a fever and we couldn't do anything for her."

"She seemed to be recovering when I left," John said. "What happened?"

"Something in the wounds from the cat-dogs," she replied. "She was delirious, hot and cold. We couldn't care for her here. John Ten took her back. He figured 7351—Universe Champ—had the best medical facilities."

"I'm sorry," John said.

"Why are you apologizing?"

"Because all this . . ." He lifted his arms up to indicate the entire settlement.

"Oh, yes, Grace Home did say you like to take responsibility for everything that goes wrong," Englavira said.

He nodded. "I guess I do sometimes," he said.

"With all these Johns around, there's not a thing that goes wrong that a couple of you don't beat yourself up about it."

"Yeah, sure," John said. "I should go see how she is. I worry about Kylie and the cat-dogs now."

"We know what they look like, we know what their dens look like," Englavira said. "We've sent the ATVs out on patrol at a five-kilometer perimeter and have not seen another nest of them. The little girl is safe. And we're glad you brought her here."

John remembered his question. "Where are all the Alarian children?" The youngest from the seraglio was still in her teens. There should have been a gaggle of young ones.

Englavira looked away. "Our children were raised elsewhere," she said.

"Oh," John said.

"The children went through with Charboric," she said. "Liuvia and Radeheva are pregnant. Remember we were left as a harem for Gesalex and the remaining half-breeds."

"I'm sorry. I wish we could do something."

"There you go taking blame for things."

"I'll go see how Clotilde is doing," he said.

"If you do want to take some blame for something, how about the lack of bacon?" Englavira said with a smile.

"Bacon?"

"I love bacon. We need more of it."

Before he left, he checked in with Melissa and Kylie. Melissa was standing atop the small hillock that rose above the settlement a few dozen meters, enough to see most of the surrounding plains and the river.

"I know this land," she said. "The grade, but not the view. We're not far from where downtown is."

"No, not far."

Below them, Kylie was running back and forth in the town square with the dog, "Dog." They had brought through just the one shepherd mix, but John saw that they could use a dozen more for protection and hunting.

"It's going to be hard work," John said. "And maybe deadly. As bad as the universe you're originally from."

"You think so?" Melissa said. "So much suffering there, so much hatred. I see none of that here."

"But—"

"Stop backpedaling," Melissa said. "We'll be fine." She hugged him then.

"Good," he said.

John transferred from Pleistocene to Home Office. 7650 was the only universe that had a Pinball Wizards location mapped over the top of the Pleistocene site, a huge, open warehouse near downtown Toledo. From the warehouse he drove one of the company cars down to the quarry site.

"Hey, John," Henry Home said as he entered.

"Hey, Henry. How's Clotilde?"

"Ah, well," Henry said, shaking his head.

"Is she all right?"

"She's at McKinley Hospital in Columbus in 7351," Henry said. "They couldn't treat her in Toledo. It's some sort of infection that they've never seen before here."

"Shit!"

"Yeah."

"Have we unleashed some sort of disease here?" John's mind started working. How many other diseases were unique in the universes? How many strains of innocent viruses in one universe would be virulent in another?

"I hope not," Henry said. "We'd have noticed before, wouldn't we? I mean, we've been traveling for months."

"Exactly. What about all the viruses we've inadvertently brought between universes?"

Henry shrugged. "What can we do? Stop traveling?"

John said, "I want to know if there's been any outbreak of flu or any type of infectious diseases around our transfer zones in all the settled universes."

"How are we going—"

"Henry, just do it," John said. "If we've been spreading disease, we'll stop all of this now."

Henry sighed. "Right. But if it was a problem, there wouldn't be transfer devices."

"Maybe the reason they aren't common is that all the travelers die from universe-local disease."

"Crap," Henry said. "I'll send a research request in the next packet."

"Priority zero."

"Right, priority zero."

John drove down to the hospital and found John Ten sitting in the waiting room.

"How is she?"

"Recovering." John Ten looked weary.

"She'll be all right," John said, though he had no real idea.

"She will. She's through the worst of it," John Ten said. "But . . ."

"What is it?"

"They didn't know what it was," he said. "And before they put her in isolation, three nurses and six patients in Toledo caught it. And two patients here. The doctors have no idea what it is."

"Did anyone . . . ?"

"No, the mortality rate is zero," John Ten said. "But—"

"Yeah." John nodded. "I've asked Henry to look into infections near all our gates in the settled universes," John said.

He watched John Ten's eyes focus for a second. He came to the same conclusion John had.

"We can't have that," he said. "We can't allow viruses through."

"Exactly."

He spent a moment watching Clotilde through the window of the isolation ward. She seemed to be sleeping peacefully in her bed.

John Ten stood beside him, and John squeezed his arm.

"This is a fluke," he said. "I'm sure of it."

"Let's hope. The alternative is unfathomable."

CHAPTER 28

Snow swirled around as they walked toward the house. The snow in Home Office had only been a few centimeters deep, the result of a meandering collection of huge flakes. But the snow here was a vertical pelting that drove into John's eyes and forced him to walk with his head down and his parka hood pulled tight. The wind pulled at the backpack full of canned food he carried.

"Up here," Melissa said. "This is the house." John and Casey followed in Melissa's tracks.

The difference in weather between Pleistocene and here—7538, or Universe Winter as they called it—was even more marked. The Pleistocene world was experiencing a warm December with little chance of snow, or even temperatures below freezing.

They stamped up the steps toward a single town house among a row of them. Orange light flickered in the window and smoke rose from its fireplace. It was just after sunset, and the temperature was dropping fast.

Melissa pounded her fist on the door.

John saw that all the windows were covered in plastic. The door was fronted by a solid glass pane.

"They might have moved," Melissa said. "I hope not, but this was a good house. Fireplace. Good insulation. Close to two drop-off points. I don't think Devon would have left it."

The door opened a crack, and a bearded face looked out.

"Yeah? We don't have any extra food, okay? Sorry. No extra," he said.

"Devon! It's me, Melissa!"

The door swung open.

"Melissa? Melissa?"

Devon stared. He was thin-faced, with a weak beard. One arm of his glasses was broken. He had a bent look to him, an old look, though Melissa had assured them that he was only a few years older than she.

"Yes, it's me!"

He looked sharply at John and Casey.

"Who are they?"

"Friends, Devon," Melissa said. "We'd like to come in. We have food."

Devon stared at her as if the words were lies, impossibilities. The glass was fogging up as he held the door open.

"Where's Kylie?" he asked after a long moment.

"She's safe," Melissa said. "Please let us in. We do have food that we can share."

"Only you! They can wait here."

Melissa turned and shared a look with John. He nodded. The porch was freezing, but for the most part the wind was blocked.

Melissa entered the house and the door closed, clicking and clanking with thrown bolts.

Casey leaned close to him.

"This is worse than I expected. So much fear," she said, stamping her feet.

"It's been two years, and it looks no better," John said.

They stood there for a long minute, then two, before the door opened.

Melissa motioned them in. "Come on."

Inside, the room was frigid. John's breath hung in the air. A fire burned in the fireplace, but it was no roaring blaze. Pieces of finished wood—from furniture, John guessed—were stacked cordlike, ready to be burned next. Devon stood at the far end of the room, near a door that led into a kitchen. He was dressed in an unzipped winter coat. Beside him were a woman and two small girls. All of them were dressed in winter coats. The girls wore mittens that were no longer pink, but rather a dingy gray.

"Devon has agreed to listen to us," Melissa said.

"We've come—" John started to say.

"Food first," Devon said. "Melissa said you have food."

"Yeah, sure." He dropped the backpack on the floor and unzipped it. He pulled out a tin of tuna and handed it to Devon. A look of incredulousness grew upon his face.

"Where did you get that?"

"We have access."

"They look well fed," the woman said, speaking for the first time. "They must have a cache."

Devon turned the can upside down, reading the label. "Conestoga Tuna," he said. "I've never heard of it. And this expiration date is next year. This isn't from a cache."

"Like I said, we have access." John reached into his bag and drew out two candy bars, milk chocolate, which he handed to the children. They looked to their mother.

"No, they'll be sick," Devon said. "They can't have that. It's too rich for them."

"Devon!"

"It is, Jane. It is."

The woman—Jane—took the candy bars. "We'll save them for later."

John lifted more cans from the backpack. Fruit cocktail, potatoes, carrots, hominy corn.

"What is all this?" Devon cried.

"Food, and we have plenty of it," Casey said.

Devon dropped the can of potatoes he had been holding.

"What do you want for it?" he said sharply.

"It's a gift," Casey said. "We don't want anything, except for you to listen."

"We've got enough religion," he said. "Enough of chances and faith and hopes that don't work out. So we'd just as well not take your food if that's the price." He took the candy from his wife's hands and gave it back. "You can leave now."

"But—"

Devon drew a pistol from his coat pocket.

"Devon!" Melissa said.

"You all have to go now," he said calmly. "Or you die as looters and no one cares."

"Devon! This is real!"

He raised the pistol. "Go now."

John had no idea where to go with this. He couldn't just force Devon to use the device and prove that they had a paradise of bountiful food in the universe next door. How could a person who refused to listen be shown the possibilities? Maybe Casey was right; there was too much fear here. The fear was too ingrained, too severe. He turned to leave. There were others on Melissa's list of contacts besides this long-ago friend from college.

Casey, however, folded her arms across her chest.

"Don't be a fool," she said. "We're not peddling religion or false hopes. Look at Melissa. Look at her." Casey turned toward Melissa. "Take off your coat."

She did so, standing in the cold living room.

"Now you take off your coat," Casey said to the wife, Jane.

She looked at Devon, who made no expression or motion. She nodded and removed the coat. Her clothes looked two sizes too large and hung on her. By contrast, Melissa looked to be thirty pounds heavier, while Jane seemed an emaciated prisoner.

"Does she look starved?" Casey said, nodding at Melissa. "We have food, we have warmth, we have a community. And you can either pass it up or hear us out."

Devon looked at Melissa and then away. His pistol wavered, and John saw that his eyes glistened with tears.

"It can't be for free!" he shouted. "Nothing is for free! You want something from us. And we don't have anything else to give. Nothing."

Jane put her arms around Devon's shoulders. "It's Melissa, Devon," she said. "We can trust her. She says it's okay, then it must be. And one of these chances has to work out, right? One of them does."

Devon shook himself like a horse, loosening Jane's grip. Her hands dropped away.

"What's the deal?" he said. "A boat to Brazil? How? Lake Erie has been frozen for five years! Greenhouses? The sun hasn't shined in months! Geothermal cities under the earth? Foolishness! We're all going to die, and there's nothing anybody can do about it!"

One of the girls started to sob, and Devon's fierce face showed a gap of sadness, of empathy.

"There is no panacea, no golden hope." He kicked a can, and it rolled against the wall, where it thunked.

John started to speak, but Casey raised a hand.

"You're wrong, Devon," Casey said. "And for the sake of your daughters, you need to listen."

He sobbed again. Jane squeezed his shoulders so tightly he couldn't shake her off.

"For the girls, Devon."

He put the gun in his pocket, and then sat heavily on the couch.

"Speak. Say what you wanna say. I don't care anymore."

Casey nodded at John, letting him know he was free to begin his argument. John reached into the backpack and pulled out three newspapers and three news magazines. He handed them to Devon.

"So?"

"Look at the dates," John said. All the dates on the magazines were that week. All the newspapers were from the day before. On the cover of one magazine was the picture of downtown Toledo, the winter sun high overhead, casting rays down on the skyline.

Devon just looked at the newspaper.

"Open it to the weather."

He turned it over in his lap and looked at the forecast.

"'Temperatures in the tens Celsius, an expected heat wave in December,'" he said. "Tricks! Just tricks!"

"I bought those today," John said. "In a universe not far from here. Where the nuclear exchange never happened. Where winter doesn't stay year-round."

"Bullshit!"

"Where do you think Melissa was for two years? Not here!" John said. "She was shot. I found her, took her to a parallel universe, and she lived there with Kylie for two years."

"Hogwash," Devon whispered.

"We've built a community, one where there's abundant food, abundant warmth, and good people," John said. "We're asking you to join it."

"Lies!" Devon said. He placed the newspaper on the coffee table.

"Why us, Melissa? Why taunt us?" Jane asked.

"I'm not taunting you. It's real. I was there two hours ago. In the warmth of the winter sun," she said. "And you, because I know you'll be good for the settlement. I know Devon. I know you. Tough situations have warped you both. But with us, you can reclaim yourselves."

"It's . . . it's . . . too much to fathom," she said. "I can't understand it."

"Please, try to hear how true our words are," Melissa said.

"We're done," Devon said. He still sat sideways on the couch. "We've listened and now we're done."

"But—" Melissa said.

"It's okay, Melissa," John said. He stacked the rest of the cans on the table. "You keep these."

Lastly, he placed a piece of paper on top of the cans.

"Here's the address," John said. "Come tonight. Or tomorrow. Or the next day."

"Get out."

"Let's pack it up," John said, just before midnight.

"I hate this goddamn universe," Melissa said.

They had waited the night before for Devon and Jane to arrive, and now tonight, but to no avail. They weren't coming. They had grown accustomed to their plight. Learned helplessness, ingrained desperation. They were unwilling to move beyond their situation and so indeed were doomed because they thought they were.

"A self-fulfilling prophecy," Casey said.

"I guess we'll look at the next people on my list," Melissa said. "But they would have been perfect. Devon and Jane were so active in college, so interested in the right thing. They'd know so many other people we could help. I just wish . . ."

"We can't lead people to happiness, Melissa," John said.

"You led me," she said.

"I provided the facts. You made the decision."

"We should have provided other facts. Helped them to make the decision. Free will be damned."

"'For your own good.'"

"Yeah," she said, and then stopped short. "Yeah, I guess acting like the mother of a toddler with everyone leads to some totalitarian decisions."

"I guess so."

Casey said, "Luckily there are millions of other people to save here. I know you want to save everyone, John."

John startled at the loud bang outside. He was certain it was the wind, but then Melissa said, "The door."

She dashed across the concrete floor.

"Careful—" John started to say. He reached into his shirt for the device, stepped close to Casey.

Melissa flung open the door. Snow swirled in, but also four bundled forms. They shuffled in, shaking snow from their feet and bodies.

Devon removed his hood.

"We're here," he said.

CHAPTER 29

By February, there were over a thousand immigrants in New Toledo, nearly all of them from Universe Winter. Word spread there slowly, from person to person, family member to family member, friend to friend. But not all settlers came from there.

After the first of the year, John traveled to 7423, Universe Super-prime.

Snow crunched under his feet as he climbed the stairs to the porch. He pushed into the apartment building as someone from the downstairs apartment pushed past in the doorway.

"Hey, John," the college-aged girl said. "New coat?"

"Hey," John replied to the person he'd never seen before in his life. "Yeah."

He stamped his feet and climbed the stairs. He hadn't told Prime he was doing this. But then why should he? Should he feel some guilt for coming here without him?

He knocked on the door. Silence within, no blaring TV, no radio. John knocked again. Nothing.

John looked around. Where would he hide a second key?

He glanced at the doorframe, the doormat. No and no. Too obvious. He clomped back down the stairs. The mail slots were a rack of squares, in a three-by-three grid, some full of mail. John reached in, turning his hand over, and felt the top of the slot. There, taped to the wood, was a key.

He ripped it off and climbed back up to the apartment. The key fit in the lock. He turned the key and entered.

It was neater than he remembered. The drug paraphernalia was gone. The coffee table was clean. The TV had been removed too. No empty cereal boxes lined the counter. The room *smelled* clean.

John heard a snore from the bedroom. He wondered why he felt so matter-of-fact breaking into his doppelganger's apartment. Maybe John Superprime's life was just an extension of his own, a room in a mansion that he choose not to live in. The possibility he did not choose.

He pushed the bedroom door open. John Superprime lay sprawled on the bed, the covers tangled around his torso. He might have been John lying there, except that the body was too thin. Except that this John Rayburn had let drugs violate his body.

"Hey, John Rayburn," John said.

His eyes fluttered open. He paused, then sat bolt upright in the bed.

He looked at John with no real surprise or alarm.

"Which one are you?"

"John Home," John said. "The one after the one after you."

"Ah, yes, the one who cracked the code. What do you want?"

"To ask you what you want."

Superprime stared at him. "My goddamn life back!" he cried.

"Why? It would be far more foreign than this is by this point. You think you can just drop back into it after so many years?"

"I can try."

"I can give you something else, if you want it," John said with a sigh. "In a community we've made in an empty universe."

"Paradise? Eden? No, wait, Rayburn's Utopia."

"Yeah, something like that," John said. He almost turned around and left. But the apartment was clean, no booze, no drugs. "Whatever, John. Be an ass about it. You want your life back? It's right here in front of you. This is your life. This is it. There's nothing more. No magic panacea. No place you'll suddenly be happy. You want a chance at doing something new, something different, then I can give it to you. You want to stay here and molder in your self-pity, do it. And if you really want to go back to 7312, I'll take you there, but you'll be no different there than here. Your home is an alien planet by now. No one will know you. Your parents will have grieved and moved on. You'll be an intruder. But I'll take you there if you want."

"I . . ."

"What?"

"I just don't want to be by myself anymore," John Superprime said.

"That I can help with," John said. "Pack your stuff. You're probably not coming back."

A city of a thousand. John was not a citizen. Oh, he was welcomed. He was lauded, even. He was listened to, but he did not belong. Which he found was fine with him. The responsibility of governing the New Toledoans would have been too much for him. He was happy to have created the place, to have seeded the population and let it go.

But when the first crime occurred, it was he who was asked to carry out the justice. It was he who decided the criminal's fate.

It was rape. A man from Winter forced himself on an Alarian. He claimed the advances were encouraged. He claimed it was a game of sexual dominance. She claimed . . . to remember nothing. The marks claimed otherwise.

The mayor of New Toledo invited John and Grace to her office to discuss the problem. Melissa had been elected to a one-year term in December. One year was as far into the future as the burgeoning community dared plan for.

"We don't have a judicial system," Melissa said. Her office was in one of the new buildings spreading down the Ottawa River from the original settlement. It had a view of the brown river from a small rise. "Who thought we'd need one?" She stood by the window looking at the river, a spot where she probably spent too much time. John wondered if she was enjoying her job. Englavira was her vice mayor.

"What have you done with him?" Grace asked.

"Nothing," Melissa said.

"Nothing?"

"Yes, it's Amalona's word against Jason's," Melissa said. "He says it was consensual. She says it wasn't. They were both drunk."

"Drunk?"

"Yes, drunk. Someone has been smuggling hard liquor in," Melissa said. That was something John had never considered, cross-dimensional smuggling in their daily shipments to New Toledo. Someone was sneaking alcohol across. He wondered if drugs were coming through too. The magnitude of what they had created threatened to overwhelm him.

"I guess the foibles of human society will follow us anywhere," he said.

"You can't stop humans from being humans," she said. "Shit, that came out wrong. If she was raped, he needs to pay."

"It seems like you're unable and unwilling to have a trial," Grace said.

"We can have a trial. No doubt. He has witnesses that say she was coming on to him. She . . . has remained remarkably quiet once she made her accusation."

"She's an Alarian," Grace said. "She's been the victim of sexual abuse from puberty. Of course she's confused."

"Yes, I know," Melissa said. "I'm not unsympathetic—"

"You're sounding like a politician," Grace said.

"There are more sides to this than the woman's," Melissa said. "Shit! I know he probably did it. But what about innocent until proven guilty."

"We're not in the United States," Grace said. "We don't have a constitution."

"We don't have much of anything," Melissa said. The only rules they'd come up with were practical ones for making sure everyone was working on the things that needed to be done. "The Council meeting notes, but how formal are those? We've been using peer pressure to get things done. We don't have any police. We don't have any judges. We've been pretending at this."

"So what choices do we have?" John asked.

"It feels like a cop-out having you here, like we can't do this ourselves. But you two are outsiders. You can have a neutral perspective. And the community looks up to you, John. Heck, most people worship you around here."

"What?"

"You're here enough to know it," Melissa said. "But if you needed a chair, half the settlement would get on their hands and knees so you could sit on their backs."

"I hope you're exaggerating," John said.

"A little," Melissa said. "But the point remains. If the justice comes from you, it might be easier to swallow."

John shook his head. "Me? That's a lot of responsibility. Deciding the fates of these two people . . ."

Grace snorted. "You decided the fate of everyone out there." She waved in the direction of the New Toledo town square. "You, and no one else. You can't back out now."

John sighed. Grace shrugged at him, as if to say that, yes, indeed this was your idea.

"Tell me everything about this Jason Grayborn," John said. "And everything about Amalona."

Grace snorted. "Fair and balanced, sure," she said. "She might have a history of false rape allegations."

"Grace," John said.

"Right, right. Innocent until guilty."

"He's a third degree," Melissa said.

"What?"

"Third degree of separation from Devon and Jane," Melissa said. "I've started thinking of our community as it relates to our first settlers from 7538. The Alarians and Devon and Jane and the two girls are zero. Anyone they recruited that they knew are one degree. Those recommended by one degrees are twos, and so on. The farther out the separation, the less likely the recommendation gets acted on. Family takes priority over friends."

"I didn't realize it was so complicated," John said.

"Recommended immigrants are placed up for additional positive or negative recommendations. Three negatives will sink you. Ten positives will get you a visit from the emigration team. Jason Grayborn was recommended by a second degree, Cecil Inkster. He received ten positives by other third degrees who may or may not have known him. He has EMT skills, which made him a strong candidate. We still don't have a doctor and just a single nurse. If a murderer had an M.D., he or she might still get ten recommendations. Jason Grayborn emigrated in January, and has been a productive member of the settlement until now, as far as I know."

"And you keep track of how many people personally?" Grace said.

"I manage by exception," Melissa said. "Whatever comes to my attention, I deal with."

"And Amalona?"

"She's twenty five, sweet, kind, and twisted from ten years in the Alarian seraglio," Melissa said. "She works in the greenhouse. She commutes to Universe Ten one day a week for an agriculture class. Otherwise not on my radar."

"And what happened?"

"We have a problem in the ratio of men to women here," Melissa said. "It started with the Alarians, and we haven't managed to balance it out. There are two females for every male here, and some of the men think they can have the pick of the litter."

"There have been other incidents like this?" Grace said.

"No, no, nothing like this," Melissa said. "But there's an attitude that any man can get the woman he wants, or at least, a woman. And I'm not willing to lower our threshold to get more men just so everyone can have a date on Saturday night." She sighed. "Anyway, last Friday evening, there was an impromptu party. Liquor was available. I'm still not sure where it's coming from. Nor am I sure it's breaking any rules. At least not until the Council makes a decision on alcohol. Jason shows some attention to Amalona. Witnesses say they danced. All in fun according to some. A little hot and heavy according to others. Jason and Amalona disappear and no one really notices when. No one really notices when Jason reappears and Amalona doesn't. Two days later, Englavira comes to my office saying she has a problem."

"Amalona never came forward?" John asked.

"Why does that matter?" Grace said.

"I'm just asking a question, Grace."

"She didn't. Englavira said she was chipper, same as always, went to work the next day. Came back. No one noticed anything. Until she happened to run across Grayborn in the cafeteria. She collapses, hysterical, and Englavira doesn't get anything out of her until she sedates her. Then Amalona explains that she had 'performed poorly,' which I have come to find out is Alarian male code for a generic reason to beat and torture an Alarian female."

"Shit," Grace said.

"Englavira checks her out. She has bruises on her inner thighs—"

"According to Englavira," John said. "Did anyone see them?"

"John," Grace cried. "How can you—"

"No. No one else saw them," Melissa said. "But Englavira said she was bruised on the throat as well. Handprints around her throat."

"He doesn't deny the sex?" Grace said. "He doesn't deny that?"

"No," Melissa said.

"Fry him," Grace said.

"Grace," John said.

"You chicken. You're scared of doing the wrong thing. You males are all the same."

"Grace, we have to be sure!" John said. "We have to know for sure."

"And when we know for sure?" Grace said. "What do we do?"

John shrugged. "I don't know. Send him away."

"We can't send him back to Winter," Melissa said. "He knows too much."

"Some other universe?" John said. "We have a lot of choices. We can banish him for suspected wrongdoing, can't we?"

Grace looked at him and shook her head. "Make it someone else's problem? No dice, John. No dice at all. He doesn't get to do this to some other woman. I won't allow that."

"What are you saying, Grace?" John said.

She stared him in the eye. "We end his life," she said. "If he's guilty of this, we end his life."

John felt his body weakening. He sat heavily in the chair across from Melissa's desk.

"Execute him?"

"If we know for certain he did it, yes."

"And if we don't?"

"If you can't convince yourself he did it," Grace said, "then you can banish him to some random universe."

"I don't know if I can—"

"Then who? Prime? Henry? Some other you?" Grace said. "You started this game, Rayburn. You gotta play the hand."

"How about you?" John said.

"Don't even suggest it," Grace said, a grim grin on her face. "He'd never stand a chance of justice from me."

"Okay," John said. He stood and looked out onto the river. "I'll do it. Tell Grayborn I'm meeting with him tomorrow. He can have anyone he wants with him."

John met with Jason Grayborn and Cecil Inkster the next morning. Grace refused to be there, not even to take notes. John used a cassette recorder to tape the interview.

"So what the hell is this all about?" Jason said. He was a tall man, undoubtedly handsome to women. Dark-haired, sharp-featured. His face was symmetric and thin. He moved fluidly, gracefully as if he could have been a gymnast in college or high school.

"I think you know," John said.

"It's bullshit, is what it is," Cecil Inkster said. He was shorter, pudgy, a dull-looking man compared to his friend. He and Jason had been roommates in college. Cecil was a friend of Devon's brother.

"It must be something if the legendary John Rayburn is here," Grayborn said.

John felt himself recoil at the flattery. Would it have worked if the man's life wasn't in the balance? No, it seemed so insincere, in all respects.

"Jason, I need to tell you what you're up against," John said. "If you raped that girl—if you raped Amalona, the penalty is death."

"What?" Grayborn cried. "That's bullshit! Did she say it was rape? Did she say that? Because she was coming on to me!"

Cecil stared with dark eyes in his pudgy face.

Grayborn stood up then. "Screw this! I'm outta here."

He stood and pulled open the door, stopping short as he saw John Superprime standing there with a gun in a holster. John had asked Superprime to be his master at arms.

"Interview ain't over yet, Grayborn," Superprime said.

"Sit back down, Jason," John said. "We have to do this."

Jason turned, a look of rage on his face.

"Ask what you want, Rayburn," he said. "My story is the same. She wanted it. I gave it to her. Anything else that's said is a lie." He sat on the chair.

Cecil wrung his hands, nervous at what he was suddenly a part of.

"Tell me what happened."

"When?"

"On the night you and Amalona had sex," John said.

"She was into me. I was into her. It was clear from the get-go," Jason said, his inflection flat. "We danced. We drank. Then we found a dark corner in one of the barracks. She initiated it. She reached into my pants. We had sex. It was pretty hot." He nudged Cecil, who only returned a blank stare. "Then I came back to the dance. That's it."

"She had handprints around her neck," John said.

"You've had sex. I've seen you with that Casey girl. You know that things happen. It got a little wild. It happens."

"She was bruised."

"Things . . . happen," he said, enunciating each word slowly.

"Did she say stop?"

"Never."

"Did she try to get away?"

"The door was open," Jason said. "She could have left."

"How do you explain her reaction to you in the cafeteria?"

"Post-traumatic stress syndrome," Jason said. "You know what crap those Alarians have been through. Normal sex with a normal man probably was too alien for her. How should I know?"

John stared at him. He was too smooth. He had easy answers for everything. As if he'd been through this all before.

"Who else have you dated here?"

"Dated?"

"Who else have you had sex with?"

"Oh, no. That doesn't work. You can't use details from another case for this one. That's inadmissible evidence."

"You sound like you've been through this before," John said.

"Bite me, Rayburn."

They sat staring at each other for a long minute. John knew Jason's story wasn't going to change. He'd have to talk to Amalona next.

"Don't go near her or another woman," John said. "Not until the investigation is over."

"Or what, Rayburn?"

"We'll banish you, as far away as we can get you."

Dark circles banded Amalona's eyes. She sat hunched on the chair in Melissa's office. He had met her once, other than the mass escape from the seraglio. He couldn't recall her being anything but a happy young woman. Now she looked haunted.

As he watched her sitting there, John decided that he would make Jason pay if she agreed he had raped her. Impartial judge be damned.

"Tell me what happened between you and Jason Grayborn," John said.

Amalona looked at him with blank eyes. "Who?"

"Jason Grayborn," John said.

"I'm sorry, master, but I don't know who that is."

"I'm not your master," John said.

"I'm sorry to offend," she said, looking down at the floor.

"Jason Grayborn gave you alcohol at the dance last Friday. Do you remember?"

Amalona shrugged.

"You two danced. Then he led you to the barracks where you and he had sex."

Amalona blushed. "I don't think that happened."

"People saw you together. Jason claims you two had sex."

"Why would he say that?"

She seemed to honestly not remember what had happened between her and Jason Grayborn.

"Because it happened. Because he plied you with alcohol and then raped you."

Amalona looked at him in horror. A look of revulsion passed over her face, followed by a rictus of pain. She groaned and flopped from the chair. She began to keen, curled in a ball on the floor. John tried to lift her back up but she recoiled from his touch.

The door opened and Englavira appeared. She had walked Amalona over from her dormitory.

"What did you do?"

John shook his head. "I tried to get her to remember."

"Fool."

"I'm sorry," John said. He stood up while Englavira scurried to lift Amalona to the chair. "But I need her statement."

"We all know what happened," she said coldly.

"We know what probably happened," John said. "A man's life is at stake."

"It is no life," Englavira said sadly.

"Please take her back to the dormitory." As Englavira helped the weak and befuddled Amalona away, John motioned to Devon.

"That was quick," Devon said.

"She doesn't remember anything," John said. "I can't . . . hurt her more."

"Now what?" John looked at the fleshy man dressed in khaki pants and sweater, such an odd contrast to the paranoid man shivering next to a weak fire in Universe 7538. They were doing something good here, weren't they? Would he and his family have died this winter in 7538 if Casey hadn't convinced him? Had it been Casey or had it been Jane, his wife, who convinced him?

John's thoughts turned back to Grayborn's case. Who would convince Grayborn?

"Devon, get me Cecil Inkster."

"Inkster? You got it."

John stood at the window, leaning against the rough wood frame. Melissa was right. This was all his doing. He should have expected something like this to happen. When a thousand near strangers come and live together, people would clash. He had just willy-nilly brought the immigrants together and now they were having problems. And no little problems. Life-and-death problems.

"Maybe John Prime is the better man for this," John said to himself.

He saw Devon dash back toward the community building. Cecil Inkster walked slowly, reluctantly behind. He looked like a man who was in over his head and with no easy way out. What had Grayborn said to him after the first interview? John wondered. The roommate would know the history of Grayborn. He'd know all the foibles. But he was in awe of Grayborn, that was clear.

John waited for Devon's knock, wondering what he could hope to get from Cecil.

"Come in," he called.

Cecil entered, ill at ease.

"Yeah?" he said. Then more boldly, "What do you want? Shouldn't Jason be here?"

"Why? Does he speak for you?"

Cecil flushed.

"So, you know Jason better than anyone, right?"

"I guess."

"Then you know the answer to this question."

"What?"

"How many women has he done this to?"

The color ran away from his face.

"I . . . I . . . don't know. He . . . hasn't ever."

"Really? This is the first time?"

Cecil looked out the window. He was sweating, even in the cool air of the mayor's office. He swallowed.

"He's never raped anyone . . ." Cecil said. Cecil almost added "before" but he held back.

"Never in college with all the women he dated. All those women he hated. This can't have been the first."

"There were a lot of women," Cecil said. "It was all consensual!"

"No bruises, no crying, no begging for him to stop? No alcohol or rohypnol?"

"Never!"

"No hands around the throat? No forced sodomy?"

"No!"

"Did you watch?"

"No!"

"Did you help!"

"Shut up!"

"Did you?"

"Shut the hell up!" Cecil screamed. His face was red. He wheezed, with hunched shoulders.

John fell silent and watched Cecil. He was as much a sociopath as Grayborn, but Cecil was a victim as well.

There was a knock on the door.

"Come in," John said into the ringing silence.

Grace stood there, a folder in her hand.

"I have some research for the case," she said, glancing at Cecil.

"Research?"

"Yeah, you'll want to read this right now." She handed him the folder and then shut the door behind her as she left.

John took the folder, sat behind the desk, and opened it. He knew immediately what it was, a Pinball Wizards, Transdimensional, research report. Grace had sent a request to every settled universe and requested a detailed examination of Jason Grayborn's history in each. Inside the legal-sized envelope were ten separate manila folders.

The first, labeled Quayle-7510, had a single piece of paper that read, *Subject does not exist. No records of parents.* The second, labeled Low-7322, read, *Subject exists and lives in New York City. No police record.* The third was thicker. In Universe 7462—Universe Pinball, so named because it was the only universe they'd found with the traditional pinball game John remembered from 7533—Jason Grayborn had been arrested for sexual assault and released. No charges were filed. The woman's name was not listed.

In Universe 7625, Jason Grayborn had spent two years on probation for sexual assault. The woman's name was listed as Yolanda Kishtan. He raped the same woman in Ten and spent four years in jail. It happened during his college years, time when Cecil Inkster would have been present.

"What happened to Yolanda Kishtan?" John asked quietly.

Cecil's body jerked as if he were on marionette strings.

"What? Who?"

"Did you help Grayborn?"

"I . . . I . . . thought this was about Amalona!"

"How many times has Grayborn done this? How many times have you helped?"

"I never helped! I really liked Yolanda. I'm the one who asked her over, but he's the one who . . . who . . . made love to her after I fell asleep."

"'Made love'?"

"That's what he said. That's what he said. I didn't know."

"How many others?"

"I don't know."

"How many do you know about?"

"I . . ." Cecil dropped his face into his palms. He was bawling; spittle and tears dripped on the floor.

"You let that happen to Yolanda, a girl you liked and that he hurt. How could you do that?"

"I was asleep."

"But you know he did it."

"Yes! I know he hurt her. I know he hurt Yolanda. She cursed me when I visited her in the hospital. I didn't do it. He did." Cecil looked up. "I didn't know he was going to do that to Amalona. I swear. I swear I didn't know he was going to do anything to her."

"But you knew what he was capable of?"

Cecil Inkster nodded sadly. "I knew."

"What did he do to Amalona?"

Cecil shook his head.

John said, "You were there, weren't you?"

Cecil nodded again.

"What did he do?"

"We left the dance with a bottle of booze," Cecil said softly. "They started kissing, but she wasn't into it. She pushed him away. He kept kissing her. Then he lifted up her shirt and . . ."

"You watched," John said flatly.

"Yes," Cecil whispered. "He lets me."

John stared at him. Cecil stared at his hands.

"Did she tell him to stop?"

"Yes."

"Did she try to fight him off?"

"Yes, but . . ."

"What?"

"That's what he likes."

John exhaled.

"Stay here, Cecil. Don't leave this room."

John wrote a note on a piece of paper, folded the paper, and placed it in an envelope. He opened the door to Devon and said, "This needs to go to Home Office right away, and then find me John Superprime."

"You got it."

John shut the door to the office, leaving Cecil inside.

Grace Home came first, as he waited for the others to arrive in Melissa's office.

"He confessed?"

"No," John said. "But Inkster admitted to witnessing it."

"Then it's open and shut."

"I know!" John said sharply. "It's just that . . ."

"It's not murder, John," Grace said. "It's a state execution." Grace's calmness horrified him. She had already accepted Grayborn's death as inevitable.

"I accept that he must die," John said. "He's guilty. It's how we ascertained his death that worries me."

"Cecil Inkster witnessed it."

"But what made Inkster admit that?" John said. "Evidence from another universe."

"It's still Grayborn," Grace said. "He's still guilty of those crimes."

"Then I'm guilty too," John said.

"What? Oh," Grace said. "Prime."

"Yes, if we hold a person guilty of any crimes his or her doppelgangers commit, then I committed every crime Prime did. I am no better than he."

Grace nodded and looked away. "No."

"What do you mean?"

"You aren't Prime," she said simply.

"But we're on the slippery slope—"

"No," Grace said. "Inkster witnessed the rape of Amalona. Case closed. It doesn't matter how we obtained the leverage to make Inkster implicate Grayborn. The fact is, he did it. This Grayson is guilty. There is no doubt. You can't be held accountable for anything Prime has done, nor can Grayborn in any other universe be held accountable for Amalona's rape."

"By the argument, Prime's crimes could be used to implicate me in another crime, simply because it raises a doubt of my innocence."

"But if you weren't guilty, there'd be no problem," Grace said. "John, Inkster was there. He saw it. He says Grayborn did it."

John nodded. "He's guilty. I know it."

"Then we do what has to be done."

Casey came next.

"Come on," she said, staring at him behind Melissa's desk. "Let's walk."

She led him to the northeast along the river.

"How many times have we crossed this river to get somewhere downtown?" Casey said. "And here there's no bridges, no roads, no university. It's amazing, really."

"Yeah." This was a small downtown in nine universes out of ten. But what they saw here was as it had been thirty thousand years before man.

There was a path of sorts, a game trail widened by the colonists who followed the river. Casey kept hold of his hand as they walked.

"Everyone knows what's going to happen," she said. "Everyone here and in every colonized universe."

"I figured when I sent the note, everyone would know pretty fast."

They flushed a quail that chirped at them as it ran into the brush.

After watching it disappear, Casey said, "We think you shouldn't do this thing."

"Grace convinced me he's guilty. I—"

"No, it's not about the guilt," Casey said. "It's about the execution. We don't want you to do it."

"'We'?" he asked.

"Some of the Caseys. Casey Low, Casey Pinball, Casey Case."

"Casey Prime?"

Casey shrugged.

"He's hurt a lot of women. And he will again," John said. "It's our duty to put a stop to this."

"Really? Our duty, and that means your duty? Who made you king?" Casey said. "All you did was find a device. All you did was be in the wrong spot at the wrong time. It's not *your* duty at all."

"When we decided to bring those colonists here, we took on this responsibility," John said. "Maybe not explicitly, but it was there. Society demands we do this."

"Exile him," Casey said simply. "Send him to 1000 or 2000 or 3000. Someplace far away."

"He'll hurt someone else."

"So?"

"You can't be callous to that! He'll rape again."

"No, I'm sympathetic," Casey said. "But you're my concern. This path—where you are arbitrator and executioner—I don't want it for you."

John nodded. "I can't ask someone else to do it."

"If you won't exile him, have Prime do it."

John swallowed. Prime would do it. Prime would pull the trigger.

"No, I can't do that."

Casey turned and faced him. "I'm begging you, John, not to do this."

John looked into her eyes. He'd told himself that he'd do anything for her. Yet, Jason Grayborn was a vile human being that had to be put down. He'd made the decision.

"They'll be here soon," he said. "I need to go back."

He turned to go, but Casey didn't follow.

John waited until all of them arrived. Ten John Rayburns stood on the hill across the river, with Jason Grayborn standing in the middle of them, shackled at his wrists and ankles. They'd used the one boat to cross the river. John had wanted their destination to be within a short walk, but not easily accessible. Only John carried a gun.

On the far side of the river, near the boat dock of the settlement, a group of settlers stood and watched silently. It had not taken long for the news to spread. Among them, he spotted Casey Home standing next to Grace Home.

"Let's go," John said.

He led the way. John Superprime took Grayborn's shoulder and guided him forward.

"I didn't do anything!" he cried as he took a step. "It's her word against mine! You can't do this!"

"Shut up, Grayborn," John Superprime said. "Or we gag you."

"There are rules! You can't punish me like this!"

Superprime punched him in the gut and Grayborn doubled over. He drew back to punch him again, but John stopped him.

"Don't. Let him whine his last minutes away if he wants to," John said.

Grayborn stood erect slowly. He didn't try to speak again as they set off toward the copse of trees.

No one else spoke as they walked slowly to the line of trees, limited by the short gait of Grayborn's shackled legs. Once, he fell, stumbling in a gopher hole. He grunted, but none of the Johns stepped forward to help him up. Gritting his teeth, he stood and the group continued on.

"I'll go on alone," John said when they reached the trees.

"No," John Ten said. "We'll come."

"No," John said. "This is my job."

One hand on the pistol in its holster, one hand on the shoulder of Jason Grayborn, John led him into the trees. The winter sun, already weak, disappeared behind the masses of gray tree limbs, but not so much as to leave them in darkness. The air was musty.

The land sloped down into a small hollow, a gorge three meters deep that ran to the northeast, dug out by spring rains over the years. John helped Jason down and stood him against the dirt wall.

"This isn't justice. It's just her word against mine," he said. "You're creating a fascist state where you're the godlike leader. Fear is what you'll get out of this. Not justice."

"This isn't just for Amalona," John said. He took a sheet of paper from his pocket and read a list of names, "Yolanda Kishtan, Jennifer O'Reilly, Cathy Reese, Quinn Pollank, Martha Abble, Julie Balusha, Gabriella Freeman."

Jason Grayborn looked at him in shock. "Where'd that list come from? Who'd you talk to?"

"You're the same in every universe."

Jason looked at him dumbly, and then he smiled. He laughed, a huge belly laugh of pure joy.

"You fool!" Grayborn cried. "Punishing me for things I didn't even do. This is worse than fascism. This is thought control."

"I'm sure you raped Amalona," John said. "Cecil Inkster confirmed it. There's no doubt that this instance of you deserves to die."

John Rayburn took the gun from the holster, turned off the safety, and aimed the revolver at Grayborn's chest.

Jason Grayborn stared into the mouth of the gun, and said, "And every one of us in every universe will continue to live, and breathe, and be the despicable beasts you fear. There's nothing you can do about—"

John fired a single shot into Grayborn's heart, and he was flung backward. His body twitched in the collection of brown leaves and then he lay still, dead.

Nausea rocked John's body, and uncontrollably he fell forward onto the wet, leaf-covered ground. He vomited bile.

He felt a hand on his back. A John stood above him. Another John lifted him up by his shoulder. The first handed him a handkerchief to wipe his mouth. John turned to find all nine of the others standing there.

"What have we done?" John said.

No one spoke, but they all crowded close, each placing a hand on his shoulder or chest or back. John breathed in deeply. He felt his guilt and nausea drift away.

In unspoken agreement, they left Grayborn's body to the elements and animals. His would not be the first body to be buried in the New Toledo cemetery. There would be no honor for the guilty.

CHAPTER 30

After getting Henry's frantic call, John drove straight to the quarry. He found Henry engrossed over a video camera.

"Tell me," John said.

"This is 7351. John Champ's world."

John peered over Henry's shoulder. He wasn't certain what he was looking at. The camera was panning over a blackened, charred ruin. Then he recognized the back wall of the quarry transfer building in 7351.

"What happened?" John said.

"We hadn't gotten a packet from 7351 in three days," Henry said. John tried to remember details of 7351. The seventh settled universe, where John's basketball team had won the state championship. Thus its nickname, Universe Champ. All four of them were in that universe: John, Grace, Henry, and Casey. They'd taken Clotilde there when she'd fallen ill after the cat-dog attack. Otherwise he could remember nothing about it, who was president, what the key technologies were. His mind was a blank.

"What happened to the transfer gate?"

"I'm getting to that!" Henry snapped. "Sorry. I'm trying to figure it out. I sent an emergency packet. No response. That's the packet right there on the ground," Henry said, pointing to the leather satchel.

"So I set up a reconnaissance camera," Henry said. John remembered that Henry was devising various ways to gather intelligence on a remote universe. He'd settled on a helium-filled balloon with onboard stabilizers. Even in a twenty-kilometer-per-hour wind, the balloon would remain motionless in relation to its starting position. He'd added a rotating mount for the video camera that panned the local area. "I cycled it through for thirty seconds. This is what I got."

"It's a total mess."

"I think someone triggered the self-destruct on the transfer gate."

"No!" Their argument for the self-destruct devices had been simple. They couldn't let the technology get into the hands of a local government. It was too easy to build a transfer gate and if an entire universe had access to it, there'd be travelers everywhere. Henry had added an explosive device to each transfer gate with a simple double switch to activate it on a thirty-second timer. John had never expected that anyone would have to use it.

"Yeah, I think so."

"And there's been no sign of John Champ or anyone else in that universe?"

"None. Their gate is down. There's no way they can get to us."

"Send me there," John said.

"Hold on," Henry said. "The quarry area has been compromised in that universe. You can't go there from here. It's too dangerous."

"I can't use my device to go backwards," John said.

"Transfer from Pleistocene," Henry said. "The gate at New Toledo is close to Toledo." The problem with the transfer gates was that they were fixed in their location. The gates located at the quarry would always transfer to the quarry in another universe. John's personal unit was not so hampered, only it transferred upward in universe number; it could never go back. Positioning the devices at the quarry in all universes was convenient until situations like this came up.

"Send me through to 7322," John said. 7322—Universe Low— was their farthest downstream settled universe, the only one farther downstream than 7351. "I'll come into 7351 from there using my device. If things are no good, I'll come back here."

"Okay," Henry said. "You gotta be careful. Maybe we should send a couple people. Or—"

"It'll be okay. Send me."

"Okay, okay." John waited while Henry powered up the gate. "Be careful!"

"I will."

"Oh, wait!" Henry ran and grabbed a backpack off the wall. "Survival pack. In case. It has a gun."

John took it, though he was unsure how he felt carrying a firearm after the events with Jason Grayborn.

"Who knows about this?" John asked.

"Just us, and my Grace."

"Better put together a warning not to go near 7351 until we figure this out."

"Right," Henry said. "Here we go. Three . . . two . . . one."

The room shifted, and he was in 7322. Grace Low looked up.

"Oh, I wasn't expecting anyone, John," she said.

"I'm John Home," John said.

"Oh, sure," she said, but John already felt the odd change in manner—an odd reverence—he could expect from people who didn't know him, even from these versions of Grace, Henry, and Casey who he felt he should know. He wanted to shout that it was just dumb luck that put the transfer device into his hands. Nothing else.

"We have a problem in 7351," John said.

"I haven't heard anything from them in three days," Grace said. "I was beginning to worry."

"The self-destruct on their gate was triggered."

Grace's eyes went to the switch near her desk.

"Oh, shit."

"Yeah, I need a ride out to Grover Estates, in Toledo," John said.

"Is that where Grace and Henry live in 7351?"

"Yeah," John said. "The quarry site is probably compromised. I'll try reaching them at home."

"Right. I'll call John to drive you over."

As darkness approached, John found the address in 7322, Universe Low, for Grace's and Henry's house in 7351. He had no idea if the floor plan was the same or even if the house was in the same exact location.

"How about that line of trees there?" John Low said. A clump of old trees marked the boundary between two subdivisions. With any luck the trees were there in both universes.

"Okay." It would be a three-hundred-meter jog back to the house from there. "Drop me off right there."

"Good luck."

"Thanks." He shook hands with his doppelganger.

"Let us know what's going on, okay?" There seemed to be real fear in John Low's voice.

"As soon as we know."

The car turned around and disappeared around the corner. John found a moss-covered boulder among the trees, something that looked like it had been there for millennia. He stood next to it, changed the universe count to 7351, and pulled the lever.

The same boulder, the same subdivisions.

"Good," he whispered. He knelt and dialed the device to 7535—the Pleistocene world. In case he had to transfer out, he wanted the device ready. John peered up the street toward Grace's and Henry's house. Nothing moved.

He walked slowly, nonchalantly down the sidewalk, his eyes open for some sign that something was amiss. Nothing on this late-winter night. Old gray snow clumped in piles near mailboxes, having melted in the day's sun and ready to freeze again at dusk.

A car turned down the street. The beams of the headlights danced past him. The car continued on.

He stopped in front of the house. No lights were on. He opened the mailbox. It was crammed with mail. No one was home, and no one had been home for days.

John paused. He took a step toward the front door. Then he saw the driveway. When had it snowed in 7650? Two days ago? Their driveway was clear. The walkway was clear. The house had a northern exposure—the walkway to the house would not have seen the sun. Someone had shoveled since the incident at the transfer gate three days prior.

It didn't mean anything, his mind said. They could have hired a neighborhood kid to do it whenever it snowed.

John took a step up the driveway. He looked around. Nothing. No alarms. No one was watching. The street was clear.

He walked up to the door, tried it. It was locked. He remembered where Grace and Henry of his universe hid their spare key, in a magnetic box under the rail at the far end of the porch. He found the key there.

He turned back toward the door and stopped.

There were tracks in the unmelted snow under the window. Boot prints.

Soldiers—or armed persons of some sort—had been here in the last two days.

Maybe it was just the police.

But why the police?

Because the quarry was owned in the name of Pinball Wizards, Inc., in this universe, and Henry and Grace were part owners. That's why. They were just looking for answers.

But would the police shovel the driveway?

John turned and walked down the driveway.

Over his breath, over the scrape of his shoes on the concrete, he heard the whoosh of wind above him.

He ran.

They'd been discovered by the local government! Somehow they'd tipped their hand and been found out. One of the team here had triggered the self-destruct and was either captured or dead. And the police—maybe the army!—had staked out the house to find their associates.

John had walked right into it.

He left the sidewalk behind, dodging between houses. The sound seemed to follow him. Helicopter. He risked a glance over his shoulder.

A faint light dipped over the roof of the house to the right.

He ran across the backyard, between trees, past an aboveground pool, over a hedge.

He realized he had to stop and transfer out. Was he safe here?

He ducked around the corner of the next house, sucking in air as he leaned against the cement. The whirl above him was muffled. He heard footsteps.

John crouched lower between the trash can on one side of him and the hose reel on the other.

A dark shape appeared in front of him. The soldier was dressed in all black, with no insignia. He carried a rifle, but it seemed too sleek, too rounded. He didn't recognize the model.

The soldier stood there, scanning the area. His eyes seemed to pass right over John but didn't stop. The man waited ten seconds, fifteen, peering into the darkness. Then he reached to his shoulder and tapped something.

He spoke words that weren't English, and then he ran forward into the darkness.

John pressed the switch on the device and transferred to 7535.

They convened in the common room of the New Toledo settlement. Though one of the other universes would have had more modern conveniences, 7535 was the only one where ten sets of identical people could meet and not cause a disturbance that would have to be explained.

Grace took a roll call. All four of them from 7322, 7462, 7512, and 7650: quartets from Low, Pinball, Gore, and Home. John and Henry from 7458, Universe Gold. John, Grace, and Henry from 7510, Universe Quayle. John Prime and Casey from 7533. John from 7601, Universe Ten, though he spent a lot of his time in 7535, the Pleistocene. John, Henry, and Casey from 7625, Universe Case. And Grace and Henry from 7651, Universe Top. Twenty-nine board members, with four missing from 7351: John, Henry, Grace, and Casey Champ. John Superprime was there as well, though they had yet to vote him onto the board.

This was the first time they had all met together in one place.

When the last of them arrived, John stood and raised his hands for their attention.

"I wish this were a better time for us," he said. "I wish we were all meeting under perfect circumstances. But urgent matters have come to our attention." He paused. "I think we can dispense with introductions," he said with a smile. There was an abrupt bark of laughter from the group. "You all know me as John Rayburn, originally John-7533 and now John Home. You all are the board members from every settled universe of Pinball Wizards, Transdimensional, except for one universe."

His colleagues looked around at each other.

"Four days ago, the self-destruct on the transfer gate in Universe Champ was triggered, obliterating the transfer mechanism. I traveled there yesterday, going to Grace's and Henry's house in 7351. It was empty. Worse, it was a trap. Soldiers were watching the house, waiting for someone to come."

There were mutters and quiet words.

"The local government?" a Henry asked.

"Not the local government," John said. "I thought so at first. That we had somehow let ourselves be spotted in that universe. But I think it's worse than that. The soldiers did not speak English, or any other language I recognized. Not even Alarian."

"Shit."

"We've been avoiding the truth, I think. We thought with Visgrath dead and Charboric banished, with Grauptham House under our control, we'd be safe. But the fact remains that someone put the Alarians in 7650. Someone banished them to one of our universes for transgressions. There is an entity—called the Vig—that takes it upon itself to police the multiverse."

"Who?"

"I don't know. But I think we've run afoul of them somehow."

"Where are John, Casey, Henry, and Grace Champ?" someone asked.

"We don't know."

"We have to find them!" This was Grace Home, he knew, fearing for anyone who might have been held captive.

"We have to be careful," John said. "But, yes, I want to go back to 7351 to find them."

"Not by yourself!" one of the Johns said.

"No, not by myself."

"We need to take it to these bastards!"

"Yeah!"

"Hold on, hold on!" John said. "They probably have a lot more resources than we do. They are organized and mean and have professional soldiers."

"But we're smarter," a Henry said.

"And we have ten universes to call upon," Casey Gore said.

"And a multibillion-dollar corporation," Grace Top said.

John sighed. "I have faith in every one of you. I do. But I fear we've run across something too great for us to handle. I couldn't stand for any of you to be hurt. I will not—"

"—allow it?" Grace Home finished for him. "We are not all your responsibility, dork. Stop trying to make everything perfect."

"Uh, yeah, I guess so."

"Yeah, that's right. What's your plan?"

"Here's what I think," John said. "They need to remain as secret as we do." The Johns returned his smile. They knew where he was going.

CHAPTER 31

"That's the last of the gold," Grace Home said. "We have a hundred thousand in cash in this universe ready. If we need more, we can convert more gold."

"That should be enough," John said. They had rented the same warehouse in Universe Champ that they used in Home Office to reach the Pleistocene universe. It was the command center, and the site of the biggest gate they had ever built. Henry Home and Henry Top were managing the construction of two more secondary gates in other corners of the city. One was near Grace's and Henry's house at Grover Estates in Universe Champ, about three kilometers away in an old textile factory. And another was near Casey's and John's apartment about fifteen kilometers to the northeast of Grace's and Henry's house. The warehouse was about halfway between the two auxiliary sites.

A circle to mark incoming transfer zones was in the center of a mass of supplies and equipment. John Prime had shown up with M16 rifles, body armor, and grenades.

"Where did you get that?" John had asked.

"Uh, trade show in my universe. No licenses needed for this stuff," he said. "Do you believe it?"

"Uh, I guess," John said, but before he could ask more questions, someone shouted out.

"The house across the street from Henry's and Grace's house is up for rent. I've got a call in to a broker. We should have access by the evening."

They'd put a bank of phones in that morning, a rush order with the local phone company. John wondered what the line jockeys had thought putting ten phones on a table in the middle of an otherwise empty warehouse. One of their surveys had run across a world in which portable phones were commonplace. Not so in any of their settled universes, though it would have been very convenient to have pocket-sized walkie-talkies to let people know what was going on.

"Good," Grace Home said.

These transactions were going through the Pinball Wizards company in this universe. John hoped no one was tracking that. How much influence and power did the Vig have in a random universe? Did they keep a presence in every universe?

John Case entered the warehouse and motioned to John. Each of the Johns had taken to wearing a unique identifier, a beard style, a haircut, that made differentiating easier. The Caseys all wore their hair differently. But the Graces and Henrys might as well have been just two persons for all he could tell them apart.

"We have some bad news," John Case said. He carried a stack of newspapers in his hands. "Here's the Findlay papers from three and two days ago. There was a body in the wreckage of the quarry warehouse."

"Who?"

"Undetermined. They don't say in either of these two papers."

"Call the coroner. Then call the sheriff. See if there's been an identification."

"Right."

He grabbed a Grace's shoulder. "How much activity are we putting through the company here?"

She nodded. "You think it might be tracked?"

"The quarry site was owned by Pinball Wizards here. They all worked for the company. Whoever's after us may be watching the company."

"That would require some sort of warrant, some sort of government interaction."

"Yeah, but . . ."

"Right. Cash transactions where possible."

"Yeah."

"We'll go through our cash faster that way."

"Then we'll have to launder more money."

"Right."

John turned as a Henry came up to him. "We've got the courier set to deliver the package to John's and Casey's apartment in twenty minutes."

"And they'll ring the doorbell for five minutes?"

"Yeah, I told them to get a signature and that the occupants are hard of hearing. They'll wait at least five."

"Who's watching?"

"We've got a private investigator watching the front of the complex. He knows about the package."

"He's taking pictures?"

"Yeah, he's got line of sight of the door through a window. Not perfect, but he can see if anyone opens the door."

"Good."

There were a lot of pieces in play, John thought. Too many things for him alone to keep straight. Yet, he had the most dedicated, self-directing team anyone could ask for. Consensus was easy to reach with this group, and he was likely to agree with any decision one of his doppelgangers happened to make. They were an army of Johns, a fleet of Caseys, an air wing of Henrys, and a corps of Graces.

"Have we checked the offices yet?" he asked aloud to no one.

"The office is in a business complex in Smerna," a Henry said.

"We called the office manager there, and they told us the office was locked tight, and no one had been there in three days. She was holding some packages for them."

"Let's check all the parents' houses," John said. "They could be hiding out there."

John heaved himself into a chair and watched the chaos around him. They'd find out what happened here, sooner or later.

A Henry set down one of the phones.

"That was the PI at Casey's and John's apartment complex. No one answered the door, even after five minutes. The courier left the box."

"Anything else?"

"Yeah, a guy exited a van in the parking lot, entered the building, and looked at the package before returning to the van."

"Did he get pictures?"

"Yep, of the van and of the guy. He wants to know if he should get them developed or keep the surveillance up."

"I want the pictures. And get the license plate number now."

Henry read off the license number. John wrote it down and handed it to John Prime.

"You think you can find out who this is registered to?"

"Duh." He took the number and grabbed one of the phones.

"Social engineering," John said to the Grace walking past.

"Sounds devious to me."

"Hey, yeah," John said, his mind fumbling with something. "Can someone go pick up the packages at the Pinball Wizards office in Smerna?"

A Grace and a Henry volunteered.

"Take some protection!" John called. "We need bodyguards or something."

"No sign of them at any of the parents' but they're all worried, and there have been enquiries from others," someone called.

"Enquiries?"

"Someone's looking for the four."

John nodded, taking that as a good sign. If they were in the custody of the Vig, then the Vig wouldn't be looking for them. But what about the dead body found in the wreckage of the transfer gate?

"That van," John Prime said, "was rented three days ago to an Agnes Ulysses, along with three other vans."

"You got the license plates on those, make and models?"

"Of course. All are black, all are the same Tucker Comet van."

"Pass the descriptions and license numbers around. We know what they're driving at least."

"Where'd they get the helicopter, though?" Prime asked.

"Probably brought that through a transfer gate. Cars are hard to disguise if they're a weird make and model. Aircraft? Not as easy to say it doesn't belong here."

"True."

Four vans of bad guys and one helicopter. They needed to apply some heat, make it hard to operate.

"What can we do to make the police help us by flushing these guys?" John asked.

A Grace said, "Call in crimes with the vans as the getaway car? Hit-and-run incidents?"

"We need bodies to make that real to the police. A fake hit-and-run won't work," Prime said.

"Think on it," John said. "If we can get them tripped up, it'll free us to work more in the open."

"I'm on it," Prime said.

John Prime took an overcoat from the rack and hid explosives in the huge inner pocket. He looked over his shoulder as he did so, making sure no one noticed. Farmboy had asked him to trip the enemy up, and that he could do. The explosives were something he'd found at an army base in 9000.

The wind swirled around him as he left the warehouse. A meticulous Henry marked his exit on a pad of paper.

"How long will you be out, John?" he asked.

"Sixty minutes."

"Okay."

The warehouse was on the edge of Toledo's small downtown.

Prime headed away from it, into a grungy, run-down area. He wanted to be a good distance from the warehouse, but he also wanted a desolate unpopulated area.

He found it, fifteen blocks away—an empty factory off the main thoroughfares. The for sale sign on the chain link fence meant the place was empty. He slipped through a hole in the fence, and, looking around for anyone who might be watching, jogged across the lot to the nearest door. It was locked, but twenty meters around the corner, a garage door was partially open. He slid under and blinked at the sudden darkness.

The building smelled of oil and rust. He listened and heard nothing but silence. Perfect.

He took the explosive device from his pocket. It was a simple device, with a timer and huge yield. He had spent an afternoon in Universe 9000 blowing up houses, buildings, and cars.

There was a press machine in the middle of the factory floor. That was as good a target as any.

He set the device on the press and set the timer for five minutes: long enough for him to get away but still be a witness for the next part of the plan.

Prime ran for the garage door. He rolled under it, ran across the lot, and dashed through the hole in the fence. Then he slowed his pace, looking around. A car drove slowly down a cross street, but the driver didn't look his way. He walked casually down the sidewalk.

He was three blocks away when the blast rumbled over him. The concussion pushed his lungs and made him feel like he needed to cough. The fireball rose into the sky like a mushroom cloud. There was a second explosion, then another.

Apparently there'd been some combustibles in the old building.

By the time he got back to the building, there was already a crowd standing at the fence. He slipped in among them. The building crackled and burnt.

"Did you see those Tucker Comet vans that just drove away?" he asked no one and everyone.

"No, man, what did you see?"

"Four vans were parked outside the building just before the explosion. Did you see that? They had stickers from Allbright Rentals," Prime said.

"Yeah, I think so."

He moved away to the other side of the crowd.

"Where'd those black Tucker Comet vans go?" he asked aloud.

"What vans?"

"They were right here before the explosion. Then they just drove off."

"Four vans?"

"From Allbright Rentals, I think," Prime added.

"I think I saw them."

When John Prime heard the sirens, he slipped away, a smile on his face.

"You're sure?"

John turned at the change in Grace's voice. She was on one of the phones.

Her face was pale. She saw John looking at her, and she returned his look with one of dejection. She nodded at something said on the other side.

"His parents saw the body? There was . . . it was identifiable." She paused, her hand shaking. "Thank you."

Grace refused to look up at him as he neared.

"What is it? What happened?" John asked.

"John . . . John Champ is dead," Grace said. "His was the body found in the transfer gate wreckage."

"Oh, no," John said. "Oh, no."

The warehouse floor seemed to waver, and he found himself sitting heavily beside the bank of phones, Grace's hand on his shoulder.

He'd been to universes where he was dead. He'd known universes where he'd never existed. But to know that his decisions had led to the death of one of him. That he was dead and gone in one universe . . .

Everyone was looking at him. He met the eyes of each John. He knew they were all feeling the same guilt, the same anger. He stood

up, and Casey was there to steady him on one side, while Grace
was on the other.

"John in this universe is dead. He died in the explosion of the
transfer gate four days ago. Based on what we know, it was to defend it and our technology from some interuniversal force." He
swallowed. The Vig? "That this . . . entity is still here, still actively
pursuing who is left in this universe, means that Grace, Henry,
and Casey of this universe are probably still alive. We have to do
everything we can to find them. Let's redouble our efforts. I'm
counting on all of you to do everything possible to save them."

John Prime entered the door, looking at the faces, hearing the
last of the speech.

"What happened?" he whispered to a John.

"John Champ died at the transfer gate."

"Oh," Prime said. "At least it wasn't us."

CHAPTER 32

John examined the photographs that the private investigator had
taken earlier in the day.

A sharp-faced, bulky man had walked into the apartment building, looking left and right, and then bent to examine the package
that had been delivered. There was a picture of him waving a wand
of some kind—metal detector?—over the package, then he'd walked
back to the black van. There were pictures of the van, the van's
license plate, and even an interior shot when the van door opened.
There were three other men inside the van. The image of them was
too vague to make out features.

"Ever see him before?" John asked.

"Never," Grace said.

"Is the van still there?"

"As of thirty minutes ago when the PI called in," she replied. He
was back in place after developing the pictures and couriering them
over.

"What if we roust the van?" John Prime asked. He nodded at the rack of automatic weapons.

"These guys are skilled soldiers," Grace said. "We'd lose more good people."

"But we'd have some people to question. We'd get some god-damn answers," Prime said.

"Torture, John? Really?" Grace said with contempt.

He shrugged.

Casey looked up from one of the phones.

"Hey, get this! One of the packages at the office in Smerna has an address listed as 'Pinball Wizards, Transdimensional.'"

John rubbed his scalp. "That may be a clue for us. Bring it in."

"We have a team in the house across the street from Grace's and Henry's house," Grace reported.

"No one noticed?"

"Gray beard and gray-dyed hair," she said. "Canes and a walker. Hopefully no one saw anything but an older couple."

"What is the plan?"

"They've already noted a black van in the neighborhood. Same Tucker Comet model. License plate matches. They can watch it from an upstairs window."

"Do we have direct communication with them?" John asked.

"Yep. Phones were turned on today as well."

"Good."

Another Grace put down a phone. "That was the private investigator. Police just rousted the people in the van. Hauled them all off in a paddy wagon."

"What?" John turned until he found John Prime standing with a smile on his face. "What did you do?"

"You said to apply some heat."

"I said to think about it."

"Thought and done."

"What did you . . . Never mind. Don't tell me."

"They pulled some heavy weaponry from that van," Grace said. "I think they'll be held for a while."

John nodded, his thoughts turning for a moment. "Have the team in the house across from Grace's and Henry's report a suspicious van to the local police. Let's use this situation to our advantage."

"On it," Grace said.

"We know where two of the vans are," John Prime said. "I wonder where the others are?"

"One is probably watching John Champ's parents' house," John said. "The other?"

"Should we drive by the farm and see?" Grace asked.

John shrugged. "Maybe. Let's wait on that." He felt how thin they were. Half the team was out in the field. He didn't want any more unaccounted for.

"Let's check on everyone's location," he said. "Just to . . . check."

"Right."

"Package from the Smerna office is here," Grace said. A Grace and Henry entered carrying a box about ten centimeters on a side. They placed it on a table.

John read the label. "'Pinball Wizards, Transdimensional.' No one but one of us would know to use that name. Dated the day after the attack."

He lifted it. It weighed less than a pound.

Taking a knife from his waist belt, he slit the packing tape and lifted the flaps open.

Inside was a sheet of paper.

He read it aloud, "'We're at the place it all began for us.' It's signed with the letters C, G, and H."

"Casey, Grace, and Henry are okay," Grace said.

"As of five days ago."

John's mind raced. Where it all began?

"The farmhouse?" he said aloud.

"That's where it began for you," Grace said.

"The quarry?" a Henry asked.

"No, the school lab," Grace said. "They probably still have their student IDs, probably are still enrolled in classes. There will be lots of students around. And they have those cots for when you pull an all-nighter."

"Send a team over," John said.

"Hold on," John Prime said. He was standing by one of the windows, peering at the street. "We got trouble."

The window to the street was mostly frosted over, except for one pane of glass that gave an abbreviated view of the sidewalk and curbside out front of the warehouse. John Prime had been keeping a lookout there when he didn't have anything better to do. They were dealing with professionals here, and he'd had a feeling something bad was about to happen. They'd been running over the opposition too easily.

A black Tucker Comet van pulled up to the curb just outside the door. They must have had the Smerna office under surveillance. What did they expect? The Wizards had no idea how to shake a tail or even know for sure that someone was following.

"Hold on," he said. "We got trouble."

"What is it?"

"Black van just pulled up outside."

"All right, team, let's bolt," John Farmboy said. "This site—Site A—is compromised. We have two other locations—Sites B and C—fed by locations in the Home Office. Let's abandon this place now."

John Prime surveyed the room. There were twelve people left in the warehouse, too many for just one transfer. Maybe six could squeeze in the large zone and not worry about severed limbs.

Prime slammed the lock on the door. He ran to the gun rack and grabbed an M16.

"Grab what you immediately need!" John Farmboy screamed. What had started as an orderly evacuation was turning to panic as Graces all grabbed papers and Henrys all tried to configure the gate at the same time.

"Calm down, people!" John Prime yelled. "You!" He pointed at one of the Henrys. "Set the gate for 7650 and a thirty-second timer. Six of you go through first. John and I will bring up the rear."

John Farmboy smiled grimly and joined him at the gun rack. Prime watched him scan the room, looking at it defensibly.

It was far from ideal, just an open room, with several ground-level windows and two sets of doors. Prime glanced at the second set of doors. They were already locked, thankfully. But each set of windows was an easy entryway for commandos. At the far end of the room were a couple of cots for people to crash on. On the other side a hallway led to the back of the building, bathrooms, a supply closet, but what else he didn't know.

He glanced over at the group of Graces, Caseys, Henrys, and Johns milling about the transfer gate.

"Let's go, people," Prime yelled. "Count off six and transfer now!"

One Grace and one Casey were phoning the away teams, one by one, letting them all know Site A was compromised.

"Powering up," the Henry cried. "Huddle in tight."

Six Wizards huddled closely in the transfer zone.

"Fifteen seconds!"

Running shadows crossed the frosted glass near the front of the building.

"Ten seconds."

Prime found himself spinning, trying to watch every window and both doors at once. There was no cover in the center of the room.

"Five!"

There was a banging on the door. The locks rattled. Muffled words echoed as everyone looked in that direction.

The six Wizards disappeared to Universe 7650.

"Reset the gate!" Farmboy said.

Prime aimed his rifle at the door and fired a single shot into the metal.

It thunked there, leaving a depression.

"Thick door," Farmboy said.

"I'd feel safer if the windows were all the same material," Prime said.

"They wouldn't be windows."

Six Wizards remained. Farmboy, Prime, two Henrys, a Grace, and a Casey. Not his Casey, Prime knew instantly. The ring that he had brought her from 9000 wasn't on her finger. Maybe she was Farmboy's Casey.

"Thirty seconds!" the Henry cried.

Farmboy put his weapon down and pulled Grace and Casey into the transfer zone.

"Twenty seconds!"

"Faster!" Prime called.

A pane of glass shattered and a spirally, billowing gas grenade entered the warehouse.

"Tear gas!"

"Transferring!"

The box disappeared and with it Casey and Grace. That left the two Henrys and the two Johns.

Prime realized he should have brought gas masks too. The gas spun out of the gas grenade in clouds. He backed away from it.

Farmboy urged one of the Henrys to the transfer zone, while he reset the device. As soon as he was in the center, John transferred him out.

Prime felt the sting in his eyes. His throat constricted. He forced himself to remain calm. It was just a chemical irritant. Rubbing at it would only make it worse.

Prime backed away from the center of the room until he was against a cement wall. He coughed.

"You next," Farmboy said to the last Henry.

Henry doubled over in a coughing fit. He couldn't even stand in the middle of the transfer zone.

"Lift him!" Prime said. "I'll send you through."

Farmboy lifted Henry up over his shoulder. Prime ran to the control board and cycled him through to 7650.

The window shattered and dark shapes entered the warehouse. And Prime was on his own.

John doubled over as soon as he appeared in the clear air of the warehouse in 7650. Coughing shook his body. His nostrils and eyes burned.

"Don't rub your eyes," Grace said.

Cold water flooded his eyes and face.

"Get him out of the zone!"

Hands dragged him away from the transfer zone. He leaned

heavily against the wall, breathing. The same warehouse, but empty of tear gas, empty of assaulting troops.

"Who's left?" Grace asked.

"Just—" His throat spasmed. "Just—Prime," he managed to say.

Grace snapped orders.

"Someone get to the Pleistocene and make sure no one—no one!—comes through to Universe Champ," she said. "I want everyone who was in Champ accounted for. There are Wizards who don't know the warehouse has been taken. I don't want anyone going back."

Casey—his Casey—handed him a bottle of water.

"You okay?" she asked.

"Yeah, I'm good." He coughed after he spoke. "Well, maybe not."

"Why isn't Prime back here already?" she said softly.

Grace—super-competent Grace—looked over at John, worry on her face.

"Do we send someone back?" she asked.

John shook his head.

"No, we don't have gas masks. Anyone we sent back would be a target."

She nodded. "But where's John Prime?"

John Prime reset the system and powered it back up, setting the timer to ten seconds. His eyes burned, and he realized he couldn't tell where the transfer zone was marked on the floor. The gas as well as his watery eyes made it impossible to see.

"Crap," he said, instantly regretting the flow of gas into his mouth.

He fired the M16 into the windows, blowing them out, one after another. He needed to air the warehouse out, and noise might bring the police. Though how he'd explain the mess was beyond him. That was the least of his worries.

He ducked behind the controls, half hidden by the table they sat on, but not safe. He counted three dark shapes in the warehouse, advancing, scanning. They were probably expecting a more docile, surprised quarry. The Wizards were lucky he'd spotted the bad guys arriving or they would have been taken by surprise. Now the only one to be taken was him.

The system activated and Prime looked up in surprise. The timer had reached ten, and he hadn't realized it.

Cold wind was coming through broken windows. The air was actually clearing, and with it, his cover. He aimed and fired at one of the approaching figures. All of them took cover behind boxes or flush against the floor. They returned fire, and Prime was forced to duck.

He glanced toward the second door. A soldier blocked the way. He was trapped. He couldn't stand in the middle of the room and transfer out. He couldn't reach a door.

One of the soldiers was advancing on him, nearing the transfer zone.

He smiled grimly, reached up, and reset the gate again. No timer. He pressed the switch.

The soldier couldn't even scream as half his body jumped to 7650, while the other half remained in 7351.

Surprise, Farmboy, Prime thought.

One down, four more to go. Five?

Blood flowed across the transfer zone, further obscuring the location.

What now?

The self-destruct mechanism. Enough charge to destroy the device. Enough to concuss everyone in the room. Prime looked behind him. He had twenty meters of empty warehouse behind him. He caught sight of a pile of blankets, next to the cots where some of the Wizards had been sleeping. Maybe it would afford enough of a shelter from the blast. How much C-4 had Henry used?

He reached up with both hands, dropping his weapon first, to press the two buttons on the self-destruct system.

"Bomb!" he cried. "There's a bomb in the room!"

Then he ran, firing blindly into the air. How long was the countdown? Thirty seconds, he remembered.

He skidded into the cots and draped the blankets over his head, burrowing down.

He heard the soldiers moving, barking muffled orders. They weren't panicking. They weren't running.

"Throw down your weapon!"

Prime looked up from under the blanket. Two soldiers stood over him. He couldn't see their faces due to the mirrored masks they wore.

"Yeah, sure. But there really is a bomb over there," he said.

"It does not look like a bomb," a soldier said. "Roll over onto your stomach." In the distance two soldiers were looking at the device. He shrugged and rolled.

Then the device blew.

"Jesus!"

John looked up to see a body appear in the transfer zone. Half a body.

He stood, dragging a blanket off a nearby cot, and threw it over the corpse. It wasn't Prime.

"Get a mop and bucket," he said. "And trash bags."

He and another John donned rubber gloves and dragged the corpse from the transfer zone. Then they forced it into a doubled plastic bag.

"Universe 7535," he said. "We'll dispose of it there." The Pleistocene universe was far too convenient for dumping bodies.

Prime was using the gate as a weapon.

"Keep the zone clear!" he shouted.

Another emergency transfer could happen at any time.

But as the minutes ticked on, nothing more came through. The urge to go back to help Prime became overwhelming.

"Have we heard from the team that we sent to the university lab?"

"Not yet," Grace said. "I don't even have confirmation that they know the warehouse is taken."

"Did you send someone to meet them to let them know that?" John said.

"Yes, of course, John," she said.

"Sorry."

"It's okay."

John checked his watch. It had been fifteen minutes since he'd come through from 7351.

"Do we own this warehouse in Low?" John asked.

One Grace looked at him and shrugged. Another paged through a notebook. She said, "We don't but it's empty."

"Send me there," John said, entering the transfer zone.

John Prime's ears rang. His eyes, filled with grit and dust, hurt when he blinked. His head throbbed. He lay under something heavy. Something black. The world had reverberated, thumped as if it were a giant drum.

He felt a moment of panic and pushed and clawed at the weight atop him.

It was the body of a solider, deadweight. He pushed it away, scrambling back and away. He coughed, but couldn't hear himself do it.

Blinking, he looked down at the soldier.

Deadweight was right. The soldier had shards of wood embedded in his back, debris from the explosion. His arm was nearly shredded.

"Too many pieces of people today," he mumbled. "Too many."

Prime stood up and grimaced in pain. Red flowed from his thigh where a piece of the table that had held the transfer gate controls had embedded itself. It looked like vampire slayers had decided his leg was Count Dracula. The stake of wood pointed perpendicular to his muscle.

"Ouch."

He yanked it out.

"Shit!"

Blood flowed down his thigh, and he felt woozy. Prime looked around for something to stanch the flood. The soldier had a backpack, and when he unzipped it, Prime found a package of bandages. He sat heavily, but when he began to apply the wrapping, he found that the blood had stopped. He wiped the wound and found that already the edges had knitted together.

It must have been a really clean puncture, he thought.

He stood on it, groaning, and wrapped his coat so that the blood on his pants wasn't obvious. Then he wondered what had happened to the other soldiers.

Limping, he walked toward the transfer gate.

It was a ruined hulk. The table was destroyed, scattered like shrapnel. If he had been hit twenty meters away, he was certain everyone closer was dead. All the windows he hadn't shot were broken out.

"Jesus."

He edged near the window, looking for the black van. It was gone.

He heard something, the wail of a siren. His hearing was coming back, but even so that siren had to be very close.

He turned toward the back door and limped toward it.

He unlocked and pushed it open. He exited onto the empty back street and walked as fast and nonchalantly as he could. He got about ten meters before he seemed to fall through the sidewalk. His leg had stopped working. His consciousness fluttered away from him, and the cold disappeared.

The warehouse in Low was dark and quiet. It smelled of dust, undisturbed for weeks and weeks. Good, John thought.

He took off his backpack and rummaged for the flashlight. Finding it, he poured it around the warehouse, until he found the door.

Unfortunately, it was chained and padlocked. He walked to the other door. No padlock on the inside. He pushed at it, but it was locked from the outside.

A door led from the open warehouse floor into some stockrooms and offices. He had no idea what was back there. Maybe another door. He'd hate to have to break a window.

A hallway beyond, drinking fountain, the squeak of a rat. He passed restrooms, another door with a window and a metal grate across it. Then an emergency exit. He pushed the door open and was out in the open, but inside a chain-link fence.

There was no barbed wire atop the fence, so he climbed up and over, startling a couple of people on the sidewalk.

"Evening," he said.

They stared at him and walked on.

He looked left and right. An empty lot was across the street, and he remembered it from 7351. It was the perfect place to transfer from.

He jogged across the road, dodging a car that came out of nowhere. He ignored the horn and jumped over a low gate. The lot had been a flat parking lot during some more prosperous time in this neighborhood. Now its blacktop was broken by brown weeds.

He stood in the center of the lot, toggled the device to 7351, and transferred.

Same lot, same weather, but here sirens wailed. A black van was across the street and someone was trying to drag a body into it. Why was there only one soldier?

John ran, again horns sounded from angry motorists.

The soldier looked up.

It was John Prime he was trying to lift. His bloody body was collapsed on the sidewalk.

The soldier lifted a rifle.

John dodged to put the van between him and the soldier.

Shots fired, ricocheting off concrete.

His back slammed against the van. Where were the other soldiers? Then he saw the smoke rising from the warehouse. Prime had triggered the self-destruct mechanism, and he'd managed to get most of the bad guys. Was this the last one?

John pawed inside his backpack. Did he even have a gun?

Nothing! He had no weapon at all.

He peered into the van. He could see through it to the ground behind. Prime was on the ground bleeding. Where was the soldier?

Keys dangled in the ignition of the van.

John smiled.

He pulled open the door and dove into the driver's seat. The van's engine turned over. He dropped it into drive and floored the gas.

He didn't care if he was leaving Prime. The soldier couldn't kidnap him without transportation.

In the rearview mirror, the soldier looked on blankly, his face

mostly obscured by his helmet and mirrored faceplate. Then he
lifted up his assault rifle and pointed it at the fleeing van. Bullets
slammed into the back of it. John's rear windows starred.

He jerked the van's steering wheel to the right and ducked down
in the seat.

He heard more shots, but not the same caliber, not the same
direction. John opened his door. He heard shouts. Peeking around
the end of the van, he saw police surrounding the downed soldier.
Apparently, they'd seen him fire on the van and had shot him.

John ran toward John Prime, still down on the pavement.

"Hold it!" The police were edgy after the shooting. They didn't
like coming up upon men armed with assault rifles.

"He's my brother!" John said, pointing at where John Prime lay.

One of the officers looked between Prime's face and John's,
then waved him forward.

"We have an ambulance on the way," one of the police said.
John nodded.

He knelt beside Prime and reached into his jacket. He toggled
the universe counter to 7650. He leaned in close to John Prime,
glanced around at the police. One officer was standing over them,
but his attention was diverted by an approaching ambulance. John
pressed the trigger and took him and Prime to another universe.

CHAPTER 33

They'd found Henry, Grace, and Casey in the university lab,
where they had been sleeping and hiding for four days. The casu-
alty that they had suffered was John Champ, dead when he
switched the self-destruct mechanism on the gate when the bad
guys had surrounded the quarry site.

The funeral had been hard. One of their own was dead. And not
just one of their own, one of the Johns was dead. One of himself
was dead.

They'd buried him in the Pleistocene world, in a new cemetery about a kilometer from New Toledo, a day after his parents had placed him to rest in a family plot in 7351. John had not considered their actions to be grave robbing; this was where John Champ should have been laid to rest.

The Alarians had sung a ululating dirge, and it didn't matter at all that it was in the Alarian language. After they had carried the pine wood casket to the cemetery, to a hole that the Johns had dug the night before, the group milled about until Grace Home nudged John, and he realized he would have to speak.

He cleared his throat and stood next to the casket.

"I never expected to stand here and lay a brother to rest," he said. "For eighteen years, I had no idea that I had a brother, so many brothers. And even when this all began, even though we knew the dangers that must exist for us, I never expected that one of us would die.

"I should have realized. I should have known that there are forces that have ideas contrary to our own." He paused. "We have found them because they have found us, and caused us this harm. It scares me that they will kill, kidnap, and harm the people I have surrounded myself with . . . the people that I love. I cannot allow you all to be attacked unchecked.

"We have run up against something larger than the Alarians. Something more nefarious. Something more widespread. And worse, they spied us before we spied them. We must be careful, we must be alert, and we must not allow them to destroy us."

The smattering of applause rippled the audience, and John felt his face go red.

"This is not the time for speeches of war. I'm sorry. John Champ died for us. And that is what we are here to remember.

"John Rayburn of Universe 7351 was loved by Casey of Universe 7351, by his colleagues Grace of Universe 7351 and Henry of Universe 7351. His parents of that universe grieved at his funeral. His high school and college classmates attended and grieved. And we attended in spirit though we could not show ourselves as we wished. That is why we gather here, the four of us—the thirty-three of us—and our friends the citizens of New Toledo."

John surveyed the group, nearly five hundred of them: Wizards,

Alarians, and refugees. A motley crew. They stared at him with calm faces, some tear stained, but all ready to believe him, to listen to him. He felt the crush of their optimism. He felt the sincerity of their belief. And it made his heart ache with the responsibility he had to these people.

"I—I—" John said, unable to speak anymore.

John Prime stepped forward then and took his shoulder. Then other remaining Johns did as well, just as they had embraced following the death of Grayborn. John found his voice again.

"My friends," he said. "I don't know what the future holds, but I believe a fight is on the horizon. I don't want to stand here again. But I think we will. Our enemy wants to kill us. Our enemy has found us. Our enemy has attacked us. I will not ask anyone to fight this battle who does not want to. There are universes enough for those who want to hide. But the time is upon us to find out this enemy and destroy it before it destroys us."

A murmur of approval rippled through the crowd.

"We'll stand with you, John!" Englavira cried.

"Of course we will," Melissa Saraft said. Kylie looked up at him with big eyes. He hoped he was not fooling these people. He hoped he was not fooling himself.

After his words, Casey Champ stood and spoke for a few minutes of her lost love, followed by Henry Champ and Grace Champ. Hearing their stories it seemed they might as well have been about him. When everyone had spoken, they lowered the casket into the ground, and John dropped dirt onto it with a shovel.

Is this the start of our burial traditions? he wondered. Was this how they would gather from now on upon the death of one of their own? Again the weight of his duty shook him to his core. He passed the shovel to John Prime and walked away from the group.

"How did they find us?" Henry Champ asked. "What did we do?"

"I don't know," John said.

"It could have been anything," John Gore said. "Put yourselves in their shoes. Track the differences between universes, wait for something anomalous to appear."

"Track changes," Grace Home said. "It's what we do for arbitrage.

Add more people, add more computers, they could detect anything that shouldn't be there."

"Like pinball," John said.

"Like computers," Prime replied.

"Then we're doomed," Henry Champ said. "They'll find us everywhere."

"They're not omnipotent," John said. "They used normal weapons like any of ours."

"Except for that helicopter," Grace Home said.

"But that's not too far advanced," Prime said.

"Yeah, they weren't robots or anything," Henry Home said, laughing.

"Yeah, right, robots," replied Prime.

"And there weren't more than twenty of them," John added. "One was shot dead. Five were arrested. Four killed in the blast. The rest disappeared."

"By the way, those five that were arrested," Grace Top said. "They skipped bail."

"Imagine that."

"It was a million dollars each."

"It doesn't surprise me," John said. "We have that many resources and we must be tiny compared to them."

"So, what do we do?" Henry Champ said.

John looked at him. "You're going to have to move," he said.

Henry Champ shared a glance with Grace Champ. Casey Champ wasn't there. She'd gone to rest after the funeral. "We guessed as much."

"Universe Champ is closed to us," John said. "There's too much risk of the enemy finding us again."

"If they found us once . . ." Grace Home said, trailing off.

"I know," John said. "I know. We have to curtail what we do in our settled universes. It's too late in 7650. We own Grauptham House. There's no way our shadow can be shortened. But there we have the most resources. We can hire bodyguards. Build defenses that they can't cross."

"You hope," Prime said.

"I hope, yes. I hope."

"But we're not going to sit idle and hope they don't find us," John said. "We need to find them first. We need to take the fight to them."

"How?"

"More surveys, farther afield. More universe mapping," John said.

"You gotta be careful," Prime said. "There's . . . bad stuff out there."

"We know," John said. "I know what you've run up against."

"Not all of it," Prime said softly, but before John could ask him more, Grace Home spoke up.

"So keep the idea transfers between universes to a minimum?" she said. "Don't develop new ideas. Don't make a difference in the universes."

"That's my best guess as to how they found us," John said. "We need to also protect ourselves. Travel in pairs. Go armed at all times."

"Sounds grim," Grace Quayle said. "Like we're running scared."

"Running safe," Grace Home said.

"This universe must be the safest," John said. "There's no human population here save us. There's no way an outsider wouldn't be spotted. Universe 7650 has got to be our biggest risk. We're visible there. We're in the open. We can't hide Grauptham House. But we can't give it up either."

"It's our revenue stream," Grace Home said.

"And what do we do when we find them?"

"Negotiate?"

"No!"

John shook his head. "We understand them. Then we deal with them."

John again went to see the news reporter Joe Cursky in Universe 7539.

"Oh, shit, you again," he said. Cursky looked the same as he always did—weary and wary, tattered and solid—but he had a tired feel about him this time.

"I need some help," John said. They stood at the bar of The Loose Mongoose, just a few minutes after the day shift from the newspaper had left their offices, not that John had seen any swell in the crowd at that time as he waited. The room had been packed at three and was still packed with reporters.

"You gave me a heart attack the last time I helped you. What now? I know you found Saraft. She disappeared."

"You watched for it?"

"I wanted to see what happened."

"I took her someplace safe, for her and her daughter."

Joe shrugged. "What do you want now?"

"If I wanted to see a body at the morgue, a murder victim, who would I ask?"

"What murder? There hasn't been a murder in Toledo in seven days," he said. "Oh, you mean . . ."

"Yeah."

"If it's like this . . . uh . . . place, you go to the night-shift clerk tomorrow after ten o'clock in the evening. Guy by the name of Bob Lauric. Medical student, or was about twenty years ago. Handles the night morgue shift on the weekends. Slip him fifty dollars."

"Lauric."

"Yeah, Lauric," Joe said. He reached out and grabbed John's arm. "Now you gotta do something for me."

John looked at the tight grasp Cursky had on his wrist, but didn't shake it off. "What?"

"I wanna see my dad."

"He's dead," John said.

"Yeah."

"I don't know where your dad is."

"Find it out, buddy," Cursky said. "I want to visit him."

"I'll see what I can do," John said.

"You owe me now."

John called the morgue in 7351 and asked if Bob Lauric was there.

"He's not on till tonight at six," the woman said blandly. "Wanna leave a message?"

"Nah, I'll call back."

It was Thursday, not Friday, but if Lauric was on duty, he'd take fifty dollars to tell him about the body of the enemy soldier shot by the police, or any of the victims of the explosion. John checked his watch. Three hours until Lauric was at the morgue.

John transferred to Home Office.

John sighed as he entered the apartment. Something was cooking on the stove. He heard music playing on the stereo. He couldn't explain to himself how good it felt to be there with Casey.

"Hey, baby," he called.

"Hey, hon," she called back from the second bedroom, their office.

He dropped his coat over the couch, and checked what was on the stove.

"Have you seen these sales projections for our computers?"

"No, but I can guess," John said. "I've seen universes where the personal computer is ubiquitous."

"Yeah, we're going to sell millions of them."

"And make it clear for universes around that we're here," John said.

"And deal with it, just like we dealt with those bastards in Universe Champ, just like we dealt with the Alarians."

"When did you become so confident in us?"

"I got it from you," Casey said.

John lifted the pot lid and wafted some of the smell into his nose. "Casey's famous tomato sauce?" he asked.

"World's famous, actually. I'm helping in the cafeteria in Pleistocene this weekend."

"Funny."

"Speaking of which," she said. "I think we should have the wedding there."

"You realize there are no justices of the peace, no priests, nor any ministers there," John said.

"We can do it officially here," she said. "But the real ceremony, for our friends, should be there."

"Your parents won't be able to attend."

"We'll let them throw us a big party afterwards," Casey said.

"Good thinking," John said. "I need to run back to Champ after dinner."

"Dangerous."

"There's gotta be some clue, some indication of the enemy's presence there," John said. "They lost lives there. They screwed up. But they launched a huge effort to find us, to hurt us. Something has to be left there. Some clue."

"Or this was some small expeditionary force, and now their real army is there waiting for you to come look," Casey said.

"If they had that sort of force in the first place—"

"The universe is a big place. Maybe we're in such a backwater we don't even see the wars being waged," Casey said. "We just don't know."

"I hope not," John said. "We just *don't* know. Which is why I have to look."

She kissed him, her arms wrapped around his neck. "Just be careful."

By eight that evening, the morgue was empty of all its employees save the cleaning staff. John trailed a pair of Slavic cleaners through a first-floor entrance and followed signs to the morgue. The inner room smelled of disinfectant and other less clean smells.

No one was at the front desk, but some sort of rock-and-roll music played from the speaker of a transistor radio.

"Hello?" he called.

No answer came back.

He pushed through a door that said COLD CHAMBER.

The room was twenty meters long and ten meters wide. The temperature was near freezing. Wheeled tables lined one wall and meter-square doors lined the opposite wall.

A bearded, long-haired man in scrubs was leaning over a table with a corpse on it.

"Yeah?"

"You Bob Lauric?"

"Yeah, and what do you want?"

"I want to take a look at a body you have here."

"Shit. Another one?"

"What?"

"It's been a regular turnstile in here this week," he said. "Let me guess. You want to see the death by police victim."

"Uh, yeah."

"Which paper you from?"

"No paper."

"You're not a reporter?"

"No."

The man came around the table and peered at John. "Then what do you care?"

"I'm an investigator. I'm investigating." John reached into his pocket and handed Lauric fifty dollars.

"Nah, the price is up this week. Supply and demand. I need a hundred."

John shrugged. He'd brought more than fifty in case. He fished another bill from his pocket and handed it to Lauric.

"Fine," Lauric said. He pointed at a door. "Number twelve."

There was a handle. John grabbed it and pulled. A pale cadaver lay within. Four bullet holes adorned the body's chest. He had no tattoos, no identifying marks, no jewelry, no clothing. No transfer device.

"Has he been identified?" John asked.

"Hell if I know. No next of kin have been by to see him though."

"Did he have anything on him? A wallet, tools?"

"Keep pulling."

John pulled the corpse out another half meter. There was a plastic box at the body's feet. Inside was a watch, a wallet, a flashlight. Beneath that were a folded shirt, folded pants, and a jacket.

"Police took the guns and ammo."

"Normal guns?"

"As normal as guns can be."

John looked at the watch. No logo. The wallet had no ID, no credit cards, just seventy dollars in cash. There were no tags at the nape of the shirt, nor at the waist of the pants.

"Weird," John said.

"Yep. Nothing on that guy," Lauric said. "You want to see the other one?"

"What other one?"

"Number thirteen," Lauric said.

John glanced at the drawer below twelve. He pushed twelve in and pulled thirteen out.

It looked like a slab of beef.

John realized in a moment it was the soldier John Prime had sliced in half with the gate.

"Jesus."

"Yeah, we don't have the other half of him," Lauric said. "Very odd."

John knew where the other half was.

"How many died in the blast? Where did those bodies go?"

"FBI took the bits and pieces we could find," Lauric said.

"How many died?"

"Three? Five? Seven? Dunno." Lauric looked quickly at the clock. "All right, you gotta go."

"Why?"

"Because . . . because my manager is coming by to meet with me," Lauric said. "I can't have you here then. You saw, now go."

John didn't have a reason to argue. There was no clue to be had on the corpses. They were clean of any sort of identifying mark. There was no abnormal technology. No clue. There was nothing to find here.

"Thanks, Bob," he said.

He left the morgue and headed back the way he came. Exiting the door, he found himself face-to-face with three men dressed in black leather jackets. They pushed past him and into the city building. John thought nothing of it, until he saw the black van idling near the curb.

He walked quickly, head lowered as if to avoid the cold, toward his car. He couldn't see if someone sat at the wheel of the van, but he didn't make himself obvious by staring. His rental was in the lot across from the city building, not quite with a clear view of the van. John pulled out and found another slot a little farther down and with clear sight of the front door and the van.

Ten minutes passed, and no one entered or exited the building or the van. Finally, one of the three who had squeezed past him appeared and waved.

The van dropped into gear and drove slowly down the street until it reached an alley. John pulled out of his spot and followed. He peered down the alley but did not turn into it.

The van had backed up against a loading dock. John looked in the rearview mirror; no one was behind him. He stayed there for a few seconds. Bob Lauric appeared, pushing a gurney. The three men grabbed the bagged body and settled it into the back of the van. A minute later, Lauric appeared with a second body bag.

John pulled a little way forward and waited. When the second bag had been placed in the van, the three men entered the side door and the van turned back toward the main street.

John ducked down as the van pulled past, then followed at a leisurely pace. It accelerated onto the interstate and headed north for several kilometers before it pulled off onto a state highway.

It was just John's car and the van, so John let himself fade back a little. The van couldn't go far without his seeing its taillights.

About ten kilometers along the highway, the van turned into a long driveway. John noted the address as he passed and continued on.

He pulled off at the next drive and watched the van's lights disappear into a patch of trees. Even through the trees, he could see its headlights wash tree trunks and patches of white snow on the ground. It stopped not too far into the trees.

John left his car where it was, at the end of the driveway of a dark house, hoping it would be fine there.

He ran across the frozen, tundralike field. Severed cornstalks grabbed at his feet.

John reached the driveway and paused. He could smell the exhaust smoke of the van, and just ahead, he heard the rumble of the van's engine.

The driveway dropped off to either side into a drainage ditch filled with drifted snow. He had no choice but to take the driveway. Ducking low, he followed the gravel path.

He'd only gone a few meters when he heard arguing voices.

Definitely not English, he decided, not Alarian, nor anything he recognized.

As he came nearer, lights flared. He thought the van had turned around toward him, but no. Overhead security lights now illuminated the open area in front of a large barn. Farther up the drive was an old farmhouse. But it was the barn that the van was parked in front of. Four men from the van were talking with a fifth that had emerged from the barn.

Inside the barn was a vehicle the likes of which John had never seen. It looked like a harvester at first, but no combine bristled with weapons like this one did. John could only assume those were weapons. It was dull black, two stories tall, and sitting atop six huge, studded wheels. It was wider than three normal cars. A ramp led up to a gaping doorway, but he could see little of the interior.

The vehicle was a war machine of some sort, he was certain. But what point was there to bring such a thing to this universe? Its very appearance would have excited comment and immediate response. Why bring the thing through at all?

John scooted off the driveway and into the ditch. Trying not to disturb the snow, he took shelter under a pine tree. The trunk was sappy, but the ground immediately below the branches was free of snow. It felt like a bunker from which he could observe the enemy.

Whatever conversation the five were having ended and two of them started dragging the body bags from the black van. They dumped them on the ground. There was no ceremony involved, no ritual. They hadn't retrieved the bodies to honor them.

The fifth man wore a mask over his face. John had assumed it was for the cold, but the mask looked like a gas mask. It was black and the shield was reflective. He stood back from the other four as if he were in charge.

He gestured for the two carrying the bodies to stop; he asked a question. One pointed to one of the bags, which the masked man ordered them to open. Based on the size, John guessed it was the corpse that had been cut in half.

The masked man squatted and looked at the body, but did not touch it. He asked a question, muffled by the mask. The same man shrugged a nonanswer.

The masked man barked a harsh question. He brought his hand down in a cutting motion. John guessed he was asking about the other half of the corpse or why it was cut in half. John knew the morbid answer.

The masked man made another gesture and the other man zipped the bag closed again. The two continued dragging the bags into the huge machine.

John heard a humming. A wind blew a gust of snow across the drive. The masked man looked up, and from the sky a machine landed in the drive. It was just a few meters long and a couple wide. A single pilot sat in the front of it. As it landed, John heard very little sound at all. Clearly, this silent aircraft was what had chased him from Henry's and Grace's house in this universe.

John watched as the pilot dismounted, and then began folding the flying machine, bending wings and struts into the fuselage until it was no bigger than a meter by a meter. Then he and another of the men from the van rolled it onto the large vehicle.

The masked man gave an order and everyone ran toward the machine, up the ramp, and into the machine. The leader was the last to leave and scanned the frozen drive before disappearing into the vehicle's maw.

John heard a humming, a deep throb that reached him through the ground. He wanted to flee, but he held his ground under the pine tree.

With a whoosh, the vehicle disappeared. Air seemed to suck him in, and then just as quickly it pushed him back. He gasped, realizing he'd been holding his breath.

He'd just seen a transfer device, the first time ever he'd seen one besides the one on his chest and the ones he had built from scratch. It was embedded in that monstrous machine, and it transferred it en masse. The power of it shook the earth and collapsed the air around it when it moved.

John crawled forward, out from under the tree, and stood slowly in the knee-high snow. The Wizards were truly up against someone who had the same technology they had. He had seen it, someone else had transdimensional traveling ability, and they were after the Pinball Wizards.

He'd known it, but now he'd seen it.

John stepped forward onto the driveway. He glanced at the farmhouse. It was dark and apparently empty. The snow to the side door was undisturbed. The enemy had wanted the farm for its large garage only. They'd needed someplace to store their war machine, someplace out of sight.

John pulled open the van's side door. No black-clad enemy lurked within, just the antiseptic smell of the morgue clinging to the unfinished cargo area. Otherwise the van was empty. He reached under the front seats, checked the glove. Nothing.

John peered into the garage. Indented in the dirt three centimeters deep was the tread imprint of the tires of the behemoth. Even in the cold, frozen ground, the thing had left impressions. John scanned his flashlight around the dark corners. Nothing.

He turned, glancing one last time before starting for his rental car. He'd seen them, he'd found them, and now the enormity of their enemy had been driven home. There was more, he realized. He'd seen their transfer devices. He'd seen them and how they acted. They could use all that information.

He had taken no more than three steps when he was knocked flat.

The whoosh pushed John down, and as he fell, he turned to see the machine hulking over him, just meters away.

"Shit!" he cried, struggling to get up in his bulky winter coat.

Lights flared. He ran, aiming for the tree he had crawled under. Shouts sounded behind him.

He dove under the tree, flattening himself against the ground. Something whizzed through the air near his head. A stream of bullets turned the trunk of the tree into Swiss cheese. Splinters rained down in front of his eyes. Only there was no explosion of gunpowder, no rat-a-tat-tat of machine-gun fire. The gun was using some other method of launching projectiles. Some silent way.

The tree keeled over, exposing him to the sky and light. Something heavy hit his shoulder. A webbing of some kind, sticky and thick. He tried to shake it off, but the stuff was glued to him.

He reached into his jacket to trigger the device, to get him out of there, but his right hand wouldn't move. The sticky webbing had pinned his right arm against his torso.

"Shit!"

The projectiles had stopped. Lights focused on him. He lifted his head up, trying to see what was happening.

John's left hand was plastered against the ground too.

The ramp of the machine had lowered. Two men ran out, armed with rifles, and crouched there, staring at his location.

He rotated his torso, trying to get his left arm out of his sleeve from the inside. The webbing seemed to tug tighter. He groaned. Sweat beaded on his forehead and froze there.

Suddenly his arm came loose. He exhaled.

His left hand was trapped between his coat and his shirt. He grabbed at his buttons, trying to get to the device. He could feel it under his shirt, but he couldn't work the controls through the flannel.

A shadow passed across his head. He looked up at the two soldiers. Their expressions were cold, as they aimed their rifles casually at him.

"I'm— I'm— from next door," John said. "I didn't see anything."

"Nice try," one said, in a slightly accented voice. "We know who you are, John Rayburn."

John worked at the button on his shirt.

"Who?"

He ripped at the shirt and a button popped.

John snaked his hand into his shirt and pressed the button on the device. Nothing happened.

"Freeze, Rayburn," the soldier said. "The goop is only going to get tighter."

John's mind raced. Why hadn't the device worked? Then he realized he'd forgotten to set it to another universe. It was still set to the current universe. He toggled the universe counter, hoping 7352 was a nice universe, and pressed the transfer button again.

He was back under the tree, still plastered in the sticky webbing.

John exhaled. Safe. That had been closer than he wanted it to be.

He tried to sit up. He couldn't. His predicament wasn't over. He was still encased in webbing.

Peering over his shoulder, he tried to see around his hood at his body. Blobs of white stuck to his shoulders, torso, and legs. But there was less of the gunk. He'd transferred past most of it.

John realized he'd have to crawl out of his clothes, just as he'd pulled his arm out of the sleeve to trigger the device. He'd have to squeeze out of the neck of the coat without getting any of that stuff on his body.

But not in this cold universe.

Using his left hand, he unzipped his coat and looked down at the display on the device. He dialed it to the Pleistocene and pressed the transfer button.

He was on the plain in the Pleistocene world. Dark, cold, but not as cold. The sky was cloudless and the half-moon gleamed silver, casting the waving grass as swords. Bearable, he decided, and pulled himself out of his coat carefully. To the north he saw a jutting of rock; he'd seen the same formation in 7351.

He stood shivering in his flannel shirt looking down at the gunked winter coat.

"At least the run to New Toledo will keep me warm," he said to himself.

Getting a clear bearing on the North Star, John began his run, at least ten kilometers in the dark, hopeful that he wouldn't come across any smilodons or a nest of the cat-dogs.

CHAPTER 34

He had to turn south twice to ford a river, finding shallow rapids of icy-cold water, and so approached New Toledo from the west. By chance he looked in the sky, away from the rising sun, and caught a flash of silver.

"Shit!" he screamed. It was the flying machine.

The enemy had followed him. He was a fool. He was a damned fool. He'd left his jacket on the plain, covered in goo, and probably covered in some sort of tracking device. They were facing an enemy with technology far in advance of their own. Of course they'd have means to track things across universes. Maybe even communication across universes, and he'd led them right to New Toledo.

He ran, even though he was exhausted and nearly empty.

Casey was there, to teach her class. Melissa and Kylie were there. Clotilde and the rest of the Alarians. What had he done?

He had to warn them.

His face was senseless from the cold. His lungs burned. He forced his legs to move, to punch the hard ground. He didn't care if he ran across a nest of cat-dogs, or a saber-tooth. He had to get there.

Twenty minutes later the flying machine crossed the sky in the direction it had come from.

They had time; the enemy was leaving. They could evacuate.

He should never have gone looking for clues. He'd found trouble, and he'd brought the trouble to them.

He turned at the whine in the sky.

It was bigger than the first flying machine. It thumped the sky and sounded like it looked. It bristled with gun turrets. Another war machine. Another deadly thing.

John ran harder, unsure where the strength came from. A gully appeared in front of him and he crested it with a behemoth jump. He had to warn them, stop the enemy, save everyone. . . .

The dark machine still moved on the horizon, just two kilometers away, and beyond that he saw the cooking fires of New Toledo, the exhaust of the generator, rising up into the air in plumes.

They had to see it. They had to know. There was always a sentry, always a lookout for wild animals.

Please evacuate, Casey, he said to himself. Please transfer to 7650. Please.

The behemoth flying machine rose higher into the air. John had to strain his neck to see it, and stopped looking for it, focusing on his pace.

He tripped, sprawling on the ground among a thicket of stones. He groaned, looking at his skinned elbows. It didn't matter. He forced his knees under him. Then pushed himself to his feet.

Ahead of him was a stand of trees he knew well: the site of Grayborn's execution. An unwelcome sight at any other time, but that meant he was only across the river from New Toledo.

He forced himself to his feet. Woozily, he took a step, then another.

He'd have to bypass the trees to avoid the gorge where they executed Grayborn. It was his natural instinct to go around it. Instead he aimed right through: it was the shortest distance. Damn Grayborn's ghost.

He paused at the edge of the trees, looking into the bluing sky, trying to find the aircraft. Nothing. Where had it gone?

He pushed into the forest. He expected to be going slower, but he found the tree trunks provided him with natural crutches. Instead of falling in agonizing exhaustion, he could lean against the ashes and maples, stagger from trunk to trunk.

His shoulder hit hard against a tree trunk; he whispered Casey's name. This urged him onward and he jogged forward. The gorge loomed ahead of him.

He stopped at the edge of the gorge, but the dirt was slick and his balance was gone. John slid and found himself at the bottom of the gorge, where he had shot Grayborn.

He tried not to look, but his eyes found the plaque someone—not him, never a John—had placed there. *Here Lies the Remains of the Rapist Jason Grayborn.*

He stared at the sign, the words blurring.

His ghost would be laughing now.

"Damn you!"

He reached his hands up to grab handholds in the far gorge wall.

A flash of light turned the sky white. A second later he felt a wave of heat, a shock wave of tropic sun, followed by a pounding deep thunder rolling across the top of the gorge. The heat of the firestorm forced John to drop to his belly and bury his face in the mud.

He screamed as the air above him sizzled. But it was so loud he could not even hear his bellowing.

He felt the hair on the back of his head curl and singe. Fire seemed to lick at his back and buttocks. Seconds ago he had been cold and beaten, now he burned in pain, gasping for breath as the oxygen was sucked from the air to feed a raging fire in the sky.

But no such conflagration could last for long, and it faded in intensity after thirty seconds such that he no longer screamed in pain.

After a minute he could roll over and put out his smoldering clothes. The sky, previously cloudless, was the green of an impending tornado. Debris—dirt, pebbles—rained down on him.

He blinked, took a slow breath of pain, and stood.

John had to see over the gorge wall.

He dug a hand in the dirt, gripped a loop of roots, and pulled himself up half a meter. He hung there, uncertain and suddenly disoriented, then he saw a flat bit of stone that he could push his palm against. Another half meter. His feet scrambled against the dirt wall, finding a bit of purchase. Then his right hand found the top of the gorge, grabbing crumbling grass and moss. He reached as far as he could, his hand catching a small tree.

Grunting, then screaming, he pulled himself over the edge of the gorge.

John lay there, gasping. The world smelled of char. He looked up in horror.

A mushroom cloud rose above him, less than a kilometer away, centered over what had once been New Toledo.

He screamed, incoherent sounds of rage and horror.

Casey had been there.

So many others.

Destroyed by his stupidity. His stupidity.

He stared and screamed as the head of the cloud slowly rose into the sky. Dark, murky clouds settled over the river, obscuring what had once been there on the shore. He found himself trying to find some glimpse of the buildings, hidden in the murk, some sign that they had miraculously survived, but he saw nothing but swirling dust and dirt.

So intent was he on peering into the dark clouds that he did not see the aircraft until it was nearly atop him.

Its weaponry turned toward him.

Rage filled him.

He would have his revenge, but not now. Not here.

John reached into his shirt, toggled his device, and pressed the button.

Nothing happened.

He looked down. The device was set to 7536. He pressed the right button again.

Nothing.

"Shit!" he said. Were they blocking the capability of the device? Had the detonation scrambled its circuits? He was trapped.

John turned and jumped into the gorge.

He ripped off his shirt and unbuckled the device. He pulled his shirt back over his shoulders. He jumped across the dry creek bed.

He dropped the device behind the memorial for the execution of Jason Grayborn and continued running up the gorge.

He was certain to be killed or captured. The least he could do was ditch the device.

In the gorge, it almost seemed as if nothing had happened. The trees within still stood. If he didn't look up into the dark sky, if he forgot that Casey was dead, if he forgot that New Toledo was destroyed.

He ran.

Above him, the shadow of the aircraft loomed.

CHAPTER 35

"I'll go," John Prime said.

Grace Home looked at him with evident relief in her eyes. Casey, however, shook her head slightly.

To her, he added, "I have to. We have to know."

They'd received a satchel post from 7535 twelve hours before that said, *Under attack.* Then nothing more. When Henry Home had tried to do a return transfer of a video camera, nothing had come back.

"You can't go through on top of the New Toledo site," Henry Home said. He'd been very perturbed when the video camera didn't return. Even the hovering system had failed.

"I'll go through from the south, about ten kilometers," Prime said.

"Alone?" his Casey asked.

"Yes," Prime said. "We've lost too many." John Home, Casey Home, John Ten, all the refugees, all the Alarians were now missing in action. Grace Home had sent through emergency messages to all transfer gates to shut everything down, go into hiding, and make no unnecessary transfers until they could understand everything that had happened. Then she'd asked John Prime to join her in 7650 at the original Pinball Wizards factory. Casey had dropped Abby off at her parents' and come with him. The meeting included John and Casey Prime, Grace and Henry Home, as well as Grace and Henry Top. A privy council of the Wizards to deal with the crisis.

"Ten kilometers?" Grace Home asked.

"I want a good distance between me and the site," Prime said. "I'll need an ATV and a portable gate."

"A portable gate?" Henry Top said. "We don't have a portable gate, just the one that John . . ."

He stopped before finishing his sentence. John was missing and with him the device that had started it all. They had no idea where he was, having disappeared after heading to Champ to reconnoiter. He could have been captured, killed, or lost in Pleistocene.

"I need a portable gate, one that I can transport easily with the ATV, that can get me back quickly, and that I can destroy after using if need be," Prime explained.

Henry Home and Henry Top turned toward each other and began whispering. After a moment they turned and nodded in unison.

"We can do that. Portable generator, quick-deployment rig," Henry Top said.

"Give us four hours," Henry Home said.

"I'll need to go back to 7533," Prime said.

"Why?" Grace Home asked.

"Uh, weapons," Prime said. "I have a cache of weapons I've been buying up in 7533."

"Okay," Henry Top said. "What site do we use for the new transfer site to the Pleistocene world?"

· · ·

John Prime transferred across the ATV and its wagon of equipment just before six in the morning the next day. The weather was warmer in the Pleistocene universe, but not enough for him to forego a coat. His leg, where the shrapnel had embedded itself, was pink and puckered. It ached dully when he walked, but two Percocet took care of that. Casey had been shocked that the wound had healed so quickly.

Prime wore a military-grade ballistic vest. He had three pistols strapped to his body—waist, shoulder, and ankle holsters. He had a knife and three grenades. His weapon at hand was a Heckler & Koch MP5 submachine gun. He also had an AT4, an anti-tank gun, just in case he came up against something big. All of the equipment was from Universe 9000, his personal trove of equipment. Yes, he thought to himself, my entire universe of equipment.

The ATV could go forty kilometers per hour on open ground. With the trailer, he expected the rate would be less, but he didn't expect to drag the trailer all the way to New Toledo. He'd set it up halfway there, near an outcropping of rock that was in a metro park in Home Universe: a safe, clear place to transfer into 7650.

His backup plan was to have the team activate the new transfer gate in 7650 every ten minutes until he returned.

Prime marked the transfer zone with small flags.

"Okay, here goes," he said.

He dropped goggles over his eyes, started the ATV, checked his compass, and headed toward New Toledo.

Even with the goggles, tears ran from his eyes at the wind against his face. He blinked his eyes clear and focused on avoiding any ravines.

The trip was quicker than he expected. He stopped after five kilometers, near the outcropping of rock. He unloaded the generator and the new gate. The Henrys had built something quick and dirty, but it would work fine. It was big enough to transfer two persons in a hurry. Any more travelers and there was danger of someone losing a limb in the tight fit.

Prime verified that the generator would run and power the gate, and then he left it ready to transfer him out.

He took another bearing and continued on the ATV. He stopped repeatedly to scan the sky and the horizon, ahead and behind. Prime saw nothing.

Finally he was near enough to New Toledo that he felt he should see some sign of it. He thought he had the right location. The landmarks to the west seemed right, but the hills on the banks of the river where the settlement should have been . . . were absent.

He slowly drove closer.

As he crested a rise near the settlement, he stopped, staring at the sight.

Where New Toledo once stood was a huge glass bowl.

The entire settlement had been nuked.

"Jesus," Prime said. They had all been killed, murdered by a weapon of mass destruction.

No wonder the video camera Henry had sent through didn't come back. There was no hard ground to transfer onto. Just a drop fifty meters into a glass bowl.

John Prime felt his rage boil.

This was his multiverse too. What right did any goddamn shitheads have to kill his friends? Who put them in charge? And if they were in charge, why the hell weren't they doing a better job? The Wizards hadn't hurt anyone. The Alarian women certainly had suffered enough. Why did they have to die?

Tears were running down his cheeks. He felt impotent, useless, a burden. And stupid. Idiotic for letting this all happen. He had given Farmboy the device. Prime had set this all in motion. Farmboy liked to take responsibility for everything, but it was just as much his fault. So many deaths laid on his shoulders.

"John!"

He turned.

A woman, with a walking stick, was coming toward him. She was one of the Alarians, and he remembered her name—Radeheva, one of the pregnant Alarians. She was gravid with her baby, at least eight months pregnant.

As she neared, John Prime saw that the stick was a broken branch that she had picked up to help her walk. A scratch ran across her forehead. Her leg was clearly stiff from another wound on her thigh.

"Radeheva," Prime said. "You're alive."

"For the moment, John," she said. She looked at him closely. "John Prime."

"What's happened here?"

"Atomics," she said. "I expect we're getting a good dose standing here. Let's be off."

"Shit!" Prime said. Why had he not thought of that? He was standing on the edge of an atomic blast site.

"Are there any others who survived?" Prime asked.

"Two others," Radeheva said. "Though I doubt for long. We were hunting. We saw the ship approach. We saw the explosion. It knocked us flat. The other two are worse than me."

"You shouldn't be so close to the site in your condition."

"What else were we to do?" Radeheva said. "Neither Audofleda nor Brenasontha can walk. And this is where a rescuer would come."

"But your baby—"

"—still kicks. Let's go."

She led him to the west.

"We were a kilometer to the east. The ship rose high, dropped its warhead, and came low. It sighted a survivor to the north, across the river, and pursued."

"A survivor?"

"Yes, it was John Rayburn—John Home."

"Farmboy? He was here."

"Not that I knew of when I left that morning. He was coming to New Toledo when the blast occurred."

"He's captured then, and with him the device."

"Perhaps. When someone is pursued, they often drop or destroy the things they want to keep from enemy hands."

"There is no way to destroy the device easily."

They drove the ATV two kilometers to the west, where they came upon a formation of rock under a small waterfall in a stream. In the depression behind the falls were Audofleda and Brenasontha. Audofleda was unconscious, her head bruised at the temple. Brenasontha was conscious, but her leg was broken.

Together, Prime and Radeheva carried the two women and placed them in the trailer of the ATV.

"I need to see what's happened to John," Prime said. "Can we wait an hour?"

Radeheva nodded. "We can wait. Where is the transfer gate?"

Prime explained where it was and how to use it, in case something happened to him.

"Give me an hour to look for him."

"We will give you two."

Prime had brought an inflatable canoe, which he used to cross the river to the far side. His mind kept coming back to the reality as he rowed: three survivors of a thousand. Just three.

They were facing monsters.

He reached the shore and pulled the light canoe up the bank where he set two large stones, fore and aft, to keep it from blowing away. He was still a kilometer or two upstream of the settlement site. No, not a settlement. The crater site.

He jogged easily toward the trees where Radeheva had last seen Farmboy John. She said she'd seen no sign of the enemy since. Had they found what they wanted in Farmboy? Had they left a few survivors to spread the word?

Radeheva had said the aircraft had pursued Farmboy from the trees northward. She'd seen him here, in front of the trees, facing the settlement. He was shocked to see footprints in the ash. Farmboy's footprints. They came forward from the trees a few meters, then they turned back into the trees.

Prime followed. Farmboy had run back, jumped down the gully, and that's where his tracks ended.

Prime hopped down and, by chance, found charred bits of clothing. This was where Farmboy had survived the blast, here behind the dirt of the ravine wall.

He looked left and right, spotted the stone someone had put up for that bastard Grayborn. That way, Prime thought. He would have gone that way.

John Prime ran past the memorial, taking the slanting gully slowly northeast and upward. When the gully was just a meter high, he found where Farmboy had scrabbled up the side. Ashes at the top of the gorge had been disturbed, and his footprints led off to the north.

Farmboy had been running; the length of his stride made that clear. Prime went five hundred meters, following the footprints straight, until the tracks veered suddenly to the left, then the right. Farmboy had been dodging something. The ground became a chaos of dirt, leaves, grass, and ash.

Something had swept the burnt-out land in all directions, something that had landed here. There was no corpse; they'd captured him. Then they had taken him away, leaving Radeheva and the two others to their fate. They had wanted John Farmboy specifically or just one captive. Prime had no idea which.

There was nothing to be done here. Prime turned around and followed the track back.

As he passed the memorial to Jason Grayborn, he paused. It was odd that this one thing was all that survived of New Toledo. Prime decided that it should not be so. He grabbed the memorial and tilted it over, shattering the stone.

His eyes settled on the device lying there.

"There you are," he whispered.

Farmboy had ditched the device here, knowing he was about to be captured. Why hadn't the enemy found it? His trail was easy to backtrack. They weren't looking for the device for some reason.

But he had it now.

John Prime had it again. He smiled.

It was back in his hands again.

CHAPTER 36

John awoke in a cell. His head was pounding. His body ached. Sliding his feet over the edge of the bed he laid on, he pulled himself to a seated position.

The room was three meters square, with a bed against one wall and a toilet across from it in one corner. A door, with a metal screen window, was to his left. There was no other window. A vent in the ceiling blew cool air. He caught the scent of ammonia.

He leaned forward, head in hands, remembering. He had run, not to escape, but to draw the enemy away from the device. It hadn't worked! Panic had flooded him, the same panic when Prime had first given him the device and it hadn't worked, it hadn't let him go back home. This time, it hadn't let him transfer forward.

Sitting in his cell, he guessed why. The enemy had some suppression tool, some way to stop the transfer from happening. The aircraft had emanated some field that suppressed the transfer process. They had trapped him and hunted him and captured him. But maybe they didn't have the device.

They had chased him from the gorge. The aircraft had moved slowly, not via a fixed wing, but some other means that kept it aloft. John wondered if they had some sort of antigravity science. As the shadow of the thing overtook him, he'd dodged left and right. Again a chunk of sticky webbing landed on him, and he fell in a heap.

The ship settled above him, its three struts forming a triangle with him in the middle. He could barely turn his head to see it, but it bristled with antennae and weapons. It was not aerodynamic in the least.

John lay there beneath it for long minutes. He was sure he'd been there for half an hour when finally he heard voices.

A booted foot pushed him on his thigh.

He said nothing, didn't react, didn't move.

Someone spoke in words he couldn't understand. It could have been the same language he'd heard at the farm in 7351. Someone else laughed. It was not a humorous sound.

A hand reached down and lifted some of the webbing off the ground and tossed it on his shoulder. John caught sight of the gloves the man wore; the webbing seemed to slither around the gloves, but it didn't stick.

A bit of webbing landed on his cheek, sticking dangerously close to his lips and nose. He tried to shake it loose but it wouldn't budge.

Another laugh. The man slung a wad of the webbing directly on his face.

John panicked, struggling to free himself. His mouth and nose were covered. He couldn't breathe, and he could do nothing to clear his face. He struggled on the ground, breathless, and certain he would die.

With that thought, his mind cleared, and he stopped his motions. John forced the panic down. He'd die with dignity.

His lungs burned, but he waited in calmness.

Casey was dead. What more could he do but die here?

Green and yellow swirls stained his vision. Then splotches of light, until his consciousness faded.

He awoke here, in the cell.

Casey.

The light did not waver as he sat there. No sound rose above the hum of the fan in the ceiling. No one looked in the wired window of his cell. He had no watch. His shoes were missing and his pockets were empty. He had no way to tell the passage of time, but he must have waited several hours before the door opened suddenly.

A tall woman entered.

Without thinking, he launched himself at her. His fingers were curled in claws. His teeth were bared. He screamed sounds of inarticulate rage.

His fingers never reached her throat. A soldier stood behind her and fired a weapon at him.

Something slammed into his chest and he fell to the floor.

Air couldn't fill his lungs. Again he could not breathe.

He heard the woman speak in their language. A soldier entered, dragged him to his cot, and handcuffed his hands behind his back. John slumped forward, trying to get air in his lungs.

A chair was brought in, and the woman sat.

The woman was tall, as tall as John, dressed in a dark blue jumpsuit, and severe in feature. Her black hair was pulled back. Her fingers were long and thin as they lay in her lap. She crossed her legs.

"The penalty for attacking an officer of the Vigilari is death," she said in accented English.

John snorted. "As long as you die too."

Her eyes grew slightly round as she heard these words, surprised perhaps at his wish for her death.

"Where is your iaciorator?" she asked.

The word meant nothing to John.

"You killed my wife-to-be," John said. "You'll get nothing from me."

"We know you have obtained one. We detected the attempt to translate," she said. "Yet it was not in that . . . town we destroyed. Where, then?"

Did she mean the transfer device? John was confused by her questions, but tried not to show it.

"Why couldn't you just leave us alone?" John said. "We weren't bothering you."

The woman considered this.

"You know why," she said. "Now, tell us where the iaciorator is located."

"I don't know that word," John said. "Who are you?"

"I am Imperator Luigiantia of the Order of the Vigilari," she said. "You are John Rayburn, a duplicate, present in thirteen percent of the fallow universes. Twenty years old, a student usually, a backwater boy. Except where you have found an iaciorator."

"What does it matter to you what we found?"

Luigiantia exhaled through clenched teeth. "You don't know much, do you? You're just some farmboy."

"A farmboy you attacked."

"It is our job!"

"Says who?"

"If we don't do this, there will be chaos!"

"The argument of every dictator."

"You fool! The multiverse will be destroyed if we don't do what we do! It is for the good of everyone that we do this."

"You nuked us for our own good! Excellent."

Emotions passed across Luigiantia's face. Whatever an Imperator was, one didn't expect this sort of response, apparently. John felt nothing but disdain for her and her organization—this Order of the Vigilari.

"Where is the iaciorator?" she asked. "It is crucial that we take control of all such devices. Where is the one you found? Once we take control of it, you can tell us how you found it."

"Is your organization responsible for banishing the Alarians?" John asked. "If so, I owe you for my friend Grace too."

"The who?"

"Alarians. Really messed-up Germanic people. Got ahold of some transfer devices—some iaciorators—and built an empire."

She took a small handheld device from her pocket, and began typing on it with one hand.

"Ah, the residents of Universe 2119," she said. "They were exterminated."

"Not all," John said. "Some of them were marooned and set up shop in my universe."

"But they had no iaciorator," Luigiantia said. "Therefore not an issue for us."

"They were an issue for us."

Luigiantia shrugged slightly.

"If we did not do our job, there would be chaos. Nothing would be unique. Everything would be merged. Universes that were in sync would be different. Order would be destroyed."

It sounded like cant to John, some ritual response to questions.

"So? Singletons are more valuable than duplicates? That's what the Alarians believed. Is that what this is all about?"

"No!"

"Power does not give you the right to decide how to exploit people," John said. "The fact that you have transfer devices does not allow you to be kings of the multiverse."

Luigiantia laughed. "I should have known. So many of you 'Americans' believe as you do, in the inherent rights of humankind. A parochial view, John Rayburn, when the whole multiverse is on the edge of oblivion. When one wrong transfer will destroy everyone human, duplicate or singleton."

"Freedom matters," John said.

"You are not free to murder, you are not free to rape, you are not free to infect," she replied.

"But we're free to live our lives otherwise."

"In your own damned universe, you are," Luigiantia shouted. "But when you get out, you're my problem. And I will not allow it."

John looked at her. "It's too late. We're out and there's nothing you can do about it."

"We'll see."

She motioned at the soldier in the doorway. Before John could move, a hypodermic needle had been punched into his shoulder. He gasped, shuddered, and then released his consciousness, the last thing on his mind an image of Casey smiling at him.

CHAPTER 37

While Grace Champ drove Radeheva, Audofleda, and Brenason-tha to a local hospital, John Prime explained what he had seen.

"Nuclear weapons?" Grace Top cried. "They nuked us!"

Though there was a moratorium on travel between universes, it seemed that every Grace, Henry, Casey, and John had come to 7650, to the Pinball Wizard factory.

"But you saw no body," Grace Home said. "They didn't kill John?"

John Prime shrugged. "There was no body there. But it was clear where he had been caught."

"And the device too," Grace Home said, not as a question, as a statement. "They have that too."

"Yeah," Prime said, though the transfer device was strapped to his chest right then. It was his once again. He touched his chest absently.

"We have to get him back," Grace Top said.

"No sign of Casey?" Grace Home asked.

"None," Henry Home said. "No one has seen her."

"A thousand people," Grace Home said. "A thousand people dead." Her eyes were red from her crying, but her face was dry now.

"Some may be alive," Henry Top said. "They might have kid-napped others as well as John. . . ." His voice trailed off. No, the New Toledoans were dead. John Ten, John Home, John Superprime, Casey Home, Clotilde, Englavira, Melissa, little Kylie, Devon, Jane, and their two children. One thousand emigrants, eighty Alar-ians. All dead or missing. "Shit," he said.

"Yeah."

"What do we do?" Casey Low asked. Her tears were on her face, and John Prime felt a pang looking at her.

"Where did they take him?" Grace Top asked.

"Where do we attack?" John Gore asked.

John Prime nodded at that. Those were his sentiments.

"How do we know?" Grace Home asked. "There's no way for us to know. We're so . . . so ignorant of everything."

Prime said, "There are people we can ask."

The statement hung there for a full minute.

"Charboric," Grace Home said with clear hostility.

"They'd know," Prime replied.

"The Alarians we know are dead," Henry Case said. "And they didn't know the history of their banishment any more than folklore. Charboric is gone."

There was a pause.

"I know where the Alarians went."

Prime looked at Grace Home. "You know?"

"John and I found the stolen transfer gate that the Alarians were trying to build. It was set for Universe 2219."

"No!"

"Yes. That's where they went."

"We know where the Alarians went," Prime mused. He grinned. "It's time to have a talk with Charboric."

In the end, Prime convinced Grace Home she wasn't coming.

"One person will have more luck than two," he said. "And I've had the most experience with jumping universes, now that John is gone."

"You think I'll go nuts and kill Charboric? Is that it?"

"No, I don't," Prime said, though he was unsure.

"I could help you," she argued.

"You could hinder me," Prime said. "I'm going alone."

"Fine."

They started by scanning the location near the quarry in 2219. It was where the Alarians had gone through from Home Office, near the abandoned Rayburn barn, where John had built the first transfer gate.

"See? There," Henry Home said. "A shack."

John Prime leaned close to the video image. "That's pretty close to where the transfer gate was, about three hundred meters from the quarry."

"They're waiting for the rest of the Alarians to come through," Grace Top said. "Long wait."

"Looks abandoned."

"It's been months, and Charboric knows the transfer gate was moved to Columbus," Prime said. "This is just in case someone comes through here. I bet there's a guard shack near the Columbus site too."

"We can check," Henry Home said.

"Let's see what's in that shack first."

Prime transferred through with the ATV and the portable gate. He stood there for a long time, waiting for some alarm, some sign of life in the shack. Ten minutes passed. Nothing.

Prime set the portable transfer device up first. He had the device on his chest, sure, but he wasn't going to let anyone else know that. Then he walked over to the shack.

Snow had drifted against the door, shielded by the sun and unmelted. The shack was empty.

Prime pushed the door open and looked inside. A piece of paper was tacked to the wall. On it was a crudely drawn map and some characters in an alphabet he did not know.

He grabbed it and walked back to the transfer zone. Checking his watch, he found the hemispherical depression of earth where the gate had cut away the dirt. The quarry did not exist here, so their transfer had cut through the earth. Prime put the piece of paper under a rock on a platform in the transfer zone.

Three minutes later the platform disappeared.

In five minutes he could expect another transfer and hopefully a response. They'd decided on a five-minute increment on transfers between here and 7650 until he returned safely.

He spent the five minutes scanning the horizon. There were no jet contrails, no power lines or telephone lines, no signs of any civilization. It was another empty universe. Unpopulated, just like the Pleistocene one. Hopefully it wasn't a plague world like 9000. A bolt-hole universe for the Alarians.

There was a pop and a new platform appeared. Atop it was a notebook. Prime grabbed the notebook. Inside was a message.

Radeheva translated. Directions in Alarian to the base. Five kilometers to the southeast. Want help?

It was signed by Grace.

His reply was, *Going to look on foot. Leaving portable gate. If not back in four hours, don't send reinforcements.*

Not that Grace would listen.

Five kilometers was a no-sweat jog. He set off, submachine gun slung over his shoulder, backpack full of munitions and supplies.

The Alarian bolt-hole fortress was a warehouse of corrugated metal built in a valley with a small river. There were no guards, no towers. Beyond the warehouse were several rows of wooden houses, recently built.

It looked no more advanced than New Toledo had.

"They left 7650 for this?" Prime said to himself.

He lay on the hill and scanned the little town with his binoculars. Here and there, Alarians moved about, always men. None of them appeared heavily armed. He spotted one man with a sidearm, no one else.

Then out of the largest wooden building walked Charboric. He looked like a smug son of a bitch, that was for sure. King of this empty little pocket universe. Charboric turned and shouted orders at one of his aides, and then he sauntered down the center of his town.

He walked right past the warehouse and started up the valley wall to the north, not forty-five degrees from John and only three hundred meters away.

What luck! Could it be this easy?

He took no guards with him, as if he was certain he'd be safe here. The fool.

John Prime ran along the bowl of the valley, just over the edge and hidden from sight. He came across a well-worn path. The Alarians came this way often. Charboric appeared, just a few meters down the path. Prime pulled the taser from his belt and ran at him.

Charboric turned at the sound of Prime's pounding feet. His

mouth formed an O as Prime tasered him in the chest. The man fell over and twitched.

Prime turned at words behind him.

Two of Charboric's aides had come after him for some reason. They were aiming guns at him.

Prime slung Charboric over his shoulder and transferred the two of them to Universe 9000.

Prime cuffed Charboric and left him next to a fire hydrant while he went in search of a vehicle. He found an SUV that started in a garage not too far away.

Charboric was awake when he returned.

"John Rayburn, you useless dup—"

John aimed an elbow at Charboric's chin.

"Just shut up."

He dragged Charboric's limp body into the passenger's seat. He undid the cuffs and recuffed him to the handhold above the passenger's window.

John drove toward his camp just north of Findlay.

Charboric shook himself awake after a few minutes. He didn't speak again, just looked out the window.

Prime felt the man's tension grow.

"Where is this?" he cried finally. "Where are we?"

Prime glanced at him.

"9000."

"There are no people here," he said.

"Everyone is dead here."

"Plague world!" Charboric lunged at him. "What have you done, you idiot?"

Only the cuffs kept him from knocking into Prime.

Prime slammed on the brakes. Charboric danced like a puppet on his cuffed arms. Prime pulled the taser off his belt.

"We're here, we'll be fine. I've spent days here and I'm fine. No plague."

Charboric frothed and lunged at him again. His face was wild and unrecognizable. Prime tasered him again.

John Prime tied him to a tree at the camp and then drove to the quarry where he transferred through to Universe 2219 and from there transferred himself with the portable gate to Home Office.

"Did you find them?" Grace Home cried when he appeared.

"I found their camp," Prime replied.

"You were gone a long time! We almost came through to get you."

"It's too well armed," Prime said. "We'll have to think of a good plan."

"What can we do?"

John Prime thought quickly. "I can go back at night, with night-vision goggles, kidnap one of their guys and get some answers."

"How heavily guarded is it?"

"They have guns, lotsa guns, vehicles, Jeeps, machine guns."

"Sheesh," Henry Top said. "This may be a dead end."

"Not yet, Henry, not yet," Prime said. "We gotta try for John's sake."

Prime said he was going to take a nap until that evening. Then he jumped to 9000 and drove back to the campsite.

Charboric was unconscious. His hands were purple where the cuffs had dug into his wrists. Prime let him down, dragged him into his tent, and recuffed him to a cot. Prime started a space heater.

Charboric's forehead was hot to the touch, feverish. His tongue looked swollen.

"Shit!" Prime said. He couldn't be sick. The plague had died out with the humans. This universe was fine. Prime hadn't caught a thing!

Charboric's eyes fluttered open. He said something in Alarian.

Prime got water and held it to his face.

Charboric's expression focused and he stared at Prime.

"You've killed me."

"I'm fine, why are you sick? It's all psychosomatic."

Charboric barked a laugh, and in seeming response vomited over the side of the cot. His body was so contorted and violent that he turned the camping bed over. He choked and vomited and then lay still.

"Why . . . why did you come for me? Revenge? If so, well done. Well done."

"No, we need— we need information," Prime said. Doubt was eating at his bravado. His confidence was draining away as it became clear that Charboric was infected with something.

Charboric laughed again.

"Information! You fool! Fools! All of you in every universe!"

"The Vig found us."

Charboric's laughter died.

"Of course. Of course. It was just a matter of time."

"Where are they from?"

Charboric laughed until he began vomiting again. This time there were flecks of blood in the green bile.

"You're going to take them on?" Charboric said. "You're going head-to-head with the Vig?"

"Yes."

"Teiwaz!"

"You don't even know."

"I know! Everyone knows, but you. You killed me for something every goddamn person who's anyone knows! But it won't do you any good. None at all."

"Then tell me."

"I'll tell you," Charboric said. "I'll tell you because then I'll die knowing you will die too."

"So you think."

He laughed.

"Universe 0010, John Rayburn. You'll find the Vig in Universe 0010."

An hour later Charboric was dead.

Prime burned the body and covered it in a shallow ditch. He returned to 7650 and lied to his friends and colleagues, even his wife. As he did so, as he fabricated a desperate offensive against the Alarians, he wondered why he felt no qualms, no remorse for what he did. All to protect the device. His device.

He transferred to 2219 and waited two hours in the brush

before returning himself and all their supplies to 7650. He sat there in the cold, pretending to raid the Alarian camp. Instead he just counted the minutes until two hours were up and then he transferred back to 7650.

"Universe 0010," Prime said.

"0010?"

"Yes, Charboric told me himself. Universe 0010."

"How do you know he wasn't lying?" Grace Home asked. "You should have brought him back."

"No. I had a gun to his head. He begged for his life, and I gave it to him in exchange for the information," Prime said.

"He could have still told you what you wanted to hear," Grace Home said.

"He didn't. I know it's true."

"We can check it out anyway," Henry Top said. "We'll send probes through."

"We'll need weapons," John Prime said. "Weapons as strong as theirs."

"What do you mean?"

"We need nukes."

"Pinball Wizards, Transdimensional, has a lot of money, but we can't buy nuclear weapons," Grace Home cried. "Besides, that's insane."

"We don't have to use it on them, we just have to prove we have the weapons," Prime said.

John Case said, "They nuked us. We should do the same to them."

"No!" Grace Home said. "We will not nuke our enemy! We don't even have nuclear weapons!"

"I do."

Everyone looked at John Prime.

"You what?" Grace Home said.

"Universe 9000 is empty, but all the infrastructure is there. Including nuclear weapons, missile subs, bombers, anything."

"How did you . . . how could you know?" Grace Home said.

Prime glanced at his Casey, who looked back at him with an unreadable expression.

"I knew about it before. But I went recently," he said. "To check it out. It's all there, for the taking."

"How could you—" Grace Home started, but John Gore interrupted.

"We know where they are and we have the weapons to get their attention," he said. "I say we show them we're not going to lie down. We nuke them and demand John back."

Johns and Henrys cheered, while Graces frowned. Caseys shared glances. But the sentiment toward using the weapons against the enemy was strong, strong enough to carry a vote. The Pinball Wizards were going to be a nuclear power.

CHAPTER 38

John Prime flew to Amarillo on the corporate jet.

"I didn't know we had a corporate jet," he said to Grace Home as he, she, and Henry Top took off from Toledo's airport.

"Largesse and extravagance of the last administration," she said. "We're taking care of the obvious items."

"But a jet is useful," Prime said.

Grace shrugged. "You sure you know what you're doing?"

"No idea," Prime said.

"I'm serious."

He opened his briefcase. "This is the manual I took from the army base in Columbus. It covers everything I need to know."

"Have you read it?"

"Three times."

"We'll expect you in three days."

"It's only a twenty-hour drive," Prime said.

"Yes, I don't want you falling asleep with a nuclear bomb in your trunk," Grace said. "And you'll need a day to find the damned things."

Prime looked at Grace. She'd taken the vote well, but it was clear she wanted nothing to do with the nuclear devices.

"This is the best way to show them we mean business," Prime said. "They nuked us first!"

"I know they did," Grace said. "But do we have to strike back with the same force?"

"We're not trying to kill any of them. We're just showing we can."

"Fine."

"Henry is going to find us a clear spot."

"He will," she said. The Henrys were building robotic scouts to examine Universe 0010 for an unpopulated area. Prime hoped that the Vig had no defense mechanisms such as Universe 1214 did. "And we'll have the demand note ready for release too."

"Okay."

"You sure you don't want help with this?"

"If 9000 is a plague world, I don't want to risk the chance someone else might get infected."

"You didn't."

"Maybe I have some immunity."

"Then we send another John."

"Maybe one of the universes I visited gave me the immunity."

"Maybe."

From the airport, Grace and Prime headed directly to the Pantex site in Home Office, while Henry drove to the warehouse they had rented.

"We have a site tour just before noon," Grace said. "Did you study the material? They won't let you on-site if you don't pass the safety test."

"Yeah, I read it."

"Good."

The limo let them off in the parking lot in front of a cement-block visitor center. The lot was half full with cars. Prime and Grace were escorted to an overly-lit room where they were given a number-two pencil, an answer sheet, and a set of fifty questions. Prime hadn't read the material, but by guessing the most reasonable answer possible, he managed to outscore Grace by five points.

The tour was led by an army sergeant, who loaded them onto a bus and trekked them across the brown earth from one end of the site to the other.

The spiel he recited seemed geared toward the concept of non-proliferation of nuclear weapons, not the creation and storage of them, which is what Prime and Grace were interested in. Prime noticed that the bus seemed to avoid certain areas, including several widely-spaced concrete hangars.

He asked, "Sergeant, what's in those buildings there?"

"Those are assembly sites, sir," he replied.

When he didn't add anything more, Prime said, "And what is done there?"

"We disassemble nuclear devices at those locations, sir."

"And assemble them?"

"When necessary. With current disarmament treaties, we spend far more time disassembling than assembling, sir."

"And what about storage? Where do you store the backpack nukes?"

"The what, sir?"

"The SADM portable nuclear devices, Sergeant," Prime said.

"I can't discuss those, sir. I'm sorry," he said, and that was the end of that conversation.

When they were done with the tour, however, they were caught from behind by a captain, who motioned them into a smaller room.

"May I speak with you briefly?" he asked.

"Of course," Grace said.

"I must ask if you are with the press," he said curtly.

"We are not," Grace said. "I'm Grace Shisler, president and CEO of Grauptham House. Mr. Rayburn is a senior vice president in the research and development division."

"Ah, the personal computer people. And how did you come to learn of the SADM program?"

"We do have government contracts, Captain," Grace said.

"Is that why you're here? To look for contract work?"

"It is. We're interested in providing on-site vendor-managed services in safety, security, and maintenance."

"You're the CEO?" he asked, nodding at Grace.

"Yes."

"Let me see what I can do."

He left, and Prime said, "What do you think that all meant?"

"We're a company with a female CEO. We match some criteria for contract work," Grace said.

"Is that it? We get a pass because you're a woman," Prime said. "Awesome."

"We'll see what it gets us."

He came back a few minutes later.

"Since you're here now, I've been authorized to give you the real tour. Afterwards, you can meet with one of our procurement officers. If you're inclined to bid on some of our open subcontracts, we'd greatly appreciate it."

In the end, they received a tour of the SADM facility, even coming within a few meters of one of the nukes, though it was behind a Plexiglas wall. Prime made mental notes of locations so that he could find his way back here.

"We could probably help them quite a bit, actually," Grace said in the limo on the way back. "Their security could use some advances."

"Sure, let's diversify even more," Prime said.

"You don't think it's worth it?"

"What profit margin would we have on this compared to a technology such as personal computers?"

"It could still be worth doing," she said.

They arrived at the warehouse. Inside Henry had assembled a transfer gate.

"This building is old," he said. "So it probably exists on the other side."

"You got everything you need?" Grace asked.

"Yeah, of course," Prime said.

"You sure you don't want company?"

"I'm sure."

She looked at him. "You kept this from us," she said.

Prime met her gaze. "I did."

"What do you do there? What use is an empty world?"

THE BROKEN UNIVERSE 343

Prime shrugged. "Art."

Grace snorted.

"Three days. Then we're coming to get you."

"Three days."

The warehouse was dark in 9000. John Prime flicked on his flashlight and played it across the walls. Empty, utterly empty.

He listened. Nothing but the Panhandle wind. Prime wasn't perfectly certain Universe 9000 was empty. He'd not picked up any shortwave signals, nor had he found any trace at all of another living person. But his survey had consisted only of parts of Ohio. Perhaps Amarillo, Texas, was the last bastion of humanity in the otherwise plague-ridden universe.

He pushed open the emergency exit. Weeds had sprung up in the sidewalk and street. Nothing. No bastion.

Transportation was the first requirement. Prime found it right outside the warehouse in a white delivery van for a general contractor. He dumped the tools, wood, and material out onto the street and drove the van to a hardware store where he picked up wire cutters, a knife, and other things he might need. He had marked the location of the Texas National Guard headquarters and drove there next.

The door to the armory had been ripped from its hinges and the weapons looted at some time during the plague. The place was barren. He tried the commandant's office and found a shelf unit of assault rifles, grenades, and pistols. He broke the glass to the unit and took what he needed.

The Pantex site proved trickier. The gates were locked tight and spike strips had been deployed in front of and behind the gate. There was no way to get near the fence; short, stubby poles blocked access off the road. Furthermore, there was a cement culvert that made driving near the fence, even if he got past the poles, impossible. He'd have to go through the gate.

John Prime donned thick leather gloves. He grabbed the first spike strip and tried to drag it off the road. It proved almost too heavy for him. Finally he managed to drag it into the grass. There were three more on this side of the gate. He was sweating heavily by the time he took his cutters to the chain and lock. It snipped with a grind of metal. He unlooped the chain and pulled it off.

Four spike strips were on the other side.

"Jesus. Were they expecting zombies?"

He encountered no more obstacles on his way to the concrete bunker that housed the SADM devices. On the tarmac near the entrance to the bunker were six skeletons, picked clean by the elements and the animals. They were soldiers, Prime saw as he edged closer, with GI tags that hung from their ribs. One of the soldiers had died of a gunshot wound—his skull had a jagged hole in the temple.

Had there been some last stand here? Had someone come to take the nukes and these soldiers died here defending the trove? Were the nukes gone?

"Shit!"

The door to the bunker was locked. That was a good sign that the special atomic demolition munitions—the backpack nukes— were still inside. But getting through the door was a problem.

He couldn't grenade the damn door. The last thing he wanted to do was to have explosives near nuclear devices, regardless of the fail-safes.

The door opened outward, but the hinges were machined flush with the wall. There was a handle, however.

He weaved the van among the skeletons and ran a chain from the trailer hitch to the door.

Slowly he eased the van forward, putting tension on the chain. The door held. He applied more gas. The van leaned forward. The wheels suddenly spun and the van lost traction, fishtailing a bit to the left.

"Damn."

Prime slowly backed up a meter or two. Then he slammed on the gas. The van lurched forward, hung there for a moment, and then jumped forward. Something smacked the back window of the van, shattering it. He slammed on the brakes. The door was intact. The chain was not.

He drove to the machine shop and found a pneumatic drill

powered by a gasoline engine. With it he was able to dig the three hinges out, though he ate through a bit to do so. This time when he yanked the door by its handle, the locks' tongues bent and the door tilted out of the frame to rattle on the tarmac.

Prime had to use the drill three more times, twice on a mantrap that required a person to stand one at a time in a particular spot before the doors would open or close, and then the vault door. He had to go back to the machine shop for more drill bits.

The vault door came off with a clank, slamming onto the tile floor. He reached in and hit the light switch. Lights flickered on, illuminating a room with twelve alcoves. The captain had explained that the SADM facility had its own bank of batteries in case of power failure. Apparently they still held a charge after two years.

Each alcove was separate from its neighbor by a meter and a thick wall of lead. Inside each alcove was an olive-drab cylinder. Straps hung from the front and each stood on a pedestal that would make it easy for a soldier to back up to it and strap it to his back. The cylinders were about seventy centimeters tall and half as much wide. From the manuals he'd been able to find in 7650, he knew they weighed nearly seventy kilograms.

"Jackpot."

An hour later, John Prime was heading toward Ohio in an M35 cargo truck with six nukes in its bed.

CHAPTER 39

John squinted against bright lights. He tried to raise his hand to wipe away the tears, but something held his arm down. He needed to blow his nose; snot was collecting in his throat. He groaned and tried to sit up. He couldn't move.

A shape blocked the light.

"John Rayburn, can you hear me?"

"Luigiantia," he mumbled. His brain felt foggy. He couldn't think right, and he was pinned down. Panic rose in him.

"That's right. I am Imperator Luigiantia—"

"—of the Order of the Vigilari," John finished. The words came unbidden from his mouth. He'd been here before, days ago or hours ago. He couldn't tell.

"Drugs?" he said, slurring his words.

"That's right. We've drugged you, John Rayburn," Luigiantia said. "So that you answer our questions without unwanted emotion."

"Casey."

"Where is your iaciorator, John Rayburn?"

"Everywhere."

"What universe is it in?"

"Every one we settled."

"No, the specific universe where the iaciorator is located," she insisted.

John felt himself grow angry, but in an abstract way.

"I told you, every settled universe!"

"Which ones?"

"That's a secret."

"You need to tell me," Luigiantia said. "Do you have two? Did you find two of them?"

"Didn't find any," John said. "It found me. I found me."

"Did someone give you the iaciorator?"

"Yes! But it's broken. Only goes one way."

"What?"

"Broken. Can only go up. One-way trip."

"If your iaciorator is broken, how can you travel anywhere?"

"Made my own," John said.

"What did you say?" Luigiantia asked, incredulous.

"I made my own iokinatinator, whatever."

"You made your own iaciorator? Without fail-safes? You can travel anywhere?"

"Haven't tried anywhere," John said. "Induction suggests I can. Can't you?"

"There are limits. Practical and otherwise," Luigiantia said, but quietly, as if she were speaking to herself.

"I had a limitation. I reverse engineered it." John's mind was slowly coming unfogged. He'd been drugged. He felt the freedom of it dissipating, and with it a dread that he had revealed too much. Had he told Luigiantia where the settled universes were? But she knew who he was. By a process of elimination—by the process of eliminating every John Rayburn—she could eliminate the Pinball Wizards.

"Leave us," she said to someone beyond John's vision. A door opened and shut.

"What does your iaciorator look like?"

"It's—"

John forced himself to remain silent.

"It's—"

"What does it look like?"

"Negotiate!" John shouted.

"I'll drug you and get what I want! Answer the question."

"No! You attacked us. You attacked us! You killed us! You killed Casey!"

"Vermin!"

"Murderers!"

"You want to be left in peace?"

"Yes!"

"You can't be! You'll kill us all, and you have no idea why!"

"We won't!"

"You've never heard of the Vigilari, have you?"

"Never."

"You're from a fallow universe."

John didn't answer as he had no idea what that meant.

"One where there is no idea of transdimensional travel," she added.

"None."

"And you found some—machine—that allows you to move from one universe to another."

"My doppelganger did."

"Your dup."

"My doppelganger."

"What does the device look like?"

"A disk, ten centimeters in diameter, just a centimeter thick. With controls and a display."

Luigiantia gasped.

"That small?"

"It fits under my clothes."

"Where did your dup—your doppelganger—get it?"

"No more answers! We deal! You leave us alone!"

"That can never happen, John Rayburn. You're too dangerous for the universe."

"No!"

She reached for something, a needle.

"I need to know where that device is, John Rayburn. I need to know where you have been. Your traces have to be sterilized before it's too late."

"No!"

A door slammed open and there were words spoken quickly, breathlessly, in a language John didn't recognize.

Luigiantia turned back toward him.

"Do your doppelgangers know which universe this is?"

"No."

"Then why has there been an unauthorized incursion?"

She barked orders in her own language. He was unbelted from the bed and helped into a wheelchair.

"I don't know how we could know where you are. We only knew vaguely of you from Corrundrum and the Alarians."

"The Alarians? Of course.

"Take him to his room," she ordered. "We'll finish this, John Rayburn, and you'll tell me what I need to know."

He was too weak to lunge out of the chair, too weak to try to run. His body was limp and useless. The orderly pushed him into a white hallway. Sunlight streaked the floor through high windows. It felt like he was in a hospital. It smelled like a hospital.

An incursion! The Wizards were looking for him.

They passed a window. A small rock garden with a fountain stood in a courtyard. This world seemed artificial, not real. He'd been to the Pleistocene world enough to know what an empty universe felt like. This wasn't the Vigilari's home universe. It was a staging universe. A firewall between them and the rest of the multiverse.

Why?

"What universe is this?" he asked, not expecting an answer.

There was a flash of light. The orderly gasped. Then a roll of thunder slammed across the world, a wave of density that plugged his ears and made him gag. He'd felt this before, only much closer.

The orderly pushed him quickly to the next window, one facing the other direction—outside.

A mushroom cloud rose on the horizon.

"Prime! You son of a bitch!" John said. Oh, what had they done?

CHAPTER 40

"It's an empty world," Henry Home said. "Not Pleistocene. No megafauna or megaflora. It's like our world, only empty."

"How could they be from an empty world?" Casey Low asked. "That makes no sense."

"It's a staging world," Grace Home said. "Not their home world, but something in between."

"For protection," Casey said.

"A firewall," Henry said.

"I feel better about nuking it," Grace Home said. "No collateral damage."

"So no sign of them?" Grace Top said.

"Well, we sent a probe through from our Columbus site, from our Findlay site, and from our Toledo site," Henry Top explained. "Simple camera probes. Scanned the entire horizon. Neat stuff. Let me draw it on the chalkboard—"

"Henry," Grace Home, Grace Top, and Grace Champ said at the same time.

"Right. Nothing at the quarry. Nothing at Columbus. But we got a sighting at Toledo," Henry Gore said.

"About six kilometers to the southeast," Henry Low added.

"Huge structure," Henry Case said.

"Nothing else," Henry Pinball said.

"That's the spot then," Prime said. "Six klicks away and downwind. That'll get their attention. Next one will be right on top of that structure if they don't give us John."

Grace Home held his gaze. She nodded.

She said, "Set up another gate near the structure on this side. And another halfway there. And one more to be safe, on the other side. We'll have nukes at each location. We'll escalate if we have to."

"Got it," the Henrys said in unison.

John Prime and John Gore transferred over at the first Toledo site into Universe 0010—Site #1. They placed the SADM device next to a tree on a level spot of ground.

"How long?" John Gore asked.

"Ten minutes."

Then Prime looked up and saw the rise of an aircraft in the distance coming their way.

"Better make that two minutes."

"Then we've got to make the next transfer cycle!" The gate at Site #1 in 7650 was flashing every sixty seconds to bring them back. Prime checked his watch. They had twelve seconds until the next one.

"We'll make the next cycle. Two minutes."

"Okay."

John Gore set the timer, and together they turned their switches.

"One, two, three!"

It took four hands to activate the SADM, all toggling switches within a second of each other. No single person could activate one. There had to be two madmen. *Not to worry,* Prime thought, *Pinball Wizards has a plethora of madmen.*

The Site #1 gate cycled with a small whoosh of air, the result of whatever pressure differential than existed between the two universes. They ran to stand in the transfer zone, holding each other's shoulders and counting to sixty.

"Get ready," Prime said.

"It's fast. It's gonna get caught in the blast."

Prime eyed the aircraft coming toward them. It wouldn't reach them within sixty seconds. "Screw 'em," he said.

He glanced at his watch.

"Here we go," he said.

The universe jumped and they were in Universe 7650.

"Mark site one as radioactive in Universe 0010. Don't transfer there from here," he said to the Henry working their gate.

"Noted."

"Tell the teams that they have some sort of detection system," Prime said. "Don't send a nuke through—or anything else—unless we plan to use it."

"Right."

"Let's get to Site Number Two."

Site #2 was three kilometers to the southwest toward the structure they had spotted in Universe 0010. Prime hoped it was far enough away from the first explosion.

"Did you notice which way the wind was blowing?" he asked John Gore.

"From the southwest," John Gore replied.

"Good."

They had a car standing by and reached the abandoned high school in minutes. The gate was in the gymnasium.

"What's the word?" Prime asked the Henry who was attending the transfer gate. It was the largest transfer gate they'd built so far, a marvel that three Henrys had worked all night on, that would cast a transfer zone fifteen meters in diameter. Henry put down the phone as the two entered.

"They dropped the pamphlets from Site Number Four," he said. "Right next to a boom box blaring static noise."

"Someone will notice that," John Gore said.

"I don't know," Prime said. "That nuclear bomb is probably a pretty large distraction right now."

The Henry added, "And we have confirmation on the explosion. They've moved the transfer gate at Site Number Four a hundred meters north of the drop site and are watching the site every ten minutes via a remote camera."

"What do the pamphlets say? What did Grace settle on?" Prime asked.

The Henry handed him a piece of paper with large-type font on it. It read, *Parlay at 41.5, -83.6 at noon local time. Bring John Rayburn and all his belongings. Otherwise we will detonate nuclear bombs on your facility. The Wizards.*

"Let's hope they know how to use our grid system and our time system," Prime said.

"They attacked us in 7351," the Henry said. "They must."

"What's at this location there?"

"Prairie, we think. We haven't looked."

"And how far is it from here?"

"About one hundred meters west."

Prime checked his watch. Noon was two hours away, and enough time for him to gather enough firepower.

"Send me through to Universe 9000," Prime said. "I'll drop something through over there when I need you to transfer me back through." He pointed to the far corner of the gym.

"Are you sure?" the Henry said. "That isn't part of the plan."

"We could always use more firepower," Prime said.

It took him far less time to gather his firepower. He had it waiting when the rest of the team showed up.

"Where the hell did you get that?" Grace Top shouted. She looked flushed and flustered, exhausted from coordinating four transfer sites across multiple universes.

"Same place the nukes came from," Prime said. "Universe 9000." He patted the M1 Abrams tank on its desert-camo-painted flank. Inside were a dozen assault rifles, a handful of grenades, and a bazooka. He didn't mention that part to Grace.

"We're bargaining for John's life!" she screamed. "We can't escalate our chances away."

"We sorta escalated it already," Prime said with a grin.

"What sort of bloodthirsty bastard are you?"

"One who's going to get our Johnny Farmboy back," he said. "Is it time?"

"Five minutes," a Henry said.

"Let's go now," Prime said. He jumped up to the hatch of the M1.

"We check with a camera first," Grace said. "That's the plan."

Prime reached down and started the tank. It rumbled to life, drowning out Grace's words. Grace turned toward the Henry and mimed the number five to him.

One of the Johns motioned Prime forward in his behemoth, and he rumbled it into the transfer zone.

Prime lifted his head out of the hatch and shouted, "Everyone who's coming better find a place aboard."

The Henry manning the gate controls glanced at Grace Home. Her face was grim, but she nodded and Graces, Henrys, Johns, and Caseys, all armed with rifles, grenades, pistols, and Kevlar jackets, climbed aboard the tank, clinging to handholds.

The Henry climbed aboard and shouted at John Prime, "I'm sending you through. Then I'll transfer again in exactly sixty seconds. Then I do it at five-minute intervals. Get out of the zone fast, unless you need to come back right away."

"Got it."

The Henry got down. He counted down from five on his fingers and flipped the switch.

CHAPTER 41

Luigiantia reappeared dressed in a black cloak. She wore weapons and devices at her belt. Six soldiers escorted her into the huge bay where John had been wheeled and left to wait for an hour. The mushroom cloud had risen into the stratosphere and dissipated slowly as he and the orderly watched. Even so, the eastern skies remained dirty and dark.

After what seemed like ten minutes—though it could have been longer, they were so mesmerized by the explosion—a runner found them and shouted an order in the Vig language.

The orderly turned the wheelchair around and headed deeper

into the facility. John saw black walls ahead as high as ten stories. It looked like an enclosed stadium or hangar.

They came to a checkpoint that separated the facility he had been kept in from the hangar. Four soldiers covered in battle gear and armed with weird-looking weapons took the orderly's laminated ID. They stared at John, and their harsh words made it clear that they had no interest in letting him into the hangar. The orderly shrugged, intimidated.

Finally after some conversation on a two-way radio, they let the orderly push John into the hangar, but not without an escort of one soldier. John noticed that the technology of the enemy was eclectic. The two-way radios looked like something he could buy at an electronic supply store. Yet, the use of transdimensional technology was more advanced than anything his own universe might have. John had assumed that the level of technology he had seen of the enemy in 7351 had been to match the technology in that universe; anything too advanced would have stood out and caught attention. Other than the transfer technology—the iaciorator—there was no great differentiating technology—nothing that made him think these were superintelligent overlords.

The soldier led the orderly and John into a hallway. A pair of glass doors opened before them, and then closed with a hiss as they passed. They were in a small airlock. The pressure changed; John felt his ears pop. He smelled some sort of antiseptic smell. The doors ahead of them slid apart, and they were in the hangar itself.

Inside, the hangar was humongous. It was at least a kilometer long and three hundred meters tall. Huge machines were parked within the structure, and smaller machines, wheeled ones and fixed-wing aircraft, were parked beneath and around the larger ones. Some of them looked like blimps. One seemed to be the craft that had attacked and captured him.

"These are all transfer devices," John said.

"What?" the orderly said.

"Iaciorator," he said. "These are all iaciorators."

The orderly snorted. "What else would they be?"

"Is this where you make them?"

"Make them?"

"Your factory?"

"What are you talking about? No one makes iaciorators!"

I do, John thought to himself.

"Are these all of them? Are these all you have?"

The orderly was about to answer, but the soldier grunted. Apparently he didn't want John to know the answer, but he had it now.

The Vigilari had found transfer technology just like he had. They controlled it, but the number of devices they had was limited. They couldn't create it.

As he watched, a crew of twenty people ran toward one of the huge machines. They were evacuating. Their cache of transfer devices was in danger. Another nuclear device on this structure would put them out of business.

Everywhere, soldiers and crewmen were rushing toward the machines and preparing them for departure. The larger ones clearly could not be started and moved quickly. But the smaller ones could. A wheeled vehicle, sort of like a six-wheel earthmover, powered up and slowly rolled down the floor of the hangar. It entered an irising door that shut behind it. Another airlock. Why?

One of the large machines powered up with a shrill intensity and then disappeared with a boom. The hangar shook with its disappearance, from the air it had displaced suddenly rushing in.

Twice more large machines transferred out, and a half-dozen smaller machines disappeared, either using the airlock or transferring directly from the hangar to some other universe. No machines came back.

The evacuation looked haphazard and slow, as if they couldn't believe they would ever be under attack.

Finally Luigiantia appeared with her escort. She pointed to one of the multiwheeled machines, and the orderly pushed John toward it. He was fairly certain he could now walk by himself if need be. His brain was clear of the drug. But he stayed put and even slouched a bit as if he were too weak to sit up straight.

A driver was already on board their machine. Luigiantia and the soldiers found chairs. The orderly strapped the wheelchair into its own spot in the center of the aisle. From there, he could see into the cockpit and out the front window.

John scanned the insides of the machine. It looked odd, as if it had been cobbled together. The metal of the floor and the walls had an odd bluish sheen. The chairs weren't even bolted into it. Instead ropes and cords lashed the chairs in place.

John was certain then that they didn't know how to build devices.

"Where did you guys find all these machines?" John asked Luigiantia.

"Shut up," she said.

"I thought you built them. I thought you controlled the technology," he said. "But you're just exploiters."

"It's our technology."

"Can you build new iaciorators?"

She didn't answer him.

The machine rumbled forward toward an airlock.

"And why all the airlocks?"

"Shut up!"

A soldier drew a pistol and pointed it at John. He looked at the barrel and shrugged.

The machine filled just a third of the airlock's area. It paused between the doors, and then the outer doors opened and the machine surged forward. Facing forward, John could see their progress better than any of the soldiers.

The vehicle turned to the northeast. The mushroom cloud had dissipated, but the sky was still a dark ruddy color that seemed similar to clouds before a tornado. There was no road, but still the vehicle could make forty kilometers per hour over the grass.

John watched as a speck on the horizon slowly grew in size.

He almost laughed when he saw it was an M1 tank.

Prime drove the tank forward.

"Mark the transfer zone!" Grace Home said. A Henry had a can of spray paint that he used to mark the edge of the zone. He was halfway done when Grace yelled, "Ten seconds." The Henry backed away. Grace threw a pad of paper a meter into the zone.

"What did you say?" Prime asked.

"That we were clear for now and to keep to the five-minute schedule," she said.

The notebook disappeared. Prime checked his watch.

"Here they come," someone said.

In the distance, a plume of dirt rose behind a black vehicle.

"That's your iaciorator?" Luigiantia cried. "It's U.S. technology! How was it fitted inside a tank?"

John shrugged. She knew the Wizards could build their own devices, but she didn't understand they had transfer gates. How could he use that?

She shouted orders to the driver. The vehicle slowed and stopped about thirty meters from the tank. John saw that a dozen people stood on or near the tank. They were armed with assault weapons and were dressed in army fatigues that seemed to be covering body armor. John Prime was in the hatch of the tank. Grace Home was hanging from the tank, and the two seemed to be having heated words.

John didn't reply.

"Did it come that way or did you fit it in there?"

John shrugged.

"A tank? How foolish!"

She didn't seem to have any concept of a transfer device that fit on a person either. They hadn't gotten his device.

Luigiantia barked a command at the orderly then exited the machine, taking two soldiers with her. Apparently John was staying in the vehicle.

She strode in long, forceful strides toward the tank, stopping ten meters away. She was wearing a microphone for the benefit of the soldiers left behind in the vehicle because her voice boomed inside when she began to speak.

"You have violated the sovereignty of the Order of the Vigilari," she shouted. "As such your lives and property are forfeit. Disarm yourselves and hand over your iaciorator."

John shook his head. "That's not gonna work," he muttered. "You guys are used to getting your way, aren't you?"

Grace hopped down from the tank. She was dressed in desert camo, but carried no weapons. She walked forward until she was just a meter from Luigiantia.

Grace looked her square in the face.

"We are at war," Grace said simply. "If you fail to deliver John Rayburn to us, we will nuke that structure into a glass-lined crater."

Before Luigiantia could answer, Grace turned on her heel and walked away.

John Prime couldn't believe how cool Grace was. He would have yelled and screamed at that amazon bitch with her attitude. Grace was handling it better than he would have, not that he'd admit that aloud.

Grace motioned at a Henry, and he wheeled the SADM they had brought with them forward.

"Arm it for four minutes," she said. "But don't start the timer."

"Right."

"The Order of the Vigilari do not negotiate with vermin," Luigiantia shouted. "Your existence is a danger to the universe! You threaten the existence of every human in every universe."

Grace didn't even turn.

"You're going to ignore her?" Prime asked.

"She doesn't see us as on her level," Grace said. "The longer she has to cater to us, the more angry she'll be, the more likely she is to make a mistake."

"You all right?" Prime asked. Sweat was beading on her forehead and she looked pale. "Henry, get her some water."

A Henry handed her a bottle of water, from which she took a long drink.

"I'm all right," she said. "Wheel the nuke after me."

Grace turned and walked up to Luigiantia. She stood there and waited for Henry to push the nuclear device up.

"If you fail to deliver John Rayburn to us in four minutes, we will detonate this nuclear warhead," she said. She pointed at the timer.

The two soldiers shared nervous glances.

"We do not negotiate with disease vectors," Luigiantia said.

"Start the timer," Grace said. Another Henry dashed forward

and the two of them held the four switches down. The timer began

Luigiantia inhaled. The two soldiers backed away.

"You're bluffing."

"No, I don't bluff," Grace said. "You've attacked us for no reason. You've destroyed hundreds of our people. We want nothing more than to live in peace."

Luigiantia stared at the timer.

"You fools. You can't be allowed to move between universes. We take our duty seriously, to keep the universes safe, not for our own personal gain. Death follows irresponsible use of the iaciorator."

"Death follows you," Grace said. "You have—" She glanced at the timer. "—three minutes and ten seconds."

"Where did you get these atomic devices?" she asked. "Do you represent a government? No. You are too young. Too many of you are just dups. Where did this come from?"

"We found them."

"Where?"

"Why does it matter?" Grace asked.

"Because they are not easy to come by!" Luigiantia said.

John Prime hopped down from the tank and walked forward.

"We got them from an empty world," he said. Grace turned on him and shot him a dark look. Still he continued. He couldn't help but gloat at the woman. "A whole goddamn world of weapons that we can use on you and your bastard friends. How do you like them berries?"

Luigiantia took a step backward.

"A plague world? You have been to a plague world?"

"She's pushing too hard," John muttered. These were fanatics, as fanatical as the Alarians were.

There was a burst of words from the radio. The driver turned and said something to one of the soldiers left in the vehicle.

A worried look passed among the remaining forward soldiers.

"What's going on?" John asked the orderly.

"We have company," the orderly said. "The big—"

A soldier barked at him. The orderly shut up, but he started unlatching John's wheelchair.

As he bent close, he whispered, "The big bitch may have finally bitten off more than she can chew."

The orderly backed John down the ramp into the grass. The smell on the wind was acrid. The orderly pushed him toward Luigiantia. She and Grace watched him approach, though Grace's smile did not match the dark grimace of disgust on Luigiantia.

John realized her eyes were focused behind him.

He turned to look over his shoulder. Another ground vehicle was approaching.

"John, how are you? Why are you in that chair?" Grace asked.

"I'm fine. I was being interrogated by my hosts," John said.

"Who are these people?"

"They're the Vig who the Alarians were scared of," John said. "They try to run the multiverse. Only they seem to be spread a little thin. They don't own the technology." This last part he said with a nod at Grace.

"Stop talking," Luigiantia said, but her heart didn't seem in the threat. Her eyes were still on the approaching vehicle. What had the orderly said? That Luigiantia may have pushed too hard? Maybe they did negotiate after all.

The second vehicle pulled up parallel to the first. It was smaller, not a troop transport, more of a personal vehicle. Two people exited the left side. They were dressed in black like Luigiantia, with one ominous addition. They wore masks.

The two walked forward, but didn't join Luigiantia. They stopped a few meters away and Luigiantia saluted them with a dip of her head and her right fist in her left palm across her chest.

The four remaining soldiers with Luigiantia suddenly appeared. They were now suited in gas masks. One of them handed masks to Luigiantia and the two soldiers who had come out first. There was no mask for the orderly, though he looked about for one.

"Sorry, buddy."

"Screw you, vermin," he said. John was sure he would have run if there weren't soldiers there with guns.

One of the new arrivals said something to Luigiantia.

She replied in tense words, but her senior replied sharply and curtly.

She nodded.

"Please disarm the atomic device," she said in English. "We will negotiate."

"We want John first," Grace said.

Luigiantia motioned with her hand. John stood and walked forward shakily.

Grace hugged him. John saw that she was pale and sweaty. She looked weaker than he felt.

"You okay?" he mouthed.

She nodded.

"Disarm the SADM," she said.

The Henrys flicked the activation switches again and the timer stopped.

Luigiantia's senior spoke again for several seconds, and then she translated.

"You must turn over your iaciorator," she said. "If you do so, we will settle you in the universe of your choice and leave you in peace."

"No," John said. "Those terms are not acceptable."

"You fools," Luigiantia said, and this was no translation. "You'll die as it is. No one visits a plague world and lives."

Her superior barked an order, and she nodded, translating what John had said.

"You cannot be allowed to travel between worlds," Luigiantia said. "You must give up your iaciorator and we will provide you with goods of a value equal to the most wealthy human in your chosen universe. That is our final offer."

"No," John said.

Luigiantia stiffened, but the mask hid what must have been a look of utter hatred.

"No," John said. "If you don't leave us alone, we will release the plans to our iaciorator to every government in every universe we can visit."

"What?" Luigiantia said.

"This isn't our iaciorator," John said, pointing to the tank. "We have as many iaciorators as we can build. We reverse engineered the one we found."

Luigiantia just stared at them until her superior said something to her.

She turned and spoke, and then the two superiors spoke quickly and furiously between themselves.

"We regret the loss of your peoples' lives," she said. "But our duty is grim and required for all the universes' safety."

"You didn't have to nuke us!" Grace shouted.

John put a hand on her arm. "Hold on, Grace."

"You have committed foolish and reprehensible actions," Luigiantia said. "But we are at an impasse. We will maintain a truce under the following conditions."

"They can't—" Grace started to say.

"Stop, Grace, and we may get out of here alive," John whispered. To Luigiantia, he said, "What are the conditions?"

"Leave this universe immediately. Do not return. Do not come to any universe below 7000. Ever. Do not share the plans for the iaciorator with anyone. Ever. If you violate these truce conditions, we will sterilize all the universes you or your dups inhabit."

"We've got them by the balls," Prime hissed. "We can't back down."

"We accept those terms," John said. To Grace he whispered, "We have a cycler going?"

"Yeah, ninety seconds until the next one," she said.

"Let's take the nuke and go," John said.

John turned back toward the Vigilari.

"We are going to leave. We'll abide by these truce conditions if you stay out of our settled universes."

Luigiantia sneered at him. "We would not go near your universes!"

"Good. Let's go."

Supported by Grace on one side and Prime on the other, he limped back toward the marked-off transfer zone.

"Sixty seconds," a Henry said.

"What about the tank?" Prime said.

"Leave it," he said. "We're about to freak them the hell out."

"Why?"

"They don't think a transfer device can be anything other than a vehicle."

"What?" Prime said.

"They have no idea how to make a transfer device," John said.

"Thirty seconds."

All dozen of them stood in the marked-off area.

Luigiantia was staring at them through her mask.

"Ten seconds."

John turned his back on Luigiantia and waited.

The world disappeared.

CHAPTER 42

John looked around at the school gymnasium.

"John!" Henry Home said, looking up from the controls of the transfer gate. "We did it!"

He nodded.

John Prime whooped. "Oh, hell yes, we did it! We own the multiverse!"

John looked around the room at his friends, his brothers and sisters. He met the eyes of one Casey and looked away quickly. His Casey was gone.

He felt no desire to celebrate.

He glanced at Grace Home, who nodded slightly, as if she recognized his mood. She still looked flushed, as if the excitement of the last day was too much for her.

She squeezed his arm.

"It'll be okay, John," she said. "We can . . . rebuild."

Even as she said it, John knew how weak the words were. He nodded anyway.

"Sure."

"I know it looks grim now. . . ."

John was looking at Grace when she collapsed.

He jumped to her side, catching her head before it bounced off the gym floor. He laid her gently on the floor.

"Grace! Grace!"

He felt her forehead. She was burning up.

Her breathing was suddenly labored. Her lungs seemed congested.

John looked up at John Prime.

"What have you done?"

"What?" But Prime was backing away.

"You've been pillaging a plague world! What the hell were you thinking?"

"It never infected me!"

"Then it must have been all right? Is that what you thought? You goddamn narcissist. You've killed us all."

"What do you mean? We'll take her to the hospital. She'll be all right."

"The Vig aren't there just to control transfer devices. They cauterize disease! They stop this from happening," John shouted. "The only reason they let us leave was because they knew we'd kill ourselves in months, if not days."

"How was I supposed to know?" Prime cried.

John advanced on him.

"You were supposed to think about someone other than yourself."

Prime backed away. He looked at his own Casey, who would not meet his gaze.

"I did this for you. They wouldn't have backed down without the nukes."

"You did it for yourself!" John said. "It was just convenient for you to help the rest of us."

Prime stopped backing up. He stood up straight.

"Screw you all, you ungrateful bastards."

He reached into his shirt.

"You all are on your own."

He disappeared.

CHAPTER 43

"We need to get her to a hospital," Henry said. "She's gonna die. Someone get a car. Get her in a car. Where's the nearest hospital?" His arms fluttered up and down like a chicken's wings.

"I have keys," another Grace said. She started for the door of the gymnasium.

"Stop," John said.

Grace looked at him blankly. "She's sick!"

"This plague wiped out an entire world," John said. "An entire world."

"But—"

"Think! All of us may already be dead," John said. "If we go to a hospital, if we interact with anyone else in this world, we may kill everyone in this entire world. Somehow, these weapons that Prime brought from his plague world have infected us."

"But we have to do something!"

"I know!" John shouted. "I know we do!" He looked down at Grace Home. Her face was pale, her breathing shallow. Her lips were colorless. "We can't take her to a hospital here."

Henry Home stared at him. "It's not one hundred percent fatal. Prime survived! And they may have an antidote here that they didn't have in 2000. We have to try."

John shook his head. "The risk is too great. We shouldn't even be here now. We need to leave this universe."

"And go where?"

"The Pleistocene universe. Universe 7535."

"But there's no supplies there! No medicine! She'll die for sure there," Henry Home cried.

"We have to keep this universe safe," John said. "You and she have loved ones here! Everyone you know could die!"

"No! We're taking her to the hospital!"

"Henry—" John began.

"Stop." Grace Home's eyes were open. She nodded at Henry.

"John's right. We need to isolate the danger. Isolate the infection. Just like the Vig."

"But—"

"It's the way it's gonna be," Grace said.

Henry looked ready to argue, but then he nodded too.

The gymnasium was filled with weapons and supplies, things the team thought might be needed in the rescue of John. Now they could use everything to survive in the Pleistocene world while they figured out what to do about Grace.

"Take everything," John said. "Food, gear, weapons. And we need the portable gates too."

"In case we want to get back," another John said.

"In case we ever can get back," replied a Grace.

In ten minutes, they had gathered up their equipment, and Henry Home was setting the timer of the gate.

"Can we leave this here?" Henry asked.

"It may not matter at all in a bit," John said. "Is this everyone?"

Henry Home nodded. "I think so."

"You held no one in reserve when you came to rescue me?" John asked.

"I guess that seems kinda silly now," Henry replied.

"No, I appreciate it," John said. "Let's get out of here as quickly as possible."

The air smelled of char.

They were only a few kilometers south of the crater that was New Toledo. Six days ago, Casey had died. Six days.

"Are we safe this close?" Henry Pinball asked.

Henry Low checked the wind with his finger. "We're not downwind of the site. We're not upwind either. Unless the wind starts coming from the north, we should be fine."

They set up tents in two locations. In one location, they placed Grace Home. Two other Graces—Grace Champ and Grace Pinball—volunteered to stay and care for her with damp washcloths and antipyretics from the first-aid kits. The rest of the team set up in the remaining tents one hundred meters away to the west.

"We're just waiting to die," Henry Top said.

"What are we going to do?" John Low asked. He looked at John expectantly.

John shook his head. "I don't know."

"We need to kill Prime," Casey Pinball said. "That's what we need to do."

John felt a twinge of horror at the power of her attack, though she wasn't his Casey or Prime's Casey.

"He's long gone," Henry Top said.

"Can we risk a hospital in any universe?" John Low asked. "Maybe some universe has a cure."

"How do we know which?" John asked. They had been stupid. The Vig didn't exploit the universes. They protected them from infection. Each universe was its own petri dish of germs. It was lucky they hadn't infected their colonized universes sooner.

"Maybe the Vig know," John Low said.

"Would they help us?" Casey Pinball asked.

"They want nothing more than for us to kill ourselves off," John said. "They were scared of disease. They only traveled to known safe universes, and they used airlocks even then to keep their base clean."

"What about that Corrundrum guy? He was a traveler," Henry Home said.

"They rented Vig technology, I think. Or paid heavily to use it," John said. "They must have. But they went to known safe universes."

"Prime never got sick," Casey Pinball said. "He traveled to Universe 2000 and he never got sick. He should be dead."

"He should be," John said. Why wasn't Prime dead?

"Why isn't Prime dead?" John Case asked.

Why wasn't Prime dead?

"How do other travelers deal with disease?" John asked. He looked at each of the Wizards clustered around him.

"Avoidance," Grace Low said.

"Expendables," Henry Quayle said.

"Airlocks and airtight vehicles," Grace Gore said.

"We're travelers," Casey Case said, "and we ignored it."

"What else?" John asked.

The Henrys shrugged as one. "What other travelers are there?"

"The one Superprime got the device from," John Low said.

"Yes," John said. "And he had no airlocks. He had no vehicle. Corrundrum spoke of a vehicle. Everyone but us and the singleton traveler have vehicles and we based our devices on his."

"Maybe he just avoided the plague worlds," Grace Gore said.

"How do you know ahead of time if a world is a plague world?" Henry Quayle said.

"You can't," John said. "Any universe could be a plague world. Any petri dish could breed a killer bug."

"And a universe that was safe the last time you visited could be infected the next time," John Low said.

"The singleton died from a malfunction or sabotage of his device," John said. "Not from disease. He had no enclosed vehicle. But his device was different than the Vigs'. He had different technology."

"Better technology."

"Yes, better. He didn't fear disease like the Vig did," John said.

"You're guessing," Grace Gore said.

"What else do we have at the moment?" John said. "But if what we've just deduced is correct . . ."

"Then he had some other method to defend against disease," Henry Quayle concluded. "We need to find Prime."

"Where's Casey Prime?" John asked, searching the faces of the remaining Caseys.

"She's not here," Grace Gore said.

"Did she even come through from Home Office?"

"She must have slipped out."

John looked at the Wizards. "I need to find John Prime, and she's our best bet."

Before John left, he had Grace Gore take his temperature three times over thirty minutes.

"I'll do this for all of us," she said.

No one seemed sick except for Grace Home, nor did her two caretakers appear to be catching any virus. However, Henry Quayle became pale just before John left. He excused himself and stumbled the hundred meters to the other tent.

"I hope we've given ourselves enough time to be sure I don't have it," John said.

"You're taking a chance," Grace Gore said. "Is it worth it?"

"Casey Home was exposed," John said. "She's already risked it."

"So that makes it okay to do it again?" Grace Gore said.

"It's Grace over there," John said loudly. "I figured you'd be more concerned about saving her."

"I am," she said. "We all are. But not at the risk of billions of people. If you feel unwell, come back immediately."

"Though it'll probably be too late," Grace Case said.

John nodded.

He used the portable gate to transfer to Home Office. He found himself in a field outside the abandoned school. He hitched his backpack over his shoulder and trotted around the school toward the parking lot to one of the cars they had left there.

The desolate school building startled him. The place was silent and empty, just as a plague-ridden world might appear. But then he was on the highway heading north and he was surrounded by people in their cars. He refused to think of the viruses streaming from his lungs, the bacteria shedding from his skin.

No, they would not die.

He drove to the quarry site and transferred to Universe 7533—Prime's universe, or rather his own first universe. He found a company car in the quarry lot and the keys for it on the wall inside the building. John headed north toward Toledo.

He turned off toward Prime's house, parked in front of it, and waited. The house was quiet, all the blinds pulled shut. Had Casey managed to get to 7533 yet? Had Casey had keys for one of the cars at the school or had she had to take a taxi or call for a ride to the quarry? Perhaps he had beaten her home. Perhaps she hadn't gone home at all. Was Prime within, watching him, ready to jump to a new universe if John pressed him?

John was about to try the front door when his father's old beat-up truck pulled into the driveway. Casey Prime got out and walked to the passenger's side where she pulled Abby from her car seat. It was then that she saw John.

She stood staring at him for a moment, then shrugged, and motioned him to follow her into the house.

It had been a little less than a year since he had been in Prime's house, but he saw in an instant that the décor had changed. The paintings on the walls weren't prints. The furniture was well made. A huge TV dominated one wall of the living room.

Casey was in the kitchen, where John saw all new appliances. He stuck his head in Prime's study, not expecting to see him. A pedestal held a sculpture of a female bent and doubled over under some sort of pressure from above.

Plunder from a dead world.

"You snuck out," John said.

"I wasn't leaving her," Casey said. She nodded at Abby.

Abby was three now, she smiled up at John. "Hi, Daddy."

"Hi, Abby," John said. He didn't correct her. John reached out and touched her forehead.

Casey glared at him and lifted her out of his reach. "We don't have a fever."

"You sure? No weakness, nausea?"

"No, none. We're fine," Casey said. "How about you? Did you bring the plague here?"

"No, I'm fine," John said, but he wondered. Did he seem flushed? Was his breath too fast?

"Go play," Casey said, shooing Abby toward the playroom in the back. To John, she said, "I know why you're here. You think I know where my John is."

"Yes, we need him."

"Why? For revenge?"

"No, he spent the most time in the plague universe, but he's uninfected. I think I know why."

"He's not here," Casey said. "You know I just got back, so how could I know?"

"You know Prime better than anyone. You must have some idea where he went."

"You're him. You must have some clue," Casey countered.

"Did you know he had the device?"

"No," she said. She paused. "How do you do it?"

"What?"

"She died a week ago."

John felt a lump of sorrow in his throat. Yet he was looking at Casey right in front of him. A million Caseys existed though his was dead at New Toledo. And more would die in the Pleistocene world.

"I dunno," he muttered.

Casey slipped close to him. She smelled like his Casey. Not the perfume, but the tang of her skin. It was overwhelming. She reached around him and drew him closer.

He found himself sobbing.

"Shush, shush," Casey said. "It's okay."

She rocked him back and forth gently while he cried. Finally he quieted, and she looked up at him with eyes that were damp as well.

She rose on her tiptoes and kissed him.

Without thought, he responded, kissing Prime's Casey deeply. It was not a polite kiss. Their tongues touched.

She had been his Casey before she had been Prime's.

She felt right in his arms.

"Casey," he said.

"John," she whispered. "There's a place for you right here."

He blinked, stepped back, and looked at her closely. It wasn't right.

John pushed her away.

"You're married to him."

"I'm married to John Rayburn," she said. "Aren't you John Rayburn?"

"I can't stay here. I can't slide into his place."

"He slid into your place," Casey said. "Abby would never know. You could be her father. She'd never know her real one left her."

"Did he? Did he leave you?"

"I know he did," Casey said in disgust. "I know he left, now that he has the device again. He won't have to stay."

"I need to find him, Casey. I have to find him now. Before he runs."

"And then you'll come back here," Casey said.

"Casey, stop it."

"If you want to know where John Prime is, say you'll come back to me."

"Casey, I can't do that."

She bit her lip. "John is nothing without a Casey. You'll come back to me. You're the one I loved."

"No."

She stepped closer, reaching for his face. John took her wrist and held her at arm's length. "I won't do this, Casey. I will not. Tell me now where Prime is. You have to."

Casey glared at him. She yanked her wrist free.

"Forget it. Leave."

"Grace is going to die," John said. "Unless you tell me where he is. And every other one of us in the Pleistocene universe. We're going to die."

Tears were running down Casey's face. "It's not fair, John, that I got him instead of you. It's not fair that I got the bad one. I should have had you."

John nodded. "I know."

She sighed. "He owns a tract of land near Findlay. He doesn't know I know, but the bank called because the insurance changed. He's got a workshop there, and a gate. I checked."

"What's the address?" John asked.

"I have it here."

John took it from her and turned without another word.

"John . . ."

He paused at the door.

"I mean it," she said. "I'm done with him. I thought he was the same as you, but he isn't."

"Okay."

John nodded and left.

John knelt in the brush and watched Prime's corrugated metal lab.

Nothing moved. There was no sound. He crept closer.

A car was in the dirt drive. He felt the exhaust pipe with his palm. Cold. He couldn't have beaten Prime here. Or had Prime gone somewhere else first?

John ran to the door and looked through the small pane of reinforced glass. Overhead halogens lit the long room inside. He saw workbenches, tools, equipment, and an early-model transfer gate. John Prime wasn't inside, unless he was very near the doorway and out of view.

John waited, and then tried the door. It opened and he slipped inside the Quonset. No Prime.

He checked the gate. The matrix was set to Universe 9000. The plague world. That didn't mean he was there; Prime had the device now. He could have gone anywhere. Though no farther ahead than 9000. He had to have a return gate in 9000. Probably on this exact site in that universe. John didn't dare go to Universe 9000. He'd surely become infected if he did.

John rifled through the lab tables. He paged through a notebook with notes on Prime's exploration of Universe 9000. He paused at a list of artwork. On the next page was a list of banks in Toledo. Next to the table was a heavy safe on the floor. It was locked. Probably full of money.

A stack of photos lay on the next table. John stared at the robotic figure at the center of each. What had Prime found? Aliens?

There was a pop of air.

John spun.

Prime was standing in the center of the lab, looking in the opposite direction. He was dressed in fatigues and carried a rocket launcher over his shoulder.

John ran and jumped at Prime. He had no choice, if Prime used the device, he was gone forever.

John tackled Prime and grabbed him around the neck. They sprawled across the floor. The rocket launcher skittered into the corner.

Prime turned in his grip and grunted when he saw it was John.

He reached into his shirt to activate the device.

John leaped at him and clung to his chest.

The world shifted.

They were in an abandoned farmhouse.

Prime stumbled. The device had sheared a circle from the

decrepit floor and the two were standing knee-deep in the floor-boards. If the house had had a basement, they would have fallen through.

Prime struggled up and onto the floor. John grabbed for his leg and missed.

Prime scuttled away from him, grinning. He reached into his shirt to trigger the device.

"You won't get it back, John," he said. "And you're stuck in 7534 now."

He threw the switch. Nothing happened.

He hadn't toggled the universe number forward. It was still set to 7534.

John lunged at him.

The world shifted, and they were on a grassy plain.

7535, the Pleistocene world.

John slammed his elbow into Prime's face, momentarily stunning him.

He reached into Prime's shirt and started ripping at the belts holding the device in place. John couldn't get a grip and he couldn't find the buckles.

Prime regained his focus and pushed John away. John came back at him, but Prime planted a foot in John's chest and kicked him.

Prime toggled the device. John leaped, afraid he'd be cut in half if he was outside the radius of the device. He had to stay with him.

The universe stuttered, and they were in a farmhouse, not a ruin.

Someone screamed. A woman turned from the stove to stare at the two men who had materialized in her kitchen.

John slammed his shoulder into Prime's face. He ripped Prime's shirt open and started unbuckling the device's straps. He had one buckle undone when the frying pan smacked him atop the head.

His vision wavered, and he slumped forward.

"Wait!" he said, but the words seemed slurred.

Another blow careened off his back.

He reached up and toggled the device one universe forward. He pressed the button and he and Prime flipped to the next universe.

Twilight on a sloped hill.

John's head throbbed. His vision was doubled. He wanted to

vomit, but struggled to crawl up Prime's body to his throat. He couldn't let Prime go anywhere without him.

He settled a forearm across Prime's windpipe and held him down while he attacked the buckles.

Prime struggled and John couldn't keep ahold of his neck. Prime was as strong as he, as massive as he, had the same reactions and the same skills.

Prime forced a knee up between them and pushed John off him. John found himself sliding down the hill, away from Prime, away from the device. He struggled to grab something to slow his descent. His fingers found the stem of a bush; it bent under his forceful grip, but held. He drew himself up, getting his feet beneath him.

Prime toggled the device. John was too far away to be in the radius of the machine. If he missed the area, he'd be sliced into two pieces, one going on with Prime to the next universe and one staying here on this hill in some unknown universe.

He didn't pause to consider. John launched himself at Prime, screaming in fury.

Pain in his foot.

They fell.

The air flew from his body and he gasped. His foot throbbed. He looked down expecting to see a stump. No, his foot was intact except for a slice off the tip of his big toe. He'd barely made it inside the radius of the device.

Beneath him, Prime groaned, his eyes closed. John had landed atop him, knocking him momentarily unconscious.

John unbuckled the device and rolled Prime over to get the straps out from under him.

He held the abnormally light device in his hands. It was in his control again. He set the device for Universe 7650, Home Universe, and waited for Prime to wake up.

Prime groaned and tossed as he lay unconscious.

John nudged him with his foot.

"Wake up," he said.

Prime groaned again. He fluttered his eyes and they settled on John. Then he glanced at the device in his hands.

PAUL MELKO

"So you got it back. So what."

"I need something from you, John."

"Forget it. I saved your ass twice now. We're done. I don't need that anyway," he said, nodding at the device.

"No, I still need you to save Grace."

"I told you I had no idea the world was still infected!" Prime shouted. "Everyone had been dead for years!"

"I don't care," John said. "I need the artifacts from the lone traveler."

"The who?"

"Where Superprime got the device. Everything that he had on him."

"That shit? It's worthless."

"It's not."

Prime looked at him, and John watched as he came to the same conclusion he had. "You think . . . ?"

"I do."

"Wow." Prime leaned forward, and then groaned. "Ow, I think my ribs are broken."

John leaned in to give him a forearm to hang on to. Prime grimaced as he pulled himself up, and then he was coming faster than John expected. He shouldered heavily into John. An elbow caught him in the nose.

Prime reached for the device in John's other hand. John tucked it into his chest and yanked it away. Prime clung to his shoulders with one hand, and clawed at his throat with the other.

John toggled the device.

They were in Universe 7650.

Shade trees blocked the setting sun. They were in near darkness under a canopy of ashes and maples.

John dropped to the ground, trying to dislodge Prime. Prime's grip loosened and John swung his leg out, kicking at the other's knee.

Prime grunted and fell. John scuttled back.

He toggled the universe counter to Universe 7651. Maybe he should run now, lick his wounds, and find Prime later. But how much time did he have before Grace Home died? Not enough to play things that way. He had to get what he needed from Prime now.

Prime swung something at him. A tree branch, and he was dazed from it. He lost hold of the device, and it slid away from him into the underbrush of shrubs and sticker bushes.

Prime must have seen it fly, because he leaped past John. John grabbed at his feet, but missed. Prime grunted and John was on him, and then the world shifted and they were in 7651.

The trees were gone, and they were in a barn. A horse lifted its head to stare at them. The smell of manure settled in John's nose.

Prime crawled away, catching John with a foot to the side of the head. John sat back dazed. Before he could right his equilibrium, Prime kicked him again and he fell flat on the dirt floor of the barn.

John could see Prime's feet as he lay there. He said something, but he had no idea what. His ears were ringing.

Prime's feet disappeared.

He was gone. Prime had gotten away with the device, and John had no idea where the lone traveler's artifacts were.

He rose to his feet slowly.

He'd blown it.

"Crap!" he said.

At least he was in Universe 7651 and not some unknown universe where he'd have to build a transfer device from scratch. If they'd gone any farther, he and Prime would have been past the settled universes and effectively stranded.

Wait.

Prime had transferred out. The device only went forward; he'd need a transfer gate to get back into the settled zone of universes. Of course, he had one in 9000. Prime had his own gate there.

John scanned the barn. He considered for a moment saddling the horse and racing to the quarry on that. But then he saw the small dirt bike, just like the one Billy Walder had when they were kids.

He grabbed it, and then poked his head out the door of the barn. No one was in sight. John jumped on the starter and the dirt bike fired up. He climbed on the seat, his knees almost knocking the handlebar, and accelerated down the dirt driveway.

Prime's base was on the north side of Findlay. The quarry was on the south. He could keep to the country roads and dirt paths and make it to the transfer gate in Universe Top in fifteen minutes. Then to 9000.

If he wasn't infected now, he would surely be then. He was betting it all on catching Prime in 9000 by surprise. John accelerated down the country road toward the quarry.

CHAPTER 44

John Prime stared at himself in the little handheld mirror. His right eye was swollen shut and one of his teeth was loose. Farmboy had laid into him good, and he'd almost gotten the device back. But no, Prime had managed to get away finally and he was safe in Universe 9000. No one would chase him to a plague world, not even the Vigilari.

He had a first-aid kit in his mobile home. He found it, under the butane stove, next to the cans of beans. The antibacterial ointment stung his knuckles when he applied it. He wrapped his left hand in gauze.

"You should see the other guy," Prime muttered.

His ribs really did feel broken. He'd only overacted a little to draw Farmboy in. There was nothing in his first-aid kit for that. He'd need to find a doctor in a populated universe.

Back in Universe Prime maybe. Where the lone traveler's artifacts sat in a safe in his Quonset hut.

He needed those things. He'd thought they were useless, but they had saved his life, if Farmboy was to be believed. They'd played with the things, microscoped then, X-rayed them, photographed them. They'd shown no sign of internal structure. Yet something saved his life. Something was keeping him from dying in 9000.

Had anyone else worn the ring? No, he only remembered himself wearing it, and then he'd forgotten he'd had it on and had worn the gaudy thing to dinner.

Apparently they hadn't been looking closely enough at the artifacts. The transfer device had been a mystery too, until Farmboy had cracked it. The other things were clearly as interesting, clearly as useful.

How much wealth, fortune, and fame would a healing device bring him?

He'd have to get back to Universe Prime—carefully!—and retrieve the artifacts.

But first he'd need to arm himself again. He'd left his tank in Universe 0010. He chuckled.

Prime had an army truck parked next to his base in Universe 9000, filled with one nuclear bomb, assorted explosives, and a plethora of automatic weapons. He hadn't handed all the SADMs over to the Wizards. He'd kept one for himself, and that made him a nuclear power.

John Prime laughed at the idea.

Him, a nuclear power!

In a fit of violent glee, he took an M2 machine gun and expended two hundred bullets into a pine tree. The tree toppled gently until it hung at forty-five degrees. He couldn't have that. He loaded another belt of five hundred bullets, and shredded the tree of all limbs and cones.

The belt ended and the gun stopped abruptly, though the sound echoed in his ears. Prime felt better after the outburst. Farmboy had almost got him, but he proved he was a better person, a better John.

He filled a backpack with handguns and grenades. The M2 was just too bulky to carry, but he knew where to come to get it if he needed it. Right here in his weapons depot universe.

He rearranged the weapons in his backpack. Prime had never felt better. He had the device again. He had the ability to travel backward, to go anywhere, to take anything. He wasn't trapped anymore. He never had to see Casey again. Or Abby.

That stung him, but just for a moment. He'd been a fool to stick down roots. He should have kept going, kept roaming. And now he would. He'd build an empire in some universe. He'd do the things Farmboy would never let him do.

Prime glanced up, looking at the southeastern horizon. He thought he'd heard something. It had happened before in this ghost world, some odd sound, some echo. He realized it was just the sound of the machine gun still ringing in his ears.

He had to fetch a flashlight to finish his work; the sun had set, leaving the camp in twilight. He entered the portable cabin he had built for the transfer device to look for it.

"Hello, Prime."

He jumped.

Farmboy stood next to the controls of his transfer gate.

"You! I left you hundreds of universes back!"

"Only one place for you to go."

Prime reached to toggle the universe counter on the transfer device on his chest.

"Where you going to go with that, Prime?" Farmboy asked.

"Away from you! Someplace far."

"I wouldn't do that," Farmboy said, "unless you have a gate waiting farther up the line."

Prime grimaced. He realized he was stuck. He couldn't use the transfer device to get back from a higher universe to a lower one; he could only go forward. To get back he needed a transfer gate, and he'd never traveled past 9000.

"So, I could build one."

Farmboy smiled. He pointed to the plans for a gate sitting on a table, plans that Prime had stolen from Henry to build this gate. He grabbed them and wadded them up.

"Can you do it from memory?" Farmboy asked.

Prime said nothing. He couldn't and Farmboy knew it.

"So, an impasse," Prime said.

Farmboy shrugged. "Naw." He lifted a hammer and held it over the transfer device. "Tell me where the artifacts are, or I strand you here forever. You could always keep going up, always running like before. But I don't think you can stand that."

Prime began to sweat. The only thing that made the transfer device valuable again was his transfer gate that allowed him to go backward. He'd tried to exploit the multiverse going forward only and failed.

"I'm not giving up the device," Prime said. "It's mine."

Farmboy stared at him for a moment. "I just want the artifacts You can keep the device and this godforsaken universe."

Was that some trick? "You'll let me keep the device?"

"It's yours, in exchange for the artifacts."

"Fine."

"And you never come near the settled universes."

Prime hesitated. He'd never see Casey or Abby again.

"You . . . You want Casey."

Farmboy shrugged. "I want you gone. Take the device and go. Just give me the artifacts."

"They're in the safe in Universe Prime, not far from where you're standing," Prime said.

"Combination."

Prime told him, and Farmboy wrote it down.

"If you've lied to me," Farmboy said, "I will hunt you down across the multiverse."

He set the transfer gate for Universe Prime, stood in the transfer zone, and ten seconds later was gone.

Prime exhaled. Done, he was done with Farmboy and the Wizards for good. And Casey. That Casey at least. There were a million more. A million universes.

Done.

CHAPTER 45

John arrived in the Pleistocene universe to find that Grace Home was delirious and one of her attendants—Grace Quayle—was sick now as well. Henry Quayle had a fever but was sitting next to Grace Home, holding her hand. No one else showed any symptoms of the plague yet.

The lone traveler's ring seemed too big for Grace's ring finger, so John slid it over her thumb.

"What is it?" Grace Pinball asked.

"Magic," John said. "I don't know. Nanotechnology? Serums? Antibodies?"

"So you have no idea if it will work."

"Just a guess. Prime survived in the plague world. There has to be a reason."

Grace Pinball laid a wet cloth on Grace Quayle's forehead.

"You have a backup plan, John?" Grace Quayle asked. She wasn't delirious as Grace Home was, but she was flushed with a fever, weak, and aching in her joints.

John grinned as earnestly as he could. "I've got a few more tricks up my sleeve."

Grace Quayle laughed. "Don't lie to a Grace," she said. "We know you too well."

John placed a thermometer under Grace Home's tongue. It had only been a few minutes since he had slid the ring on her finger. He checked the level of the mercury in the thermometer: forty degrees Celsius.

No change.

He had no idea if the effect would be instantaneous or if Prime had slowly built up an immunity by wearing the ring over days. He felt the remaining artifacts in his pocket. Maybe it was one of the other devices. No, Prime had worn the ring; John had seen it. But not the other stuff.

Grace was right. He had no backup plan. This was his only idea. The plague had destroyed a whole world. He had seen it as he rode the minibike through the desolate streets. It was an utterly deserted world. There was no other hope. None that was quick enough to save Grace Home.

He checked her temperature again. A little bit above forty now. It was getting worse.

He sat heavily on the ground next to Grace. There had been so many deaths because of him. New Toledo and with it, Casey. Gesalex. His foster parents in 7650. And now all the Wizards.

The only one likely to survive was John Prime.

He had squandered this wonderful gift. He had the ability to cross universes, to save people, to help those who suffered, and he had wasted it. But what could he have done differently?

He'd built his transdimensional company. He had used it to make billions of dollars. He had recruited an army of Johns, Graces, Henrys, and Caseys. But what had they *done*?

Perhaps the greatest thing had been the creation of New Toledo, where the refugees from 7538—the nuclear winter universe—had immigrated to. But it had been only a drop in the bucket. The people who had come had only been a small fraction of those who suffered. Universe upon universe, stacked to infinity, humanity suffered. What could he do?

What could he have done differently?

He remembered Abby's smile when she had called him Daddy, the warmth of Casey Home's kiss. Was it for him to solve those problems? Was it for John Rayburn to do anything more than live his own life?

"It can't be that bad."

John looked up into Grace Home's clear eyes. Her labored breathing had slowed. He face had lost its flush. She looked normal, though tired.

He reached over to place the thermometer in her mouth, but she batted it weakly away.

"Stop poking me," she said.

John laid the back of his hand on her forehead instead. It was cool to the touch.

"It worked," he said.

"What worked?"

John slid the ring off her thumb. He handed it to Grace Pinball, who placed it on Grace Quayle's hand.

"Something new, something that'll change everything," John said.

"Again?"

"Again."

John knocked on the door and waited.

He could have sent Henry or even another John, but he'd come himself with the lone traveler's ring. Every Wizard in the Pleistocene had been inoculated with it. Now they were watching Home Office for any sign of an outbreak of the plague. If they saw one, John wasn't sure what they would do.

"Cauterize it?" Henry Home had asked. "Like the Vig?"

So far, there had been no sign of any fevers, no alerts from the local hospitals. Only one Wizard remained to be dosed with the ring's magic.

The door opened, and Casey Prime looked at him.

"You found him?" she asked.

John nodded.

Casey stared at him for a moment, and then nodded.

"He's not coming back," John said. "He's got the device and he's going to leave forever with it."

"You came to tell me that?"

"And another two reasons," John said. "One is to inoculate you and Abby against the plague."

"And the other?"

John looked at Casey—his first Casey—then leaned forward and kissed her on the lips.